MONSTROUS

NICOLE M RUBINO

MONSTROUS

A novel

By: Nicole M. Rubino

For Mila & Michelle

And for all the girls with teeth & claws - don't be afraid to use them

AUTHOR'S NOTE

Thank you so much for deciding to read *Monstrous*. I want to make sure every reader enjoys the book and feels comfortable reading it, and so I have included a list of content/trigger warnings.

Monstrous is best enjoyed for readers 18+ as it contains graphic, consensual sex; blood play, some graphic violence and gore, cannibalistic thoughts described in detail, reference to off page sexual assault, on page light sexual assault (kissing), anxiety/panic attacks, and character death.

Although I believe I've covered every detail, if you feel there is something I've missed or if you have any questions or concerns, please contact me at authornicolemrubino.com.

CHAPTER
ONE

I've never been afraid of the dark.

I've never needed reassurance that there isn't a monster in my closet or under my bed.

Perhaps it's because a part of me always knew I was the only monster in the room.

I glance down at the paper between my fingers, the corners of it rustling as a slight breeze caresses my skin. But it does nothing to alleviate the oppressive August heat in New York making it difficult for me to breathe.

Sweat pools beneath my arms and in my palms, though the latter has more to do with what I read on the paper than the weather.

Dear Rhiannon Owens,

It is my sincere pleasure to inform you of your acceptance to Alystair University. Our Admissions Committee takes great care in considering every application, and your outstanding qualities and impressive character have set you apart as truly exceptional.

I snort, not bothering to read the rest like I have every single day since I received the letter the morning after my eighteenth birthday in June. *Outstanding qualities.* And what would those be? The monstrous claws that hide beneath the chipped varnish of my nails?

Impressive character. The only thing impressive about being an actual monster is this ridiculous school I'm forced to attend as a result.

Now, *truly exceptional,* I get. After all, how many people can say they are half-monster?

Everyone at this school, apparently.

A soft chuckle breaks me away from my rumination. "Are you reading that letter again?" My mother throws an arm around me. "It's not going to change. You've been accepted to Alystair!" Her voice pitches high at the end. I tear my eyes away from the paper to look up at her forcing my lips into something that resembles a smile.

My mother's dark eyes are wild with excitement, and my father stands beside her, a proud smile splitting his face.

"You didn't even tell us you applied, Rhi," he scolds softly, lifting his baseball cap and running a hand through his light blonde hair.

It's because I hadn't. I fold the letter and stuff it into a pocket inside my Sailor Moon tote bag.

"She probably didn't want to jinx anything," my mother suggests, and they both turn their gazes away from me to take in the campus.

We stand on a large, grassy knoll surrounded by four ornate stone buildings. Spires scrape the cloudless sky on each building, with pointed arches interspersed among them. Paved gravel forms a perfect square around the greenery, with one stone path that cuts through the middle toward a building with a large iron door set back into an arch.

The luscious green lawn, so vibrant in contrast with the dark gray buildings, is peppered with students. Some are sunbathing, others reading or laughing in small groups. They all look so normal, it's hard for me to picture any of them with claws. But, I know they're there, the same as my own, hiding just beneath the surface.

My parents smile at each other, and my heart skips knowing how happy they are. Maybe I can learn to be happy here too, and who knows? Maybe I can lead a somewhat normal life. Or whatever passes for normal around here.

"Are you Rhiannon Owens?" A gentle voice asks, and I turn my attention to the direction it came from. Two girls approach me; one is blonde, hair the color of spun gold, eyes a bright, gleaming sapphire ringed in light green. She stands at least two heads taller than the other, a fair-skinned brunette with dark mahogany hair and a full hour-glass figure.

"Who wants to know?" I reply, and immediately bite my tongue. It's probably not wise to get snarky at a new school that's full of creatures from my worst nightmares, but I've never really had a filter when it comes to speaking my mind.

The blonde's eyes narrow, but the brunette smiles, her hazel eyes warm and comforting.

"I'm Scarlett." She holds out her hand. Her dark hair tumbles over a white tank top tucked into belted, high-waisted denim shorts. Blondie ignores me completely, her stunning eyes dancing about the campus, and I take a moment to assess her. She's incredibly tall, lean, and her facial features are hard as stone. Everything about her is unwelcoming, her arms crossed over a black T-shirt. It's then I realize that she's wearing black leather gloves.

Interesting fashion statement, considering it's August and the heat is sweltering, but I don't comment on it. She might have a medical condition or even more likely, knowing what crawls beneath her skin, it could be anything from claws to scales.

I shake Scarlett's hand. "Rhi. Nice to meet you."

"This is Astrid." She jerks her head toward her companion, who finally settles her gaze on me. Astrid doesn't offer her hand.

"Are you both freshmen as well?" My mother chimes in.

Scarlett nods. "We started at Alystair Academy for high school, though, so Astrid and I have known each other for a few years now." She flashes an endearing smile at Astrid, whose hard gaze softens when she looks at Scarlett.

Ah. I know *that* look. Astrid's stony, territorial stare makes a lot more sense now.

"These are my parents," I say. My mother rushes forward to shake Scarlett's hand with such eagerness one would think *she* was attending Alystair.

"I'm Angela, and this is my husband, John."

Scarlett smiles as she returns the handshake, but Astrid remains in her statuesque position with her arms crossed. A blush creeps into my mother's cheeks as her palm hangs midair in front of Astrid. My blood heats with anger at her blatant rudeness towards my parents. A familiar dull ache in my fingertips serves as a warning my claws are about to emerge, and I take a deep breath in as I wipe a dark brown strand of sweat-drenched hair from my forehead. My fingers tremble and my chest tightens with the effort of forcing my claws to remain hidden.

Scarlett throws a friendly arm around my shoulders and ushers me forward. "Well, we have so much to do! Tours, meetings with professors, you know." She says hurriedly. "It was lovely meeting you both!" She urges me on, and Astrid joins us without a word. I glance behind me to find my parents' bewildered faces.

"I'll call you both later!" I shout and throw another fake smile on my lips. Scarlett leads me toward the gravel path and through a stone archway that places us behind the building with the Greek columns. We pause as we round the corner. I drop my bag as I lean back against the wall, shaking out my still-trembling fingers in an attempt to keep the claws at bay.

"It would be helpful if you would just let them out," Astrid says placidly.

I throw her a venomous glare. "I've spent the last two months trying to keep them *in*."

Scarlett softly places her hand on my shoulder. "You don't have to hide here, Rhi." She holds her free hand up, and long, curved claws shoot from her fingertips, exactly like mine. "We're all like you."

I let out a shuddering breath. It's surreal to see the claws on another person, even if I have a set of my own. I've fought so hard these last two months to keep them hidden, often crying into my pillow at the pain it caused. But Scarlett's words start to chip away at the shame and horror that's followed me since my eighteenth birthday. *You don't have to hide here.* The tightness in my chest slowly dissipates. *We're all like you.*

A sharp bite of pain reverberates through the tips of my fingers, and I glance down to find my fingernails have been replaced by claws. At least two inches long, they curve to a sharp tip, blood leaking from my nail beds. The weight of my hands feels different, heavier at my fingertips with my new manicure. My thoughts wander to the night of my eighteenth birthday, the night they first emerged, as blood dripped from my clenched hands onto the gray carpet of my living room. I recall a pair of golden brown eyes wide with horror as they took in the blood that stained the floor in small droplets.

Astrid hisses, dragging me back to the present. "Well, that's what happens when you don't let them out regularly."

I open my mouth, ready to rip her head off, but Scarlett interrupts. "Your parents don't know what you are, right?"

I shake my head. "How did you know that?"

Her answering smile is warm and reassuring. "Professor Talbot, the President of the University, he's the one who told us about you. He sent you your acceptance letter." A bell of familiarity rings in my head as I picture the signature at the bottom of the letter. Scarlett's hazel eyes fall to the bag at my feet. "I'm guessing you still have it?"

I nod. "How did Professor Talbot know about me? Even *I* didn't know about me."

Scarlett shrugs. "He knows a lot of things. He's mysterious like that. Rumor has it he can even tell when people are lying."

Of course, he can. Before I know it, someone will be telling me unicorns are real too. I shake my head, flexing my fingers, trying to shake the dull ache from my claws. This is definitely going to take getting used to.

Among a thousand other things.

"I know this is all...a lot," Scarlett pats me gently. "Why don't we give you a tour of the campus like we're supposed to, and we can go over everything mentioned in your acceptance letter?"

Scarlett keeps saying "we" as though she anticipates Astrid being somewhat helpful, but considering all she's done thus far is pin me down with her condescending stare, I'm guessing Scarlett will be doing most of the explaining.

I blow out a breath. "Fine." Because aside from the first page of the acceptance letter welcoming me to Alystair, the second page rambled on about how the school was a safe-haven for monsters like me *and* a school of magic. I'd thought I'd gone half-insane when I first read it, seeing as up until my eighteenth birthday, I, and the rest of the mundane world, thought Alystair was an exclusive college for the kids of CEOs and neurosurgeons.

I push away from the wall, voicing my thoughts. "And to

think, I thought this school was nothing more than a presti-gious, wannabe Ivy League for stuck-up rich kids."

Astrid snorts. "Oh, it is. But being descended from monsters puts us above being an Ivy League legacy, don't you think?"

Fair point. I grab my bag and start to follow. "What about all my stuff?"

I'm gifted with a blank stare from both girls.

"My clothes, bedsheets...you know, the stuff I brought with me from home that I left in my parent's car?"

Astrid's sapphire eyes glisten with understanding. "Oh." She waves her hand dismissively. "Don't worry. That will all be taken care of. It's probably at your room already."

I open my mouth to protest, but Scarlett flashes me with one of her reassuring smiles, and we begin walking back toward the stone archway to return to the perfectly manicured campus lawn.

"So, what monster are you descended from?" I ask Astrid, my voice tinged with mockery. Despite the fact I have claws and have now seen yet *another* person with claws, the skeptical part of my brain still screams that none of this is real.

The corners of Astrid's lips curl, and the girl is as terrifying as she is beautiful when she smiles. "Medusa."

I stop, nearly barreling into Scarlett, who's been leading us. "Is that the one with snakes in her hair?"

Astrid wrinkles her nose in disappointment. "She's one of the most famous monsters in history - a Gorgon who turned people to stone just by catching their eye."

Scarlett chuckles. "I think my girlfriend expected more awe from you."

"Oh. *Wow.*" I draw out the last word, earning a vicious glare from the Gorgon. Ignoring her completely I turn to Scar-lett. "And what about you?"

"I'm a Lamia," she says with another heartfelt smile that makes me think she's less of a monster and more of a teddy bear.

"I don't know what that is," I say.

Scarlett winks, her mouth curving into a sinister smile that removes any thought from my head that she might not be dangerous. "You'll find out soon enough."

I ping pong my gaze between the two girls and swallow the hysterical laughter threatening to pour out of me. "How do I know that I haven't just gone insane?"

Scarlett lets out a deep sigh. "Let's take a seat on that bench over there. We'll hold off on the tour until we've talked through this."

I follow her lead, fiddling with the strap of my tote.

Once we sit, me and Astrid on either side of Scarlett, Scarlett hands me the school's pamphlet. My clawed nails graze Scarlett's arm as I take it from her.

"Is there an easy way to get rid of them?" I ask.

"Transmogrification, which you'll take this semester, will teach you how to control all the side effects."

I gulp. Side effects? As in, more than *one*? What else is going to happen to me?

"I still can't believe this is my life," I say, taking deep breaths.

Astrid rises from the bench and stands beside Scarlett. "Well, believe it, or else you're going to end up eating any guy that comes near you when you're horny. Or girl." She cocks her head. "Do you like girls?"

I nearly choke at the question. "What?"

"It's not a hard question. Do you prefer men or women? Both?"

"That's not what..." I shake my head. "What do you mean, I'm going to 'eat' them?" I think of my birthday party, of the bloodlust that consumed me when I merely breathed in the scent of my best friend, Jesse. My heart is dangerously close to beating right out of my chest.

"Don't listen to her," Scarlett says. "She's just trying to scare you."

Astrid puts her hands on her hips. "No, I'm not."

Scarlett glares at her girlfriend. "If you're not going to be helpful, can you at least keep your mouth shut?"

"Fine," she huffs.

A half smile adorns Scarlett's face at the scowl on Astrid's mouth. Before Scarlett turns her eyes back to me.

"I thought about it, you know," I admit. "The night of my eighteenth birthday, I kept thinking about what my friend Jesse would taste like." A rude noise erupts from Astrid's throat. "*Not* sexually," I clarify. I shudder as bits and pieces of that night bombard my brain. How I had a sudden, insatiable craving for Jesse's lips on mine. And how that craving turned into something ominous when a pang of hunger pierced my abdomen as I imagined what his blood would taste like if my teeth pierced his skin.

Scarlett nods. "It's normal for us, but as far as I know, no one has ever eaten someone they were attracted to."

"Don't forget about Milton," Astrid pipes in.

Scarlett winces. "Yeah. That was unfortunate."

I give Scarlett a concerned look.

"I'll tell you another time," she waves her hand. "Though I have to ask, was this the first time you had thoughts like that?"

I nod and reach into my tote bag for a bottle of water.

"Did you...and I'm not trying to pry, but did you get your period?"

Heat rushes to my cheeks. How could she know that? "Yeah." I take a sip.

Scarlett's eyes grow serious. "That's when it starts for us, for the girls at least. The urges, the claws, the teeth-"

I nearly spit out the water. "Wait, teeth? What teeth?"

Astrid flashes another evil grin. "Your monster teeth."

"Astrid," Scarlett warns.

"You're no fun," Astrid scrunches her nose and flops back down on the bench.

"It's hard to say exactly what other features you'll have since we don't know what you are yet," Scarlett explains.

I finally swallow a large gulp of water. "Why's that?"

"I'm guessing your parents are completely human," Astrid pipes in, staring at her gloved hand. "If they weren't, you would have been at the Academy with us for high school, and you wouldn't be finding out all of this just now."

"I was adopted," I offer.

"Ah," Scarlett says. "That definitely explains it. Our specific blood type isn't discernible with human testing, so your blood type would appear human. If you'd grown up with your biological parents, you would have been tested at birth and known what monster you were descended from."

This feels like a soul-crushing blow. My parents still have no idea what I am or what the school really is. I'm sure that when they adopted me there wasn't a checkbox for "part monster" on the adoption papers. My birth parents didn't want me, and they were *like* me. Would my adoptive parents want me if they knew what I really was? Another unsettling thought worms its way into my head, and I realize this school is the only place I will ever be able to be myself. Once I leave, I'll have to hide what I really am for the rest of my life.

Perhaps the stories are wrong. Maybe monsters aren't lying in wait underneath beds or inside closets to devour unsuspecting children. Maybe the monsters are just hiding from a human world that would do monstrous things if it ever found out the truth: that we live beside them in plain sight.

TWO

Scarlett decides it's finally time for my tour to begin, and I spend nearly two hours in quiet contemplation as her and a reluctant Astrid guide me around campus.

The building with the columns is the Northgate dormitory, its hallways carved out of stone and marble—far more luxurious than the ones I'd seen while visiting other college campuses. Long rectangular windows are set within each arch, flanked on either side by marble columns wrapped with an ornate golden chain. The windows are draped in thick, blood red curtains held open by gilded ropes. Chandeliers drip from the ceiling, spaced every few feet. White orbs peek out from the serpentine arms of the chandeliers. The effect is stunning.

I feel a burst of gratitude that isn't my own and am struck with the realization that the hallways have a sentience.

Which is utterly ridiculous.

Then, again, I got claws for my eighteenth birthday and was invited to attend a school for monsters.

As we continue the tour, I'm told two of the other three buildings are where classes are held, Eastbourne and Westbourne, and the final building; Southgate, which is home to the cafeteria, gym and other recreational spaces.

"Westbourne has a dungeon, which I'm sure-"

I cut Scarlett off with an incredulous stare. "Did you just say 'dungeon?'"

"Of course," Astrid chimes in. "Where do you think they put the unruly monsters who try to eat other students?"

My mouth parts, and I'm momentarily fazed until Scarlett gives Astrid a sharp *thwack* across her chest.

"This campus is old," Scarlett explains. "Westbourne *was* a dungeon at one point, until they built the actual building on top of it. I think it's only used in the most extreme circumstances, but it's definitely not used to detain students." She shoots Astrid a warning glare.

Astrid merely flashes a wicked grin. "Rhi is looking a bit pale. I think it's time we pass her off to Talbot."

My heart stammers. "The President of the University? Why would I need to see him?"

Scarlett shrugs. "He asked us to bring you to his office once we were done. Probably wants to see how well you're processing everything."

I groan. "Can't I just send him an email?"

Scarlett and Astrid shake their heads simultaneously.

We head toward the Eastbourne building as the sun starts to dip behind the dormitory, bruising the sky in a dusky pink and deep purple. The inside of Eastbourne is no different to the inside of the dormitory, its halls gleaming from perfectly sculpted marble floors. Tall arched windows let in the last of the sun's fading rays. The hallway looks as though it belongs in a palace rather than the classroom building of a university.

The girls and I take a left as soon as we enter Eastbourne and stop at the first door set back into yet another stone archway. Words are etched onto the door itself in an elegant script, and I squint as I make out the writing: *President Gene Talbot.*

Scarlett faces me. "It was so nice meeting you, Rhi! Here," she takes out her cell phone. "Take my cell number down. Call me if you need anything, or you want to hang out!" The exuberance in her voice is genuine, and I smile as I type her number into my phone.

"Thanks," I say.

As I pocket my phone, Scarlett pulls me into a hug. "Good luck with Professor Talbot!"

Astrid smirks knowingly, tilting her head as a form of goodbye. I sigh, watching the girls leave, and raise my fist to knock on Professor Talbot's door.

It opens before I even get the chance.

"You must be Rhiannon."

I blink furiously as I take in the body that belongs to the voice. Handsome and appearing to be somewhere in his thirties, his wavy, chestnut brown hair is combed away from his face, revealing piercing gray eyes. A close-shaven beard traces his jaw line, chin and upper lip, accentuating his devilish smile as he shakes my hand.

"It's Rhi," I correct him.

His gray eyes find mine, that devil-may-care grin widening. "Ah, so you prefer your nickname. Got it. Well, we are very excited to have you, Rhi. I hope you are just as thrilled to matriculate at Alystair University."

I don't comment further. Excited is too bold a word to describe how I feel about Alystair.

Professor Talbot steps aside to let me in, and I take a seat across from a large Edwardian desk littered with manila folders and various loose papers. There is a soft *click* as Professor Talbot closes the door, and when he reappears in my line of vision, I find he's blotting his forehead with a white handkerchief.

"Whew. I don't remember the last time I kept up a glamour of that magnitude."

"Glamour?"

"An illusion, Rhi. One of the many things you will learn here, at Alystair University." The grin is back on his face. "But first, let's go over a few things." He sits down and opens one of the folders on his desk. "Angela and John Owens are not your biological parents, am I correct?"

I eye him warily. Scarlett said he mysteriously knows things, but that only makes me uneasy around him. "How do you know that?"

"Neither of them has a sliver of magic, and yours had to come from somewhere."

"Then, how did you find me?" I lean forward, my curiosity piqued. "How did you even know I exist?"

This time, he grins with his teeth. "We can sense things, Rhi. Once you begin your lessons, you will strengthen this sense."

"'We' as in all monsters, or 'we' as in you and I?"

Talbot returns my suspicious gaze, his expression considering, and I get the feeling he's struggling with how to answer.

"You and I," he finally says.

Something stirs in the pit of my stomach, a new but familiar sensation that had been quelled by the shame and horror I've been drowning in since my eighteenth birthday: excitement.

"Are we the same kind of monster?"

Talbot chuckles at that. "No. We aren't."

I pull my ponytail forward, tugging at the ends of my hair and avert my gaze. My voice drops to almost a whisper. "Do you know what I am?"

There's a pregnant pause. And then, "yes."

I whip my head up at his response, that fluttering sensation returning. My heart thumps wildly as my brain saddles on to the realization that this is *real*. This is real, and I will finally discover this other part of myself, the one I've been fighting since I discovered my claws.

"Well?" I press.

Talbot has the manila folder open. His gaze bounces between me and something in that folder. I'm on the edge of my seat waiting for him to tell me.

And then he closes it.

"Rhi," he begins, and disappointment floods through me. "Finding out which monster you are descended from is a big deal. Most children of our kind grow up with this knowledge. You are about to have it thrust upon you. I think the better approach would be first to acclimate to your surroundings here, and as your abilities progress and reveal themselves, you can discover for yourself which monster you are."

I tap my leg furiously, wanting to argue. How could he have that information at his fingertips and not share it with me?

"Are there any others like me?"

Professor Talbot narrows his eyes in confusion. "What do you mean?"

"Are there other monsters that grew up with humans, not knowing what they really are?"

Professor Talbot inhales through his nose, those gray eyes swimming with an emotion that resembles something strangely close to pity. He folds his hands on top of the folder.

"No, Rhi. Not all of us grow up with our birth parents, but we do at least grow up with others like us. I don't know why your birth parents gave you up, but it's strange that you were unaccounted for until now. The only reason we found you was because your monster side emerged, allowing us to sense magic where there originally hadn't been any."

Ah. So, *that's* how he found me. Not so mysterious after all. I want to push him further on what kind of monster I am, but the discovery that I'm an anomaly among those who are already anomalies stops me. It's one thing to be different, but to be different among people you're supposed to belong to only makes me feel more alone, just when I'd thought I found a place to belong.

"Ok."

Professor Talbot raises his brows in surprise. "That's it? I thought you would put up more of a fight for information."

"I'm tired." The truth of that statement buries itself within my bones. My head feels ladened, my thoughts swimming with all that has been happening. Tired is an understatement.

Talbot nods. "Well then, let's get you to your room."

He rises from behind his desk and I follow suit, allowing him to lead me through the door and out into the hallway. He takes out the white handkerchief from earlier and folds it into a neat square that he tucks into the top pocket of his gray jacket. That prompts me to recall his earlier statement.

"Professor Talbot? Earlier you said something about a 'glamour.' What exactly were you, uh, glamouring?"

"Ah, yes. That reminds me." He turns his back and gestures for me to follow. "The hallways move—tricky little bastards."

"I'm sorry. What did you just say?"

"Tricky little—"

"No, I meant about the hallways moving. Move *where*?"

He shrugs. "Sometimes to another floor, maybe even another building. Ah! See?" He gestures vaguely to the hallway and the arched window to my right. "My office is in East-bourne, but now, we're in Northgate."

I look around, not noticing much of a difference in the

hallway from before, but when I look out of the window, I realize the view has changed. I'm now looking out at the campus from the front of the Northgate building. *Unreal.*

"I had to glamour them to stay put when you came into the building, just in case they tried to play tricks on you." Talbot continues, taking off without me. I quicken my pace in an attempt to keep up. "It seems they know exactly where you need to be."

"So, they're helpful then?" I ask incredulously. I'm talking about *moving hallways* for fucks sake.

Talbot chuckles darkly. "Not necessarily. But they always move—"

Professor Talbot comes to an abrupt stop, and I nearly crash into him before peering over his shoulder to see what caused our sudden halt.

This school may house terrifying monsters with human faces, but right now, leaning against the marble wall is a boy, far from monstrous, with the most gorgeous face I have ever seen.

CHAPTER

THREE

"Ah, Nicholas Cervallos, interesting that I should find you here."

Nicholas looks up from a book he'd been reading, amber eyes so bright I'm not sure if it's the sunlight or his eyes themselves that light up this corridor. The corner of his mouth quirks up, drawing my eyes to his sensuous lips.

"Come on, Professor Talbot. You know I like to be called Nick." His tone is playful yet commanding.

"What a coincidence, our new student here also prefers her nickname." Professor Talbot moves to the side, beckoning me forward with a tilt of his head. "Nicholas, this is Rhi."

Nick flashes Professor Talbot a warning look, then breaks into a smile. He clamps the book down from the spine, and pushes himself off the wall with the back of his foot, holding his hand out to me.

"Nice to meet you."

Standing upright, Nick towers over me, the top of my head level with his chest. He's close enough that I tilt my chin to look up at him. "You too." I find myself holding on to his hand a moment longer than necessary.

"You have blood on your hands," Nick says nonchalantly, as though that's perfectly normal.

Stunned at his remark, I pull my fingers from his and note, with a jolt, that my claws have disappeared, leaving only blood that still coats my fingers.

"Oh." I clench my fists in an attempt to hide my blood-stained fingers.

Nick's mouth tugs at the corners, a devilish gleam in his eye. "There's no need to hide them." He pulls his attention from me to address Professor Talbot. "What can I do for you, Professor?"

"If you wouldn't mind showing Ms. Owens to her room, I'm sure she'd rather you accompany her, than myself," Professor Talbot suggests.

Nick skewers Talbot with an annoyed gaze and scrunches his nose. "Actually, I was just about to-"

"And that's why I thank you in advance for being so accommodating." Professor Talbot fishes around in his gray pant pocket, pulling out a slip of paper. "Here are the details." He hands it over to Nick, who looks like he'd rather have me actually eat him alive than play tour guide.

"Have fun. Rhi, if you need anything, my office is in the Eastbourne building, first floor, first door on your left." He winks and walks off, leaving me alone with Nick.

Nick eyes the paper, then crumbles it up and tosses it over his shoulder. He shoves the book into the back of jeans. "Come on."

Then he takes off, not bothering to wait for me.

"Thank you," I say.

"Don't mention it," he says sharply.

His long legs create effortless strides down the hall, and I rush to keep up.

"Is something bothering you?" I ask.

He stops and turns at that, brows raised. "Why would something be bothering me?"

"You have a *bit* of an attitude."

A half grin twists his face, eyes flashing. Nick starts walking again at a faster pace.

Before I know it, I tug the hem of his shirt. He stops again, turning to me with such a thunderous look it would stop a hurricane in its tracks. "What?"

"Don't bother showing me to my room," I snap as I walk past him. "I'll figure it out."

Nick releases a throaty laugh, then catches up to me in two quick strides. "Didn't Professor Talbot tell you that these hallways move? We should have been at your room already. Why do you think I'm so annoyed that I had to be the one to take you there? We could be here for hours, and I have somewhere to be."

My anger deflates a little. "Well, that's no reason to be rude to me. I didn't do anything. Blame these stupid hallways." I throw my hands up.

Nick covers my mouth with one hand and pushes me against the wall with the other. I let out a muffled scream of protest. My fingers throb, my claws threatening to emerge to come to my defense.

"Don't piss them off! You want to wander around these hallways forever?"

I shake my head. Nick removes his hand from my mouth. "No more insulting them, okay?" he says gently.

A strand of blue-black hair falls onto his forehead as he straightens. "I'm sorry for being rude. Let's just walk and see what happens."

I nod, peeling my back from the wall and follow him. We walk in silence, me being far too nervous now to say anything out loud that might insult the fragile egos of the hallways. It occurs to me just how much I still don't know about this place.

I take a moment to eye Nick peripherally, trying to decipher from his human - and *blindingly gorgeous* - looks alone what type of monster he might be. But it's no use. As far as I can tell, the only thing dangerous about him is that he's brutally beautiful. And that alone can make a person monstrous.

'What's Rhi short for?" He finally asks, turning to me.

I snap my gaze forward, silently praying he didn't catch me looking at him. "Rhiannon."

"Oh, like the witch."

"No, like the song."

"The song is about a witch."

I sigh wearily. "I didn't know that."

He glances at me quizzically. "You never wondered what your name means?"

"Not really."

"*Dreams unwind. Love's a state of mind.*" He hums.

I glance at him, raising a brow.

"It's from the song, *Rhiannon*," he says, somewhat exasperated.

At this point, I'm only partially paying attention to what Nick is saying. I realize we've been walking, but the hallway hasn't changed. It's as though we've been in the same spot for the last few minutes, despite how far we've walked.

Nick falls silent again, which means I guess it's my turn to keep the conversation going.

"What does your name mean?" I ask.

His answering smile is dazzling. All white teeth against golden skin, his full lips curving into a wolfish grin. "For that, you'd have to know my real name."

"It's not Nicholas?"

"No."

"Well, then what is it?" I try to keep the intrigue out of my voice but fail miserably.

Nick – or whatever his name really is – pauses in front of a dark slate door. "That," he says as he knocks, then places a hand on the doorknob, "is information you have to earn, Rhi."

A voice yells "come in" and he swings open the door, but I don't look inside; I stare at him, the echo of my name on his lips playing over and over again in my head, sending a delicious shiver down my spine.

He steps inside, thankfully oblivious to my stunned state, and greets the person already waiting. "Hey, Scar, I've brought you your new roommate."

I break from my trance, finally noticing a familiar dark-haired girl sitting on an ivory bedspread. "You're my roommate?"

"Surprise!" Scarlett squeals in delight.

"You know her?" Nick asks Scarlett.

Scarlett jumps off the bed and throws her arms around me. "We're old friends." She releases me with a wink.

"Ohhhh," Nick drawls, as he crosses his arms over his broad chest and leans against a tall, dark dresser at the foot of Scarlett's bed. "This is the girl you showed around earlier." He regards me with renewed interest, eyes roving slowly over my body.

"Sasha came by looking for you," Scarlett says.

That disrupts his scrutiny of me as he groans. "What did you tell her?"

Scarlett flashes him a mocking smile. "I said I'm not your keeper."

"Can't you be nice?"

"No."

The dynamic between them is interesting. There's an easy playfulness between them, yet their tone with one another is almost acerbic.

Nick sighs. "She's gonna be a monster to deal with."

"Figuratively or literally?" I ask.

He laughs. "Both." Nicks runs long fingers through his hair. "Those damn hallways."

"I wondered what took you so long," Scarlett mutters with a glance at me.

I reach for my phone in the back pocket of my jeans. "We couldn't have been that long." Upon seeing the time, I suck in a sharp breath: Nick and I walked those hallways for almost an hour.

"But...that's impossible. It didn't feel like more than five minutes!" I sit down on a bare mattress across from Scarlett's, taking in the boxes of my things stacked throughout the room with wide eyes.

"Yeah...that's another thing. Time moves differently in the hallways, as well. Sometimes it stays the same, but sometimes it speeds up," Nick offers.

"Or slows down," Scarlett chimes in. "But the real question is...why did the hallways spit you out an hour later?"

I have no idea what she's talking about.

Nick must. He rolls his eyes and straightens. "Knock it off, Scar. I gotta try and smooth things over with Samantha."

"You mean Sasha," I offer.

He blinks. "Right. I'm seeing Samantha tonight." Nick moves toward the door, and I flash a look of disgust at his back. As he opens the door, he looks at me. "It was nice annoying you, Rhi." He turns to Scarlett. "Catch ya later, Scar."

"Good luck in the hallways, Nicky Boy." Scarlett blows him a kiss when Nick scowls, then shuts the door.

"Nicky Boy?" I question.

She shrugs. "Pet name. Do you want help unpacking your things?" Without waiting for an answer, Scarlett uses a long claw of her pointer finger to slice open the top of a box.

"Did you two date or something?" I remain seated on the bed as she pulls my books out of the box.

"Ew. No. And what was all that talk about Nicky annoying you?"

"He just got on my nerves a bit." And not entirely in a bad way, if I'm being honest with myself.

Scarlett lets out a whooping laugh, throwing her head back. "Oh, Rhi, I knew I liked you from the moment I saw you. You're probably the first girl I've met that hasn't fallen all over themselves at the sight of him."

It's a good thing I didn't tell her how viciously beautiful I think he is, despite his attitude or the fact that I nearly came undone when he said my name.

"Well, *you* seem immune to his charms," I observe.

"That's because it's easy for me." She continues removing books from the box and stacking them on the floor.

"Why's that?"

Finally, she looks at me, hazel eyes shimmering with amusement. "Because he's my brother."

FOUR

er *brother?*

I replay Scarlett and Nick's exchange and recognize it now. Each of them was somewhat playful with the other; a bit competitive, yet comfortable. That genuine camaraderie wasn't friendship or even the remnants of an old relationship. It was something much stronger than that: the bond of siblings.

And yet, they look nothing alike.

"Well, half-brother, to be exact," Scarlett explains, as if reading my thoughts.

So, Nick is her half-brother, and I'm over here complaining about him.

"I'm sorry. I didn't mean-"

Scarlett waves her hand. "Don't apologize. Nicky usually comes off as abrasive. He's not great with meeting new people, especially girls." Her eyes twinkle. "But to be fair, he's not really a player. He's completely upfront with everyone regarding his feelings on relationships. Most of the girls he dates know about each other."

"So, he dates multiple girls at once?" Scarlett nods. "And they're okay with that?"

"Like I said, you're probably the first girl I've met that didn't fall over herself at the sight of him. So, yeah, they're okay with it." She sighs. "Anyway, Nicky has abilities that don't lend themselves well to relationships."

At first, I'm wrapping my head around all of Nick's names. First, it was Nicholas. Then, Nick. After that, Nicky Boy, and now, just plain Nicky. Not to mention that evidently, Nicholas isn't even his real name. But the mention of Nick's abilities yanks me from my previous thoughts with a sharp tug.

"And what are his abilities?"

Scarlett's lips curl.

There it is. The resemblance. They both have the same smile.

She sits beside me, grinning. "I thought he got on your nerves?"

I frown at her conspiratorial smirk. "He did."

"You seem very interested in him."

Blood rushes to my cheeks. "I'm not. It's just...well...is he dangerous?"

Scarlett's eyes darken. "It depends." Before I can ask her to elaborate, she continues, "If you want to know about him, ask him. He won't hurt you if that's what you're worried about."

That's exactly what I'm worried about. What sort of monster hides underneath his skin? What do those devastating features really conceal? These questions run through my brain on a loop, and it irks me just how interested I really am in Nick Cervallos. But I raise my chin and eye Scarlett coolly. "I'm not afraid of him."

The lupine grin returns. "Good."

. . .

It's well past nine in the evening by the time I finish unpacking. Scarlett helped unload every bag and box, happily refolding any clothes that had gotten crumpled in my suitcase and even running to the cafeteria to bring us some pizza when the grumbling of my stomach interrupted our light conversation.

My bed sits across from Scarlett's, the two beds creating an "L" shape. A nightstand is perched to the left of my bed, while a beautiful, stone-finish fireplace sits to the right. Its rough-hewn wood mantle is already adorned with pictures of Scarlett and Astrid, as well as pictures of Scarlett, Nick, and a beautiful woman I can only assume is their mother. She shares the same flawless golden skin as Nick, but that's where the similarities end. Scarlett inherited her mahogany hair and hazel eyes.

"I'll make room for your pictures," she offers. "There's enough of Astrid and I in this room to fill a gallery."

I smile as I look around. That's true. More pictures of Astrid and Scarlett decorate the dark dresser at the foot of Scarlett's bed and the nightstand next to it.

"How long have you guys been together?" I brush my hair in the full-length mirror suspended on our shared closet door.

Scarlett sits at the desk next to her bed, dabbing her lips with cranberry. "Four years."

"Wow."

She shrugs. "It doesn't ever seem that long." In the reflection, I see her turn and face me. "You have beautiful hair. It's such a gorgeous color."

I smile, grateful for the compliment. I've always liked the color of my hair: a dark brown threaded with natural gold highlights. "Thanks."

Scarlett gets up from the desk and admires an outfit she'd placed on her bed. "Tonight is a 'welcome back' bonfire. Even though classes don't start until late August, almost everyone comes back at the end of July. Do you want to come?"

My blood hums with excitement at the thought of a party. But then I remember how the last party I went to turned out, and the idea of being around large groups of people sets my nerves off like a minefield.

"Everyone here is *exactly* like us?" I know this question has been answered for me time and time again, but two warring thoughts battle for dominance inside my head: what's more terrifying - having another monstrous characteristic reveal itself in front of a large group of people, despite the fact that they are monsters like me?

Or...the fact that said large group of people are *monsters,* and I'll be surrounded by them.

She nods enthusiastically. "I can't wait to introduce you to the gang." It's hard not to fall prey to Scarlett's bubbly optimism, and my anxiety takes a back seat for the moment.

Scarlett begins peeling off her clothes. While I'm no stranger to undressing in front of other girls, I don't know Scarlett that well, and I turn to avoid seeing her in the mirror.

I hear a chuckle. "Don't tell me you're embarrassed?"

I clench my jaw and turn. "I'm not."

"Excellent. Then help me with this zipper."

A short, black dress clings to her curves, flaring at the waist. I tug the zipper up and ask, "So, you said you were a Lamia. What exactly is that?"

Scarlett faces me with a shark-like grin. "Well, there are different kinds of Lamias. Some Lamias excel at seduction and our powers lend themselves well to that type of ability."

She stops there, turning to admire herself in the mirror.

"Ok, and what can the other types do?"

"Eat children," she says calmly, catching my horrified expression in the mirror's reflection.

Her mouth lifts at the corners, and I'm silently praying that Scarlett is the seductive type of Lamia just as a knock at the door interrupts my spiraling thoughts.

"Come in!" Scarlett shouts as she fastens the three buttons on the front of her dress. When the door opens, Astrid and another girl walk in. The girl has shoulder-length jet-black hair and rich, dark skin. A black choker wraps around her thin neck, her full lips painted a dark purple shade I wish I could pull off.

"Zo! I didn't think you were back yet!" Scarlett squeals and hugs her.

This girl is very fond of hugging.

"Decided to come back a little early," Zo replies. "Anything to get away from the step-monster." Her coal-black eyes find mine and she holds out a hand. "Hey, new girl, I'm Zo."

I take her hand, my eyes drawn to the dark ink adorning both of her forearms from wrist to elbow, some of the designs resembling unfamiliar symbols while the others are pictures of what look like...

Monsters.

"Rhi."

"Nice to meet you. Do you know what is seen in the middle of March and April that can't be seen in the beginning or end of either month?"

I blink and tilt my head. "What?"

Astrid snickers, but Scarlett releases an aggrieved sigh. "Zo, can you give her about five minutes before you start with your riddles?"

"Riddles?" I question.

A mocking smile curves Zo's lips. "I'm half-Sphinx. I like riddles."

"Like from Oedipus Rex?"

She nods. "You got it. So, do you know the answer?"

"Zo," Scarlett groans.

"What happens if I don't?" I ask, my intrigue spiking as I attempt to recall the play. Oedipus was able to answer the Sphinx's riddle. But what happened to those that couldn't?

Zo leans into me, flashing a mouthful of razor-sharp teeth. "Then, I'll eat you."

I snap back faster than a rubber band, stumbling into Scarlett's desk. Zo and Astrid are a riot of laughter, but Scarlett's normally sweet face is now murderous, the heat from her eyes nearly tangible.

A solemn chill sweeps over the room, as if someone turned the dial down on anything joyous and fun. And though I don't feel anything in particular, my blood ices when I catch Astrid and Zo's vacant expressions.

Just as quickly, they snap out of it, and Astrid turns an angry, stony glare on her girlfriend. "Really, Scar? Persuasion?"

"Do *you* like being fucked with?" She snaps back.

Astrid continues to glare at Scarlett, but her face softens. Zo suddenly finds something on the floor in need of scrutiny when Scarlett glances at her.

"I didn't think so," she says.

Zo looks up at me. "Sorry, Rhi. It was just a joke."

"Don't worry about it." The Sphinx gives a slight upturn of her mouth, and though she doesn't say it, I sense she's relieved I've accepted her apology.

We can sense things, Rhi. Professor Talbot's words echo in my head.

"Let's just get down to the party," Astrid suggests as she wraps an arm around Scarlett, the black leather glove on her left hand lightly squeezing Scarlett's shoulder.

"Fine." Scarlett's tone is rough, but she doesn't shake Astrid's arm. The two head for the door, Zo trailing behind them.

I take one step when another thought strikes me like a lightning bolt.

"It's the letter R" I say to Zo, answering her riddle.

Astrid and Scarlett pause, but Zo whirls, a wide smile on her full lips. She approaches me, and I watch her cautiously, waiting for another prank. But she wraps her arm around mine and says: "Welcome to the girl gang, Rhi."

CHAPTER

FIVE

The four of us trot down the marble and stone hall, Zo's arm linked in mine as she rambles off the different species of monsters at Alystair.

"Let's see, so you've met a Gorgon, a Lamia and a Sphinx." She taps a clawed fingernail on her chin. "Tonight, you'll meet Olivia, who's a Charybdis."

A what?

"A type of sea monster," Zo explains, noticing the bewildered look on my face. How do you even spell charibee - never mind.

"I'm also part Gorgon," she continues, breezing past my still perplexed expression.

"Do you have the same abilities as Zo?" I ask Astrid, who walks in front of us with Scarlett.

"No. I'm a descendant of Medusa. Zo's ancestor is Euryale." Astrid doesn't elaborate, and though I'm familiar with Medusa, I have no idea who Euryale is.

Always observant, Zo adds, "Euryale was Medusa's sister."

"Oh," I reply, waiting for some type of elaboration. When it doesn't come, I press, "So, Euryale, what could she do?"

"Her screams would kill anyone who heard them" Astrid answers placidly, as though she were commenting on the weather.

Fear licks my spine, and I whip my head towards Zo. "Can you-"

"My screams will hurt you, but not kill you," Zo reassures me, offering me a warm smile.

I release a breath, keeping my gaze straight ahead. Regret churns in my stomach at not pushing Professor Talbot to tell me exactly what kind of monster I am. Being around these girls who are so comfortable and self-assured with their monster heritage has tendrils of jealousy taking root in my chest. For once, it would just be nice to know who I truly am.

We exit the dormitory and head right, traveling through a large archway in the back corner of the building where it connects to the classroom structure. The hallways were mercifully lenient as I check my phone and realize only about five minutes have passed since we left the room. Astrid and Scarlett lead us down a grassy hill, and even before I glimpse the large bonfire raging toward a the night sky, cedar and smoke inundate my nostrils.

At least fifty people hover around the fire in small groups, and I'm struck by how normal they appear. Some of them have drinks, while others are smoking, and they could easily be my own friends from high school. Bubbly laughter and carefree smiles lend themselves well to this breezy summer evening, the night sky flush with stars. The normalcy washes away the rest of my lingering nerves, and I start to relax as we approach the party.

We pause in front of a girl with long, wavy hair that is a piercing aquamarine with eyes to match. She wears a white linen sundress, contrasting well with her deep olive skin, which is a shade darker than mine.

Zo smiles. "The gang's all here."

"Liv, I'd like you to meet Rhi. She's my new roommate," Scarlett beams.

Aquamarine waves shyly. "I'm Liv. How do you like Alystair so far?"

"It's okay."

"Do you know what your abilities are?" Liv's bright eyes are endearing, her voice soft and childlike.

I shake my head. "Just the claws. I haven't seen the teeth yet."

Zo's smile is sharp. "Oh, just wait. They're so much fun."

For what feels like the first time since my eighteenth birthday, I genuinely smile. We stand in a close-knit circle, the five of us, and an unfamiliar sensation settles upon me. It's subtle, but I think I recognize it: *belonging*.

Astrid's trademark stony glare hardens – if that's even possible – at something behind me.

"Ladies," a smooth voice drawls.

A small turn of my neck introduces a new boy in my vision. Not much taller than me, bright red hair and sparkling green eyes. If Nick was fire and shadow, this boy is fire and sunlight.

It takes me a moment to realize that not one of the other girls greets him, but he holds out a hand to me. "Kieran."

"Rhi." I don't take his hand.

I don't like the way Kieran looks at me. Like a snake, ready to devour its prey. Nick might have been a bit rude, but he didn't leave me feeling so...

Unsettled.

"Get lost, Kieran," Zo growls.

His eyes flick toward her, glinting in cruel amusement. "Jealous?"

From the corner of my eye, I see Astrid peel off her gloves. Immediately, each of the girls steps back.

"Kieran, I really don't think you wanna start something." She wriggles her fingers.

Kieran scowls. "I just wanted to introduce myself to your friend." His gaze falls back to me.

Zo steps forward. "You've done that. Now leave us alone."

Kieran doesn't move. His poison green eyes dance between each of us, lingering on Astrid and her bare hands. A sneer turns his mouth, but he remains where he is.

"Kieran, what English word has three consecutive double letters?"

At first, I'm appalled that Zo is asking riddles at a time like this. But then I remember that if he can't answer correctly, she'll eat him. I think.

He doesn't miss a beat. "Bookkeeper," he replies with a malevolent smirk, and Zo curses.

"Get out of here, Kieran." Scarlett's claws are out.

Kieran gives her a mocking smile, as though daring her to use them.

Astrid cracks her knuckles and walks toward him. "Oh, I have been *dying* to get my hands on you."

His eyes widen, his features twisted in fear. "Bitch," Kieran snarls, but leaves to join another group on the other side of the fire.

I turn my attention to the girls: Liv is rubbing Zo's back, her eyes searing across the courtyard where Kieran retreated to. Liv and Scarlett exchange nervous glances, while Astrid tugs her gloves back on, daintily adjusting the hem at her wrist like a refined lady at afternoon tea.

My voice breaks the silence. "Should I even ask what that was about?"

Scarlett darts a cautionary stare at Zo, whose temper still

hasn't ebbed. Her chest rises and falls in a rhythm similar to the lid on a pot of boiling water, and I can sense the anger building inside her.

"Kieran is an incubus," Scarlett explains. "He can travel into people's dreams." Her eyes fall to the floor, and she bites her lip.

While that doesn't sound terrible, I also get the feeling Kieran's notoriety with this group exceeds his creepy ability. Or his smug demeanor.

"It's ok, Scarlett," Zo says. "I'll tell her."

Her ebony gaze is penetrating when she looks at me.

"Kieran and I went out almost all of last year. He was sweet – different from the guys I usually go for. Or so I thought." She shifts uncomfortably. "I knew he was an incubus, but Kieran can't enter your dreams unless you give him permission." A reluctant sigh escapes her throat. "But we'd been going out for months, and I thought it would be fun. Imagine the things we could experience together while dreaming?" Zo clenches and unclenches her fists, and Liv gives her an encouraging squeeze. "I never thought..." She shakes her head.

My stomach plunges seeing the turmoil on her face "Zo," I hold up my hands, "you don't have to tell me anything. Believe me, after what just happened, I can't say I even remotely like him."

Astrid chuckles, but Zo gives me an adamant stare. "No. You should know *exactly* what he's capable of. Though we'd been dating for a while, we weren't having sex. I knew it frustrated him."

That sharp plunge in my stomach dips even further, and the hair on my arm prickles as I realize where this is going.

Zo takes a deep breath. "After he kept pressuring me, I broke up with him, and I thought that was it. But I'd forgotten that I allowed him in my dreams. He broke into them one night and *attacked* me. He turned into something from one of my worst nightmares." She shudders.

Before I can stop myself, I throw my arms around her. "I'm so sorry, Zo." I pull back to find her eyes glistening with tears, residual fear lingering there. The fury that lances through my blood is unrestrained, and I turn to search for the literal green-eyed monster.

He stands self-assured and dignified among another group of students, smiling like he's campus king. The claws are out before I can stop them, but the usual ache in my fingers is absent. Instead, an unsuspecting throb pierces my gums and a coppery, metallic taste washes over my tongue. I clamp a hand over my mouth.

A leather-clad hand rests on my shoulder. "Rhi, are you okay?"

I face Astrid, slowly bringing my hand from my open mouth.

She grins. "There you are."

I press my tongue to my new set of fangs, gliding it along a sharp tip. Fear's icy fingers grasp my heart at the feel of the once flat spaces now sharpened points, and in my head I can't help but to picture the mouth of a shark.

"I wouldn't do that if I were you," Astrid warns. "You can slice your tongue open."

I cement my tongue to the bottom of my mouth, resisting the urge to groan. What is with these monstrous abilities and them coming forth at parties?

Scarlett rushes toward me, pulling me away from the girls. "Do you want to leave?"

"No," I tell her. "Maybe just some water? I need to wash the taste of blood out of my mouth."

Scarlett nods and leads me back toward our group, before disappearing into the crowd.

"What a terrible time for them to come out," Zo comments. "This is the first time they've ever emerged?"

"Yeah. My claws came out on my eighteenth birthday."

"Hmm." Liv taps her chin. "What were you feeling when your teeth came out?"

I wait before responding, looking right at Zo. "I wanted to rip Kieran's throat out."

Liv's mouth drops open, while Zo stares at me in wonder. But Astrid looks positively beside herself with glee. Her grin returns, mouth wide and showing off her own sharp teeth, sapphire eyes sparkling.

Just then, Scarlett returns, a bottle of water in hand. "Sorry," she says, breathless. "I had to find Nick so he could-" She pauses, taking in the group's awed expressions. "What's going on? What did I miss?"

"Scar," Astrid says, her mouth growing impossibly wider. "I think we've just discovered what our dear Rhiannon is." She steps toward me, running her tongue over her lips. "I think we've just found ourselves a Scylla."

SIX

"N*ooo,*" Scarlett's voice calls out in amazement.

"No way," Zo shakes her head. "There hasn't been a Scylla at this school since..."

"Ever." Astrid finishes for her.

"That means we're cousins!" Liv bounces on her heels.

I hold up a hand. "Whoa, whoa, whoa. Wait a sec." I take a sip of water, swish it around my mouth, then turn my head and spit it out. "What's a Scylla?"

"You've never read the Odyssey?" Astrid draws her brows together in disbelief.

"SparkNotes, maybe. But what does that have to do with me being a Scylla?"

Zo steps forward. "Scylla is like, one of the most famous Greek monsters." Astrid snorts. "Besides Medusa, of course," she quickly amends.

"In the Odyssey, Odysseus sails his ship into the lair of Scylla rather than take his chances on Charybdis. Scylla eats six of his men," Liv explains.

"Hmm. Doesn't sound like he made out that well, then," I answer sarcastically. "What would have happened if he took a chance with Charybdis?"

For the first time since I've met her, Liv's gentle demeanor vanishes, replaced by a ruthless smile. "Then *all* of them would have drowned."

I frown. "And what makes you so sure I'm a Scylla?"

"Most of us get our teeth with our claws," Zo quips. "But only the more...*scary* monsters get them when they are angry." She nods in Liv's direction. "Like our Liv over here."

I turn to Liv half expecting her to be insulted, and I'm thrown for a loop. She looks pleased, that ruthless smile still gracing her features.

"Then why couldn't I be a Charybdis?" I argue.

"Have you shown any sort of affinity for water?" Liv asks.

I think back to the night of my party, and then to my most recent urges. The only affinity I have seems to be the desire to eat boys. How convenient.

"No," I say with a breath. "I think I need a minute." Or several. I turn my back on the group as I make my way to a secluded area I find behind some trees.

I don't know how long I stay there, resting against the bark, contemplating the fact that not only am I a monster, but according to the girls, I'm one of the "scary" ones, and I don't know how to feel about that.

"Everything okay?" A concerned voice asks.

I raise my eyes to find Nick looking absurdly handsome, even in a pair of jeans and a *Fleetwood Mac* t-shirt. Moonlight brushes across his blue-black hair, his sharp, chiseled features accentuated by the glow of the fire behind us.

"Fine."

He takes a step toward me. "Scarlett told me you met Kieran."

I take a sip of water. "Yeah. Charming guy. Why is he still allowed to go to school here?"

"Zo didn't tell anyone except for the girls."

I don't comment on that. It was something I assumed the minute I'd asked the question. Zo wouldn't be the first – or the last – girl to not report assault of any kind. I think of the fear on Zo's face and anger threatens to consume me. It's unfair how boys like Kieran keep getting away with shit like this, and girls like Zo continue to live in fear and sometimes, misplaced shame for thinking they allowed it to happen or feeling too vulnerable to come forward about it.

A familiar sting reverberates throughout my gums, my teeth once again piercing through the sensitive flesh, as I picture Kieran acting carefree and innocent. Saliva pools in my mouth, the strange taste of almonds overwhelming my tongue while visions of me tearing into Kieran's throat and ripping apart his chest have the corners of my mouth lifting in a satisfied grin.

"Hungry?"

My attention snaps to Nick, his own lips twisted in a knowing smirk. I lick my lips hastily, praying to some greater power I also haven't been drooling.

"Why do you say that?"

He juts his chin in my direction. "Your teeth. Those are some fucking fangs."

A blush creeps into my cheeks at what sounds like the strangest compliment ever. My stomach somersaults as Nick's eyes linger on my mouth before I finally realize that yes, that *was* a compliment. What is my life?

Thank you feels far out of reach as an appropriate response, so I decide to change the subject. "I don't understand. How could Kieran attack Zo in her dreams?"

Nick shoves his hands in his pockets, a tendril of dark hair falling onto his forehead. "You don't have any abilities in your dreams. Essentially, Zo was powerless to stop him. And once an incubus latches on to your dreams, they control them. Her roommate, Liv, was away at the time, so there was no one to wake her up."

A shiver wracks my body. "But he can't hurt her now?"

"No. And there are a few reasons he wouldn't hurt her again."

"The girl gang," I answer, thinking of Kieran's terrified face when Astrid threatened him with removing her gloves.

Nick nods. "Zo also has a tattoo on her wrist that prevents Kieran from entering her dreams. And there's one more thing."

I raise my eyebrows.

He takes one more step, all but in my personal space. Amber eyes seem to glow in the firelight. "Me."

Scarlett's words echo in my mind when I asked her if Nick was dangerous: *It depends.*

I fold my arms across my body. "And just what makes you so terrifying?"

Nick flashes a sharp smile. "More information you have to earn, Rhi."

"Um, Nicky?" A high-pitched voice rings out. "Am I interrupting something?"

Nick continues to look at me, eyes searching for something as he answers the girl, hidden from view by the trees. "No, Sam. I'll be there in a minute."

"So," Nick crosses his arms over chest causing the sleeves of his shirt to strain against his biceps. "Scar tells me the gang thinks you're a Scylla."

That explains the inquisitive look in his eyes. Like his sister and her friends, to him, I've become a shiny new toy.

"Like they say, it's all Greek to me." I shove my own hands in my back pockets.

Nick's eyes drag up my body to my face, lingering first on my lips before settling on my eyes, a bored gleam to them, as if he's not impressed with what he sees.

"Well, *I* don't think you're a Scylla," he says in an authoritative tone.

Despite the fact that I don't know exactly what a Scylla is, I'm irrationally annoyed at his claim.

I cross my arms over my chest, mimicking him. "And what makes you such an expert on the subject? Are *you* a Scylla?"

Nick laughs, a smug, arrogant cackle that has my gums aching around my fangs. My claws are also pushing their way through my nails.

"Nickkkyyyy," A shrill voice complains.

His jeering ceases, and Nick's face twists into irritation as he drops his arms.

"Better get going, *Nicky.*" I can't resist flashing my own mocking smile, complete with my new sharp accessories.

If my taunting bothers Nick, he doesn't show it. "At least walk back with me. I don't want to risk Kieran finding you alone."

We aren't far from the party, but I take his offer, nonetheless. "Well, aren't you quite the mother hen."

He chuckles. "The result of having a younger sister."

I'm surprised to feel my heart fall. Of course, his being here isn't out of interest in me – it's brotherly concern. He probably does that with all of Scarlett's friends. Except, maybe Astrid.

Wait - why should I care what this pompous pain in the ass thinks of me, anyway?

Nick drops me off with the girl gang and stands several feet away in a large group of nearly ten people. Naturally, seven of those ten are girls, one with tawny, short hair that gives me a look of disdain.

That one must be Samantha, I muse.

I come into the gang's conversation just as Zo is iterating a story about her step-mother, whom she continuously calls "step-monster," and my thoughts turn from wondering if she means that literally when the tawny-haired girl from Nick's group speaks in a loud, crooning voice I can't help but overhear.

"It's *so* nice of you to look after your little sister's friends like that, Nicky."

In my periphery, Nick shrugs. "You remember being a freshman. Making good choices seems to escape them." He speaks with that same aloof, pretentious tone he'd had with me in the hallway. The entire group laughs as if he's just told them the most hilarious joke, even though nothing about his comment was remotely funny.

At this point, I'm seething. Exactly how old is Nick, to be sharing sage advice like he's Gandalf? Besides, *I* didn't ask him to come check on me. He took that upon himself, and some-thing tells me it was more than looking out for his "little sister's friends."

"Rhi, earth to Rhi!" Scarlett gives me a gentle shake.

I blink. "Sorry." I stretch my mouth wide, still feeling the throbbing in my gums.

"What's going on? You look like you want to eat someone. Was Nicky being rude again?" Her hazel eyes are bright and worried, and my anger ebbs.

"Not exactly." I think of the entire group's laughter. "Though it would be really excellent if I had extra heads with long necks and razor-sharp mouths to pick an entire group of people off at once."

The gang apparently misses my scornful glance over to Nick and the others. They're too busy staring at me again, excitement evident on each of their faces.

"*Yes*, you're definitely a Scylla!" Zo exclaims, and Liv nods enthusiastically.

"Let's just hope she still wants to hang out with us after everyone else finds out what she is," Scarlett says.

Astrid rolls her eyes. "Yes, yes, she's a fucking legend. Let's not stroke her ego even more."

I shuffle my gaze among the four girls, not bothering to address Astrid's comment. I'm learning the best way to deal with her is to ignore her completely, especially since whatever she can do when her gloves are off scares the shit out of everyone else. "Again, you've all lost me. What did I say that makes you absolutely sure I'm a Scylla, and why is that so exciting?"

"You tell her, Liv. You're her cousin," Zo prompts.

My eyes go wide. I'd forgotten about that. "Are we really cousins?"

Liv nods, smiling. "Well, we aren't cousins the way humans are cousins. Our monster ancestors were cousins, so we do share some common ancestral traits. But I wouldn't mind calling you my cousin if you don't." Her aquamarine eyes are hopeful.

I smile back at her, that kernel of belonging sprouting again. "I'd like that."

"Personally, I think Rhi should do her own research and decide herself if she thinks she's a Scylla," Astrid suggests.

I'm not one to shy away from a challenge. "I think that's a fantastic idea, Astrid." My smile is wide and sharp as I let my teeth show.

Scarlett laughs. "Uh oh, Astrid. This one's not scared of you."

Zo joins Scarlett's laughter, tucking the loose tendril of dark hair behind her ear. "Just promise me that when you know for sure you're a Scylla, you'll still hang out with us, okay?"

Again, my gaze travels to each girl, taking in the characteristics that make them unique. As different as they are from each other, from me, we all share a common thread, something that binds us inexplicably.

That welcoming comfort is there, wrapping itself around my shoulders, a silken shawl settling upon my skin. I smile and for the first time since my eighteenth birthday, hope blossoms in my chest, like a flower that has just found the sun after spending too much time in the dark.

SEVEN

The soft glow of my laptop lends a dim light to our otherwise dark room. Scarlett gently stirs in her bed opposite mine, but I'm confident she's more asleep than awake. Unfamiliar words dance along the screen like dark pixies as I research my supposed monstrous ancestor, Scylla.

According to myth, Scylla was once a very beautiful sea nymph that was loved by the Greek god Glaucus. He enlisted the witch Circe, for help in making Scylla fall in love with him. But Circe loved Glaucus and in her jealousy, turned Scylla into a hideous monster. Another source claims it was a sailor that was struck by Scylla's beauty, rather than Glaucus, but the message is still clear: Scylla was never born a monster. She was cursed into one.

Sources also differ on what she looked like in her monstrous state, but the description that stuck with me was Homer's account of Scylla having six long necks with heads lined with rows and rows of sharp teeth. And at the party, didn't I voice a desire to have just that as I stared venomously at Nick and his posse?

The answer is yes. Yes, I did. That's why the girl gang were so gleeful as soon as the words left my mouth. They obviously knew what Scylla looked like.

But it's not my (hopefully never visible) monstrous form that has the girls so excited; it is allegedly what a Scylla would be able to do. What I discover about my alleged ancestor is fascinating, but also resonates with me on a personal level. It's like discovering you perfectly align with your zodiac sign.

The next morning, I take my findings to Professor Talbot, eager to have someone else confirm my assumption. Professor Talbot glances at me from behind his Edwardian desk, opening a familiar manila folder filled with sheaves of paper.

"I must admit, I'm very pleased to see your enthusiasm in researching your heritage," he says.

"So, it's definite then? I'm a Scylla?"

He nods, that a fiendish grin lighting up his face.

The confirmation should excite me, but all I can think about is sprouting six heads the next time someone cuts me off on the highway.

"You don't look pleased," the Professor observes.

"I won't..." I struggle to get the words out. "I won't turn into one, though? Right?" My anxiety takes a tangible form in the sound of my shaking voice.

"Of course not."

I breathe a sigh of relief. "Then why is everyone so excited that I'm a Scylla?"

Professor Talbot places both hands on the desk, rising from his seat. He then clasps his hands behind his back and paces the length of the desk. "I'm sure you know that we've never had a Scylla at the University before."

I nod.

"Well, that would make you interesting enough, except that it's been said Scylla possessed a form of telekinesis."

My mouth drops open, and the wide expanse of my blue-green eyes must alert him to my incredulousness because he clears his throat. "The description of Scylla you read claimed she had six heads, yes?"

Again, I nod.

"So, think of it as you having six invisible heads that stretch from your mind, allowing you to move things you are not touching."

"That's fucking amazing." I clamp a hand over my mouth in letting a swear word slip in front of a professor.

But Professor Talbot grins wider and for the first time, displays his own set of razor-sharp teeth. "I'd have to agree with you. It *is* fucking amazing. Scylla, herself, was able to train one of those heads to watch *behind* her."

I tap my knee with frenetic excitement, finally looking forward to starting classes where I'll be able to tap into these abilities. But with all that talk of powers, I'd forgotten one important thing: I was still a monster.

That's the problem with power, and magic being a form of it. It seduces you into a state of comfort. It allowed me to momentarily forget about the fact that the body I'd been familiar with my whole life has a completely different side to it. One that is foreign and arcane. It's a body I will have to reintroduce myself to, and it feels strangely like having to go through puberty all over again.

My face falls, and Professor Talbot, whether he sensed my apprehension or saw it, asks, "What's wrong?"

I chew on my bottom lip. "This all sounds so incredible, but at the end of the day, we're still monsters. Dangerous, terrifying-"

He comes around the desk to face me. "Who said we were dangerous?"

"Well, no one actually *said* that," I confess. "But I wanted to eat a friend of mine last month. I have teeth and claws-"

"A kitten has teeth and claws. Does that make it dangerous?"

I think about that for a moment. "I guess that depends."

"On?"

"A kitten that's not provoked isn't dangerous. But if you get too close and piss it off..."

"Ah." His impish grin returns. "Let me make something very clear: We are no more dangerous than your provoked kitten. We are no different from humans. Like them, we have weapons to defend ourselves should we need to. They have their guns, bombs and knives. We have teeth and claws. And, like humans, some of us are bad apples in the bunch, that *do* have a desire to hurt and maim independent of the desire to defend ourselves." Kieran's face comes to my mind. "But our heritage doesn't make us evil," Professor Talbot continues. "Humans decided that of us long ago, just as today they decide what skin color or religion or sexual orientation is the subject of their hatred."

His words sink into me, filling a small void in my heart. For months, I've been swimming in a rapid torrent of shame. For each moment I'd found comfort in my new lifestyle, I had another where I suffocated myself beneath waves of guilt and fear.

But Professor Talbot was right. I'd let the generic definition of the word *monster* consume me, constantly wrought with worry and sorrow that I wasn't a person anymore. Yet, haven't I still been the same girl? The one who, at age ten, wanted nothing more to be Sailor Moon and run off into the sunset with Tuxedo Mask.

I'd been so preoccupied with the notion of *what* I am, but

the teeth and the claws, the abilities, none of those things change *who* I am.

THREE WEEKS LATER, the day before the first day of classes, I sit on my bed, frowning at my schedule.

"Uh, Scar?"

Scarlett pauses leafing through a magazine. "Hmm?"

I hold up my phone, displaying my schedule. "One of these things is not like the other."

She gets up and sits beside me, eyes creasing as she studies the schedule. "I don't see a problem."

"Really? Tell me which one doesn't belong: Beginner's Transmogrification, Ancient Myths and Legends 101, Intro to Poisons, and *Economics?*"

Scarlett blinks, unmoved. "Well, this is college after all. We have to take regular college courses like everyone else." She rises. "I'm going to meet Astrid for coffee. Wanna come?"

I shake my head. As much as I love hanging out with the girl gang, I'm not fond of being a third wheel, and I *know* Astrid will not appreciate my presence. "No thanks. But I'll meet everyone for dinner later."

Scarlett shrugs and leaves. She's gone for barely two minutes when someone knocks on the door. Without thinking, I open it.

Nick stands in the doorway, all broad shoulders and arrogance. One forearm steadies him against the doorframe, his other hand in the pocket of his jeans. A *Rolling Stones* graphic t-shirt hugs his biceps and chest, and that maddening, wayward lock of hair falls against his forehead.

He straightens when he sees me, peering over my shoulder. "Is Scar here?"

"You just missed her."

"Okay." He eyes the phone in my hand. "Is that your schedule?"

I didn't realize I'd kept my phone with me when I answered the door. "Yeah." Long, muscled legs sweep past me.

I didn't invite him in, but I don't plan on kicking him out, either, even if Nick has studiously avoided me since the night of the party.

He holds out his hand. "Can I see it?"

"Sure."

Silence follows as Nick studies my phone, and I keep my mouth shut for reasons being I have no filter, and ever since the bonfire, I've been dying to tell him what a smug prick I think he is.

A beautiful smug prick. But a smug prick, nonetheless.

"You've got Cicero for Trans. That's excellent. He's cutthroat, but whatever abilities you have, you'll excel in no time," he tells me, eyes still glued to my phone.

I resist the urge to snort at the "whatever abilities you have" comment. Nick still refuses to acknowledge that I'm a Scylla, for whatever reason.

"Steffens likes to give a pop quiz every week, so for Ancient Myths, make sure you keep up with the reading."

I nod, though he's not looking at me.

"I didn't have Lang for Economics, so I can't really help you there, but Wilde for Poisons will be tough." He finally looks at me, a hard expression on his already chiseled face. "Standard grades don't count in Poisons. Whether you become violently ill or not is how you're graded."

Hearing that, I'm almost positive my olive skin has turned alabaster.

Nick puts a hand on my shoulder, his fingers touching bare skin exposed by my tank top. Warmth like drizzled honey trickles from the spot his fingers touched.

"Listen, you'll be fine. Stay alert in that class. Make sure you pay attention to *everything* Wilde says. She likes to drop hints in her lectures. This is not the class to zone out in or skip, even once."

I swallow. "Okay. Thank you."

"No problem." He drops his hand from my shoulder and hands back my phone, my skin tingling from his touch. But Nick doesn't move toward the door, just continues to stare. Assessing? Judging? Or after avoiding me for nearly three weeks, did he forget what I look like?

The silence grates against my bones. "Do you actually listen to those bands you wear all the time?" This is a ridiculous thing to say, but one of us had to speak, and it's better than insulting him.

He gives me a bemused grin. "Why would I wear the shirt of a band I don't listen to?"

My brows shoot skyward. "You'd be surprised. Apparently, it's a trend."

Another quirk of his lips. "Do I look like someone that follows trends?"

No. You look like someone that would set the world on fire, I want to say.

"Not really," is what I come up with.

Rather than respond, his hand brushes away a strand of hair that escaped my ponytail, fingers grazing my collarbone. Nick does this absently, as if it's second nature to him. My breath hitches at the contact, shattering the moment.

Snapping out of his daze, he hastily goes for the door.

"Should I tell Scar you were looking for her?" I blurt out, amazed I'm able to formulate words.

"Uh. No," he replies, not meeting my eyes. "I'll talk to her later."

Nick leaves, and I flop down on my bed in awe. I have no

idea what just happened. Despite the fact that I'm supposed to be able to sense how people are feeling, Nick is a blank canvas. Yet all I can think about is Nick's fingers on my skin.

I let out an aggravated huff. I should be getting a head start on reading for Poisons, now that I know this class could end with me in a hospital bed. But I do the far more important thing and go on Instagram to find Nick.

Surprise, surprise, his social profile is absent. At least he has the whole dark and mysterious thing going for him.

Screams and muffled shouts echo from the hallway, and I leap from the bed in alarm. Opening the door throws me into a frenzied chaos of students running throughout the corridors, banging on doors and whispering frantically with one another. Everyone has a look of undiluted terror on their faces. Some are crying.

Still unsure of what's going on, I take off down the hall, when strong fingers wrap tightly around my wrist.

I smell him before I even see his face: Cedarwood and Vanilla, a scent that teases my nose with equal promises of danger and safety.

Slowly, I turn and bring my eyes to Nick. His breathing is rapid, and the relief in his amber eyes leaves me confused.

"You're okay," he says, eyes darting around my face, trailing down my neck and arms.

"Of course, I'm okay. It's barely been half an hour since you left. What could possibly-"

His fingers tighten around me. "Scar. Where is Scar?"

A sinking feeling settles in my stomach, and my confusion turns to worry. "She's with Astrid. Nick, what's going on?"

Nick doesn't answer. He races past me, pulling my hand and forcing me to go along. I will my feet to move as quickly as his legs, other students nothing but blurs in my periphery.

Finally, a voice shouts, "Nick!"

I turn before he does, spotting Scarlett and Astrid at the other end of the corridor. Nick squeezes my hand, but his fingers release mine as he runs to his sister. I follow tentatively, still wondering what's the cause of all this madness.

"What's all this fucking anarchy?" Astrid echoes my thoughts.

"It's Sasha Nichols," Nick says shakily. "They found her about half an hour ago."

Something about Nick's statement sounds ominous, as I'm pretty sure Sasha wasn't missing. So, if they "found" her, what does that mean?

Nick turns a sickly shade of green, and suddenly, I don't want to find out.

"Found her where, Nick?" Scarlett presses.

"In the garden, at the back of campus." His eyes shine with unshed tears. "In pieces."

CHAPTER

EIGHT

A myriad of thoughts barrel into me all at once.

The first thought is a gruesome picture of Sasha Nichols. It doesn't matter that I hadn't met her before, because all I envision is a slew of body parts strewn about the campus garden.

The second thought is the first time I heard her name was in my room – she was supposed to meet Nick, but the hallways toyed with us and he'd been late to their meeting and said he had to smooth things over with her. Was that the last time he saw Sasha?

Normally, I'd wonder what kind of animal is capable of this. But at a school filled with monsters, an animal, or even a homicidal maniac doesn't need to be the culprit when all your peers have curved, sharp claws specifically designed to pierce flesh, and teeth that put a great white shark to shame.

And I'm surrounded by hundreds of them.

My heart beats frantically, feeling as though it's trying to escape my chest. Cold sweat gathers at the back of my neck, my vision spotty at the edges. Nick and Scarlett are talking, but

56

their voices are muffled, sounding further away with each unsteady breath I draw. The ground feels unsteady beneath my feet as my knees tremble.

"Rhi's going to pass out," someone says.

Nick is behind me just as I sink backward. His chest is broad and firm against my back, one arm looping around my waist and the other grasping my left arm to keep me upright.

"Maybe she should lie down," another voice comments, this one strained and concerned.

But Nick's voice is the only one I recognize, and I wonder if it's because I can feel his lips at the base of my ear. "Rhi, just breathe," he says softly.

Breathe. Right. How do I do that again?

I swallow gulps of air rapidly, my breath coming short and quick.

"No," he says. "Slower." He takes a deep breath. "Longer." And lets it go, caressing my neck with a warm brush of air. His chest rises and falls against my back, and I mimic the motion.

Astrid and Scarlett slowly come into focus; Astrid of course, with a perfectly neutral expression on her face, and Scarlett just the opposite: cheeks flushed with worry, eyes large and troubled.

I'm keenly aware of being pressed against Nick's body, and crimson burns my cheeks as I gently push his fingers from my waist and stand upright.

"I'm okay," I say as he steps to my side. "Thank you."

"Why don't we go back to my room?" Astrid suggests. "It's close."

Scarlett throws an arm over my shoulder, guiding me away from her brother. "Nick, aren't you coming?"

"No. I...uh...should really go check on Samantha."

My mouth doesn't have a filter, but apparently, neither does my face as I inadvertently wrinkle my nose in jealousy.

But Nick already has his back to us, pace picking up to a light jog as he disappears around the corner.

"I just texted Zo and Liv. They're coming, too," Astrid says. The three of us walk, the earlier frenzy having dimmed a bit, giving me time to focus on the surprising feeling of envy I'd felt when Nick mentioned he needed to check on Samantha.

I tell myself I have to stop taking these moments with Nick and turning them into something they're not. Each encounter with him is nothing more than him being concerned for his little sister's friends. He'd said as much to me back at the bonfire.

Thoughts of Nick and his motives leave my mind as Liv and Zo come out of nowhere, wrapping us in a giant hug.

"Oh, thank the gods!" Zo exclaims. "We're all in one piece!"

"Too soon, Zo," Scarlett mutters, shaking her head. "Too soon."

Liv glances at me. "You okay, Rhi? You look like you've seen a ghost. *Have* you seen a ghost?" The way in which she phrases the question has my already addled brain contemplating whether or not ghosts are real.

We file into Astrid's room, a single. Apparently whatever Astrid can do with her hands merits the Gorgon having a room all to herself.

Another terrifying thought.

"Just because she's a Scylla, doesn't mean she can see Shades," Astrid says as she heads to a desk that sits against the wall opposite the door. Scarlett and Zo sit down on Astrid's dark green bedspread flush against the left wall, while Liv gestures for me to sit with her on a small, cream-colored sofa across from the bed.

"What's a Shade?" I ask.

"A ghost," Zo replies.

I feel myself pale again, and Liv catches on. "No one's

ever actually seen one, though," she reassures. "We aren't Oracles, so the likelihood of any of us seeing a Shade is slim to none."

Good grief. Oracle?

"Oracles are humans who receive prophecies from the gods," Zo quips, noticing my vacant expression. "Occasionally, they can see Shades."

"Are there any at this school?" I ask.

"Just one, and she's part monster, of course," Scarlett answers, looking over at Astrid, typing furiously on her laptop. "What are you doing?"

Astrid knows Scarlett is talking to her without looking up. "Hacking into Professor Talbot's files to see what I can get on Sasha Nichols."

This new information clings a bell in my brain like a pinball machine, different sections of my brain glowing as more unsettling information strikes: ghosts - I mean *shades* - are real; there's someone at this school that receives prophecies, and finally, Astrid is a hacker.

The last part is really the only thing that makes sense.

"Yeah, let's get back to that." Zo gets up and paces. "What the hell is happening here?"

"Someone's lost their damn mind," Scarlett answers.

"You guys definitely think it was one of us? Like, someone from school?" I pass a nervous glance around the group.

Astrid turns from the desk, her face drawn in disbelief. "What other kind of creature would hack a girl into dozens of pieces? Oh, and according to Professor's Talbot's report here," she jerks her head to the computer screen, "the body parts were cleanly severed."

My stomach flips, imagining Sasha's tendons and muscle exposed through the end of her elbow.

"That doesn't necessarily mean it was one of us," Liv's

voice leads me away from body parts. "A skilled swordsman is capable of making a clean cut."

Zo stops pacing and snorts. "Please don't tell me you're referring to the Sons of Hercules?"

I'm too overwhelmed to bother asking who the Sons of Hercules are, but Zo assumes a challenging stance in front of Liv. "And what if I am?"

Liv chuckles. "Then, I'd say you're bat-shit, Zo."

Zo tilts her head in an avian manner.

It's very, very disturbing.

Scarlett leaps from the bed, placing a hand on Liv's and Zo's shoulders. "Listen, obviously, tensions around here are high. But it doesn't make sense for us to argue amongst ourselves. This could be an isolated incident, but if it's not, we all have to be on high alert."

Watching Scarlett, I can tell she's doing something with that ability of hers. It's extremely subtle; her hazel eyes turn slightly greener, and she doesn't blink. Liv and Zo immediately relax and back away from each other, but both remain standing.

"So what do we do now?" Liv asks.

"I don't think any of us should go anywhere alone," Scarlett answers.

Astrid stands behind Scarlett, wrapping her arms around her waist. "I don't think that will be a problem for us." She kisses Scarlett's neck.

Zo nods. "Good idea. Let's compare schedules."

It takes a half hour to lock down our routine. We stand in a circle, phones in our palms. To my delight, I discover at least one of the girls is in each of my classes. I have Trans with Astrid, Ancient Myths with Liv, Economics with Zo, and Poisons with Scar.

"We can be lab partners." Scarlett winks at me.

"Do we decide now what extracurriculars we're going to sign up for at the Activities Fair on Friday?" Liv asks.

Zo groans. "Let's save that conversation for later."

"Activities Fair? I have to engage in something other than trying *not* to get murdered?" I say in disbelief.

There's a collective chuckle among the girls.

"It's ok, Rhi." Liv places a manicured hand on my shoulder. "The Activities Fair is fun. There's a lot to choose from, and it will be nice for us to have something to take our minds off everything that's happened."

Doubtful. It feels like it would be difficult for almost anything to take your mind off potentially getting torn apart. The pace of my heart quickens as it had earlier, before the feel of Nick's lips at the base of my ear ebbed my anxiety. The frantic beating immediately slows.

Apparently, there's a specific *someone* that takes my mind off getting killed.

"Can we just...talk about something else?" My voice comes out breathy, and I'm not sure if it's a looming panic attack or the memory of Nick's lips on my skin.

"Sure," Scarlett begins, a wicked gleam in her eyes, "especially because I'm *dying* to know why you were alone with my brother."

The girls turn their attention to me. I open my mouth but nothing comes out.

"Like, in bed?" Zo says with a smirk.

"No!" I exclaim, looking from one girl to the next. They all seem equally intrigued, sly grins on their faces.

"Damn," Liv mutters. "Another one bites the dust."

"I did *not* sleep with Nick. He came to our room looking for *you*." I point at Scarlett.

She blinks. "When?"

"Like, two minutes after you left."

She cocks her head, confusion scattered all over her face.

Just then, the door crashes open and a hysterical blonde stumbles in, brown eyes crazed and dangerous. She steadies herself and raises a long, clawed fingernail in our general direction. In a somber, chilling voice, she proclaims: "One of you is going to die."

CHAPTER
NINE

A cold feeling of dread settles in my abdomen as the girl leaves, having delivered her death sentence.

I let out a breath. "Who the fuck was that?"

Zo waves her hand. "Oh, don't worry about her."

I skewer Zo with an incredulous gaze. "She just said one of us is going to die!"

"Yeah, but she's an Oracle," Zo explains, like that's supposed to soothe me. Like she just told me this girl's birthday, or something equally trivial.

"Yes, and didn't you tell me Oracles deliver prophecies?" The cavalier attitude from the gang is scaring the shit out of me. Not one of them looks perturbed, and while I expect that kind of placidness from Astrid, I'm shocked that no one else seems as worried as I am.

"Yes, yes, but Kassi's a descendant of Cassandra, the Oracle who was cursed not to be believed," Zo further clarifies.

My blank stare must alert her that I need more information before I can write off that death sentence as inconsequential.

Zo sighs. "Cassandra was offered the gift of seeing the

future from the god Apollo in exchange for love. But she reneged on her offer after he gifted her visions of the future, and since he couldn't take back her powers, he cursed her. So, the prophecies she gave were never believed."

"But were they true?" I question.

Zo shrugs. "I don't know."

"And Kassi has the same...er...gift? She can see the future?" I press.

"Yeah, but no one believes her either," Scarlett interjects. "I really wouldn't worry about it." Her gaze finds Liv. "Remember what she said about Milton?"

A chorus of chuckles erupts from the girl gang.

Milton. Why does that name ring a bell? I think Scarlett or Astrid mentioned that name after telling me that no one had ever eaten someone they were attracted to. "What did Kassi say about Milton?"

"Who cares?" Astrid says dismissively. "You won't believe it anyway."

Liv smiles warmly. "We'll tell you another time."

Why does everyone keep saying that? But I don't get a chance to ask my question. The girl gang scatters, picking up their belongings to head back to their rooms. Scarlett, Zo, Liv and I bid farewell to Astrid, planning to meet her in a little while for dinner. Zo and Liv take off in the opposite direction once we are in the hall, leaving Scarlett and I alone.

I sense her scrutiny before I look at her. Her hazel eyes are creased, studying me. "What's up?"

"Nicky said he came to our room looking for me?"

"Yeah. Why would I lie?"

"You sure you didn't misunderstand him?"

I open the door to our room, letting Scarlett in first before I close the door and cross my arms in front of my chest. I'm not trying to be abrasive, but the last few hours have been somewhat taxing, and I just want Scarlett to spit out whatever she's taking too long to say.

"No, Scar. I understood him perfectly well." I'll leave out the fact that I can't help but listen to him when he speaks. "He came here and asked where you were. Why are you giving me the third degree?"

"Sorry," she replies, eyes drifting to the floor. "It's just that I told Nicky I was going to get coffee with Astrid." She brings her gaze up to me. "He knew I wasn't here."

A small ember of heat grows in the pit of my stomach, climbing and burning hotter until it settles in my chest. Was Scarlett implying...

She takes a step toward me. "He came here to see you, Rhi."

Electricity courses through my veins. But I force myself to quell it, remembering Nick's obvious disinterest in me at the bonfire and his arrogant, condescending attitude at me being a Scylla. Or, more recently, his leaving to go check on Samantha.

That one still kind of stings.

I throw a callous glare in her direction, one that would make Astrid proud. "Scar, I don't know if you think I need a guy, or whatever, but I really don't need you to play matchmaker." Her cheeks turn scarlet. "And I'll admit, your brother is gorgeous, but I'm not interested in him, and he *definitely* isn't interested in me."

There. I said it out loud. I admitted that Nick is stunning, and I said I wasn't interested in him. Though, I might have said that last part more for myself.

The room grows colder, similar to how it felt when Scarlett performed her tricks on Astrid and Zo, but yet again, I don't feel anything.

"What are you doing, Scar?"

Scarlett looks like a giant despite her small frame; chin

raised, eyes cool and assessing. "This doesn't affect you, does it?"

"Whatever you're doing? No."

I expect her to be angry. Frustrated, maybe. But the warmth in the air returns, and Scarlett smiles, wide and satisfied. "*If* you discover my brother is interested in you, can you promise me one thing?"

My eyes narrow. "What is it?"

She chews on her bottom lip, dropping her voice to a whisper. "Promise me that you'll give him a chance, okay?"

That wasn't what I was expecting. "I don't know, Scar. You said he was dangerous."

"I said 'it depends,'" she counters, but her countenance remains hopeful.

What, on this side of the River Styx, is happening right now? Is this one of those things where because Scarlett and I have become fast friends, she thinks I'm the perfect match for her brother?

Yet, the next words leave my mouth almost instantly. "Alright, Scar, I promise."

A MELODIC *PING* sounds from my phone the next morning revealing an email from Professor Talbot, addressed to the entire student body. It informs us to keep Sasha and her family in our thoughts, which, truthfully, is the last thing I want to do. In fact, I want to keep Sasha's murder the farthest thing from my mind.

The rest of the email asks us to remain calm and assures us that we have nothing to fear. The faculty is using everything and everyone at their disposal to bring the perpetrator to justice.

I raise my eyes from my phone, new questions flooding my

brain. Does monster school have their own version of the secret service to handle these kinds of situations? Or do they involve the human police? I'm sure the NYPD has seen some shit in their day, but even New York City, with all its uncanny characters and oddballs, pales in comparison to a school crawling with monsters.

Nearly an hour later, Astrid, Zo and Liv greet Scarlett and I at our door, and we leave to head to our classes. Astrid and I have Transmogrification together, and as I sit down at my desk next to Astrid, I glance over the syllabus. It reads like a workout routine, if said workout routine included things like: "Flex back wings; contract muscles: 20 x 5."

How does one flex wings? And what sort of creatures *have* wings? I try to get Astrid's attention, but her nose is stuck in a book.

Professor Cicero enters, a burly man with salt and pepper hair and legs so thick I imagine he must spend most of his free time doing squats. He places a briefcase on the desk in front of the class and holds a piece of paper between his fingers.

"Good morning, class. I am going to start by taking attendance, which I will only do once. Because frankly, I don't give a shit if you're here or not. This is an opportunity to become the best version of yourselves, to excel at whatever abilities your ancestors have lent you, and if you choose to squander that, then you're a bunch of morons."

Cutthroat, indeed.

"I am going to call your name, and then I'd like you to tell me your monstrous ancestor."

I cringe as he begins the roll call. I'd been dreading this part, anticipating the reactions of my fellow classmates. But maybe no one will care.

"Astrid Abrams," Professor Cicero calls.

"Medusa," she answers, not bothering to glance up from the book.

Professor Cicero doesn't seem bothered by Astrid's lack of attention. He checks off her name and continues down the list. I'm practically sweating by the time he gets to me.

"Rhiannon Ow-"

"Scylla!" I shout, unable to keep it on my tongue any longer.

Cicero brings his gaze up to me, smiling curiously. "Welcome, Ms. Owens."

The whispers start immediately.

As he finishes taking attendance, I make a mental tally of the various monsters I'd heard: a Harpy, another Sphinx, a Hydra, two Chimeras and a Cyclops - I had to actually seek out the voice that belonged to that one, desperate to see if he only had one eye. Alas, he has two - three Lamias, and another Gorgon, but she didn't specify if she was a descendant of Medusa or Euryale. Of those that I remember, not one other person said they were a Scylla.

"The next few weeks will consist of you working tirelessly on the abilities you may already know, and those you have yet to discover." Cicero looks directly at me as he says this. "Therefore, I am dismissing you all early." Collective whispers of excitement sound about the room. "However," he continues solemnly, "to fully excel at your abilities, you must have a keen understanding of your ancestor. I would like a report detailing the history of your ancestor, together with a clear description of their documented abilities – five-page minimum, due tomorrow."

The collective excitement turns into groans, and I can't help but join them. It's our first class, and there's homework.

Welcome to Monster College.

I gather my belongings, aware of students eyeing me and

whispering amongst themselves. Despite Cicero's initial curiosity, he keeps his head down, occupied by another piece of paper that he fished out of his briefcase. Astrid is already ahead of me, and I struggle to catch up with her when a body appears at my side.

"Hey, Rhi, right?" A friendly voice inquires.

It's the Cyclops. Messy blonde hair covers his forehead, and I try to peer through the fringe to spot an eyeball.

He offers a toothy grin. "It's right here." He holds up his left hand and staring back at me in his palm is a bright blue eyeball.

"Oh!" I gasp, and the eyeball blinks rapidly, as though startled. The boy laughs, his cheeks turning a brilliant shade of scarlet. "I'm sorry. That was rude," I admit.

He raises his right hand, this palm mercifully lacking an organ. "No worries. That's the typical response Boris elicits."

"You've named him?" The Cyclops and I linger near the door, Professor Cicero still engrossed in whatever he'd been reading.

"He sort of named himself," he replies bashfully. "I'm Josh, by the way."

"It appears you already know my name." I shake the eyeball free hand.

"You sit two seats in front of me. It's definitely not hard to remember the name of a Scylla."

At the mention of my ancestor, I'm instantly annoyed. Would he not be introducing himself if I were something else? "What is it with you people and Scylla's? Am I the second coming?"

Josh snorts. "Nothing like that. It's just...well..." As his voice trails, his honey-colored eyes settle on something behind me. It takes me a moment to follow his gaze, discovering that the students slow down as they pass, in the same manner cars slow on the road trying to glimpse an accident, eyes searching me with blatant curiosity.

"News sure does travel fast around here," I murmur.

"Alright, okay, nothing to see here!" Astrid shouts at everyone, settling by my side. The students that had slowed their pace now pick it up, avoiding Astrid's eyes.

"You're welcome," she says to me, admiring her gloved fingernails.

"Thanks Astrid. I wasn't aware you assigned yourself my public relations rep."

"Consider yourself aware." She whips her sapphire eyes to mine. "Now, can we get going? Your next class may be on this floor, but mine is three flights up."

"Astrid, do you know Josh?" I gesture to the Cyclops.

"Hi," he says somewhat shakily. I notice he doesn't offer his hand to her in the same way he had done to me moments earlier.

Astrid waves a gloved hand at him, then turns to me. "Rhi, let's go."

"What class do you have next?" Josh asks me.

"Ancient Myths."

Josh chews on his bottom lip as he addresses Astrid. "I have that class, too. I can walk with her."

Astrid tosses her gaze between Josh and me. "Fine," she says and turns quickly on her heel.

"Wait!" I call to her. Astrid faces me, one eyebrow arched. "We aren't supposed to walk anywhere alone, remember?"

Astrid's lips curl into that terrifying smile. Backpedaling, she holds up a gloved hand and wriggles her fingers. "Don't worry, Rhi. No one would *dare* to fuck with me."

The snarky grin is still on her lips as she turns, golden hair catching the sunlight through the windows before she disappears around the corner.

Josh lets out a long breath. "She scares the shit out of me."

I smile wryly as I face him. "I think she scares the shit out of everyone."

He nods. "Shall we?" Josh gestures in front of him, and we begin our short journey to Ancient Myths.

And when I say short, I mean *short*.

The class is three doors down from the one I just left.

I glance at my phone. "Well, we have fifteen minutes to kill before class starts."

"I don't have this class. I lied," he says with a sheepish grin.

"Why am I not surprised?" I grin back at him. Josh is cute, in this just-fell-out-of-bed- type of way. Endearing. Adorable, even. But interacting on that level with the opposite sex seems ill-advised, at least until I can curb my carnivorous urges.

And yet, despite my undeniable attraction to Nick, not one of my alleged monstrous heads reared themselves in his direction.

Still smiling, Josh drops his chin, toeing the ground. "Maybe once you're finished with classes, we can meet in the library, and-"

A slimy male voice slithers down my spine: "Cheating on Nick already?"

Josh's eyes narrow at the intruder, and my claws are already out, teeth sharp and eager to tear into flesh. I know the voice without having to see his face.

Kieran perches beside me, lips curled into a malicious grin. I whip my head toward him faster than I thought was possible.

"What do you want, Kieran?"

The incubus folds his arms, green eyes flashing. "I see you believe the gang's version of what happened between me and Zo."

My entire body enters defense mode. Saliva pools under my tongue, again bringing with it a strange taste of almonds. A different type of hunger emerges: one of anger, of revenge. One that demands I remove Kieran's head from his body.

Gods, this kid really brings out the worst in me.

Kieran drops his shoulders as I face him; a small flicker of fear crossing his face. "Kieran," I smile, carefully running my tongue over my pointed teeth. I invade his personal space, a delicious thrill running through me as Kieran's fear becomes a savory scent that teases my nostrils, something like smoked meat. Saliva dribbles out of the corner of my mouth. I catch it with my tongue.

I briefly flirt with the idea of eating him. My brain teases me with images of my teeth tearing into the pulsing vein at his neck and ripping the flesh from his body. I imagine my lips coated in his blood, my tongue lapping up the red liquid like licking the juices from a steak. I wait for a feeling of horror, of disgust to creep in, considering I'm eyeing this asshole like he's my next meal. But oddly, only more thought comes to mind.

He would probably taste like shit.

"I can sense things, Kieran. And I sense that you're a lying piece of shit." I only need to raise my eyes to level my gaze with his, and Kieran takes a small step backward. I won't lie and say I'm not surprised at his behavior. What is it about me that's so terrifying? I have claws and teeth – same as Zo. Same as all the other monsters.

And then I realize the advantage I have that other monsters don't: I'm an extraneous variable. No one has encountered a Scylla before; therefore, no one knows what I'm capable of. I understand Kieran's fear. Even *I* don't know what I'm capable of.

Judging by the look of terror on Kieran's face, I can tell that it's going to be fun finding out.

Despite his palpable fear, Kieran stands his ground, his stare unwavering. Admirable, really, considering I'm exerting every ounce of self-control to refrain from tearing him to pieces.

I'm grateful for Zo's courage in telling me what happened. How many other girls has he taken advantage of that haven't spoken out? That didn't know what he is capable of and fell for the same vulnerability Zo witnessed?

Kieran forces the smile back on his face, eyes slitting towards Josh. "I didn't think blonde and boyish was your type."

"Assholes aren't my type, Kieran."

One side of his mouth curls; a snake slithering upright. "Then why do you want Nick so badly?"

My initial instinct is to deny it, but something tells me this is one of Kieran's abilities. If an incubus has the power to seduce people, he must have a knack for knowing their desires.

My neck and face heat before I have a chance to quell it, giving Kieran the confirmation he needs.

The prick winks. "Sweet dreams, Rhi." He walks away, his last statement reeking of something insidious.

A threat.

TEN

"I thought Astrid was scary, but you're terrifying," Josh says.

As Kieran disappears, my claws and teeth retract, and my body relaxes. I marvel at the control my body suddenly exhibits, as though it knows I've acknowledged what I am and can finally function as I was meant to all along.

When I turn to Josh, his cheeks are flushed, and he fidgets, adjusting and readjusting the strap across his body, looking everywhere except my face.

"I didn't know that you and Nick-"

"There is no me and Nick," I cut him off.

He nods, scrunching his nose. "Okay.

Students file into the classroom. Josh peeks over my shoulder, then meets my eyes for the first time since Kieran left. "Well, Kieran seems like he deserves whatever's coming for him." He offers me a sly grin.

I can't help but smile back. There's something about this kid. "See you tomorrow?"

His grin widens, a spark of confidence in his eyes. "Maybe sooner." With that, he moves past me.

Now, I understand that all of us here fall under a category far removed from normal, but I've never met so many cheeky guys in my entire eighteen years.

Before I go in, I spot Liv and Zo walking toward me.

"Excuse me, where is your chaperone?" Zo demands.

"I traded her in for him," I jerk my head in the direction of Josh. "And Astrid deems herself too terrifying to be fucked with, so she went to her next class alone."

"Leave it to Astrid to make her own rules," Zo sniffs in disapproval.

"What about you?" I ask her. "Liv and I have class together, but who's walking you to your class?"

"My class is right there," she gestures to the same room I'd come from. "And then you and I have like an hour to kill before Econ, so Astrid and Scar are going to meet me after their class, and we'll probably just go back to our rooms."

"I've got some time after this class, too," Liv pipes in. "Want to go to the library after this class and catch up on some reading?" She asks me.

"Sounds good."

Zo says goodbye to Liv and me, and as we enter class, I hear Zo call the name of someone farther down the hall and shout a riddle at them: "What has hands but can't clap?" I smile to myself as the answer appears in my brain: *a clock.* This riddle was easier than the first one she'd given me.

Just like Trans, a syllabus greets each student at their desks. At least this one looks relatively normal. A schedule of readings, papers, and tests fill the pages. I notice that pop quizzes are conveniently left out. Then again, they wouldn't be "pop" quizzes if we knew about them.

As I fall into the familiar, dry routine of a syllabus explanation, my thoughts are invaded by Nick and my private conversation with Scarlett. I know I made a promise to her, but I'm not sure how well I can keep it. A jittery sensation flutters about my stomach when I think of the fact that Nick came to the room to see me. But why pretend he was there to see Scarlett? Nick seems too suave and sure of himself to worry about whether a girl likes him or not, judging by the cadre of girls that appear to always surround him. So, why the games?

My only conclusion is that Scarlett must misunderstand Nick's interest in me. Maybe he's finally acknowledging my monster heritage, and that's what piquing his curiosity. I'd be lying to myself if I said that didn't sting, that for all of my attempts of a cavalier attitude when it comes to Nick, the reality is I *want* Nick to be interested in me. I want Nick Cervallos to be interested in Rhi, not the Scylla beneath my skin.

Just like Trans, we're dismissed early, with reading up to Chapter Five in our textbook titled "Mythological Monsters: A Bestiary," as our only assignment. Fantastic. I was just getting used to calling myself a monster, now I get to call myself a "beast" as well.

"Nick said Steffens likes to give pop quizzes, and I have a feeling we might get one tomorrow on the first five chapters," I tell Liv as we head to the library after class.

She cranes her neck and turns her lips. "That was nice of him to warn you." Her aquamarine hairs twist away from her face in two braids fastened at the crown of her head. The rest of her hair falls in soft, luxurious curls. She looks like a mermaid, which I realize I can't rule out the existence of.

I shrug, feigning indifference to her comment. "That's what he told me when he came to our room looking for Scarlett."

"Ah. Looking for Scarlett. Right."

Time to change the subject. "So, I know Zo can hurt someone with her screams, as well as recall information at the drop of a dime, Scar can alter people's moods somehow, and Astrid everyone is just scared of whatever Astrid can do with her gloves off. What can you do?"

Liv stops, flashing me that rare ruthless smile. "It's better if I show you." She leads me outside, stopping by a fountain that sits between the classroom building and the library. It's rectangular and large enough to fit about twenty people in it, though shallow enough that the water would only reach my knees. A statue of a woman with the bottom half of a snake sits upon a sculpted marble throne. She holds her arms out to her sides, palms up, in a welcoming gesture. Water falls from her fingertips into the rectangular pool below.

"Echidna," Liv tells me. "Mother of all monsters."

That explains the throne.

Liv perches on the side of the fountain, running her fingers along the surface of the pool. "Do you know anything about Charybdis?"

"Just that it's a cousin of Scylla," I reply, as I smile and take a seat beside her.

Liv returns the smile, but it wavers. "If you ever Google it, you will get some pretty horrifying images. But Charybdis was beautiful, once. The daughter of Poseidon and Gaea. Charybdis aided her father in his quarrel with Zeus, flooding large amounts of land with water. So, Zeus cursed her and turned her into a monster."

Yet another tale of a woman being cursed by a man. I'm seeing a pattern here.

"In her monstrous form, Charybdis eternally swallowed sea water, creating whirlpools." Liv dips one finger into the pool, creating a circular motion. Though her pace never increases, the waves in the water do, moving faster and faster until a hole large enough to swallow a person forms. It thrashes and whirls, spraying water into my face.

"Holy shit." I lean over carefully, staring into the endless black pit of the whirlpool. "Where does it go?"

Liv stares at the whirlpool, smiling. "I don't know. Nowhere good, I'm guessing."

"Well, cuz, that's seriously cool." My voice carries a genuine appreciation, reflected in the way Liv's eyes light up.

Liv and I head to the library. The entrance is almost completely glass windows and doors separated only by white paneling.

The main floor is flooded with light, an information desk to the left and several long desks scattered on the right. We descend the stairs almost immediately upon entering and nestle ourselves at a long wooden desk behind some shelves.

That comfort is there again, but this is something all too familiar to me: the comfort of books. If I could bottle up the smell of walking into a bookstore, I would.

I open my "Mythological Monsters" textbook and immerse myself in the mandatory reading. The monsters are presented in alphabetical order, and I come upon the letter 'C' before I have a chance to fully digest monsters 'A' through 'B'.

A picture of a "centaur" catches my eye. I immediately think of Professor Cicero and his massive legs, built like a horse.

Unlike the other monsters I've so far become acquainted with, specific names of Centaurs are listed down the page, each with a brief description:

Agrius: fought with Hercules.

Amycus: fought at the Centauromachy

Asbolus: Seer who read omens in the flight of birds.

And on it goes, listing about twenty different Centaurs. I

hope Steffens doesn't include all of these on the pop quiz, because there's no way I'm remembering every single one.

Finally, I get to Charybdis, and the picture plastered underneath the title monster is enough to give me nightmares.

A monstrous sea creature, with the height and girth of about seven eighteen-wheelers side by side and a mouth large enough to swallow the Titanic with room to spare. It presents as a giant worm bursting through the surface of an angry, churning sea, mouth lined with rows upon rows of razor-sharp teeth. I read its history, its description, all matching up with what Liv told me. But nowhere does it mention Charybdis used to be a beautiful woman, cursed to this form by a vengeful god. No, it reads as though she was *born* this way.

Anger flares in my chest.

"Hey," Liv disrupts my rumination. "Ready to meet Zo?"

I nod, packing my things and follow Liv out of the library and back to the classroom building. Astrid, and Scarlett are already with Zo, discussing something in front of a bulletin board.

"What's this?" I look at the board. The papers broadcast different clubs and activities available at the college, everything from Honor Societies and fraternities to a crocheting club.

"It's sort of a prelude to the Activities Fair this Friday," Scarlett explains.

Right. The Activities Fair. We'd briefly discussed the Fair the night before, but everyone was too preoccupied with Sasha Nichols' death to give it much thought.

Besides, not one of us wanted to join the same club. I severely lack any hand-eye coordination, so anything to do with sports is out for me.

Honestly, nothing leaps out at me.

"Do we *have* to pick an extracurricular?" I ask.

"Yes," Zo supplies. "In Alystair, everyone is required to have an extracurricular."

I vaguely remember the Advisor who helped me make my schedule saying that.

"You'll find something," Liv assures.

The group moves a few feet away from the board while I linger, hoping something will grab my attention. It's then that a picture of two people in white garbs with what look like caged masks on their faces catches my eye. They're locked in a duel stance, a thin steel weapon in their hands. The word "Fencing" blazes in large, ostentatious letters across the top of the page.

My brain automatically equates fencing to sword fighting, which, in my head, sounds really fucking cool. But then I remember my severe lack of hand-eye coordination, which I assume this sport requires.

I sigh regretfully, eyes moving across the board to see if something else elicits the same amount of excitement in me.

Something does, though it's not what I expect.

"You should do it." Nick's voice behind me sends jolts of electricity through my blood.

"I don't think I'd be any good," I admit without facing him, half hoping he'll just leave.

Nick is undeterred by my body language. He settles next to me, my peripheral vision bombarded with the corded muscle that creeps below the sleeve of his shirt. Hunger stirs in my abdomen, a hunger I'm familiar with that has nothing to do with my carnivorous urges. Against my will, I bring my gaze to his.

There's a small, triumphant grin on his lips, as though we'd been engaged in battle I was unaware of, and he'd come out victorious. "You won't know until you try."

This kid is infuriating, but I'm more furious at myself for falling prey to the enigma that is Nicholas Cervallos.

"Thanks, Jedi Master," I say, my voice dripping with sarcasm. "I'll be sure to practice using the force while I'm at it."

Nick gives me a mollified smile, as if he knows I'll take his cliché advice. But he surprises me as he leans in, his breath warm on my neck. "Come to the dark side, then. It's much more fun." He straightens and walks past the girls, waving. "Hey Scar. Ladies."

I stare after him, stupefied, replaying my series of encounters with Nick: first encounter, acts like smug prick; second encounter, acts like concerned smug prick; third encounter, graduates to helpful smug prick, followed by scared and anxious hero. Which brings us to our most recent encounter, where we explore familiar territory: smug prick.

Yeah, keeping my promise to Scarlett is going to be *extremely* hard. I don't like playing games, and Nick is volleying for carnival master right now.

Still, there has to be a reason he acts this way with me.

With the exception of Astrid, who looks gloriously bored, the girl gang all look pleased with themselves. Scarlett, specifically, looks like the cat that got the cream.

"I know what you're thinking," I say to all of them. "And unless you count Star Wars banter as erotic, then quit looking at me like that."

If anything, my statement only makes them look more self-satisfied.

"History generally shows banter as erotic," Zo informs me.

I cast my eyes skyward. "Of course, it does."

Yet for all my protesting of Nick's interest in me, I can't ignore the small ember that sparks inside me at the thought and for once, I don't snuff it out.

CHAPTER
ELEVEN

The dread that has been following me ever since Sasha Nichols' murder intensifies as I take in my professor for Poisons class the next day.

Wilde is not what I was expecting. For some reason, I expected an elderly woman with leathery skin whose lethal smile she reserved for some unfortunate soul right before she killed them.

But Professor Wilde is something out of the pages of a gothic vampire novel. Skin so pale it's nearly porcelain, with granite eyes cut from steel. Platinum hair flows down to her waist, unencumbered by anything to anchor it; yet it stays put, like it's afraid to defy her. Like Professor Talbot, she appears no older than thirty, but the wisdom in her eyes tells me she's much older.

And unlike my imaginary elderly Professor, Wilde wears a sharp smile, one that beckons you close with dreams and thrilling promises but will cut you down faster than cyanide.

Wilde is Poison personified.

That sharp smile never wavers, simultaneously welcoming

and warning our class that she is not to be trifled with under any circumstances.

I equally love her and am terrified of her.

As the last of the students take their seats, Wilde says, "Well, look at all this fresh meat," in a voice that's all bells and chimes, so you'd never know just how deadly she is.

Terror inches over loving her. She laughs as some of the students shift uncomfortably. "Can anyone name a well-known poison?"

No one answers. Wilde's smile sharpens. "Don't make me pick you."

Scarlett raises her hand. "Arsenic."

"The King of Poisons. Good. What else?"

Another boy raises his hand. "Cyanide."

Wilde nods. "Almost as famous as Arsenic. Keep going."

Someone else calls out, "Hemlock."

Wilde's smile practically glimmers. "Excellent."

Cold panic sets in as I realize everyone must have read the textbook already to know these poisons. I mean, arsenic and cyanide are well-known enough, but hemlock? Who would know that without having read the textbook?

I curse internally as I recall planning to read the textbook before I became distracted by Sasha and Nick.

Wilde glides from behind her desk to stand before the class, a hair's breadth away from the front row, her cutting smile straightening. I've never been so happy to be in the third row.

"These poisons you've all mentioned, you know what they are?" She surveys the room, meeting every one of our eyes. No one answers her. We all know the question is rhetorical.

"Child's play," she says. "Humans trying to be gods." Her mouth turns into a wry grin. "Or monsters." She paces the length of the first row. "What you will learn in this class, no one outside of this school knows. No one outside of this school can recreate. You will not only learn how to mix poison to kill, but more importantly, you will learn what can kill *you*."

Wilde pauses her pacing in the center of class, her stare grave. "All of you, every single one of you, have more enemies than you realize. Unfortunately, the very essence of your being forces you into a role of hunted, as well as hunter." I shiver at her words. "But there is no room in this class, in this school, in your *life* for fear, and I am here to make sure the only thing you fear is my wrath should you ever forget it."

Her tirade is both inspiring and frightening. I sense her words are the tip of an iceberg, a sliver of truth with a mountain of secrets underneath.

Wilde's signature smile carves her face, and her gaze slices to me. "If you haven't already, I suggest you read Chapter One of your texts before lab later. Otherwise, some of you won't be returning to your classes until holiday break."

My face pales as I remember Nick's words: *Standard grades don't count in Poisons. Whether you become violently ill or not is how you're graded.*

Professor Cicero might be cutthroat, but Wilde *cuts throats.*

Or, rather, poisons them.

Scar and I leave Poisons in silence, afraid to open our mouths, as though the air itself might be tainted with toxicity.

"Holy shit," I breathe once we are in the hall. "That was nerve-wracking."

Scarlett nods, face grim. "I'm so nervous for lab later.

Fuck. Lab. The place where I may or may not end up poisoned. "I need to do some reading," I tell her.

"I'll come with you."

Scarlett and I go back to our room, and I relax as I finish Chapter One, which was just an introduction to the science of Poisons but mentioned nothing about specific poisons or how to make them. There was, however, one piece of information worth mentioning: *While there is no cure-all for all poison, the venom of a **Scylla** will either slow down the effects or eradicate most generic poisons.*

I have venom?

I bring my teeth down, pressing my thumb over every sharp point and feel nothing but my own saliva. Unless, my saliva is laced with venom.

Isn't venom itself poisonous? If Wilde didn't scare the shit out of me, I'd go ask her about it right now.

Our afternoon lab class is upon us before we know it, and Scarlett and I are once again silent as we head to the basement of the classroom building, running into Nick along the way. A pretty blonde girl is at his side, her posture shifting from fawning to territorial when she spots us.

"Why do you two look like you're off to the guillotine?" he asks.

"Poisons Lab," Scarlett explains.

The blonde laughs, relaxing as she dismisses us as threats. "Oh, I remember my first class. The terror is real. Nick, is this your little sister?"

"Amanda, meet Scarlett and Rhi."

"You guys will be fine!" She says in a cotton candy voice that sounds like it's reserved for toddlers. I expect her to coo at us any minute. "No one has ever gone to the infirmary on the first day."

How reassuring.

Scarlett looks as though she is going to faint; I grab her hand in mine. "We've got this," I tell her and shoot her a winning smile.

She shakily returns it, and I look back at Amanda and Nick, triumphant. But my heart sputters and goes into overdrive when I see Nick is also smiling.

Directly at me.

His smile really is something to behold. I can see why, as Scarlett put it, 'girls fall all over themselves.' He smiles with a lazy confidence, in a way that makes you think that particular smile is reserved only for you.

Scarlett is too nervous to notice, but Amanda isn't so distracted. She tugs at Nick's arm. "Let's go, Nick. I have something I want to show you."

I don't miss the innuendo in her voice and neither does Nick. He pulls his smile from me and focuses on Amanda, rewarding her with that wolfish grin.

My stomach does that thing again where the acid boils and lurches, and angry heat spreads throughout my chest and the back of my throat. I refuse to continue to call it jealousy.

I'm almost grateful for the possibility of being poisoned as a distraction. I force down a fit of irrational laughter as I take in the Poisons lab, which looks exactly like a chemistry lab. Large black desks are arranged in two rows, eight in each row. Bunsen burners, clear glass bottles with labels, glass stirrers, thermometers, and everything else you can think of that should exist in a chemistry lab. At each station also sits a bulbous flower in a pot. It grows from one long, thick dark-green stem, absent leaves. The flower itself is closed - a purple so dark it's almost black.

Scarlett and I take the second desk, with me standing closest to the aisle. There are no seats, so we stand side by side, watching the room fill up as we wait for Wilde.

Ten minutes after the class should have started, she still hasn't appeared.

"Isn't there some sort of rule that if a teacher is more than ten minutes late, we can leave?" I recognize the girl from Ancient Myths. A Chimera, I think.

I frown, not quite sure that's true. But the Chimera heads

for the door, her dark ponytail bouncing behind her. She tugs at the handle. "It's locked!"

Scarlett stirs nervously beside me. I'm not too calm, myself. Why would the door be locked?

Just as the thought crosses my mind, each flower on the desks snaps open, revealing sharp teeth on petals that whirl like a windmill while emitting a dark, rancid gas in our faces.

Screams and curses sound in my ears. The gas hovers near each station before spreading like a thin veil throughout the entire room. I bring my hand to cover my nose and mouth, watching several other students, including Scarlett, do the same. Then, it starts.

The first slump comes from the back of the room. A boy with spiky black hair lies on the floor convulsing, blood pouring from his nose.

Panic fills the room as more bodies hit the floor, all of them twitching and convulsing, blood trickling from their nostrils. Those who are still standing run to the door, screaming and begging, banging until their knuckles bleed. Until they too, join the bodies on the floor.

A death grip clasps my wrist, and I beg to whatever gods exist that I don't see what I know I'm about to see.

I hesitantly face Scarlett. Her hazel eyes are ringed with red. Dark, coppery-scented blood falls from each nostril.

"Rhi," she chokes, falling into me. I catch her as her body seizes, her grip on my wrist now loose.

"Scarlett!" Tears streak uncontrollably down my face. What the fuck is happening?

Scarlett's hand latches on to the ends of my hair, pulling at a desperate attempt for help. The fear in her eyes nearly causes me to fall apart completely.

I struggle to push my own fear to the side as Scarlett's eyelids flutter and finally drift closed. Her breathing is short and rapid, but she breathes. Yet, I can breathe perfectly, realization dawning that the poisonous gas has no effect on me. I can search this room. I can find a cure.

I lay Scarlett down as gently as possible, dumping my bag on the ground beside her, and I reach for the textbook. I nearly tear out pages as I turn, looking for something, *anything* that counteracts the effects of this poisonous gas.

I throw the book across the room in frustration. What am I missing?

Scarlett wheezes. Her breathing stops for three whole terrifying seconds, then resumes.

The solution hits me like a sledgehammer to the gut: *While there is no cure-all for all poison, the venom of a **Scylla** will either slow down the effects or eradicate most generic poisons.*

Chapter One. I'm the cure.

I cradle Scarlett in my arms, her body completely limp. My teeth emerge with fervor, saliva dripping and ready, like they know they're needed. My mouth floods with the taste of almonds, but before I think any further on it, I sink my teeth into Scarlett's neck.

I don't drink her blood, but some of it washes over my tongue, tainted with toxicity. It tastes like spoiled milk, and I bile rises in my throat.

I pull away just as Scarlett awakes with a jolt. She sucks in a large gulp of air, which, I now observe, is clear of the gas.

"Are you okay?" I ask.

She nods, eyes wide with residual terror.

"Stay right here." I leave her side and work on the remaining students. By the time I'm finished, I've bitten about fifteen people. The feel of my sharp teeth piercing their skin is jarring, not to mention how disgusting it is to taste another person's tainted blood. I run over to a large trash bin and vomit, that horrible, spoiled milk flavor lingering on my tongue. I wipe the back of my hand over my mouth just as Scarlett approaches me with a bottle of water. Beads of sweat dance across her forehead, and she hasn't bothered to clean the dried blood under her nose.

"Thank you," I say. She says nothing, just glances around at the rest of the students looking at me in a mix of gratitude and awe.

And fear.

The door creaks as Professor Wilde steps through. It takes every ounce of my self-control to not chuck the water bottle at her head. As it is, my claws have now joined my teeth.

"What the fuck was that?" I demand from the back of the room.

Wilde raises a pale eyebrow, that too-sharp grin on her face. She scans the class, no one daring to move or scream or ask her why she almost killed an entire classroom of students.

But no-filter Rhi is here and raging and does not give a shit.

"Are you fucking insane?" I continue as I barrel toward her.

"Ms. Owens," she says in a tone that implies I'm very much overstepping.

But again, I really don't give a shit.

"I don't care what lesson that was supposed to teach us. You're unhinged. A complete fucking nutjob-"

"Ms. Owens," Wilde says again, her voice accompanied by a low growl that's not at all human.

That ceases my tirade, but I'm still seething, standing inches from her perfect porcelain face. She pins me with her gunmetal eyes and dismisses the rest of the class. "You," she jerks her head toward the door, "in my office. *Now.*" Wilde turns on her heel and though I don't want to, I follow.

Astrid waits for Scarlett in the hall, so I relax as I realize Scarlett won't be walking anywhere alone. Her sapphire eyes search me questioningly, and I shake my head and mouth *later.*

It's no surprise that Wilde's office is in the basement, probably so she can be close to her murder chamber. Besides, isn't that what basements are for? To house terrifying, murderous monsters?

Oh right. That's the school's dungeon. Silly me.

I sit in a brown cushioned chair as Wilde perches on the edge of her desk, scouring me like a bird of prey. She crosses one leg over the other, black leather pants clinging to her thighs like second skin.

"Ms. Owens," she begins, "you must realize your outburst was not only inappropriate, but unnecessary?"

Un-fucking-necessary? Fifteen students almost died in her class, and she has the audacity to tell me that my "outburst" - as she called it - is unnecessary?

I clear my throat. "I'm afraid I have to disagree Professor. Watching nearly fifteen students – one of them a good friend – almost die I think justifies my 'outburst,'" I make air quotations, "as both appropriate and necessary."

Wilde chuckles, the monster. I take back what I said about loving her and being afraid of her.

I just fucking hate her.

"They wouldn't have died, Rhi." Wilde sighs, rises from her perch, and crosses her arms. She glances down briefly before dragging her eyes up to mine. "You needed to know what you're capable of. You needed to know that you could save them."

"And you couldn't have just told me that?" I ask, bewildered.

She shakes her head, platinum hair unmoving. "No. Your venom would not have released if the circumstances weren't dire."

I give her a blank stare. She cocks her head. "I'm guessing you didn't know that."

I close my eyes, sighing heavily through my nostrils. "No. I didn't." My eyes flutter open. "But isn't venom poisonous?" Wilde nods. "Then how-"

"There's a reason Scylla's are rare, Rhi, and a reason they are revered by our kind. The tetrodotoxin in your venom is paralyzing and deadly, but when crossed with any other poison, it acts as a healing agent. It also makes you immune to *most* poisons."

"I'm sorry. Tetro what?"

Wilde looks behind her to her desk. She reaches with one hand to grab a book, then holds it out to me. "Here," she says. "Read this. I'm sorry you had to see your fellow classmates suffer, but I can't promise that it will be the last time. Please be assured, no one has ever died in my class, and no one ever will."

With that, she turns her back to me and sits in the chair behind her desk. "Do you have any more questions?"

I have one more question. One that cannot wait for me to read to have an answer. "You said my venom is deadly and causes paralysis. How will I know when it's released? What if" –and my cheeks flame as I say this –"what if I'm kissing some-one? Will they die?"

I expect Wilde to look amused, but she looks sympathetic. "According to the literature, your venom tastes like almonds. That's how you know it's been released in your saliva."

My mouth falls open as I recall the taste of almonds in my mouth right before I bit Scarlett and during my confrontation with Kieran.

"And," she continues, "Your venom will only appear in dire circumstances. When you feel threatened."

"Thank you." I'm warming up to her a bit.

"If you don't have any more questions, you're free to go."

I nod, rising from my seat.

"Rhi," she begins, rising with me, "if you need help with anything or have any more questions, please see me first. I've got more expertise in this area than most of the other professors."

"Okay," I reply, but my head is spinning with a tangled web of thoughts. The debacle in lab was more a test for me than anyone else. I'm poisonous, but only when threatened. Yet, I'm immune to almost all poison.

Good grief. I'm exhausted.

I'm too busy ruminating on the last hour's events that it takes me a moment to realize that my light footsteps are echoing in the otherwise silent hallway. Panic spears my abdomen.

I'm alone.

Well, not quite.

A second set of footsteps trail behind me, lighter than mine. My claws unsheathe and my teeth sharpen, the deadly flavor of almonds washing over my tongue. I spin to face my alleged attacker, claws raised to strike, but I stifle a scream instead.

The Oracle; Kassi stands inches from me, a milky white veil over her dark brown eyes. Her lips slightly parted, she stares at me unblinking, as though in a trance.

I wave my hand slowly in front of her face. With lightning swiftness, she catches my wrist in a clawed grip.

Her voice is a low rumble of thunder, her words a thousand times more frightening than the first ones I heard her speak: *"They're coming for you."*

CHAPTER

TWELVE

I yank my wrist from her grip and run down the hall. Each thud of my footsteps on the floor reverberates in my ears, drowning out the Oracle's ill-boding words. I glance only once behind me as I continue to run and crash into someone else.

A scream tears from my throat before I realize it's Nick.

"Rhi," his hands are surprisingly gentle as he grabs my arms. "What happened? Are you okay?"

I force myself to breathe the way he instructed me to two days ago: slowly, in and out. "I think so." I shoot another glance over my shoulder. "Kassi...she..." I shake my head. "It's nothing."

His amber eyes crease into slits. "What did she say to you?"

"I...I can't remember," I lie. Nothing in this world can erase those chilling words from my memory: *They're coming for you.* But I decide to keep this from Nick. For some reason, this feels too personal, not to mention, it sounds ludicrous.

Nick doesn't buy it, either. He purses those full lips in protest but says nothing as he places a hand on my lower back.

"Come on," he directs with his free hand. "Let's go."

I walk beside him, the hand at my back dropping. "What are you doing down here?"

"I saw Scarlett with Astrid on their way back to your room. She had blood under her nose, and her eyes were completely bloodshot." He side-eyes me. "Scar told me what happened in class, and how you saved everyone."

"I'm just your friendly neighborhood Scylla, saving the school one venomous bite at a time," I mumble.

Nick lets out a surprised laugh. "Spiderman fan?"

"Not my favorite Avenger, but I like him." I tilt my head towards Nick. "You still haven't explained how you ended up down here."

"The girls said you'd be alone and told me you all made a pact not to go anywhere by yourselves." He shrugs as we ascend the stairs. "Figured I'd walk with you."

"I bet Amanda wasn't too happy about that."

He nearly stumbles climbing another step and turns to face me. "That's none of your business."

I bite back a snarky remark because of course, he's right. It's *not* my business. Regardless of what Scarlett thinks, Nick really hasn't expressed any interest other than being friends.

"You're right. I'm sorry," I tell him, and the hard muscles of his face relax. I meet him on the same step. "Thank you for walking with me. Kassi really scared the shit out of me with what she said."

He inclines his head, a curious smile on his face. "I thought you couldn't remember what she said?"

Shit. This is what I get for lying. "It just seems silly. Besides, I don't believe her anyway." Another lie. Thank gods Professor Talbot isn't here.

Nick's smile twists. "You don't?"

"No."

"Hmm." He continues climbing.

I scramble after him. "Has she ever said anything to you?"

"Once."

We reach the first floor, also empty, as most of the classes are done for the day.

"But you believe her?" I press.

Nick finally looks at me. "I'm still deciding."

That's a surprise. I thought no one believed Kassi, as was declared by her ancestor's curse. I'm still deciding if I believe her, myself, but to find someone else that is on the fence regarding her prophecies is reassuring.

We traipse across campus towards Northgate, and I want to prod further at his last comment.

Nick beats me to it. "Heard you took on Wilde. That's impressive," he says with an appreciative glance.

"Yeah, attempted mass murder doesn't sit well with me."

We climb the stone steps, and Nick holds open the door, allowing me to pass through first. A little less smug today and a little more Sir Lancelot.

"Believe it or not, you fared better than I did. My first Poisons Lab, I threw up for about four hours." He grimaces, seemingly remembering the encounter.

"Yikes." We take the hallway stairs to the second floor, and I wonder with a certain amount of strange optimism whether the hallways will toy with us again.

They don't. Nick drops me off at my room.

"Thanks again for walking me back." I reach for the doorknob as Nick wraps his hand around my wrist.

"Rhi, if Kassi gave you a warning, heed it."

My blood goes cold. Kassi gave me not one, but *two* warnings. I face him fully.

"Why, Nick? What did she tell you?"

He pauses, lips parting. His hand, still wrapped around my wrist, feels like fire made flesh.

A rush of air behind me catches me off guard, and I nearly fall backwards. The feel of leather descends upon my shoulder blades as Astrid steadies me, letting out a haughty chuckle. Nick snatches his hand away, like he's just touched the scorching handle of a pan. "Special delivery," he says, regaining his composure.

Astrid steps to my side, looking from me to Nick. "I trust you handled with care, then?"

He leans into Astrid, his signature grin appearing. "I'm not the one with the deadly hands, Astrid."

Astrid remains unfazed, smiling right back. "That's not what I hear."

Nick stiffens, his body now ramrod straight. Heated fury ignites in his eyes, and I sense he's taking Astrid's comment as an accusation. *But for what?*

He leaves without another word.

"What was that about?" I ask her as I settle on my bed, and she closes the door.

"Nick's being questioned about Sasha," she replies in that causal tone of hers, as if she just said *Nick's favorite color is purple,* or something equally mundane.

I clench the sheets. "Questioned?"

"I'm sure they want to know where he was the night she was murdered, since he was with her a lot." Astrid flops down on Scarlett's bed and lies down.

"But you don't think...I mean...does Scarlett know?"

Astrid shakes her head.

"Where is Scarlett, by the way?"

"Showering."

That sounds like a great idea. I'm also not keen on being alone with "Astrid with the Deadly Hands", but this new information regarding Nick is both alarming and intriguing.

"Do you plan on telling her?"

Astrid sits up with an annoyed huff. "No, Rhi. The only reason I know this information is because of my hacking. And I don't plan on telling my girlfriend that her brother is a possible murder suspect. Nick can tell her himself."

I toy with a loose thread, avoiding Astrid's gaze. "Do you think he did it?" I whisper, as though saying it any louder might make it true.

The shuffle of her feet tells me she's up and approaching, but Astrid doesn't sit beside me. Reluctantly, I glance up, surprised to find a rare look of empathy on that stone face.

"No, Rhi, I don't. I've known Nick as long as I've known Scar. But before you get into anything with him, you should know there's a reason he's not good at relationships, and it's not because he's a player."

She finally joins me on the bed. "I'm sure Scar told you that her and Nick are half-siblings?" I nod. "They have different fathers, except, and I don't know how much of this is true, but it's been said that Nick's father is a god."

A part of me is not surprised, and yet, I still need to wrap my head around the fact that gods and monsters actually exist. Of course, the most beautiful boy I've ever seen would have godly blood flowing through his veins. He couldn't just have been *born* that ridiculously good-looking.

"Which one?

"I don't know. But because of it, he has *a lot* of abilities. More than average for our kind. Some of them are your run-of-the-mill powers, and others..."

"Others?"

Astrid's stare is grave. "Others, no one has even heard of."

Is he dangerous? I'd asked Scarlett.

It depends, was her answer.

Scarlett walks through the door as though summoned by my thoughts, holding the front of her purple robe, her hair wrapped in a white towel. Her flip flops squelch across the floor as she goes directly to her bed, not saying a word to either of us.

"Scar?" Astrid calls.

There's no response. Astrid shoots me a look of concern and walks over to Scarlett, who curls into the fetal position on her bed. Astrid sits and places a hand on her hip. Scarlett closes her eyes, a shuddering breath escaping her chest.

"I was so scared," she says.

The lab. The gas. I was so busy thinking about Nick and my prophecy of doom that it didn't occur to me that Scarlett might be suffering from post-traumatic stress after that class.

"I'm so sorry, Scar." I tell her.

She opens her eyes, a small tear bouncing down her face. "You saved my life. You have nothing to be sorry for."

"Wilde only did it to test me. She used everyone in the class as lab rats so my venom would release, and I would know what I was capable of." As I say it, the rage ignites again. What a ridiculous and careless way to let me know I'm useful.

"I didn't know that Scylla's were immune to poisons," Astrid admits.

"Not all," I clarify.

"Scar also tells me her Persuasion doesn't work on you."

"Nope."

"Interesting," she murmurs, then glances down at her gloved hands. "I wonder if you're immune to me."

I fidget, thinking of Nick's earlier words. *I'm not the one with the deadly hands, Astrid.* "What is it that you can do with your hands?"

She smiles down at them, palms facing up. "I'll show you, one day."

Saturday hits me like a bucket of ice-cold water to the face, not that I'm complaining. After a hellish week, I've never been more grateful to wake up with nothing to do.

Well, that's not entirely true.

After the rest of the week passed uneventfully (Poisons was thankfully undramatic; Trans was mostly meditation to strengthen the mind; Ancient Myths was a whole lot of reading and no pop quiz; Economics was…Economics), I decided to break out of my comfort zone and sign up for fencing at the Activities Fair on Friday night.

Okay, and take Nick's advice, I admit.

The first introductory class is set for ten this morning, and I curse as my phone tells me it's already nine-thirty.

I throw on a pair of leggings and work out attire, and *geez,* what is it with sports bras? I mean, I'm not much of an athlete so I don't wear them often, but the one I do own feels like it's choking my boobs because it was wronged by them.

After my teeth are brushed and I throw my hair into something that looks like a bun, I grab my drawstring bag and sneak out of the room so I don't wake Scarlett. I'm probably going to hear some shit from the gang about walking alone, but it's broad daylight and there's plenty of people already out and about to witness my hypothetical murder if it were to occur.

The auditorium sits on the first floor of the building between Northgate and the library. I push open the door to the auditorium, surprised to see it already a flurry of activity. Figures dressed in those same white outfits I'd seen on the flier dance on blue mats lining the floor, that thin weapon between them. I count about twelve people paired off on each mat, all unrecognizable behind the caged masks.

A flash of blonde catches my eye as I spot Josh leaning against the wall a few feet away from me, arms crossed over his chest. His eyes are glued to the fencers, but he must feel my stare. He looks at me and smiles.

I head over to him, elated that I have a friend amongst a group of strangers.

"Scylla," he greets.

"Hey, Josh." I eye his left hand, and wave. "Boris."

Josh laughs. "I don't think anyone has ever outright acknowledged him before." He holds his palm up, that electric blue eye scrutinizing me. Josh clenches his fist, and Boris disappears underneath his fingers. "Do you fence?"

That causes me to laugh. "Not at all."

"Me neither," he says with a relieved sigh.

I share in Josh's relief, knowing that at least I'm not the only entirely brand-new student trying out an activity they'll probably be terrible at.

A tall, willowy girl calls us to attention. Her hair is ink-black streaked with royal blue, and she has a regal posture, holding herself with a certain grace I assume only students who have been at this school from conception can achieve. She introduces herself as Madeline Fitzgerald, a senior, and distantly related to *the* F. Scott Fitzgerald of *The Great Gatsby* fame.

This school is something else.

Madeline gives us an enthusiastic speech about how wonderful fencing is, how it will improve our mental focus and our hand-eye coordination (major WIN, for me) and teach us discipline and *blah, blah, blah.*

Lady, just give me a sword.

To which I learn that the aforementioned sword is called a

foil. And basically, the first thirty minutes of class is learning all the fancy fencing words, which I know I'm going to forget in ten seconds. And then, I'm disappointed to learn that we aren't going to do any fencing today. Instead, we are going to observe the *real* fencers show us their stuff.

I should have slept in.

I sit cross-legged beside Josh, a few feet away from one of the blue mats. Our knees touch, and if he notices, he doesn't shift away. I place both hands behind me, leaning back on my palms, eagerly awaiting the duel about to take place.

Two masked figures approach from opposite ends of the mat, and I take in their body language. The figure to my right is jittery, footsteps light but hurried. He or she is nervous.

The figure to my left stalks to the center of the mat like a wolf. His or her posture is relaxed, the confidence of this person evident in each deliberate step.

"*En-garde,*" Madeline says. The fencers relax into position.

"*Pret,*" she says next. The sword hand of the jittery fencer shakes a bit.

"*Allez!*" At that final command, the fencers engage. The one on my right goes straight for a lunge, but the confident one must see it coming and dodges with ease. The match ensues, and I lean my body upright, fascinated with the swiftness and dexterity of both fighters. I come to view it as less of a match and more of dance. Both fencers are agile and elegant, their feet so light to the mat they almost look like they're hovering. But the confident one is winning, judging by the numerous strikes against his or her opponent.

After the fifteenth strike, Madeline yells, "*Arrêt!*" The fencers back away, and Madeline joins them on the center of the mat as they flank her.

She grins with exhilaration. "I hope you all enjoyed that demonstration. Now, I'd like you to meet two of your instructors. You'll be working with them and a few others in the oncoming weeks."

The one to the right takes their mask off first. Dark brown eyes regard us coolly, the face beneath the mask a portrait of perfect arrogance. Despite the small display of nerves I'd seen while she fenced, this instructor now looks like she would eat us alive.

I bite my bottom lip. If that instructor has the audacity to look that confident after she lost, then I don't want to see the face of the other one, the instructor who treated that mat like it was nothing more than a runway for him or her to strut their stuff.

But the confident one removes the mask, and I shouldn't be surprised to see his face.

Sweat gleams across his forehead, his blue-black hair almost saturated. It does nothing but darken the locks and makes me wonder what his hair would feel like beneath my fingertips. His amber eyes are ferocious, triumphant, the way a king's might be having just returned from a victorious battle.

I can't stop staring at him.

And regardless of the fact at least seven pairs of eyes are also staring at him, he only stares back at me.

CHAPTER

THIRTEEN

I force my jaw to stay locked and finally avert my gaze, finding Josh looking at me instead.

"Nick and Bianca will be your instructors this year," Madeline's voice draws my attention back in front. So, Bianca is the name of the instructor that is now looking at all of us like we're pesky insects she'd like to crush underneath her ridiculous-looking fencing shoes.

I'd like to shove a foil up her ass.

"You'll work with each of them, sharpening your skills. At the end of the school year, we will have a competition, a chance for you to show off what you've learned." She smiles like she has a secret. "Well, that's it for today. See you all next Saturday."

Josh is up before me, holding out a hand. I take it, making sure not to glance at Nick, though I feel his eyes on me.

Josh blows out a puff of air as we walk toward the back wall where we left our things. "A competition? Shit." He shakes his head. "Wish I would have known that before signing up."

"You can just quit," I say, my shoulders tensing at hearing Nick's voice behind me.

"Nah. Quitting is for quitters."

I laugh. "Well, then we'll just have to practice extra hard to ensure we both come out looking like Jedi Knights. Maybe our abilities can help us." I think of how useful it would be if and when I can tap into my telekinesis to make my opponent trip or stay still as I strike. Although, that's probably illegal and a form of cheating, but I'm not a good follower of rules.

"Do you know what your abilities are?" Josh asks.

"Other than I'm immune to some poisons and some powers, no."

Josh's face perks up. "Really?"

"Mmhmm. Oh, and I'm also a walking antidote. So, should you ever find yourself poisoned by a jilted lover, please come find me."

I reach down to grab my drawstring bag and sling it over one shoulder, leaving Josh to a fit of laughter.

"What's so funny?" I ask when I straighten.

"I don't think I'm in danger of being poisoned. I'm usually the jilted lover."

"Oh, so you're the one doing the poisoning, then."

Another fit of laughter. "Nah. Not my style."

"I get it. You prefer a good old-fashioned knife-in-the-back."

Bewilderment sparks in his eyes, but his toothy grin remains. "I just meant I'm a lover, not a fighter."

"Oh." Of course. Because, as always, I take things a step too far.

Without warning, I'm assaulted by the smell of cedarwood, vanilla, and sweat.

"Hey, Rhi." Gone is Nick's previous white get-up. Pity. Having a conversation with him would be so much easier if he were still in that absurd outfit. Now he wears a simple pair of black basketball shorts and socks with black sandals – a boy trend I can't figure out.

Oh, and he's shirtless. Because that's necessary.

"Hey. Nice um...moves back there." What in the world am I saying?

His lips press against a smile. "Thanks."

I do my best to rip my eyes from his chiseled bronze chest and Spartan abs – a miraculous feat, really – so I can pull my attention back to jilted Josh. "Have you guys met?"

"I don't think so." Nick offers his hand, but Josh stiffens, fists clenching at his sides. Fear widens his honeycomb eyes.

"I just remembered I have to get over the library. I'm meeting someone." Josh says this hurriedly, the words coming out in a jumble. He whizzes past me without so much as a wave. I turn my neck to follow his trail, watching as he flings open the door and disappears.

I face still-shirtless Nick. "Do you normally have that effect on people?"

"Abject terror? All the time."

I cross my arms. "Doesn't work with women, it seems."

"That's because men are cowards."

"Or you're really not that scary."

He gives me *that grin*, teeth gleaming. "Why don't you walk with me and find out?"

For the record, I want to say no. Despite my agreement with the girl gang, I don't need him to babysit me, especially when he sends these incessant mixed signals.

But he's off before I can protest, hard back muscles tight beneath his skin. He grabs a duffel bag by one of the blue mats and reaches inside, drawing out a black shirt.

Really? He couldn't have put that on *before* he came over here?

He drags the shirt over his head and makes his way back to me, bag in hand. "So, what do you think?"

We exit the building, the campus lawn littered with students as it had been the first day I arrived. Warm sunshine splashes my face as we move towards the dorms.

"Well, you could definitely use some toning in your mid-section," I say with obvious sarcasm. "If your goal is to be an extra in the next *Magic Mike* film, they'd never take you."

"I was talking about the class, Rhi," Nick says with a dramatic eye roll, but the corner of his mouth curves up.

"I mean, if you're training me, you certainly have your work cut out for you. All that fancy footwork? You might as well be teaching me to fly."

He chuckles. "Essentially, that's what we're doing. Don't worry, when it comes to me, you're in good hands."

I stumble at what I mistake for an innuendo, and he grabs my arm.

"We'll work on your balance and footing," he says, releasing me. "Was there anything you liked about it?"

I contemplate the match between him and Bianca, and how it appeared Nick anticipated Bianca's moves, and sometimes, vice versa. "I like how there seemed to be some sort of strategy involved. It was like you knew your opponent. It reminded me of playing chess."

He turns his head and smiles. Of all the things I'm immune to, why can't I be immune to *that*? "It's *exactly* like chess, Rhi," he says with excitement. "Do you play?"

"Here and there." No way was I going to get myself caught in that trap. I'm sure "chess master" is just another hat Nick wears because of his godly parentage.

"I don't know how to play," he says as we reach the dorms.

I'm genuinely shocked. "It's not that hard."

"Maybe you can teach me, and in exchange, I can give you extra fencing lessons."

These walks of ours are becoming more and more bizarre. Yet I find myself saying, "Sure," as we reach my room. "When do you want to start?"

"How about tonight?"

"Tonight?" I reply, uncertain.

"Unless you have something else to do." His jaw twitches underneath his smile. "Plans with Josh?"

Oh, how the tables have turned. I lean into him. "That's none of your business." I flash him a mocking smile as I parrot his own words back to him. "But I'll be available by nine, if you're not busy."

I don't have plans with Josh, obviously. Nick just needs a taste of his own medicine.

"Nine it is." His smile is relaxed, and I manage to keep the surprise from my face. "Common room?"

"See you then."

Nick leaves, and I open the door to my room wearing a victorious smirk.

The entire girl gang is here, scaring me out of my wits. "Gods! What are you all doing here? And why are you all so quiet?" I hadn't heard a single voice while I stood outside. You'd think five girls in a relatively small space would generate some noise.

"I need an outfit for my date tonight," Zo croons from Scarlett's desk. "And it appears you do, too."

"No, it's not-"

"And who are you meeting this evening?" Scarlett asks, hazel eyes twinkling. She sits on Astrid's lap, who is perched on Scarlett's bed.

Oh shit. This is going to cause an uproar of monstrous proportions. "Listen, I'm meeting Nick, but-"

Scarlett squeals. Astrid rolls her eyes. Zo grins from ear to ear and exchanges a knowing smirk with Liv, who sits on my bed.

"But it's not like that!" I interject. "I'm just going to teach him how to play chess, and in exchange, he's going to give me extra fencing lessons."

"Oh, I'm sure he's going to give you *lessons*," Liv says as Zo laughs. Even Astrid manages a tight-lipped smile.

I give Liv my best glower. "We're meeting in the Common Room. I don't plan on bringing any condoms unless you think it's likely I'll be getting fucked by the hallways."

Astrid nearly spits out the water she'd been taking a sip of. "Gods, Rhi, I love it when you let the Scylla show."

I turn my attention to Zo. "Who are you going on a date with?"

"Andrew DeLeon. He's a junior. I've had my eye on him since the bonfire."

"He answered one of her riddles correctly," Liv pipes in.

"Yeah, after answering her incorrectly five times," Astrid counters.

"He showed persistence," Zo says with annoyance.

As they bicker, Sasha Nichols comes to mind. We were told she'd been returning to the dorms after a night out when she was murdered.

"Are you leaving campus?" I ask.

"Of course," she scoffs. "We're going to Carbone."

"How did Andrew get reservations there? It's almost impossible." Scarlett asks in disbelief.

Zo waves her hand. "His dad is some big Wall Street guy."

She's missing the point. "Zo, do you think it's smart to be leaving campus when someone was murdered only a week ago?"

"In that case, *not* being on campus might be safer," Scarlett points out.

"Fine." I sigh heavily through my nostrils.

"If Zo doesn't return to our room by midnight, I'll start to worry," Liv says in a way that makes me think she won't worry at all.

"Who says I won't go back to Andrew's room?" Zo says with a wicked grin.

"Zo, I don't care whose room you go to as long as you go there and return in *one piece.*" I level my stare. "Got it?"

"I got it," she says softly. "I'll be careful."

"What about you?" Liv stands and tilts her head, aquamarine eyes thoughtful. "What time are you meeting Nick?"

"Nine," Astrid and Scarlett chime together.

I gesture to the couple. "You heard them."

"Scarlett and I can walk you there," Astrid tells me.

"Ok," I reply.

Scarlett leaves Astrid's lap and pulls me towards our closet. "Let's find you something to wear tonight," she suggests gleefully.

"Leggings and a Sailor Moon T-shirt is what I was going with."

She shoots me a look of disdain as Zo and Liv giggle together. "Just indulge her, Rhi," Liv calls out.

As Scarlett rifles through the closet, I can't help but acknowledge that a small part of me *does* want to look nice for our little chess match tonight. After all, chess is a game of strategy, and nothing says strategy like distraction with an outfit to kill.

FOURTEEN

The Common Room is practically empty when I arrive. Astrid and Scarlett were happy to escort me to the door but left the moment I was safely at my destination.

A fire roars from a large ornate fireplace in the wall opposite; a glossy flat screen TV hangs above its mantle. Several couches and upholstered armchairs are scattered throughout the room, the fire creating a cozy glow against the dark wood of the furniture.

Inside the room, I count only about three other people, including the one I came here to meet. Nick lounges in a corner, one arm draped lazily over the back of a chair, the other resting on its arm. His eyes meet mine as I enter, gleaming and golden and cat-like, striking against his entirely black ensemble. And though his signature wolf grin is absent, there's no mistaking the predatory shift in even the most subtle of his movements; the way his gaze hungrily searches for mine.

Perhaps this boy has a strategy of his own.

I smooth my palms down the sides of my black jeans as I

walk toward him. Scarlett decided to pair them with a white tank top, which she claimed would look magnificent against my tanned olive skin and dark golden-brown hair.

After deciding this outfit was simple and harmless enough, I obliged. Nick's eyes leave my face and dance along my collarbone before falling to my chest, each sweep of his gaze leaving a burning trail against my skin.

He rises as I approach and pulls out my chair. "You look very nice."

"Thank you." Just before I sit, he pushes the chair in, and I hold back from making a joke and saying something like "You're too kind, good sir," in light of his newly emerged etiquette.

When Nick returns to his seat, his gaze flicks to something behind me.

"We have an audience," he says.

I turn. Sure enough, Scarlett and Astrid have the Common Room door slightly ajar, the sneaky little spies.

I toss my hand flippantly. "They'll get bored soon enough. Shall we?"

His answer is a slow smile.

I spend a good twenty minutes explaining the function and rules of the pawns, the knight, the rook, the bishop, and the king and the queen, to which he asks no questions, just continues staring at me with that lupine grin.

"Now, I don't expect you to remember all that-"

"I remember everything you just said."

"Of course, you do."

Nick gives me a quizzical look. "It's hard not to listen when you speak."

I will myself not to blush as I recall thinking something similar about him. Instead of answering, I push my center white pawn out two spaces.

Our chess match begins, Nick unsurprisingly a quick study. He takes his time before each move, eyes rarely leaving the chess board. In most cases, I'd spend this time calculating my next five moves, but with Nick being a novice, I slack off a bit.

He brings his hands to rest under his chin, elbows on the table. I sense a bit of frustration in him – he doesn't know what move to make next.

"Why do I get the feeling you opened with some sort of strategy?" he asks.

I can't help but smile. "Because I did."

Nick glances at the board once more then lets his arms drop as he looks at me. "I don't have a chance of winning, do I?"

Still smiling, I shake my head. "I opened with what's called the Bishop's Opening. You countered it well in the beginning, but I saw your moves coming a mile away." Crimson stains his cheeks. "Don't take that personally," I quickly amend. "I play a lot, and you're just starting."

He regards me with a tilt of his head. "I thought you said you played 'here and there'?"

Damn. I *did* say that. "I lied."

"Evidently." Nick runs his hand along his mouth, his eyes returning to the chess board with conviction. "Okay, tell me how you're going to win."

I launch into my explanation, showing him the next three moves he was undoubtedly going to make that would result in my bishop moving in for checkmate. When I meet his gaze, he's staring at me with a look of appreciation mixed with astonishment.

"That's exactly right. Wow." He shakes his head in what appears to be disbelief before looking at me. "You're going to be great at fencing."

I tsk. "No hand-eye coordination, remember?"

"Yeah, but that's-" His eyes lock on something behind me. "Can I help you?"

Josh enters my vision as I crane my neck. "Hey," I try to cover up Nick's rude greeting.

"Hey," he replies as he tentatively approaches. "Sorry to interrupt. I was just getting back and heard your voice." He looks at me. "Thought I'd come say hello."

"Where were you coming from?" Nick doesn't hide the suspicion in his voice.

I shoot Nick an annoyed glare before saving Josh from replying. "It doesn't matter. We were just wrapping up our chess game." I gesture toward the board.

Josh glances briefly at the board before holding his right hand to Nick. "I'm sorry I left in such a hurry this morning. To be honest, you kind of scare me."

Nick raises an eyebrow and gives Josh's hand a firm shake. He then looks at me. "See? I told you. Abject terror."

The air in my lungs rushes out. I'd been preparing for some sort of alpha male showdown, but Nick offers Josh a sparkling smile and says, "Nice to meet you."

"He's not scary," I tell Josh. "Excellent fencer and mediocre chess player, but scary? Nah."

Nick strikes his chest as though he's been maimed. "Mediocre?"

Josh laughs. "Well, I'll let you guys get back to your game. Goodnight."

"Night," I reply as Josh leaves, and I return my attention to Nick.

"Mediocre?" he repeats, that wolf grin flashing boldly.

My eyes roll skyward. "I know. It must be so gut wrenching for you to discover you don't automatically excel at something. Will you be okay? Do you need anything?"

His amber eyes darken as he leans forward, his broad chest casting shadows over the board. "What are you offering?"

Okay. I walked right into that one.

"My skills as a more than decent chess player," I tell him as I roll the queen between my thumb and forefinger.

"I'm pretty sure that was part of our original bargain." His smile is sharper now.

My breath hitches at the suggestive note in his voice, and for all my strategies and calculations during our game of chess, right now, I've got nothing.

Right now, Nick's got me in checkmate.

And nothing about it is awful.

A creaking echoes loudly throughout the empty room as the door opens. I tear my gaze from Nick toward the person entering, and a trickle of fear creeps down my spine as I recognize the oracle, Kassi.

Even across the table, I feel Nick's body stiffen when he sees her. Kassi freezes upon noticing us tucked away in the far corner of the room. Thankfully, her eyes are a normal brown, not milky white the way they'd been when I'd seen her in the basement, but the emotions swirling within them are anything but tranquil. They glisten with fear, doom, and panic as she looks from me to Nick and then back to me, before her eyes widen. She inhales a sharp breath, and I wait for her to deliver one of her terrifying prophecies.

Yet, nothing comes. Kassi hurries from the room as quickly as she came, leaving a heavy sense of dread in her wake.

CHAPTER

FIFTEEN

Nick and I continue to meet twice a week, once for my extra fencing lesson and once for his chess lesson. Though Kassi has yet to show up again to either, there hasn't been another heated moment between us since.

It's at about our third fencing lesson that I finally admit to myself that I *like* Nick Cervallos. And not just because he's nice to look at either, which is definitely a plus. Like right now, he lifts the hem of a dark blue tee shirt to wipe sweat from his forehead, giving me a breathtaking view of his sculpted abs, complete with an incredibly defined 'v' that might as well be a neon sign that says "look here!"

"See something you like?"

I drag my gaze up his still exposed stomach to find Nick staring back, a familiar smug tilt to his lips.

"Oh, please. I know you do that on purpose." I scoff.

He flashes me an impish grin, full of white teeth. "I never said otherwise. Besides, you seem to enjoy the view."

I feel my cheeks start to burn, and I try to quell it. I won't let him get under my skin. "Maybe I'll start using my shirt, too." I gesture to the fitted black tee shirt I wear under my fencing gear.

Nick's brows shoot up, that sultry, maddening grin still on his face. "What's stopping you?"

I turn my face to hide my smile, and the fact that I have no quick-witted retort hardly bothers me. It's always like this with us. Always challenging each other. Always locked in some sort of duel, whether it's chess, fencing, or verbal sparring. Nick's proven to be a worthy opponent on more than one occasion, his absurd intelligence lending itself well to our friendly battles.

"Are we done for the night?" I ask, facing him again.

"Tapping out?" He counters, arching a dark eyebrow.

"Poisons test tomorrow," I say grimly, and that wipes the playful expression from his face.

"Ah. Ok then." He gestures toward the auditorium wall, where we've placed our bags and water bottles. Nick waits until I'm beside him before he starts walking, and we both retrieve our belongings.

"You nervous?" He watches me intently as he drinks from a stainless-steel bottle.

"Of course," I answer, swallowing my own drink. "Don't you remember my first Poisons Lab?"

Nick winces as we head toward the exit. "Anything I can do to help?"

My brain immediately goes to inappropriate places. I grip the bottle tightly, trying to shake the image of Nick hovering over me, sweat dripping from his brow, his hands running down my body, and his mouth -

"Tell me something about yourself," I say abruptly.

He stares at me incredulously.

"What?"

He shrugs, pushing the doors open. "Nothing." Nick goes silent for a moment, and I'm worried he's not interested in opening up to me. We take a right and walk down the hallway. Moonlight spills through the tall arched windows, painting the marble floors a sparkling silver, its glow the only light by which we can see.

"I hate Jello."

I whip my head in his direction, astonished by his sudden proclamation. "Are you kidding?"

"Nope. It's disgusting. Don't put me within three feet of it." He wrinkles his nose.

"Now I know what to get you for your birthday," I tease. "What's your favorite color and food?

"Blue and my grandmother's paella." Nick smiles, like he's reliving a fond memory. "What about you?"

"Hmm. Red and pizza." I furrow my brows. "What's paella?"

"Only the most delicious meal you'll ever have. It has rice, chorizo, mussels, saffron..." He trails off, releasing a deep sigh. "What I would give to have that right now."

"Why don't you go visit your grandmother this weekend?"

Nick laughs, full and warm. His eyes dance. "I'd love to, but she's in Spain, where I'm from."

My mouth drops open. "You weren't born here?"

He shakes his head.

"Can you speak Spanish?"

His hand grips my elbow, stopping me in my tracks. We face one another, and Nick leans in, whispering, *"quiero besarte hasta la muerte."*

I raise my gaze slightly, pulling my bottom lip into my mouth. Nick's eyes hungrily track the movement.

"What does that mean?" I ask with a shaky exhale.

Nick draws me into him, his hand still on my arm. "Let me show you."

He takes my chin between his thumb and forefinger, angling my mouth towards his. My eyelids flutter closed when an inhuman, blood curdling scream wrenches them back open. Nick places his body in front of mine, moving at an unnatural pace. My heart in my throat, I grip the back of his shirt, my eyes darting in every direction to ascertain where the scream came from.

It's then I realize the hallway looks different, and that we'd been walking far too long without realizing it. The exit is now before us, its double doors creaking open like they're waving us through.

"Shit," Nick mutters. "We need to go. I'll take you back to your room." He wraps a hand around my waist to usher me forward, but it never leaves. He grips me tightly as we leave and move quickly across campus. It's not late enough on a Thursday evening that no one might be out, yet not a single student or teacher is outside. Fear coats the back of my throat, sliding down into the pit of my stomach where it nestles itself like a poisonous snake.

"What was that, Nick?"

"I don't know," he answers, those eyes of his alert and moving in every direction. I even see his nostrils flare, as though he can scent the danger. "But that scream wasn't human." We thankfully reach Northgate and step inside. "I don't know if you are aware, but the hallways were...letting us have a moment, for quite a while."

Ah. I knew it felt like we'd been walking for far too long while we talked.

"But when the doors appeared after that scream, that was them telling us to get the fuck out of there," he continues as we make our way up the winding staircase toward the second floor.

I shiver involuntarily, too many unsettling thoughts in my brain. What kind of monster made that sound? Was it the one that murdered Sasha? Or was it someone *else* being murdered?

I stop abruptly, pausing to place my hand on the wall and catch my breath before another panic attack takes me in its claws.

"Rhi," Nick whispers. "Breathe." He gently rubs a hand down my hair. "Look at me."

I do as he says, finding his eyes wide with concern. "I won't let anything happen to you, ok? I'll tell Talbot about what we heard first thing tomorrow morning."

I nod, swallowing against a dry throat.

"Your room is right down the hall." Nick holds out his hand to me, and I take it, the feel of his warm, lithe fingers encasing my own enough to slow my erratic heart and chaotic breathing. We reach my door in a few quick strides, and I swipe my key card, relishing the view of my room when I open the door.

"Thank you," I say to Nick, who doesn't follow me in. Instead, he peaks over the threshold.

"Scar's not here?"

"She's staying at Astrid's."

"Oh."

Realization pierces me like a shard of glass. I have the room to myself tonight. *Oh* indeed.

My thoughts war with one another. Inviting him in would definitely mean *trouble*. But...good trouble. Right?

No. He's the school's notorious bad boy.

But who cares? Don't I deserve to have fun?

You like him more than you want to admit.

It's that voice I hate. The one that reminds me fucking him and forgetting him wouldn't be possible.

I sigh regretfully. "Goodnight, Nick. And thank you again."

He smiles almost ruefully. I'd forgotten our fingers were still entwined, and he brings my hand to his mouth, sweeping his lips across my knuckles. "*Quiero besarte hasta la muerte.* Goodnight, Rhi."

He turns and walks away, and I close the door in a stupor, replaying those words again in my head. *Quiero besarte hasta la muerte.* Gods, I wish I knew what that meant. Though, I have a pretty good idea. I sit with my back against the door, chewing the inside of my cheek, turning my thoughts over. Finally, I yank the door open.

I move as swiftly as I can, though Nick couldn't have gotten far. Juniors typically dorm on the third floor, so I head towards the stairwell. I slow and come to a complete stop just outside the archway to the stairs. Voices travel towards me, one undeniably Nick's. The other is female, familiar, and I recognize it as Kassi's voice.

"Stop this now, Nick," she hisses.

"Your prophecies aren't always accurate, Kassandra." Nick's tone is volatile, but there's a hint of desperation underneath, like he's trying to convince himself.

"*This* one is, Nick." Her answering sigh is heavy. Remorseful. "*Please.*" Unlike Nick, Kassi doesn't hide her desperation. It's nearly palpable - her tone so imploring it feels as though her anguish grew talons and raked them down my back.

Nick says nothing at first. And I wait- the hard, cool wall flush against my back - right outside where the two of them discuss a prophecy. And despite what Nick said in an earlier conversation about deciding whether or not he believes her, it seems as though he does.

They're coming for you. Kassi's earlier threat echoes in my ears, and I shudder. Because if both Nick *and* I believe her, does that mean what she says is true? And if so, who, exactly, is coming for me?

"Fine, Kassi. It's done." Nick answers with finality, and something within me shifts with that conviction.

"It's for the best Nick."

There's no response on his end, just the rustling and movement of footsteps heading up the stairs and fading. I blink several times before I detach my body from the wall, releasing a deep breath. I take a few steps down the hall, contemplating everything I just heard, when Kassi's sad voice permeates through the darkness.

"It's for the best."

CHAPTER

SIXTEEN

Nick passes me in the hallway without so much as a second glance the next day. I ignore the warning bells in my head and naively attribute it to him rushing to class, judging by his quickened footsteps.

My heart knows better.

It's proven correct when he doesn't show up for our chess lesson the following Tuesday, and he simply responds to my text with a generic, "Sorry, something came up."

On Wednesday, I happen to glance up from my Poisons textbook while studying in the library, and find Nick rushing past me, his chin tucked into his chest.

I'm *seething*. I slam my book closed, hastily grab my belongings, and follow him past rows of bookshelves until he finally turns a corner and opens the door to a private study room. He barely glances behind him as he attempts to close the door, but I slap my hand against it to keep it open. The blatant shock on his face when he faces me comforts my rage.

"Can I talk to you?" Though I phrase it as a question, it comes out like a demand.

Nick's Adam's apple bobs as he swallows. He inclines his head toward the room in invitation, turning away from me as he moves inside. I follow and close the door.

He turns and crosses his arms as he leans against a gleaming chestnut table, his expression cold. "Well?"

I ignore the way his detachment cuts me. "Why are you ignoring me?"

He sniffs. "I'm not."

"Don't lie. You're fucking terrible at it." Nick raises two brows at my vitriolic tone. If there's one thing I'm great at, it's reading people. Playing chess will do that. Besides, I would know. I'm an outstanding liar, myself.

Nick relieves a weary sigh. I study his beautiful face and discover dark circles beneath his eyes. "Things are complicated, Rhi. Let's leave it at that."

I narrow my eyes, any sympathy I'd had for him gone in a flash. I'm so angry at the way he's casually dismissing me. After all, it wasn't my imagination - I *know* he tried to kiss me that night. And just like the first night we played chess, I know I didn't imagine his heated gaze and the way he flirted right up until Kassi -

Kassi. She'd be there the other night too, begging him to put a stop to something. Did she mean *us?* But what could Nick and I being together have to do with anything?

Unless they have a history together. In which case, all of this makes perfect sense.

I set my jaw, running my tongue slowly over my sharpened teeth. I smile a little, letting him see those *fangs* as he'd called them.

"Sure, Nick. It's for the best, right?"

The way his bronzed skin leeches of color has my inner monster positively beside itself with glee. His answering silence solidifies my victory. *Check. Fucking. Mate.*

I give him my back and reach for the door. I'm halfway through the threshold when he whispers: "I'm sorry, Rhi."

Those words have me pause. I will my feet to move, to not give into what I initially perceive as an empty apology. But that desperation is there again, the one I'd heard the night he'd spoken with Kassi. The one that begs me to believe him.

I don't face him, but I say, "Me too, Nick," and close the door behind me before he can say anything else.

OUTSIDE OF FENCING CLASS, Nick and I no longer spend time together. I'm still his fencing partner, though our private sessions have come to an end. That pricked my heart at first, but Nick is at least friendly towards me, if nothing else. Still, every so often I think back to that night, wondering if there is more to what I heard between Nick and Kassi, and if I'm wrong in thinking his subsequent coolness was a result of the two of them being in a prior relationship.

"Concentrate, Rhi." Cicero's scolding voice hurdles me back to the present.

In Trans, we've moved from meditation – which, unsurprisingly, I was terrible at – and graduated to more exciting things, like me exploring my still-yet-to-emerge powers of telekinesis. For the last two weeks, I've spent each class imagining a gruesome head like the one I'd seen in the *Ancient Myths* textbook reaching to knock a book off Cicero's desk.

"It's been two weeks, Owens," Cicero scolds, "and that textbook hasn't moved an inch."

My eyes are strained from trying not to blink; my head pulses with the intensity I've been burning to focus on moving this book. Sweat beads on my temples and underneath my arms. This is more physically exhausting than fencing. My teeth grind as I attempt not to lose focus, but I am itching to bite Cicero's head off.

"You have a snowball's chance in hell of controlling all six of Scylla's heads," he continues to goad me. "At this rate, you'd be lucky if you're able to control one."

What a pain in my ass. I'd like to shoot him a scathing look, but that would break my concentration, and I'd have to start all over. I'm not interested in cutting off my nose to spite my face.

At this point, I'm concentrating so hard I forget to breathe. I exhale sharply just as my peripheral vision catches Wilde walking into class, finally breaking my concentration. *Shit.*

She and I have come to a mutual understanding since the first Poisons lab. She hasn't tried to kill any more students, and I haven't cursed her out in a fit of hysterics.

Progress.

Wilde side-eyes me as she walks over to Cicero, sitting behind his desk like a great big lump of meat. How does someone so wide fit in most doorways? The world may never know.

Cicero smiles at her, and she turns that granite gaze on him. Her silken blonde hair creates a screen between us and their faces as she leans with one elbow on the desk, hushed whispers poking around her veil of hair.

Astrid makes a noise in her throat to get my attention, and I catch her wriggling her eyebrows at the two teachers.

I find myself smiling despite the fact that I've made zero progress in two weeks. Astrid, meanwhile, returns to her latest victim, a Hydra boy with royal blue hair who volunteered to be her test dummy. Astrid has been perfecting what Cicero calls the Medusa Effect, a stare that causes someone to become paralyzed. So far, out of her twelve volunteers over these few weeks, she's only been able to paralyze two.

"I did it!" she exclaims, and I nearly die from shock. Astrid expressing an emotion other than bored disinterest is like hearing a dog sing Taylor Swift.

Wilde straightens, her waterfall of hair parting to reveal a smug-looking Cicero, his lips twisted in a mocking smile. "Robert, my boy. Can you move?"

Robert's night-dark eyes dart left to right. "Uh. No," he replies with panic in his voice. "I can't move at all."

His fingers shake and his shoulders twitch as he struggles to make his body obey his brain.

"Well done, Astrid," Cicero commends her. "Now, if you would-"

"How is Rhi progressing?" Wilde interrupts him.

"Abhorrently."

"I'm not surprised," Wilde says.

My gaze turns murderous, and Wilde shoots me an apologetic glance. "Well," she starts, "No other monster has ever exhibited any sort of telekinetic powers other than Scylla, herself, and our abilities have been diluted for thousands of years -"

"So you being able to use telekinesis doesn't appear to be happening any time soon," Cicero interrupts with a sardonic grin.

I resist the urge to stick out my tongue as I catch Wilde whispering in Cicero's ear. His grin widens.

"Excellent idea."

Fear pools in my belly as Cicero and Wilde fix me with mutinous expressions.

"Geraldine, my dear," Cicero beckons a Gorgon from the back of the room, "would you please come to the front of class? Oh, and bring your bow and quiver along."

Geraldine is the best archer of our freshman class, and never goes anywhere without her beloved bow and arrows, especially since Sasha's death. But why would Cicero have use of them right now?

Geraldine hesitantly picks up her quiver of arrows, slinging her bow over her shoulder as she walks toward the front of class. Her caramel hair is fastened in a tight braid that hangs down her back like a thick rope. She looks at Cicero questioningly.

The Centaur gets up and pulls his desk toward the wall with so little effort one would think he was merely pulling open a drawer. A large expanse of space now exists between poor paralyzed Robert and the windowed wall opposite.

"Geraldine, please stand over there," he gestures towards the wall.

She takes her position. The fear in my stomach explodes into terror as I realize she is directly in line with Robert, who remains paralyzed. Still, I can't fathom Cicero and Wilde's plan, and how it might involve me.

Wilde gauges the distance, then her steel eyes find mine. They seem to say, *don't fear, you can do this.*

"Rhi, I'd like you to stand beside Geraldine, please," Cicero instructs.

At first, I don't move. A part of me sees where this is going, though my rational brain is still fighting it.

"Ms. Owens." Cicero calls again impatiently.

I adversely oblige and stand beside Geraldine. Her breath is shaky, as is mine, but nothing compares to the look of undiluted panic on Robert's face.

Cicero crosses his arms and leans against his desk, now flush against the front wall. "Professor Wilde has informed me that your abilities seem to emerge when you're under duress. I'd like to further test that theory."

I narrow my eyes at Wilde. The Judas that she is wears a blank expression, no sharp smile now.

That scares me the most.

"What do you want me to do?" I reluctantly ask.

It seems Cicero borrowed Wilde's cutting smile. "I'd like you to use telekinesis to stop the arrow Geraldine is going to fire at Robert's head."

"Are you fucking nuts?" I exclaim as Geraldine says, "No way. Absolutely not."

Robert looks like he wants to cry.

Cicero ignores me, addressing Geraldine. "Some of your arrow tips are blunted, are they not?"

"Yeah, but-"

"Then there's no issue. Even if he's hit, Robert will be fine."

"It's still going to hurt!" Geraldine protests.

Cicero shrugs. "Then let's hope Rhi can deliver."

I stare at Cicero and Wilde with a mix of rage and disbelief. "Do you have some sort of fetish for maiming your students?"

Wilde at least has the decency to look vaguely reproachful.

Cicero gives zero fucks. "Geraldine, take aim."

The archer raises her bow unsteadily. The regret in her eyes is tangible, but she doesn't lower the bow.

This is really going to happen.

"Astrid," I plead. "Release Robert from the paralysis." Astrid looks at me with uncertainty, gnawing her bottom lip. It's the first time I've seen a soft emotion on her face that's not directed toward Scarlett.

"You will do no such thing," demands Cicero. "I will count down from five. Five..."

"Please..." Robert's lips tremble.

"Four..."

"You can't be serious!" I scream.

"Three..."

Oh gods. This is definitely going to happen. I focus all my

strength and energy on Robert. But even if I can move the arrow, will I be fast enough?

"Two..."

My hands shake uncontrollably. I can't do this. I couldn't even move a book. My heart thumps with such fierceness I swear it's trying to escape my rib cage.

"One...

My thoughts are an incoherent jumble; my focus entirely eradicated.

...And then I hear the whisper. Soft at first, but it grows harsher until it's hissing in my ear.

Release me.

"Fire!" Cicero roars.

Go. I answer the whisper just as I feel the rush of air when the bow string snaps from Geraldine's fingers and the arrow rockets from its hold, barreling toward Robert. This is all happening in seconds, but I feel like I'm watching in slow motion. The arrow glides through the air - a perfect shot. Though Cicero told Geraldine to aim for the head, she granted Robert a small mercy by going for the chest instead. I can see exactly where the arrow will strike – an inch to the left of Robert's heart. Even though the arrow is blunted, the force with which it was released will shatter his rib cage.

Whatever I let loose feels like cracking a whip; it jerks me forward as the invisible force lunges for the arrow, moving faster than I thought possible. But it's not going for the arrow, I realize. It's going for Robert.

It strikes Robert directly around his middle, and he's knocked to the floor, gasping for breath. The arrow sails past him, embedding itself into the wall behind him with a *thump*.

My vision fades, and I drop to my knees, sick with relief. I feel Geraldine run past me toward Robert, screaming his name.

Someone else is standing next me, the feel of leather against my back my only inclination sign that it's Astrid.

"Rhi, are you okay? What just happened?"

I have no explanation other than I used some sort of force to knock Robert out of the way of the arrow.

"She broke the paralysis," an awed voice states.

"Impossible," says another harsher voice.

Once my vision returns, I find myself staring at the floor. The nausea has abated, but cold sweat sits at the back of my neck. I raise my eyes to find Robert sitting upright, his face entirely leached of color, breathing in and out heavily as Geraldine rubs his back.

"You knocked the wind out of him," Astrid tells me, helping me to my feet.

"I didn't...I don't..." I struggle for words.

Wilde interjects herself between me and Robert. "Tell me what happened, Rhi," she says softly, eyes wide and curious.

"Maybe you can let her breathe for a few seconds before you interrogate her," Astrid snaps.

Wilde responds with a twitch of her jaw. "Very well." She turns to Cicero. "We can continue this conversation in your office." She once again faces Astrid and me. "Get her some juice and something small to eat. Then find your way to Cicero's office. We'll be waiting."

Astrid doesn't reply. She places a gloved hand between my shoulder blades and pushes me towards the door. I try to shoot Robert an apologetic glance, but he's staring at the floor, continuously breathing in and out, his skin still ghost white. Geraldine leans close to him as she strokes his back.

I sit in Cicero's office with Astrid standing to my right, my very own bodyguard. She refused to leave my side despite Cicero and Wilde's incessant demands, and I can't help but admire her persistence and loyalty.

Both professors observe us from behind Cicero's oak desk, laden with so many loose papers the disarray is giving me anxiety.

"Do you feel better?" Wilde asks.

I nod.

"Can you tell us what happened?"

I take a deep breath, throwing my hands in the air. "I don't really know. I was nervous, terrified. I wasn't concentrating at all. I kept thinking about how I couldn't do it." I lick my lips. "But right before Professor Cicero told Geraldine to fire, I heard a whisper." Wilde perks up at that; Cicero clenches his fists.

"What did it say?" he asks.

"*Release me,*" I repeat. "So, I did. And it felt like I was handling an incredibly strong whip. It struck Robert, knocking him out of the way."

Wilde glances at Cicero, a triumphant smirk on her face. "See? I told you. She broke the paralysis."

"But that's impossible," he says again, his voice heavy with disbelief. "She was only supposed to move the arrow."

He skewers Astrid with an accusatory glare. "Are you sure *you* didn't release Robert?"

"And how would I do that?" she says sharply. "I'd have to be staring directly into his eyes for that to happen, and I was nowhere near him. Stop trying to make excuses because Rhi did something incredible, and you can't wrap your narrow-minded brain around it."

Cicero's face turns as red as a tomato. Wilde tips her head back and laughs.

"Can we go now?" Astrid continues.

Cicero's large nostrils flare, giving me the perfect picture in my head of a pissed off horse.

Wilde nods, touching Cicero on the shoulder.

I rise, following Astrid out of the room and walk at her side.

"What?" she says when she catches me looking at her, a huge appreciative smile on my face.

"Gods, Astrid, I just love it when you let the Gorgon show."

She snorts. "That's not *just* the Gorgon," she says sharply. But she returns the smile, edged with a little cruelty. "That's Medusa."

CHAPTER

SEVENTEEN

Word spread fast of my telekinetic display in Transmogrification class. At one point, it felt like the entire school was approaching me at random intervals, asking me the most ridiculous questions: *Do each of your heads have names? Do the heads get along? Do you think I can meet one of them?*

Thank gods for the girl gang. Astrid remained my self-appointed bodyguard. Zo distracted nosy people with her riddles and Scar with her Persuasion, causing disinterest as soon as someone asked about my abilities. Liv simply steered conversation in a different direction as soon as anyone brought up the incident in Trans class. And Nick...

Nick's behavior is off, and not just with the way he's treating me; I haven't seen a new girl on his arm since Amanda.

Maybe he's been invaded by a body snatcher.

He's also become chummy with Josh. Like, bromance chummy. Josh is Nick's new fencing partner, and even though I'm sure Nick doesn't swing both ways, a heavy fist of jealousy unfurls in my chest as their easy laughter floats into my ears.

133

Because Nick was avoiding me again. In fencing, he passed me off to Bianca. When I questioned why he seemed frazzled, he cited midterms were coming, and he was overwhelmed. Because the only phrase more ominous than "winter is coming" is "midterms are coming."

I'm nervous about midterms. Especially because I have no doubt Cicero and Wilde have some outrageous plans up their sleeves for me. Maybe this time they'll place me in front of a speeding train and ask me to stop it with my mind. Or maybe Wilde will ask me to raise the dead using my venom.

The options are endless.

I feel a *thwack* against my chest padding. "Get it together, Owens," Bianca scolds me, withdrawing the foil.

"It's Rhi," I say, for the three hundredth time. But B, as I call her in my head, doesn't ever call me that. Always Owens, like the drill sergeant she is.

B raises her mask. "For the last time Owens, I don't care. At least, not until you show me you can master this move that we've done a thousand times."

Her chocolate brown eyes are saturated with impatience. She'd be very pretty if it wasn't for the perpetual scowl on her face.

"Something doesn't feel right," I tell her as I raise my own mask, resting it atop of my head. For some reason, the most recent move we've been working on, the *remise*, feels too hard to grasp.

"It's simply a short series of attacks," B huffs. "What do you mean 'it doesn't feel right'?"

I shrug. "I'm not sure. It's like my arm won't work that fast."

B tosses her mask and foil to the ground. She stands behind me, her breath ruffling the sweat-slicked hairs at the back of my neck. She brings her arms in front of me and grips my right wrist, turning it left and right, the foil in my right hand glinting off the auditorium lights.

"Hmm. Your wrist bends without resistance or cracking. Do you feel any pain?"

"No."

Her grip tightens around my wrist as she steps closer, all but a second shadow against my back. "I'm going to do the *remise* as if I were you. Keep your arm and wrist relaxed, and just go through the footwork."

I do as she says, feeling a little uncomfortable when she's standing so close to me. We move through the *remise*, me trying as hard as possible not to tense my body even though B is using me like a puppet.

Finally, she stops, releasing my wrist and coming around to face me. Her eyes dart between my right and left hands.

"Put the foil in your left hand," she tells me.

I do as I'm told without speaking, and immediately this feels better.

"Let's try again," B instructs, picking up her mask and foil.

I throw my own mask over my face, but not before catching a glimpse of the rest of the room. Almost everyone has stopped their own instruction to watch the exchange between me and B, including Nick and Josh, who stand only a few feet away.

B lifts her mask again. "Hey, nosy bitches, get back to your own duels," she snaps.

I grin beneath my mask; never thought I'd see the day where I'd be grateful for Drill Sergeant Bianca.

We duel and this time, the *remise* feels as natural to me as breathing. At the end of the lesson, B approaches me at the back of the room, as I take a sip of water before gathering my things.

"Why didn't you tell me you can fight with your left hand?" She asks.

"Because I didn't know that I could."

"Bullshit," she scoffs. "You can fight with your right *and* left. You're ambidextrous."

"Maybe," I admit, not understanding why this might be important. "I've never really tested it. Why does it matter?"

B flashes me a cat-that-ate-the-canary grin. "Did you know that Scylla, herself, was ambidextrous?"

I tighten my grip on the water bottle. "No."

"Didn't think so. There hasn't been a monster since Scylla that's ambidextrous." She glances around, her bravado briefly slipping. "I know you were taking extra fencing lessons with Nick," she starts.

Here it comes. This is the part where she tells me she's been fucking him, and I need to stay away from him because he's bad news and *blah, blah, blah.*

"B," I interrupt, "whatever you're going to tell me-"

"Did you just call me 'B'?"

Shit. "Yeah..."

Her trademark scowl turns into a strained smile. "It's fine. About the lessons, I was going to ask you if you wanted to continue having them with me."

I almost drop the water bottle. "Really?"

The scowl returns.

"Sure," I say quickly. "That would be great. Thank you."

"Thursday nights. Eight sharp."

I resist the urge to salute. "Got it."

B heads back to the mat just as Josh jogs over.

"Did she really just offer you extra fencing lessons?" He asks, pure shock lining his voice.

."Indeed. The end of days is near." I step aside to allow another fencer room to grab her things, but my foot becomes tangled in one of the straps of the numerous bags lying on the floor. I stumble, crashing into Josh. We go down in an unceremonious heap which ends up with him lying directly on top of me.

His hands cradle my head, softening the impact, and my fingers hook into the back of his shirt.

Josh's face hovers inches above mine. "Are you okay?"

"Yeah," I say with a tight swallow. "Sorry. Is Boris okay?" With his palms open cushioning my head, I worry that I might have crushed the eyeball.

He gives me that toothy grin, cheeks colored pink. "Don't be sorry. Boris has never been better."

Josh pushes himself off me, helping me to my feet. I wipe the dust from the floor off my pants and look up to find Nick watching us, his expression unreadable.

THAT NIGHT I'm woken by a pounding at the door. I jerk upright, looking first for Scarlett, but her bed is empty.

The pounding is incessant. I stumble from my bed, praying to the gods that something hasn't happened to one of the girls, and fumble with the lock on the door, finding the last person I'd ever expect standing outside.

"Nick," I breathe. "What are you doing here?"

For all his dramatic pounding, he appears remarkably calm. He stands with his hands in his pockets wearing another band T-shirt, though for some reason, the name of the band is obscured – blurred out. Nick's even got on that wolf grin of his, though something about it looks off.

"Can I come in?"

That's a first. I don't think he's ever actually asked to be invited into the room.

"Okay." I pull the door wider to allow him inside. He brushes past me, and again, I notice something odd about his movements. They're less graceful, cumbersome, as if he's not sure how to move in his own body.

I close the door and turn to him. "What's-"

Nick grabs my face roughly with both hands and crushes his lips down on mine. Startled, I push him, breaking us apart.

"What are you doing?" I demand.

His eyes flash with amusement. "You don't want this?"

I wish he'd take that shit-eating grin off his face. "Did I want you to barge into my room in the middle of the night for an intrusive make-out session? No, not really."

The grin widens but then flickers, like a static television channel. Nick steps closer, his entire body pressed against mine. "Liar."

Heated rage lances through my blood as I again push him away. "What is wrong with you? First, you all but ignore me, and ever since Josh-" I stop as something dawns on me. "Oh, I get what this is about." My eyes crease into slits. "You don't want me, but you don't want anyone else to have me, either." I steel my nerves. "Well, newsflash, *Nicholas*," I poke a finger at his chest, "that's not how it fucking works. Now get the hell out of my room."

His sinister smile is still plastered on his face, unmoving. Scowling, I shove him out of my way, but in one quick motion he grabs my arm and spins to me face him, shoving me hard against the wall. He pins me by my shoulders, my hands clawing at his arms. My claws...

Where are they?

I anticipate the taste of almonds in my saliva, but that's absent, as well as the feel of my razor-sharp teeth.

Panic ensues as I realize I'm completely defenseless against him.

I look past Nick, my eyes searching for anything in the room I can grab with my telekinesis. My voluminous *Ancient*

Myths textbook sits atop my desk, the perfect weapon to strike him upside the head.

But as much as I reach, it doesn't budge. There's no feel of the whip, no force moving forward. Nothing.

I slowly drag my eyes up to his face, that wolf-grin now monstrous. His amber eyes have gone wholly dark, and his smile widens to show off his teeth.

An entire school full of monsters, and I've never seen such a terrifying mouth like the one that looks like it's going to devour me whole.

Nick has six – *six* – rows of razor-sharp teeth. In fact, it looks as though his whole mouth is engulfed in nothing but crude, pointed fangs.

An unbridled scream tears from my lips as Nick's jaw unhinges and his mouth enlarges before he brings those fangs to my neck and rips into my throat.

CHAPTER

EIGHTEEN

"Rhi! Rhi, wake up! WAKE UP!

Hands grip my shoulders, shaking me awake. I nearly throw Scarlett off me as I lurch upright.

I take in my surroundings. I'm in my room, daylight pouring through the curtains. Scarlett looks at me with terrified hazel eyes.

"It was a dream, Rhi," she says gently and sits beside me.

I touch the spot on my neck where I felt Nick's fangs pierce my flesh and shudder. Nothing but smooth skin. I let my face fall into my hands.

"Do you want to talk about it?" asks Scarlett.

I raise my head to look at her. Do I want to talk about the fact that her psychotic brother snuck into my dreams, tried to make out with me, then kill me?

Nope.

I also don't want to drag Scarlett into this. I can handle Nick by myself.

"No, Scar. It was just a stupid nightmare. I think midterm week is getting to me."

Scarlett offers a sympathetic smile and pats my back. "Well, we can study together today, if that would make you feel better."

My gut twists. Here she is trying to make me feel better, and I'm thinking about all the ways I can dismember her brother.

But again, this is separate from Scarlett. I'm sure if she knew what he did, she would take my side. It just all feels so...*odd*. So unlike Nick. But what other explanation is there? He had to be invited in, which is why he asked if he could come into the room. And then he decided to mess with me knowing I would be completely defenseless in my dreams. I assume this means Nick is part incubus.

Rage surges past confusion as I play this out in my head.

I finally address Scarlett. "Sure. There's just something I need to do first."

I LEAN next to Nick's door, arms crossed. I'd knocked earlier, but no one answered. Maybe he was still sleeping after the busy night he had breaking into my dreams.

Throaty chuckles travel down the corridor, and I perk up hearing a familiar laugh. Sure enough, Nick rounds the corner with two other guys, one I know as Andrew, the junior dating Zo, and the other I've never seen before.

Andrew spots me first. His glacial blue eyes dance as he nudges Nick. "You've got a visitor."

For his part, Nick appears absolutely stunned to see me. Not nervous or even amused, but utterly perplexed.

Give him a fucking Oscar, ladies and gentlemen.

The other two hang back a few feet as Nick approaches me, the confusion in his eyes transforming into concern.

"Rhi, what-"

I pounce like a tiger and shove Nick hard against his shoulder, pushing his back flat against the wall. His amber eyes widen and turn frantic.

"Consent. It's a thing you know," I spit at him.

His face shows no sign of remorse or shame, the concern replaced by anger. His eyes narrow. "So is assault."

"Oh, please. This is warranted."

"How so?" His gaze flicks to my hand still on his shoulder.

I let my claws unfurl into his skin. "Don't try and claim that just because it was a dream, that makes it ok."

Confusion twists his features. "Makes what okay?"

Anger consumes me at his lackadaisical attitude. Even more at the perfect display of confusion on his face. I'm angrier still that he's making me spell it out, but I won't give in to him.

My grip on his shoulder tightens, the claws now dangerously close to piercing flesh. "The next time you touch me like that without my permission, here or in my dreams, you'll find these claws in a place you'd never want them."

I don't bother to wait for an explanation or apology; I doubt I'll get either one. His cold stare is visible in my mind's eye as I turn my back and leave, ignoring the astonished looks of Andrew and the other companion as I breeze past them.

The dream replays in my head, stoking my anger like a hot poker. How abrasive he'd been with his hands, and the rough way he'd touched me. And then he had the audacity to act like nothing happened? Like I was the crazy one?

But then I'm reminded that something about him in my dream seemed off. How his smiled faded around the edges; how his grin seemed less wolfish and more serpentine.

I shake the doubt away. No. It was him. How could it have been anyone else?

Scarlett is sitting on her bed when I enter our room, books

and notes splayed all over. "What's wrong?" She asks when she looks up.

"Nothing," I lie. Again, I don't want to drag her into this. This is between me and her brother. "Worried about Poisons in a few days."

She pats the space beside her. "Then come here, and let's study."

Two hours later, the bedroom door crashes open. Nick barges into our room, throwing a mangled-looking Kieran at the foot of Scarlett's bed. Blood pours from his eyes and nose, trickling slowly from the corner of his mouth.

"Nick!" Scarlett jumps from the bed. "What-"

I haven't known Nick long, but I've never seen him look so angry. He steps over Kieran, grabbing a fistful of red hair, yanking his face up.

"Tell her what you told me," he growls.

A wet, gurgling sound squelches in the back of Kieran's throat. He's trying to speak. It's not until Kieran lets out a sputtering cough and throws up blood on the floor, that I realize he's drowning in his own blood.

Some of them are your run-of-the-mill powers, Astrid's voice reminds me ...*Others, no one has even heard of.*

Nick looks as lethal as I've imagined. Amber eyes flash in the late afternoon sunlight, and I can almost feel heated fury coming off him in waves.

Kieran finally inhales, and his next words chill me to the bone. "It was me," he confesses, voice raspy.

My jaw drops. What was the last thing Kieran had said to me?

Sweet dreams, Rhi.

"What did he do?" Scarlett asks, her voice rough around the edges.

Nick's grip on Kieran's hair tightens. "Our friend, Kieran here, snuck into Rhi's dreams wearing *my* face and attacked her."

Scarlett stares from Kieran back to me, but the only person I can look at is Nick, who releases Kieran with a rough toss and leans into me. His lips are a breath away from mine as he says, "I would *never* touch you like that..." His voice trails. "...unless you asked me to," he finishes. My breath hitches. Nick steps back from me, skewering Kieran with a look that would chill the dead.

"What do we do with him?" Scarlett asks.

Nick finally looks at his sister and smiles, that slow, lupine grin I know. I resist the urge to smack myself in the head. Some part of me knew during the dream that it wasn't Nick, and it was the smile that gave it away. No one else I know smiles like that. Like a devourer of secrets.

"That's for her to decide." He leaves without another word.

Kieran remains on the floor, gasping and hacking up the remnants of blood swirling in his lungs.

I stand beside him. "Get out, Kieran."

The incubus struggles to pick his head up, poison-green eyes shining with relief. He slowly pushes himself off the floor, wiping his mouth with his hand as he leaves.

"You just let him go?" Scarlett stares at me with incredulity.

"Yup," I say, my chess brain formulating a plan. "Let's call the girls. I have an idea."

"That son of a bitch," Liv says after I repeat the events of last night and this afternoon.

Zo rises from my bed. "This has to stop."

"I agree," I say from beside her. "But I don't want to put anyone in a situation to come forward if they don't want to." Zo cheeks flame, and I go over to her. "Zo, you don't have to-"

"Don't tell me not to feel bad." Her dark eyes glisten with tears. "If I had the courage to say something, maybe he wouldn't even be in this school anymore. And this wouldn't have happened to you."

Astrid joins me beside Zo. "You think you're the first person he did this to? The only girl to stay silent?" She places a comforting gloved hand on Zo's shoulder. "No, Zo. And you can't blame yourself for what he does or did to anybody after you."

Scarlett approaches us tentatively. "Even if you did report him, less than one-third of reported perpetrators are punished."

"That's a pretty dismal statistic," Astrid says.

Zo places her face in her hands, her shoulders shaking with sobs. Liv wraps her arms around her, followed by Scarlett, who comes from behind Astrid. Finally, Astrid joins the hug. I remain detached, seething at Scarlett's last statement.

"We're *not* a fucking statistic," I say, my voice coated with so much ice that the girls look up and break apart. "In fact, we're not even average girls. Last time I checked, we've got teeth and claws. We're *monsters*. And it's about time we started acting like it."

Astrid flashes her terrifying smile. Zo and Scarlett grin with their razor-sharp teeth. And Liv gives me her rare, ruthless smile, the one I know comes from the horrifying monster I'd seen in my textbook.

"What do you have in mind?" Zo asks.

My own lips curl into a smile of cruel amusement. "I'll need two things: first, I need Kieran's number."

"I'm on it," Astrid says, strutting over to my desk and opening my laptop.

Scarlett places a hand on my shoulder. "What's the second thing you need?"

I turn toward Liv. "My cousin."

"What do you want me to do?" Her aquamarine eyes sparkle with intrigue and loyalty.

My smile takes on a sharp edge, a mimic of Wilde's. "I need you to be Charybdis."

CHAPTER

NINETEEN

The following evening I sit on the edge of the Echidna fountain, waiting for Kieran to arrive.

Though the campus at this hour appears deserted, I'm hardly alone. My monster girls lurk in the shadows, cloaked in darkness. Moonlight drowns any remaining semblance of night around the fountain itself. It shines down on me like a beacon, a glowing star in a sea of blackness. The slithering serpent can't miss me.

I glance at my phone, the bright numbers warning me of the approaching midnight hour, and I smile. Not long now.

Kieran appears right on time, green eyes bright but wary. "I got your text."

"I'm surprised you came," I say as I stand.

"I wanted to show you that I'm not afraid of you. You, or your overbearing watchdog," he snarls.

He means Nick, I muse.

I smile with my sharp teeth, saliva bursting with an almond flavor. "You should be."

Zo emerges from the shadows, and Kieran darts his eyes toward the intrusion. "What are you doing here?"

"We want an apology, asshole."

Kieran lets out an arrogant cackle. "I'm not apologizing for anything." He invades Zo's personal space, and she flinches at his proximity. Gods, how I want to rip his insides out. "What are you going to do, Zo?" he taunts. "Bore me with your riddles? You can't scream, because if you do, you'll hurt anyone within a mile radius. You're going to do nothing, because that's what you're good at."

My teeth are *begging* me to rip him to pieces. So much venom has pooled in my mouth I'll be tasting almonds for weeks.

"Kieran, you really leave me no choice," I tell him, my voice surprisingly calm.

He scoffs, facing me. "Please. You won't do anything without Nick to back you up."

"That's where you're wrong, Kieran." I step into his personal space. "I don't need back-up, but now that you mention it..."

Liv appears from behind Kieran, paying him no mind as she walks toward the fountain. Her bright blue hair dazzles once the moonlight hits it, and I hide a smile thinking about how such a beautiful creature is so, so deadly.

"What's she doing?" Kieran asks.

Now, I let him see that smile. "You really want to know?"

I don't give him a chance to answer. I strike with the invisible whip, letting it wrap firmly around his neck. Kieran's eyes widen in fright as he claws his neck, leaving bloody trail marks where his own claws scrape his skin.

Meanwhile, I shove my hands in the pockets of my jeans, doing everything with my mind. I jerk the whip toward the fountain. Kieran stumbles before I give another hard yank, and he falls to his knees at the fountain's edge.

"Wha-wha-" he struggles to say.

I cup my hand to my ear. "What's that? Can you speak up?"

"Let me-" Kieran pauses abruptly, staring in wide-eyed terror at the whirlpool churning inside the fountain. Its mouth is wide and treacherous, funneling down into a dark nothingness.

I give the whip a little slack.

"What the fuck is that?" Kieran screams.

"That's where you're going, Kieran, if you don't cut your bullshit."

For a moment, his arrogant bravado returns. "You don't have the balls," he sneers.

I tighten the whip once more, laughing as I approach him. I give another mental tug, and his body lurches downward, chest teetering over the edge of the fountain, face soaked with water. I grab the back of his shirt.

"You're right. I don't have the balls." I bring my lips to his ear. "I've got something better."

I push him down toward the swirling darkness, the weight of his upper body causing him to tip forward faster than I anticipated. Kieran lets loose a piercing scream as he tumbles toward the whirlpool, but I pull the whip back with as much force as I can muster. He falls backward, a dark stain across his jeans.

A dark blur flashes before my eyes. In between one breath and the next, Zo is behind Kieran, his eyelids fluttering like butterfly wings. Her jaw elongates as her mouth widens, flashing her rows of monstrous fangs. She leans down and sinks those sharp teeth into Kieran's neck, his screams piercing the dead night as she tears away a large chunk of flesh. Blood pours freely from the open wound at this throat. He brings a shaking hand to cover the serrated skin.

Zo spits Kieran's blood on the ground, her face twisting in disgust.

"How does he taste, Zo?" Liv asks with a savage smile, her own fangs poking beneath her upper lip.

Zo spits again. "Like shit."

"Thought so," I say with a smirk.

"I'm sorry," he sputters, "I'm sorry. I'm sorry. It'll never happen again."

"What won't happen again?" I demand.

His breath is rapid. "The dreams. The attacks. I won't ever do it again. Not to you. Not to her," he nods in Zo's direction. "Not to anyone."

"Damn right you won't." Astrid emerges from the shadows with Scarlett. She holds open her phone, revealing she'd been recording the entire showdown.

"Looks like someone needs a new pair of pants," Scarlett says with amusement.

The five of us cage Kieran in like a pack of wolves. "Look at us," I tell him. "All of us. The next time you even so much as *think* of touching a girl without her consent, remember this night. And where you'll end up if you don't behave."

Kieran nods, his throat bobbing. The blood has stopped flowing, no doubt as his body begins healing itself.

"Get out of here," Zo demands.

He crab walks before he gets up and races from the six of us. Scarlett goes over to Zo and throws an arm around her. "How did that feel?"

Zo looks at Scarlett with a satisfied grin. "So fucking good."

"I'll bet," Astrid replies, joining them. The three girls start talking about Kieran's scared facial expressions, taking turns laughing. Liv finally stands next to me.

I smile at her. "We make a great team."

Her lips twist into a sly grin. "Of course, we do. We always have. Scylla and Charybdis. You never heard of the saying?"

I shake my head.

"'To be caught between Scylla and Charybdis means to be in a predicament where avoidance of one danger ends up exposing you to the other."

"Ah," I reason, "so it's like being caught between a rock and a hard place?"

"Precisely. Except, without the possibility of being eaten."

I laugh. "Caught between Scylla and Charydbis.' I like that."

Liv lets out a breath of air. "We really got him. For a minute there I thought he was going to go over. But you played it just right."

I don't answer, just smile.

I don't tell her that I played nothing right. I don't tell her that for a moment, I nearly lost control as the weight of his body took me by surprise. I don't tell her that Kieran almost did go over and disappear forever into that whirlpool of hers.

And I don't tell her that the thought of it doesn't bother me one bit.

THE FOLLOWING evening after Operation Charybdis is my first private lesson with B.

If I thought B's offer to train me privately meant she'd ease up with her drill sergeant behavior, well, then to say I'm wrong is like saying hell is just a sauna.

"Footwork! Remember the footwork!" she screams at me. Her standards are one *corps a corps* away from impossible.

Our hour is nearly up, but I can't take another ten more

minutes of beratement. While B's back is turned, I lift my mask. "You want to come to our party on Saturday?"

She goes rigid, then immediately relaxes as she turns. "What party?"

"Bacchanal."

Bacchanal, defined as wild and drunken revelry, is a party thrown by the freshmen and sophomores right after midterms. Apparently, it's a tradition that began ages ago, and is limited to freshman and sophomores because the juniors and seniors can't be bothered with such small parties thrown in dorm rooms. Much to the dismay of the opposite sex, our party is exclusively "girls only."

Honestly? Thank gods. Nick barely looks at me whenever he walks past me as it is.

B raises a dark eyebrow. "You want me to come to a party for freshman and sophomores?"

I try to hide a scowl but fail. "No one said you *have* to come."

Scarlet colors her golden-brown cheeks. "I didn't mean it like that. You actually *want* me to come?"

I shrug. "Sure. We're friends, right?" As soon as I say it, I'm not sure that it's true. She's my Mister Miyagi – if Mister Miyagi was a perpetually angry junior in college. But that doesn't necessarily make us friends.

Then she smiles. Really smiles. Not a forced one. "Yeah. We are. I'll come. What time?"

"Eight-thirty," I tell her, still shocked that she accepted the invitation, but a small kernel of happiness sprouts seeing the elated look on her face. "You can come to my room first, and we'll go there together."

"Ok," she glances down, fiddling with the hilt of the foil, a nervous tick to her movements. "Do you need me to bring anything?

"Lingerie."

The foil clatters to the ground. I bend to grab it. "What?" I hear B exclaim.

I hand her the foil, her brown eyes wide with worry, and I fight the urge to giggle. "It's okay. It's going to be all girls."

"Oh." The panic in her eyes regresses, but she still looks wary. "Why?"

"Let's just say we're tired of guys."

Intrigue passes over her features, but she smiles. Again. Holy shit.

"I get it," she says, still smiling. "Speaking of guys, did you hear what happened to this kid, Kieran? He's a junior, too. You might not know him."

My jaw sets in trepidation. "We've crossed paths. What happened to him?"

B comes closer, leaning into me. "I don't know how much of this is true," she whispers, "but one of the seniors said they saw him surrounded by a group of girls." I stiffen. "He was on the floor, and he'd pissed himself. I don't know what they did to him or why, but he's been keeping a low profile."

"Low profile how?" It's only been a day since we threatened him.

"He's always been very bold, very touchy when it comes to girls." She wrinkles her nose. "Now, he pretty much just keeps his head down and sulks wherever he goes."

Excellent.

"I personally never liked him," B continues.

I'm liking Drill Sergeant Bianca more and more. "What about the senior? Does he know who the girls were?" I'd thought I'd planned our sabotage late enough on a weekday that no one would be traipsing around campus.

B laughs. "No. He was apparently really drunk. I don't

think anyone would have believed him, if not for the change in Kieran's behavior."

I reach to grab my mask and remove it fully. "Well, whoever those girls were, I'm sure they had a good reason." I drop my foil and start to remove the padding. B's dark eyes flit to the bandage on my left wrist, covering the fresh tattoo I'd gotten this afternoon after classes were done that will keep Kieran out of my dreams. Zo brought us to a tattoo parlor in the city, on the West side. The female owner, another Sphinx, didn't even ask what tattoo we needed. She saw Zo and just knew.

"What are you doing?" B asks.

"Isn't the lesson over?"

B glances at the clock high on the wall behind me. "We still have five minutes." She picks up my foil from the floor and hands it to me. "*En garde.*"

I groan.

CHAPTER
TWENTY

Midterms pass without any hiccups.

Though, I may or may not have failed the Economics midterm, of all things. Go figure.

Ancient Myths is iffy. Way too much information to remember. Poisons and Trans I know I passed with flying colors, and I have a sneaking suspicion the two sadists decided to go easy on me, since our tests for those classes were designed for each individual, rather than for the collective class.

The evening of Bacchanal arrives. My Victoria's Secret bag sits on one side of me, a pair of black heels on the other, waiting for Bianca.

Astrid flips through a book while Scarlett puts finishing touches on her makeup. She turns in her desk chair, her lips a startling shade of deep scarlet that beautifully compliments her dark hair and hazel eyes. "Want to try this?" she asks me. "I think it will look really nice on you."

"Sure," I shrug. I didn't do much in the way of makeup. A

little blush and mascara. "Too bad you didn't have a sister," I say as she skips happily over to me.

Scarlett laughs, carefully applying the color to my lips. "Actually, Nick used to let me put makeup on him when we were little."

I try to remain still while she finishes applying the lipstick, but I can't help the small turn of my lips. "Really?"

"Yeah. I was about four, I think, so he was six." She dabs the corners of my mouth with a napkin and sighs. "He's a really good big brother." Scarlett doesn't meet my eyes, but a part of me wonders if she knows of his being questioned about Sasha Nichols. "Don't you dare tell him I told you that," she looks at me, a tight smile on her mouth.

Without touching my lips, I pinch my thumb and forefinger together and pass them across my mouth, twisting at the corner. "Lips are sealed."

Scarlett steps back, admiring her small paint job. "Oh, Rhi, that color is beautiful. Isn't it beautiful, Astrid?"

The Gorgon glances above the top of her book. "I'd sleep with her."

"Stop, Astrid. You're making me blush." I look in our full-length mirror. As always, Scarlett's right. The color is beautiful. A deep, dark scarlet, it pulls the green from my blue-green eyes and lets them shine like polished gems. "Too bad it will wear off after two sips."

Scarlett flashes me her brother's wolf grin. It's uncanny how they look nothing alike otherwise, but that small characteristic they share might as well make them identical. "It's a stain," she explains. "It's supposed to last twenty-four hours."

"Wonderful. I'd hate to wake up tomorrow and have to reapply before breakfast."

Astrid snorts just as there's a knock at the door.

"That must be Bianca," I say, and open the door.

Oh gods. It is *not* Bianca. It's Nick.

And he looks like he just walked off the pages of a men's fashion magazine, wearing a perfectly pressed white collared shirt, gold cufflinks gleaming at his wrists. His belted black pants show off the hard muscles of his thighs. I finally drag my eyes up to his clean-shaven face, black hair combed to perfection. He blinks twice before his gaze dips to my lips.

I'm not sure how long we stand there staring at each other, though I can't imagine what Nick finds intriguing about me. While he looks like he could hop on a plane for Paris fashion week, my black leggings and gray Alystair sweatshirt are incomparable. My gut twists as I wonder if Andrew was able to get him and his flavor of the week a reservation at some fancy Manhattan restaurant – thus the reason for his attire.

"Come in," I finally say, stepping aside. He nods his head in gratitude.

"Oh, Nicky!" Scarlett exclaims. "You look so nice! I forgot you had an Eleusis meeting."

"Thanks," he says. "Hey Astrid."

Astrid puts the book down and smiles at him. "Well, don't you clean up nice."

"It took a village."

I remain behind him, feeling awkward in his presence, until Scarlett catches my gaze. "Rhi, come here! Stop hiding back there."

It takes great effort to keep from scowling at her words as I stand next to her. "What's Eleusis?"

"It's the society I'm in," he explains, looking everywhere except my face.

"The *secret* society," Scarlett adds, and Astrid rolls her eyes.

"All the elite schools have them," Nick counters, a muscle twitching in his jaw.

"What happens at these meetings?" I chime in.

His gaze finally rests on me, his lips pressing against a smile. "That's a secret, Rhi." Nick focuses his intense stare on his sister. "I really came by to tell you guys to have fun, but make sure you only drink *one* cup of the Dionysian Frenzy."

"Why? I thought we could at least have two." Scarlett gives him a sisterly whine.

He answers her with a very older brotherly look. "Because one is enough. Two is pushing it. Three...well...I better not hear that *any* of you drank that much." Nick's eyes lock on mine.

Dionysian Frenzy is evidently the "Zeus" of all cocktails. More of a magic potion, it supposedly makes you feel amazing, though, like with anything, too much of it is dangerous.

It's also illegal, but Zo's beau Andrew knows how to make it.

I can't help the smile that comes as I meet Nick's eyes. "You really are such a mother hen."

He shrugs. "Have fun guys," he says and opens the door to reveal Bianca, fist raised in mid-knock. Her face pales when she sees him.

"What are you doing here?" he asks.

I sprint forward to rescue her. "I invited her." I tug B into the room. "Have fun at your *secret special meeting*." Nick shoots me a confused look before he steps out, and I shut the door behind him.

B is dressed similar to me, holding a black bag of her own.

"La Perla?" Astrid's eyes the bag in B's hands. "Who are you trying to impress?"

B grants Astrid her signature scowl. "I like the way their things fit, that's all."

"At three hundred dollars a bra?" Astrid pushes.

I let out an aggrieved sigh. "Does it matter?" I shoot a pointed glance at Scarlett. "It's time to leave, isn't it?"

Scarlett nods enthusiastically. "Let's get over to Zo and

Liv's. I can't wait to see how they decorated! Zo said Andrew did all the glamours."

We leave with our lingerie-filled bags in tow. Liv suggested changing once we arrived at her and Zo's room, lest we roam the hallways scantily clad and earn unwanted attention.

The four of us are the first to arrive, finding Scarlett's use of the word "decorated" to be a severe understatement.

The entire room has been transformed into a forest, not with paper decorations, but an *actual* forest. I can smell the dirt, the sap from the trees, the fresh scent of leaves and pine needles. My feet sink into a mossy floor.

"This is some glamour, Zo," Astrid glances around, wide-eyed.

Zo beams. "Andrew's good at what he does. Speaking of which," she gestures to a punch bowl over where Liv's desk used to be. It now resembles a stone altar, the punch bowl one of the many treats that lie upon its surface.

B and I head over to the bowl, leaving Astrid and Scarlett to take in the unbelievable transformation of the dorm room. I think I can actually hear crickets.

"Shit. Is that Dionysian Frenzy?" B's voice is breathless with disbelief.

The liquid in the bowl is clear, but shimmers with a crystalline quality that reminds me of scattered diamonds across its surface. The scent I breathe in is a combination of a few of my favorite things: French toast, chocolate chip cookies, and… the last thing I won't admit out loud: cedarwood and vanilla.

"Sure is," Zo's voice chimes in next to B.

B fixes both of us with a serious stare. "This shit is no joke."

I brush her off with a wave of my hand. "I know. I know. Nick already warned us to only drink one."

B bristles at the mention of his name. "Oh. Is that why he was there?"

"Yeah." Something in the way she acts around Nick makes me think they have a history. Not that I should be surprised. "Let's go change."

Astrid and Scarlett emerge from a canopy of trees Liv informed us is a private area, clad in their chosen lingerie outfits. Astrid in a pale gold slip, Scarlett in a stunning red bra and matching shorts set. B and I trade places with the couple, and I toss my heels on the floor and start to undress.

B turns abruptly, giving me privacy. I peel off my clothes, and drag a midnight black slip over my head, trimmed with Chantilly lace skimming the tops of my very exposed breasts. The area underneath my rib cage is barely concealed with sheer lace, revealing the skin to the top of my navel. The rest of the slip is solid black until it reaches the very tops of my thighs, where it once again transforms into sheer lace. I put on matching black underwear and a suspender belt on last. Hooking the straps to the suspender and thigh highs takes most of my attention, and when I finally look up, B is dressed and staring at me.

For her part, she looks incredible in a burgundy bra and underwear set, with a matching robe that is loosely tied so it remains slightly open. Like me, she has on thigh highs, but the straps are absent. Her dark hair, usually tied back, hangs in loose waves around her face.

"You look..." she trails off, then shakes her head. "Really nice."

I smile gratefully, sliding my feet into my black pumps. "So do you. Good choice on the La Perla."

I gain that rare genuine smile from her, and we step out of the canopy.

Geraldine the Archer arrives with Harper Repaci, another freshman, and gives us quick hellos before stepping inside the canopy to change. B seems nervous beside me, which I find odd, considering her usual confidence during fencing class and that she's a junior. I chalk it up to the fact that she doesn't really know anyone. I officially introduce her to the girl gang, Zo immediately bombarding her with a riddle: "What disappears as soon as you say its name?"

B gets it on the second try, much to my delight, answering with "silence."

By then, Geraldine and Harper join us, and I make the appropriate introductions. Harper's dark blue eyes hold a residual melancholy, and I remember she recently broke up with her girlfriend. Geraldine and B begin a conversation about their respective skills in archery and fencing, so I sit beside Harper on a surprisingly comfortable bench made of tree bark. She gives me a forced smile.

"How are you doing?" I ask her.

She shrugs, her shoulder-length caramel hair bending with the movement. "Okay, I guess. I wasn't going to come tonight, but Geraldine forced me to."

A pang of sympathy strikes my chest. I can't help but think of Nick. Rejection sucks, in all its forms. "Well, I'm glad you're here." Harper's tight smile loosens, and I grab her hand. "Come on."

I make my way toward the bowl with the Dionysian Frenzy. No one has dared pour themselves a cup yet, but isn't this supposed to be a party? Besides, I'm usually the first one up when the buffet line opens at family gatherings. I'm not sure how this is any different.

"I like your style, Rhi." Astrid says, coming to my side.

"Are we waiting for something epic to happen?"

"Nope," Zo grins. "Liv, turn on some music." Zo sashays to the bowl. She hands out cups to Harper, Astrid and I, gesturing to pass them back to Geraldine and Bianca, who now stand right behind us.

From somewhere above in the canopy of trees, music blares as loud as a New York City nightclub, some new pop tune I've heard on the radio once or twice.

"Aren't we going to get in trouble for this?" I yell at Zo over the music.

She shakes her head, a self-satisfied smirk on her face. "The walls are sound-proofed. Another glamour by Andrew."

"Wow, Zo," Astrid interjects. "You must give really good-"

"Drinks!" Zo yells, grabbing the ladle of the bowl. I smother a laugh and flash Astrid an amused grin.

Zo fills our cups one by one. All eight of us stand in a circle, B and Geraldine flanking either side of me. B stares into her cup and sighs; Geraldine clenches her own cup, fidgeting nervously. I'm too distracted inhaling all the scents I smelled before, the cedarwood and vanilla jumping to the forefront, to be nervous about what we're about to drink.

The music lowers enough for us to have a conversation.

"Midterms are over," Zo announces. "And I'm here drinking the most notorious drink of drinks with the baddest bitches at this school."

I giggle, joined by the chuckles of everyone else.

Zo raises her cup in B's direction. "Here's to Ms. Bianca Ramos, for gracing us with her magnanimous junior presence." From the corner of my eye, B flushes. "Here's to my boyfriend, Andrew, for doing all of this shit." Zo waves her free hand around. "Who will also be getting laid tonight for his efforts."

Scarlett claps and whoops loudly, the rest of us following suit. Zo inclines her head in a mock bow. Then, she cuts her dark eyes to me. "And to Rhi, our favorite Scylla and all around bad-ass friend."

I'm momentarily stunned by the proclamation, but I find the faces of each of the girl gang, all of them shining with gratitude, and I know they're all thinking of Kieran. Zo has a secretive smile on her face, but her eyes shimmer with gratefulness. As do Astrid and Scar, who are probably recalling the incident in Poisons lab. And Liv – Liv shares her own smile of gratitude, no doubt in my accepting her offer as family.

I hold my own cup high. "To the fiercest group of unapologetic women I've ever known."

The entire group cheers, the air an infectious buzz of crackling energy. No one seems nervous any longer.

I take my first sip of the Dionysian Frenzy.

CHAPTER

TWENTY-ONE

I feel *fantastic.*

Clear liquid lingers near the bottom quarter of my cup, and my heart falls as I realize I'm almost done.

I want more.

I don't feel tipsy, or inebriated, or any of the things I expected to feel considering Nick's warning of not drinking more than one cup. Instead, I feel elated, invincible; downright unstoppable.

"Why can't we have a second cup again?" I ask no one in particular.

"Because Nicky told us we shouldn't," Scarlett immediately answers, flashing me a warning look.

Astrid murmurs against her neck: "Because you *always* listen to your older brother, right?" Scarlett's fair cheeks redden.

Harper stares down into hers. "I wouldn't mind another cup."

"Me neither," Geraldine agrees.

Zo leaves a still-dancing Liv and heads over to the bowl,

the first to pour herself another. She meets every single pair of eyes that watch her. "Just *one* more, got it?"

The girls - including Liv - lineup, eagerly waiting their turn for a second cup. Only B hangs back, tugging my wrist. "I've seen what this shit can do when you drink too much of it." She shakes her head. "It's not pretty."

I scoff. "What? Will I turn into a monster?" I smile with sharp teeth. "Been there, done that."

"I'm serious, Rhi. Short of getting really sick, you hallucinate."

I glance toward the bowl, then back at B. "Just one more, okay? Besides, I feel fine right now."

B gives me a cautionary glare, but nods and comes with me. We refill our cups, and I clank mine against hers. "Cheers..." B brings the cup to her lips. "Drill Sergeant Bianca." She nearly chokes and narrows her eyes at me. I just wink at her.

Round Two of the Dionysian Frenzy is even better than Round One.

Although this time, I actually feel drunk. But not intoxicated, fall-down drunk. Happy drunk. Wanna-kiss-someone-drunk. That sort of thing.

Unfortunately, my options at this party are non-existent.

Geraldine sidles up next to me when I take a break from dancing. Her tanned skin is flushed, eyes wide and glassy. "I slept with Robert," she says, giggling.

"Oh, thank gods," I tell her, not surprised by the admission. "When?"

"That night, after...you know." Her face turns grim.

"Let's not think about that day."

"I'd been thinking about asking him out for a while, and when Cicero wanted me to fire an arrow at his head..."

I put a comforting hand on her shoulder. "Geraldine, that wasn't your fault. Cicero's a prick for making you do that."

She throws herself around me. "Thank you. Not just for tonight, but for what you did. I don't know if I could have handled it if I hurt him."

I pat her on the back. "It's okay, Geraldine. You don't have to thank me."

The archer pulls back, exhaling sharply. "Anyway, what about you and Josh?" She raises her dark eyebrows suggestively.

"Uh. Yeah. There's nothing going on with that. We're just friends." As I say it, I'm pretty sure I should be telling Josh this. Yet, I never discourage his flirtations. Instead, I welcome the attention, especially after Nick's abrupt coldness. But I know it's selfish.

Geraldine shrugs, eyes sparkling. "I think he's pretty cute." She takes a large gulp of her drink.

"Who's cute?" B approaches my other side.

"Josh," Geraldine and I say in unison.

B's features shift. "Oh. Yeah. If you like that blonde, pretty boy type." She busies herself with staring into her now-empty cup. "I thought you were into Nick?"

Geraldine's head snaps in my direction, lips curving upward. "Nick Cervallos? Scarlett's brother?"

My already warm cheeks grow hotter as I shoot B a death stare. "He was just my fencing partner."

"*Just* your fencing partner?" B is annoyingly persistent.

"Yes," I say through gritted teeth, then knock back the rest of my drink in one gulp.

She nods, seemingly buying my lie. "Good. Because last I

heard, he's been going back and forth between Amanda and Lila."

There it is. That tightening, churning of my stomach when I think of Nick and other girls.

This is really killing my buzz. The few drops left in my cup seem to shimmer in a sad wave.

Liv comes over in a drunken twirl, laughing, pulling the three of us to dance again. I try to lose myself in the rhythm of the music, in the infectious beat of the song, but my drunken state only allows me to focus on B's last words regarding Nick.

I slink away from everyone else, backing slowly toward the stone altar with the bowl. A cursory glance reveals there's probably just enough left for one more cup. My eyes flicker back to the girls. Everyone is still dancing. Accounted for. No one is paying attention to me.

I don't bother with the ladle, just plunge my cup into the bowl, scooping out the rest of the Dionysian Frenzy. It fills about a half-a-cup.

"I fucking *dare* you," a stony voice says.

I whirl, nearly dropping the cup. Astrid glowers down at me. For someone so tall and striking, it's unbelievable how she moves like a stealth ninja.

"This is still my second cup." A terrible, blatant lie.

"Seriously? I may be tipsy but I can still see clearly, and I saw you dunk your cup to get the last of it."

I raise my brows. "Do you want some?" I'm not opposed to sharing if she shuts up about it.

Astrid wrinkles her nose. "No. But I still don't believe you're going to drink that."

"Really?" I challenge.

She crosses her arms, her black gloves severe against the shimmering gold night gown. "Yeah. Really."

I chug the entire contents just as Astrid slaps the cup from my hand.

"What's wrong with you?" She hisses. "Nick said *two* was pushing it, and you've just drunk two and *a half.*"

"Oh, *fuck* Nick." I try to move past her, but stumble as the room tilts.

Well, this escalated quickly.

Astrid grabs my arm. "Is that what this is about? Him?" She shakes her head. "Rhi, his behavior isn't what you think, and if you're going to-"

I wave her off with my free hand. "This isn't about him. This is about *me. I* want to have fun." Lie, after lie, after lie. But I wrench my arm free of hers and head back toward my dancing friends, finding it much easier to dance this time around.

Except, I stare past Liv to the animal that pecks at the mossy floor. "Is that a deer?"

Liv looks behind her then tilts her head as she faces me. "What are you talking about, Rhi?"

I start laughing hysterically, grab Liv's face in my hands, and give her a friendly kiss on the lips. "You are so pretty, my little sea monster." I wrap her in a hug. She smells like blossoms.

"Shit." Someone says. "Rhi, did you have *another* cup?"

I turn to the hand on my shoulder and find Drill Sergeant Bianca. I salute her. "No. No. I absolutely did not." Then, I burst into laughter again. I have the funniest friends.

"Zo, call Andrew," Bianca says. "Tell him we need *mithridatum.*"

"What's that?" Scarlett says. Her eyes have split from two into four, aligned in pairs on top of the other.

"It's an antidote," B explains, examining me like a science experiment. "It will sober her right up."

Well. That certainly won't do. "No. Nope." I stumble from the small crowd of girls. I'm perfectly happy feeling the way I feel, which is carefree and fun. And if B and the rest of them are going to ruin my fun, then I'll just leave.

Their voices are incoherent babble as I squint and wobble towards the door and practically fall through it. The last thing I hear before it closes is someone yell: "Don't let her-" but the voice cuts off.

I stumble into the hallway, the cold floor biting into my toes as I take a few steps.

"Ah." I giggle. "I forgot my shoes." I'd taken them off at some point.

But when I turn toward Zo and Liv's door, it's gone. Another stretch of gray stone appears where the door had been.

"Oh noooooo," I drawl. "Please don't do this to me." I place my hands against the smooth wall and push. Maybe it's another hallucination. "Guys! Let me in!" I press my ear to the wall, silence greeting me on the other side; then I rest my overbearingly hot forehead against the cold stone, murmuring, "Why are you doing this to me?"

Unsurprisingly, I receive no response, so I take my chances moving down the hall, swaying, knocking into the wall every now and then. Making it back to my room this intoxicated would have been hard enough without the magical hallway playing tricks on me.

Though I think I've been walking for a few minutes, I'm no closer to the end of the hallway than I was before. The far side looms before me, seemingly to be half the length of a football field away, and the more I walk toward it, the farther the distance spreads.

"Oh gods," I continue talking to myself. "I'll never make it."

I try anyway, tripping and cursing, my double-vision causing my stomach to flip, and I drop to my knees.

I'm breathing in and out as slow as I can manage, clenching my eyes shut, trying to shake the nausea. I need to get back to my room. Or to *a* room, except I have no idea if I'm still on the same floor. I remember Professor Talbot's words that not only do the hallways shift corridors, but they shift floors as well.

A horrid thought crosses my mind. What if I'm on Kieran's floor, and he finds me like this? After what we did to him, I have no doubt he'll try and finish what he started in my dream, maybe more.

Or...what if whatever attacked and killed Sasha Nichols lurks in these halls?

Though the thought doesn't help with the nausea, I muster whatever strength I can manage to push myself to stand.

Nick stares at me, hands in the pockets of the pristine outfit he'd been in when I'd seen him earlier. The only difference is that the top two buttons of his shirt are undone, revealing the golden glow of his muscled chest, and his hair is mussed, as though someone had their fingers tangled in it. My stomach once again somersaults with the idea that he'd just come from some girl's room. But maybe he's an illusion, another hallucination.

"Oh, fuck." I attempt to turn, but I lose my balance and nearly fall over.

Before I hit the floor, Nick is there, strong, warm hands and that intoxicating scent of...well...*man.* Definitely not a hallucination.

"No, I'm Nick, remember? Though probably not, considering how drunk you are." One of his hands goes around my waist and the other holds my arm. "Damn it, Rhi how much of the Dionysian Frenzy did you drink?" He guides me down the hall.

"Three," I say, holding up two fingers, giggling.

Nick curses again. "Didn't I tell you one was enough?"

I stick out my tongue at him, the overbearing mother hen that he is. "Astrid dared me."

"Oh. So you did the smart thing and succumbed to peer pressure. Got it."

I try to shove him away, murmuring some incoherent, not so nice things about him, but I end up almost falling again. He catches me, and my misstep causes me to stumble into him. I'm steadied by his quick hands, his fingers falling a little higher than my hips. Heat spreads through my chest and creeps up my neck. His fingers seem to melt through the silk of my nightgown straight to my skin.

Luckily, my blush is hidden with my face buried in his neck. Cedarwood and vanilla dance into my nostrils. I pull my head away and clench my eyes shut before I throw up. Or kiss him.

"I just want to lie down." I whisper.

"Okay," he says, the sharp edges of his voice gone.

Nick guides me another few steps, steering me to the right. He opens a door, and I break away from him, half running and half stumbling toward a king-size bed covered in black sheets. I throw myself on top of it and wrap my arms around a large pillow when a familiar scent hits my nostrils and sends me rolling over on to my back.

"We're in your room," I say, opening my eyes as much as I can to look around.

It's large – larger than the average solitary dorm room. Across from the bed to the left of the door is a small entertainment stand with a flat screen TV on top of it. To my immediate left lies a nightstand. From what else I can make out through my twisting vision, a desk sits against the left wall.

"Well, there's no way you were making it to yours. Not without throwing up, at least."

He's right, but that still doesn't change the fact that I'm lying in his bed with nothing but an incredibly short nightgown that barely covers my body.

Nick must realize this too. He sighs and walks over to me. "Look, I promise nothing will happen to you while you sleep here. But if you want to attempt to go to your room, I'll help you."

I sit up slowly, dangling my legs over the edge of the bed, my head swimming. There's currently three Nicks standing before me, and I know that going back to my room is definitely not an option.

"No," I grumble. "I trust you."

A ghost of a smile haunts his lips. "Do you need anything?"

"I need to never drink again."

"I imagine you've said that before."

"Water?" I ask.

Nick nods then disappears into another hallway in the right wall.

I glance down at the uncomfortable garters strapped around both of my legs and fumble with the hooks to release them. I'm still struggling when I hear Nick's voice.

"Do you need help?"

I freeze and look up at him. He stands before me with a bottle of water, gazing down with concern at my very exposed thighs.

I nod, swallowing thickly. He places the water on the nightstand and leans over me. He unhooks the clasp on the outside of each thigh with ease but pauses when he gets to the clasps on my inner thighs.

Nick's eyes meet mine in a moment of vulnerability, and I realize he's waiting for permission.

"It's ok," I whisper, though I don't know if I'm talking to him or myself. But before I mull on it further, he stops again, eyes flicking toward the hem of the nightgown that rests high on my thighs.

"The other clasps are under there." His voice turns low and husky.

Ah. Right. The garter had to be hooked to something, and that something would be the racy black underwear and suspender belt I'm wearing.

My fingertips reach for the hem of the nightgown, drawing it higher and higher until it's bunched in my hands, exposing the final hooks.

For a moment, Nick doesn't move. His breathing is laborious, eyes trailing slowly over the bare skin of my thighs and moving up until they rest on my stomach. Finally, those amber eyes meet mine, and this time, there's no mistaking the hunger in them.

His deft fingers undo the final hooks, removing the straps and throwing them to the side. He loops long fingers under the suspender belt and pulls it down to my ankles in one swift tug. I let the nightgown fall from my palms as Nick's hands move to the thigh-high stockings.

"These too?"

"Yes," I breathe, aware I'm fully capable of removing the stockings myself, but that would mean I'd have to give up the feel of his fingers on my body, and I'm not ready to do that yet.

Instead of hastily grabbing the stockings and yanking them off, his fingers trace the lacy fabric before slipping underneath and rolling them down.

"Done this before?" It's a miracle I manage to keep my voice from shaking.

He doesn't look at me as he smiles. "Once or twice."

The stockings are off and Nick straightens, hesitation in his features. My body is screaming for his hands to touch me again, absent of the carnivorous hunger. No, this hunger is something else. Something that has me thinking about his hands in between my thighs, as well as his mouth.

My whole body ignites as he leans over me, placing his hands on my arms to guide me down to the bed. My eyelids droop as soon I hit the pillow, but before I drift off, he places a kiss on my forehead.

"Goodnight, Rhi."

TWENTY-TWO

The nutty scent of coffee creeps into my nose, and I force one eye open, then another.

I groan, placing the heel of my hand to my forehead as my head rages, and slowly push myself up with my other arm.

The first thing I notice is that I'm not in my bed. Black silk sheets pool around me, and I vaguely remember falling asleep in someone else's room.

That someone else being Nick.

He sits with his back to me, typing on his laptop. His face is slightly turned, and I watch as he brings a blue mug to his lips, tongue rolling over them as he places the mug back down on the desk. He's exchanged his collared shirt and pressed pants for a white shirt and gray sweatpants. The cuff links glisten on the nightstand next to me.

"Good morning," he greets me, keeping his back turned.

"Uh. Good morning." I glance down at my scantily clad body. My nightgown had ridden scandalously high during my fitful slumber. Good grief. I slept like this? Did I sleep with him?

"Did we...um...we didn't..."

Nick turns to me with an impish smirk on his face.

Oh gods. We *did*.

"Yeah, Rhi. We fucked until the sun came up, and then I decided to sleep on the floor, because it's so much more comfortable." The sarcasm is all but dripping from his mouth as my eyes follow his and land on a black comforter and pillow on the floor beside the bed.

Right now, I don't have it in with me to verbally spar with him, so I flop back down on the bed. "Thank the gods," I mutter and close my eyes.

Nick chuckles. "Would have it been so terrible if you slept with me?"

"Yes."

"Wow." Genuine surprise and indignance lace his voice.

I let out a long sigh. "That's not what I meant. Your sister is one of my best friends." I tell yet another lie. "Wouldn't that be awkward?"

I know for a fact Scarlett would be thrilled to hear things between her brother and I were progressing to that stage. Sleeping with him would have been terrible for numerous reasons, one of those being I was heavily inebriated last evening.

The other reason is I don't want to allow myself to become even more emotionally invested in Nick Cervallos than I already am.

"Scarlett didn't seem to think so," he counters.

I shoot upright as fast as my hangover will allow. "She was here?"

Nick nods. "Dropped off some clothes for you. I texted her

last night because I knew she would be worried about you. All the girls were."

I regard him warily. "And what exactly did you tell her?"

That staple wolfish grin appears. "Just that you came to my door in nothing but racy lingerie and begged me to fuck you."

With as much force as I can, I throw a pillow at him. "Nicholas!"

He dodges the pillow with ease, laughing. "Alright, alright. I told her I was on my way back from the meeting when I found you in the hallway, and you were wrecked, so I let you sleep in my bed. I didn't lay a finger on you." Nick holds up two crossed fingers. "I swear."

But he *did* lay a finger on me – or, er...*fingers*. My brain conjures up the feeling of his fingertips against my thighs, removing the garters as I held the bottom of my nightgown in my hands. I know my cheeks are scarlet without having to feel the burn.

Nick rises from his desk, walking over to me. He's standing so close, his scent all but enveloping me, stronger now than it had been on his sheets. He gently takes my chin between his thumb and forefinger, titling my head so I'm forced to look at him.

"Nothing happened, Rhi. I promise." His voice is so sincere, so endearing, I know he's thinking of the incident a few weeks ago with Kieran.

"I believe you."

Nick nods, dropping his fingers from my chin. "Good." He rakes the same hand through his hair. "There's a bathroom and shower over there," he jerks his head behind him.

"Okay." I reach to the side of him and grab the coffee. "Is there anything in this?"

He shakes his head. "I didn't know what you liked." There's

a trace of agitation in this voice. "I brought some of those milk pods and some sugar from the cafeteria."

I wrinkle my nose. "I'll take two sugars, please."

Nick goes back to his desk, grabbing two sugar packets and a wooden stirrer.

"So," I say as he hands me the condiments, "how did you get lucky enough to have your own room?"

A mirthless chuckle causes me to glance up from stirring, and Nick sits beside me.

"I'm lucky enough that no one wants to room with me."

"Really?"

He nods.

"Even your cadre of lusty-eyed women?"

That earns me a contemptuous glare. "*Especially* them."

"Why?"

Nick glances at his watch. It's the first time I've noticed him wearing one.

"Do you want to get breakfast?" he asks.

Hell yes, I do. I'm starving. I keep a lid on my enthusiasm and simply nod. "What time is it?"

A tug at the corner of his lips. "About noon."

"Don't they stop serving breakfast at eleven?" I remind him.

I'm rewarded with that full, dazzling smile. "We're not going to the cafeteria."

I SHOWER in his private bathroom, relishing the solitude. It's been a while since I've had the pleasure of being wrapped in silence as I wash my hair. Though, I wouldn't exactly mind if Nick came in and...

Okay, Rhi. That's *enough*.

Scarlett brought me a pair of jeans, my slippers and a black sweater that's way too tight and definitely not mine. Sly little vixen. As soon as I'm dressed, I head through the small corridor back to Nick's room, where I find him scrolling through his phone. He's ditched his T-shirt and sweatpants for jeans and a white thermal sweater that hugs his incredibly defined biceps.

Give me strength.

Nick glances up from his phone, eyes going straight to my chest that's bulging out of the too-tight, too-low sweater that Scarlett so "thoughtfully" brought for me. I make a show of using the towel I'd taken to cover my upper body and towel-dry my hair.

"I'd just like to go back to my room and dry my hair," I tell him.

"Okay. How long?"

"Ten minutes."

Nick stands, shoving his phone in his jean pocket. "I'll go with you and-"

"It's okay," I cut him off. "Just come get me in about twenty minutes."

He raises an eyebrow. "What happened to you not going anywhere alone?"

I've thought about this. Last night, the hallways could have dumped me anywhere, including my own room. Yet somehow, I ended up on Nick's floor.

And it wouldn't be the first time.

"I have a feeling the hallways are watching out for me," I tell him with a sly smile and slip out his door.

I walk with my arms crossed over my chest, concealing the over-exposed skin protruding from the extremely low-cut front. I know I look absurd, but mercifully, I make it back to my room with no interruptions.

In fact, *I* end up being the interruption as I slide the key card in and barge into my room, shocking a *very* naked Scarlett and Astrid entwined in Scarlett's bed.

"Shit." I squeeze my eyes shut. "I'm sorry, guys. Sorry."

Astrid growls as I hear them shifting beneath Scarlett's bedspread. "Don't you know how to knock?"

"This is *my* room too, you know."

"It's okay," Scarlett's gentle voice caresses the air. I can almost hear the blush on her fair skin. "We just thought you would be...tied up a bit longer." A fluff of the covers. "You can open your eyes now."

Through slitted eyes, I glimpse Astrid leaning back against the pillows in a black shirt and Scarlett snuggling against her in the red bra from last night, the bedspread concealing them from the waist down.

"What the fuck are you wearing?" Astrid's sapphire eyes widen as they take in the shirt.

"Ask your girlfriend." Scarlett just gives me a purse of her lips. "I just came back to change and dry my hair," I tell them, ripping off the sweater and tossing it at Scarlett.

Astrid throws up her hands. "You're really not going to tell us?"

"Tell you what?" I turn my back to the couple, fishing around in my drawer for a long-sleeved shirt. When I face them, Astrid is glaring at me.

"You and Nick?" She raises a golden eyebrow suggestively.

"Me and Nick are going to get breakfast." I grab the hair dryer from Scarlett's nightstand and turn it on, drowning out the series of questions firing at me.

By the time I'm done, both Scarlett and Astrid are standing behind me, thankfully wearing pants. Astrid arms are crossed in her signature abrasive posture, and Scarlett's hands are on her hips, an expectant look on her face.

I place the dryer back on the nightstand. "You saw how

drunk I was last night. Do you really think Nick would do that?"

The first smile I see is Scarlett's. It's joined a second later by Astrid's.

Nick's light knock saves me from saying anything else. "I'll see you guys in a little while."

"Text us before you come back," Astrid warns. "And bring me some pancakes!"

THE DINER NICK takes me to is within walking distance of the campus. From the outside, it looks like a dingy establishment.

Inside is a whole other story.

Less of a diner and more of a French bistro, I feel a tad underdressed. I'd swapped the tight sweater for a loose black one, kept my jeans, and threw my hair into a high ponytail. Even Nick, in his causal outfit, looks like he fits in here, with his slim fitting white shirt that glows against his golden-brown skin.

We sit across from each other in chairs of dark wood, matching the gleaming tabletop laden with pretty, white napkins and shimmering plates. The other patrons in the restaurant look normal at first glance, but a second look tells me these diners are of a different variety.

"What is this place?" I ask him with a bit of wonder in my voice.

"A diner?" The statement ends with a question mark, as if he can't understand why I would ask that question in the first place. I give him a gentle kick against his shin under the table for good measure.

He chuckles. "Okay, okay. It really is just a diner, but for... people like us." Nick flips a laminated menu between his fingers.

I take another glance around, sensing. *Some* of the patrons here are monsters. But there are others here that are something else. Something I can't identify.

Nick puts the menu down. "You don't look convinced."

"It's because I'm not." I pick up my own menu, making a show of perusing it and ignoring Nick until he tells me the truth.

Long fingers grip the top of the menu and drag it down flat against the table, until I'm staring into amber-gold eyes.

"Fine. But if I tell you, you have to *promise* you won't say a word to anyone. Not to any of the girls. Not even Scarlett."

"You mean Scarlett doesn't know?" A delicious current hums in my blood, thinking I might be privy to something he didn't share with his sister.

"Promise, Rhi."

"I promise."

Nick leans over, and I lean into him as well, resting my arms on the table, trying to focus on what he's about to tell me rather than that damn scent of his that just slapped me in the face.

"There aren't just monsters here, as you've noticed. This diner is a safe haven, the same way Alystair is, but for *all* sorts of magical creatures." He jerks his head to my right. "That girl over there? She's a mermaid."

My jaw falls. "Really?"

I can tell he's fighting a smile at my awestruck face. "Yeah. The guy she's with is a fairy."

My palms flatten against the table, and I fight the urge to look in their direction. "How do you know?

Nick straightens, shrugging. "I come here a lot."

That sours my mood. Of course he comes here a lot. With all of his dates.

As if realizing this, his eyes find mine. "Listen, Rhi. There's something-"

"Me first," I blurt out. Before he launches into his explanation of his non-committal behavior or whatever he's going to say, I have to clear the air.

He blinks, but nods for me to go ahead.

"I'm really, really sorry for blaming you about Kieran." His lips part, but I hold up a hand. "Let me finish. And I'm really, really sorry it's taken me this long to apologize to you. I was so embarrassed, and I felt really bad, and I didn't have the courage to face you."

A small smile. "So that's why you were ignoring me?"

Wait. *What?* I narrow my eyes. "You ignored me first."

He shakes his head. "Rhi, that's what-"

A plump woman approaches the table, coffee pot in hand. "Nick!" She greets. "It's been a while. Thought maybe something in the food had kept you away."

Nick immediately relaxes and gives the waitress his dazzling smile. "No way, Minerva. Everyone knows you have the best food in the city."

She releases a heartwarming chuckle, one that seems to drizzle over me like maple syrup. Minerva faces me, her wide smile further accentuating the creases in her ochre skin, but her eyes, one green and one brown, are filled with a childish enthusiasm.

"You, my dear, must be very special. Nick never brings anyone in here."

My jaw drops again.

Nick clears his throat. "Minerva, this is Rhi. Minerva is the owner of this fine establishment." He makes a grand sweeping gesture with his hand.

"Nice to meet you," I say with a genuine smile of my own.

"You, as well. Coffee?"

"Please." Minerva fills my cup and then Nick's.

"I'll be back in a few minutes to take your order." She winks, then heads to the table with the fairy and mermaid.

A heavy silence fills the space between us, which I decide to break. "Why do you come here alone?"

"I like doing things alone."

"Well, clearly not *all* things." I don't keep the suspicion from my tone. He parades around school with an entourage of women yet has never brought any of them here – except for me. This boy is as puzzling as a Rubik's cube.

"You sure are judgmental," he fires back.

"Did you bring me here just so you can insult me?"

He flinches. "That wasn't...I didn't mean..." He sighs, shaking his head.

"You just *stopped* being my friend, Nick. You wouldn't fence with me, wouldn't play chess with me. You wouldn't even walk with me to classes. Why?"

Maybe I shouldn't bother with this, but I need closure. Never mind that Nick stopped his flirtations – fine. He doesn't like me that way. But what about the friendship we cultivated?

Minerva comes back to take our order. Considering the turn this conversation just took, my appetite has waned since Nick first invited me to get breakfast. I order scrambled eggs and toast. Nick gets the works: eggs, bacon, sausage, and home fries.

Once she leaves, Nick finally speaks. "Do you know why you always see me with different girls?"

"Because you get bored?"

"No." The sharpness with which that word comes out feels like it sliced right across my skin.

I take a sip of coffee. "Then why, Nick?"

Nick leans forward again, resting his elbows on the table.

"Have any of the girls told you anything about me? About who my father is? About what I can do?"

I bite my lip and nod. "Astrid said your father is a god. And that you have abilities no one has even heard of." I think of Kieran choking on his own blood.

He lets out a mirthless chuckle. "It's the unknown godly powers that draw them to me, but the gifts from my mother that push them away."

I set the coffee cup down. "Who?"

"Amanda, Samantha, Lila," he waves his hand in the air. "All of them. Scarlett has the gift of Persuasion. She can persuade people how to feel. I can do the same thing, only I'm ten times more powerful than my sister."

I furrow my brow at him.

Nick licks those sensuous lips. "Scarlett's Persuasion is temporary. Mine is permanent. I can *make* someone feel afraid – forever. I can *make* someone feel happy for the rest of their life. And...I can *make* someone fall in love with me."

My brain puts the pieces together. "So, no one wants to be with you because...they think whatever they're feeling is an illusion - it isn't real."

A solemn nod.

"How did everyone find out? About your...abilities."

Nick cracks the knuckles of his left hand. A nervous tick. "An accident, a few years ago," he starts, sucking his bottom lip into his mouth. "I was fifteen. In love for the first time – or so I thought. It was just a stupid crush. So, so stupid."

I shift closer, intrigue and worry fighting for top emotion.

"She didn't love me," he continues, his breath shuddering. "So, I made her love me. I willed it. I had no idea what I was doing, that I was even *capable* of doing something like that." He drops his head in his hands.

"What happened to her?" I whisper.

When Nick looks up at me, the fear and hesitation in his eyes are palpable, and I sense he's weighing his options. Tell me the truth, and I might reject him. A rejection that will matter more than all the others, although I'm not sure why. But if he lies...

He lets out a long breath. "They couldn't reverse it. Tried everything. So, she went insane. She now spends her days in the psychiatric ward at some fancy hospital in Connecticut."

The shudder that wracks my spine is involuntary, but Nick notices. "I understand if you want to leave now," he says quietly.

I won't lie and say I'm not frightened. I am. But I still have questions.

"You were young, and it was an accident," I reason. "How does Persuasion work? Is it like mind control?"

He shakes his head. "It's all about controlling emotions. Have you ever heard of the James-Lange theory in psychology?"

I give him a blank stare.

"The theory is that your emotions are a result of physiological arousal. That's what Scar and I manipulate. Let's say you see something you fear...a spider. Your heart might race. Your palms might sweat. The emotion that accompanies these physical reactions is fear. So, Scar and I take that fear and twist it, turn it into joy. With Scar, that would only last an hour or so. But me?" He brings his gaze to mine. "You would never fear spiders again as long as you lived."

I blow out a breath at how incredible that is, but dangerous just the same. "But even with all of this, the guilt, the anger you keep - that doesn't keep you from sleeping with these girls."

Those amber eyes darken dangerously. "Why should it? They use me as much as I use them. So, why should I care? We hookup until they start having feelings, then they pull away *just* in case I might be the one steering the reins. And nothing I say changes that. So, I've stopped trying."

Minerva sets our plates down. My appetite has waned further.

"So," Nick says, pushing the food around on his plate. "I come here alone because none of them are worth bringing here."

My chest tightens. "But I am?"

He lets his fork clatter on his plate, pausing, as if realizing what he just let slip. He finally meets my eyes. "I see the way you look at me, Rhi. Like I'm some piece of shit. Like I'm *Kieran.*" I open my mouth to protest but he keeps going. "I wanted you to know I'm nothing like that. Nothing like *him.*"

"Why do you care what I think, Nick? You don't care about Amanda, Lila, Samantha, what all of them think – but you care about what I think?"

He chews thoughtfully, eyes slowly searching my face. "Do you remember the last night we fenced together? The night we heard that scream?"

"Yeah."

"You asked me to tell you something about myself." He shrugs. "No one's ever wanted to know anything about me before." Nick tries to keep his expression neutral and unbothered, but I can tell by the cracking of his knuckles again that it more than bothers him.

"And you decided that the most interesting thing you could summon about yourself is that you hate Jello?" I joke in an attempt to get him to smile.

It works. He smiles and throws a crumpled straw wrapper at me. I begin to relax, happy that both of us had this opportunity to clear the air, but something else nags at my brain.

"What about Kassi?"

Nick's face contorts into genuine confusion as he finishes another sip of coffee. "What about her?"

"I thought you two might have been together at some point." I grip the handle of my own cup of coffee to steady me for what I might hear.

"Kassi?" He asks incredulously, then shakes his head. "I'm not her type."

I have the itch to say something like 'I thought you were every girl's type," when he fixes me with a pointed look.

"Oh," I say, slightly chagrined. "It's just...I heard you that night." Since we're having a confessional, I might as well admit I'd been eavesdropping that night. I brace myself, waiting for some sort of admonishment or look of disapproval.

Instead, Nick's expression is solemn. "I thought you might have." He sighs heavily. "When I told you things were complicated, I wasn't lying. Kassi told me something."

I nearly drop the cup I'd been holding. "About me?"

"Maybe."

I shoot daggers at him. "That's not fair. If she said something about me-"

"I don't know if it is about *you,* and I told you, I'm still deciding if I believe her." He takes a bite of his food; the sound of bacon crunching beneath his teeth is now making my mouth water. "But you don't believe what she says to you, right?"

This seems like another good time to lie, considering he just lied through his teeth. There's no way Nick is still *deciding* if he believes whatever Kassi has said to him. He most certainly does.

"No, I don't." I lie right back.

Nick's lips curl, a cross between a genuine smile and a cunning one. "Most monsters don't. But I don't think you're like most monsters, Rhi."

Feeling hangry at his non-answer, I wrench a piece of bacon off his plate without pushing him, because I have an idea of my own forming. His eyes widen in amusement, but he says nothing, even as I shove the whole piece in my mouth.

"Sexy," he says, taking a sip of his coffee.

I hope I'm not blushing as I start to eat, but I almost choke when he says, "You're even sexy when you drool, too."

"*I do not drool.*"

"Yeah, you do. You drooled all over my pillows."

Just for that, I take another piece of bacon off his plate, and some home fries. I'm happily eating when he says to me: "I want to train you again."

I swallow the large amount of food in my mouth. "In fencing?"

He rolls his eyes. "No, in synchronized swimming."

The smile that turns my lips happens before I can stop it. "You would look amazing in a Speedo."

Nick almost spits out his coffee, but I rain on his parade. "Bianca has been training me on Thursday nights." I help myself to more home fries.

He tosses his gaze from his plate, to mine, then back to his, now free of home fries. "Why didn't you just order them?"

"I didn't want them at the time," I say through a mouthful of food. "Even if we're no longer fencing partners, I'll still play chess with you."

Nick reaches across the table, his thumb gently sweeping across my lips. I inhale sharply.

"You had a crumb right there." His thumb remains on my lower lip, lightly tapping.

Minerva pops by our table. "More coffee?"

Nick jolts his hand back, knocking his silverware to the floor. "I'm sorry Minerva," he says, reaching down.

"Don't bother yourself, Nick. We'll get you another set." She chortles and walks away after refilling our cups.

Nick watches her leave, then pins me with a stare. "You sure you don't want to tell Bianca you're switching back to me? She's tough."

I wipe my mouth with a napkin, ensuring there are no more "crumbs" on my lips. "No. B is my friend. I won't do that to her." In fact, I really should text her once Nick and I are finished.

Nick nods. "Okay, but the chess offer…"

"Still stands."

That earns me his wolf smile. "You know, the first time we played chess, I think you were going to offer something else."

The low octave of his voice trickles down my spine. My toes curl in my sneakers, but I meet his challenging stare. "Maybe. I guess we'll just have to keep playing for you to find out."

That dark hunger returns to his eyes, curling my toes even more, lightning coursing through my veins.

I think of last night. His fingers on my thighs. Underneath my nightgown. The low hum of his voice. The dark, ravenous look in his eyes; the same one that's devouring me right now. The one that tells me he's thinking of the exact same thing that I am.

And then I think of Kieran's blood on the floor of my bedroom. Nick's features transformed into a mask of rage. The girl forever trapped in a cage of her own mind.

Just what kind of monster am I dealing with?

TWENTY-THREE

We walk back to campus, Astrid's pancakes in tow. I made sure I got enough for Scarlett, too.

My emotions are raging inside me. I'm still unsure what Nick and I are, exactly, especially in light of his admission that I was the first and only girl he'd taken to his little secret dining spot. I mull over the vulnerability he showed, the honesty that came forth.

But I still can't help the sliver of fear that licks my spine when I think of what he was able to do to Kieran, or what he did do to the girl that lives in a padded cell.

An accident, I remind myself. *The involuntary actions of a foolish boy.*

Nick's hand brushes mine, but his fingertips don't hook into my own, as though he's unsure of making such a move just yet.

I could just do it. Take his hand. Save him the trouble of all that doubt and insecurity, but before I muster up the nerve, both of us are halted at the University gates by three familiar faces.

Wilde, her sharp smile dulled into a thin, hard-pressed line. Cicero, arms crossed, making his already broad frame swell. And Talbot, cloud gray eyes stormy and threatening as he takes in the two of us.

The oppressive tension in the air threatens to strangle me where I stand. Wilde approaches us, heading right for me. Nick wordlessly hands me the container of pancakes, as if he knows what's coming.

She pulls me from his side; Nick's eyes narrow at the delicate hand on my arm, nostrils flaring.

"What's going on?" His voice is a low, menacing growl.

Cicero takes a step toward Nick, hands now clenched into mighty fists at his side, but Talbot shakes his head. "Nicholas, we need you to come with us." His voice is without emotion but demanding enough that Nick doesn't question it.

Nick shoots me a desperate, pleading look - not to help him, but to make sure I don't believe whatever Wilde is going to tell me-before he walks toward Cicero and Talbot. The two professors take him by the arms like prison guards and usher him away.

At first, I'm unable to move as Nick disappears from my vision. Once he's nothing more than a speck on the campus backdrop, I wrench my arm from Wilde's grasp. "What are you doing? Where are they taking him?" I begin to follow, but Wilde's clawed hand grips the back of my shirt.

"There's been another murder, Rhi," she says in my ear, releasing her hold.

My head turns before my body. Slow. Deliberate. Reptilian. "And you think it was him?" The one Scylla head I have control of stirs, ready to be unleashed.

"The victim was Amanda Reynolds."

Shit. Of course, they think it was him. The first girl to be murdered was someone he'd been seen with. And now the second girl is *also* someone he has a history with.

This is not promising.

"When?" I hiss.

Wilde's face is stoic, no trace of emotion. "Last night. I don't know the exact time."

Last night. Where he could be accounted for. He was at the Eleusis meeting and then *I* was with him the entire night. Asleep in his bed.

Drunk out of your mind, a nasty voice replies. *He very well could have snuck out and killed her.*

I hand Wilde the container of pancakes. My feet are already thudding against the pavement, running away from her, even as she screams at me.

Running towards Nick.

He didn't do this. Despite his terrifying abilities, despite the girl he'd inadvertently harmed five years ago, I *know* he didn't.

A boy who is resigned to letting everyone think the worst of him, because he's tried so many times to prove otherwise and no one would see it.

So he gave up.

Until me.

For whatever reason, he doesn't want me to believe what everyone else does. He bared his truth. And I accept it. So now, I have to go and save him by doing something I know I excel at.

Lying.

I burst into Professor Talbot's office, finding Nick sitting in an armchair directly in front of Talbot's desk. Cicero stands like a watchdog on Nick's left side.

"He didn't do it," I pant. "I can prove it."

"Rhi," Nick warns, but doesn't look back at me.

Wilde comes barging in a second later, perfectly composed,

though I know she'd been running after me. She places the pancakes on the corner of Professor Talbot's desk.

"Damn it, Sara. You told her?" Cicero glares at Wilde.

"Pipe down, Cero," she snaps back, pronouncing it like "zero."

I walk around to face Nick. I immediately notice his forearms lie strained and flat against the arms of the chair, his wrists encircled with crude burn marks.

"What the fuck are you doing to him?" There's no pain on his face, but the marks around his wrist ignite a burning wrath inside me. The Scylla head hisses, waiting.

Professor Talbot is disturbingly placid. "Merely making sure he stays put while we question him." He tilts his head, staring directly at me. "Will you behave, or do we need to do the same with you?"

The entire chair lifts inches off the ground as Nick jerks his body in an attempt to free himself. "Don't you fucking *touch her.*"

I place a hand on Nick's shoulder to relax him. It works. Barely. "You don't need to do this to him. I can vouch for his whereabouts last night."

Cicero huffs, shaking his head. "What do you do to these girls, Nick, that have them so enraptured? Maybe you're using those Persuasion powers after all."

An inhuman growl escapes Nick's throat.

Talbot crosses his arms. "Alright Rhi, let's hear it. You begin, and I'll interrupt when I have a question. And you know you must answer honestly."

I nod. Of course, I can't lie to him. I just have to strategize enough to answer in a way that won't be lying.

"Well, as you know," I begin, letting out a deep breath. "Last night was Bacchanal. I drank too much, so I decided to leave the party early."

"What time was this?"

I shrug. "Maybe eleven? Nick found me in the hallway, trying to get back to my room-"

"Why is her recount necessary?" Cicero interrupts. "We know Nick's version before all of this happened. You place him at the Eleusis meeting by eight-thirty. What we need to know is what he was doing *after*."

Wilde clears her throat. "I believe she was getting to that, if you would let her." Cicero glowers at her, but she nods for me to continue.

"As I was saying, Nick found me in the hallway trying to get back to my room, and we went back to his." I'm lying by omission. I don't want to say "he took me back to his room" because if I do, they are going to make some nasty assumptions about what I'm going to imply next.

I pause.

"And?" Cicero presses.

I cock my head, showering him with a withering look. "You really want me to explain what we did in his room?"

Wilde places her head in her hands, shaking it back and forth. But Cicero and Talbot remain unmoved.

I pull out my best flush of embarrassment, my voice dropping to a demure purr. "Well, first, I couldn't get my garter straps off. I was wearing lingerie, you see. It was a lingerie-themed-"

"I know what garter belts are," Cicero barks. Nick's hands tighten around the arms of the chair--I can already see the claw marks.

"Then you must know how difficult they can be to remove," I say sweetly. "I couldn't get them off. So, Nick helped me. He started with the clasps on my outer thighs, but the most difficult ones were underneath my nightgown. So, he reached underneath-"

"I think we can all agree we know where this is going." Wilde pierces Cicero and Talbot with a cutting stare.

"Well?" Cicero looks at Talbot. "Was she telling the truth?"

Professor Talbot gives a single nod of his head.

It takes all my self-control not to let out the tight breath I'd been holding.

Obviously, I wasn't lying. I took a gamble that they'd stop me before I went too far and actually *had* to lie. Because I couldn't tell them Nick was innocent due to the fact that we were up all-night having sex or having sex during the hours Amanda was killed. But I also didn't want to let them think Nick took me to his room and decided to take advantage of a drunk girl. No, I'd let them think it was *our* decision to go back to his room. And leave the rest to their imaginations.

Professor Talbot doesn't say a word to me. He addresses Nick directly. "Do you understand why we had to question you?"

"Yes."

I butt in. "Because he slept with the two victims? I hardly think that qualifies him as a murder suspect. What's his motive?"

Cicero's jaw twitches, but it's Talbot that turns his stare to me. "I forget that you grew up amongst humans, utterly ignorant of our ways." My cheeks burn. "Which is not your fault." He motions for Cicero to put another chair beside Nick. Nick stirs, another low growl sounding from his throat. Talbot's gaze slices to him. "Relax, Nicholas. I just want her to sit. Your restraints have been lifted."

Nick slowly brings his hands from the armchair. The claw marks are clear now, at least six inches long, much longer than mine. He doesn't touch the tender skin on his wrists, just brings them to his lap.

I finally sit, careful to look at Nick as I do. He won't meet my eyes.

Professor Talbot moves around his desk, as he did the first time I sat in his office. He now stands front and center between Nick and me.

"I'm sure you think a crime like this is solved similar to a human crime: Blood samples, fingerprints, *motives*." He sneers at the last word. "Unfortunately for you, this isn't..." He glances behind me, to whom I presume is Cicero. "What's that human show called?"

"Law and Order." Wilde's voice offers the answer.

The mocking smirk on his lips is almost enough for me to tell him I watch CSI, not Law and Order, but I put a muzzle on myself and stay quiet.

"Yes, this isn't Law and Order, Rhi." His stormy eyes are back on me. "Amanda, like Sasha, was found in body parts, all of them cleanly severed. Short of a very skilled swordsman, there are very few things on this earth that can do something like that to something like *us*. And do you know what one of those things is, Rhi?"

I shake my head, afraid to open my mouth.

"A full-blown monster."

Laughter escapes my chest before I can stop it. "So, you're telling me that only a literal *monster*, from one of our textbooks, can be the culprit for the way those girls died, and you decided that *Nick* fit that description?" I look at Nick, who stares unmoving, unflinching, at the floor. I don't understand why he isn't defending himself. "Nick, it obviously can't be you! Our powers are diluted!" I whip my head to Professor Talbot. "You told us that since the very first monsters, our powers and abilities are watered down. We hold but a fraction of the power our ancestors did. How can you think-"

"The powers of gods are *never* watered down. Even if you

are part monster." Cicero's words grate against my ears like sandpaper.

I look once again at Nick, who finally meets my eyes with resignation.

"So, you..."

"That's right, Rhi," Cicero says with all the enthusiasm of a game show host, "Nick here can become the absolute worst version of himself. And would have no control once he lost himself to the monster."

With that tone, Cicero could be announcing lottery numbers for all I care. I can't take my eyes off Nick.

Any hope or relief he'd had since we spoke and he lifted that weight from himself is gone. His countenance is pure defeat, despondence. And anguish.

"Cero, was that really necessary?" Wilde asks.

"Yes, Sara." His voice is normal now. Stern. "The girl should know what she's getting herself into. Who she's defending." He cuts Nick an accusatory glare. "Before she's next."

Something feral crosses over Nick's face as he snaps. Swifter than an adder he's up from the chair. It clatters to the ground with the force of his departure.

I jump up in panic, but Talbot steps between Nick and Cicero before anything escalates. "That's *enough*," he snarls, but it's Cicero he bites at. "Nicholas is free to go. He wasn't lying about where he'd been prior to him being with Rhi. And Rhi wasn't lying about their....activities last evening."

I expect Nick to bolt, but he doesn't move. "What about Rhi?"

Professor Talbot smiles in a way that puts Nick's wolf grin to shame. "I'd like to speak with her, privately."

Nick sets his jaw. I place my hand on his arm before he tries to protest, and they decide to throw him in the dungeon that lies beneath the school. "Nick, it's okay. I'll see you later."

He finally looks at me, eyes searching. I school my features into a neutral expression, not wanting to give him any reason to worry. Nick takes my hand, gives it one comforting squeeze, then showers the three professors with a scathing look before he leaves.

"He's quite taken with you." Talbot gestures for me to sit again.

"I'll be sure to invite you to the wedding."

The Professor chuckles as he sits in the large leather chair behind his desk; Wilde and Cicero flank him on either side. "You're not in any sort of trouble, Rhi. I just want to explain why we needed to question Nick, and why he still remains our prime suspect."

The confusion must show on my face, because before I can open my mouth, Talbot speaks again--"Nick wouldn't defend himself against the idea that in his monster form, he could have killed those girls because he wouldn't remember. Additionally, a true monster leaves no traceable evidence. There are no fingerprints to test; no fluids to examine. All we have to go on right now is that of the three hundred students in this school, Nick is the only one that is a descendant of a god as well as a monster, and therefore, the only student capable of fully transforming."

"He didn't do it," is my only response.

He sighs wearily. "I want to believe that, Rhi. Not only is he an exceptional student, but I have known him since he started as a freshman at the Academy, six years ago. He has been nothing short of perfect – in all aspects of his academic career, and as a person. But Wilde, Cicero and I-" he motions to the other two professors, "we need to exercise every precaution. Cover every detail. For the safety of *all* the students."

I nod, speechless.

Professor Talbot places his palms flat against the table.

"Rhi, for your own safety, be alert. And if you really think Nick is innocent, be doubly vigilant. Watch him – *everyone*, closely."

"I will."

"Then, you may go."

I rise and grab the pancakes before I leave without bidding any sort of farewell. I make sure I'm far enough down the hall and around the corridor before I rest my head in my hands, struggling to grasp the tornado of thoughts and emotions surging in my brain.

"Hard to believe, isn't it?"

I'd know that voice anywhere, but it's missing its usual warmth, its fire. Still, I'm not surprised when I lift my head and Nick stands only a few feet away, shoulders slumped and his nails biting into his palms.

When I don't immediately respond, he lets out a somber chuckle. "Or maybe it isn't."

I approach him warily, like he's a wounded animal prepared to strike. He certainly looks it. "Nick, I meant what I said in Talbot's office. I know you didn't kill those girls."

"I sense a 'but' coming."

"Why didn't you tell me?"

The resignation on his face transforms into disbelief as he openly stares at me. "You want to know why I didn't tell you I can turn into a full-blown *monster?* Rhi, I had a hard enough time telling you what I could do, what I did to that girl five years ago."

I square my shoulders, taking another step closer to him. "And yet, I'm here, aren't I?"

Nick lifts his chin, eyes probing. "Yeah, you are."

"And I'm not going anywhere."

As he moves closer, the heat of him is scorching, that scent of his wrapping me like a shroud. "You really want to do this... with me?" The surprise and relief in his voice is heartbreaking.

"Yes," I say, with as much conviction as I can put into my voice.

His shoulders sag, his breath flowing unrestrained as though my words unchained him. "They're going to be watching me." He pushes a wayward strand of hair behind my ear. "You too."

I feel that smile creep upon my face, the one edged with cunning, the one with a diamond tip that cuts through glass. "Then let's give them one hell of a show."

TWENTY-FOUR

Astrid is the only member of the girl gang I seek out after what I witnessed in Professor Talbot's office. I ask her to meet me in the cafeteria, handing over her now cold pancakes.

"Shit," she breathes, chewing her bottom lip. "I can't believe they're able to keep this quiet. It must not have happened on campus."

"Can you find out?" We sit next to each other at one of the round tables, our heads bent low.

She covers her face with her black-gloved hands, sighing heavily. "I have to tell Scarlett."

I nod in agreement, fiddling with the end of my ponytail. "Nick doesn't want to tell her."

"I know. We have to find a way to prove that he's innocent."

I place my elbows on the table, creating a diamond shape with my fingertips. "I was thinking that's where you come in."

She raises a gold-dusted eyebrow.

"Your hacking," I clarify. "See if you can get into whatever files the school has on all the students."

"There's at least three hundred students in this school. Do you know how long it would take me to go through *all* of those files?"

I scrunch my nose. "So, you *can't* do it?"

Astrid huffs, pulling the container of pancakes closer to her and popping the plastic lid off. "Of course I can." She drizzles four packets of syrup over the entire stack. "I'm just saying by the time I go through all the files myself, whatever or whoever is doing this could have wiped out the entire school and half the city." She shoves a giant forkful of pancakes into her mouth.

My Scylla smile is back. "Who says you are doing it all by yourself?"

Astrid looks at me and grins--mouthful of razor sharp teeth, pancakes and all.

ASTRID DROPS me off at the library before heading back to the dorms to talk to Scarlett. I'd told her I was going there to do some research.

I lied.

I make my way downstairs, passed the tables where Liv and I studied, and into the back of the room, the darkest and most secluded spot of the library itself.

On the floor, surrounded by thick volumes of texts, I find the person I'm looking for.

"Oh, Kassi," I say in a singsong voice.

She looks up, startled. Then, her brown eyes narrow. "What are you doing here?"

"You didn't know I was coming?"

"That's not how my powers work. Besides, no one ever

comes looking *for* me," she says as I sit cross-legged next to her.

A pang of guilt strikes my abdomen. It can't be easy, being who and what she is. A person that delivers doom upon others and then, is not to be believed. I wonder why I *do* believe what she says.

"I have a question for you."

As soon as the words leave my mouth, she shakes her head, dark blonde hair swishing across her shoulders. "I know what you're going to ask, and I can't tell you."

"I thought that wasn't how your powers worked?" I pick up one of the books on the floor as she scowls. "*Hell's Princes: A Biography.* This is some pretty dark stuff you're into."

Kassi rips it from my hands. "I'm just doing some research," she says quietly, averting her gaze.

"I'm doing the same thing." I draw my knees into my chest and rest my arms atop my kneecaps.

Kassi sighs wearily. "You want me to tell you what I told Nick, right?" She lifts her eyes to mine; regret lingers there. "I can't tell you."

I let my legs and arms fall. "Why not? Nick said it might have to do with me. Don't I have a right to know?"

She shakes her head again. "Think of it like a bank account. If you were to walk into a bank and demand access to Nick's account, you would never get it, even if he gave you permission to go in there and access it for him."

"Kassi," I groan. "Are you comparing your prophecies to currency?" She must be part Sphinx to speak in riddles like this.

The look she gives me is resolute. "Absolutely. Banks deal in cash. I deal in information. But if it's not *your* prophecy, I can't help you." She returns to the book she'd been reading.

I slap my hand down on the page. "Nick said it might-"

Kassi slams the book closed; I snatch my hand away just in time before it's caught. "It doesn't matter what Nick said." Her stare turns serious. "I told him what I told him. I never mentioned any specific names."

I say nothing, astonished at her outburst. Kassi lets out a humorless laugh. "Did you even think to ask what I might be doing down here, reading books like this-" she sweeps her hand over the various texts surrounding her, "all by myself on a Sunday?"

The shame that burns my chest swelters the longer she looks at me with those dark brown eyes. Because I hadn't for one second thought of why she was sitting, hidden amongst the books, alone. I hadn't for one second thought to question the fact that every time I've seen Kassi, I've never seen her with another person.

"I'm sorry, Kass," I admit, swallowing.

She scoffs. "You just came here, looking for information. Information you have no right to know."

I bite my tongue to keep from arguing. She has a point, especially if she said she never gave Nick specifics, like mentioning my name. Which means Nick is the one inserting me into his prophetic narrative.

"Kass," I put a hand on her shoulder. "I'm *really* sorry. You're absolutely right." Kassi looks at me, the anger in her face receding. "I just want to help him."

She bites her bottom lip at that, as if she wants to tell me something but is fighting it. I decide to change the subject. "So, how often do you get these...visions?"

Kassi shrugs. "Maybe five, six times a day."

The remorse in my gut churns. I try a different approach. "Are you also a Sphinx?"

She grins. "Yeah, though the predictions tend to over-shadow everything else."

This isn't working. "What are you researching?"

Her gaze scatters over each of the tomes around us. "Monsters. Monsters that are different from us."

I pick up the *Hell's Princes* book. "Find anything interesting?"

"Plenty."

I flip open the book, my eyes scanning over the Introduction. Four crowned princes. Lucifer. Leviathan. Satan. Belial. Imprisonment. Envy.

Nothing useful.

I close the book and set it down. "Kass, do you need help with your research?"

Her eyes narrow in suspicion. "Don't pretend to want to be my friend. I still won't tell you what Nick's prophecy is."

"I just think you can use some company." I hold my palms up in defense. "I won't ask you another thing about Nick or his prophecy, I swear."

This time, I'm not lying. My heart aches for her. She holes herself up in the darkest part of the library, partly because no one else wants to be around her, and partly because she probably can't stand being around other people all the time, having visions of their future.

"Besides," I continue as she still regards me cautiously, "what you're researching looks interesting." Now *that's* a lie. "Is it for class?"

"No," she says, quietly.

"Okay." I jump and wipe down my pants with my palms. "Just let me know what day and time to meet you."

Kassi stares up at me warily, but then a large smile turns her mouth, melting my heart. "Can you do Friday's at four?"

"Poisons Lab ends at four. I can meet you here right after."

Her smile widens.

"I'll see you next Friday, if not some time before then." I turn to leave when her hand catches my wrist.

I freeze. I know this grip. This tight squeeze of her claws. This isn't some "Wait a minute, I forgot to tell you something," grip. Even before I face her, I know exactly what I'll see.

Eyes veiled over in milky-whiteness. A vacant stare, like something has taken hold of her. Something not of this world.

Kassi's not looking at me. She stares blankly straight ahead.

I force my breathing to steady, resisting the urge to scream. "Kass-"

Her head snaps up abruptly, entirely avian, those depthless eyes boring right through me. *"He's not what he says he is."*

It's the same chilling voice I'd heard in the basement. The one that ices my blood and rattles my bones.

But this time, I don't run. I steel my nerves and lean into her. "Who, Kass?"

Her lips unfurl unbearably slow, like whatever has a hold of her body is having a hard time forcing a smile.

"Not who. What."

Kassi blinks furiously, her grip on my wrist loosening. The next time she looks at me, her eyes are dark brown, widened in shame, her cheeks a rich pink. "I'm sorry, Rhi. I-"

I join her on the floor once more. "You have nothing to apologize for. *Nothing.* You warned me once. You just warned me again. Though I have no idea what you meant either time." I raise my eyebrows, hoping she'll take the bait.

"Rhi, I have no idea what I just said to you. Those kinds of prophecies..." she lets out a long breath. "Those kinds of prophecies are something different. I feel like something takes over my body. It uses me as a vessel then disappears. I have no idea what I've said once it's over."

I pat her back. "It's okay. I'll figure it out."

He's not what he says he is. I can't help but think the entity was talking about Nick. A monster that is half god, who has powers I have yet to fathom. But I already know his dark secret.

Correction. His dark *secrets.* He inadvertently caused a girl to go insane. He can change into a full-blown monster, though I have no idea what kind.

He's not what he says he is. Unless...

Unless Nick is hiding something else.

CHAPTER

TWENTY-FIVE

I trudge back up the library steps and out the doors, exhaustion weighing heavy on my bones. My hangover still lingers, and these last few hours have been less than peaceful.

I pause at the Echidna fountain, taking a seat on its edge. The statue at the fountain's center has those inanimate eyes that appear to stare directly at you no matter what position you're in. Those eyes must see a lot.

Only days ago, it was Kieran's body that hung over the fountain's edge as Liv's whirlpool threatened to swallow him whole. I wonder what Echidna, mother of all monsters, thought about her squabbling children in that moment.

I wonder what she thinks of me right now.

"I thought I'd find you here," a whimsical voice states.

I drag my eyes from Echidna's face to find Liv, long aquamarine hair loose and vivacious, her eyes soft and sparkling. The stark difference between the beautiful girl that stands before me and the ringed sharp-toothed monster in my textbook is alarming.

But then I think of that ruthless smile.

"Having a rough morning to mid-afternoon," I tell her, dipping my finger in the fountain. "Why'd you think I'd be here?"

Liv sits beside me. "This is where I go to think. So, I had a feeling you'd be here too." She flashes me a relieved smile. "A lot happened after you left the party."

I wince. "Dare I ask?"

She laughs, flicking the surface of the water. "Nothing terrible. Bianca ran outside after you, but of course, you weren't there. She ended up leaving shortly after."

Shit. I *really* need to text her. "Did anyone tell her what happened?"

Liv nods. "Nick did. Told Scar when he texted her."

I feel a tiny modicum of relief. "Okay. What else happened?"

A sly smirk. "Well, we all decided to get some air, and naturally, Astrid and Scarlett decided to go back to your room because by that time, we'd heard from Nick. Zo went to Andrew's, so it was me, Geraldine, and Harper." She pushes a strand of hair from her face. "Geraldine ended up calling and fighting with Robert, who was at different party with another *girl* who answered his phone when she called."

"Oh shit," I say, my eyes wide. "How did that go?"

Liv waves her hand nonchalantly. "Oh, he came outside like, five seconds later apologizing, and they went somewhere together. But Josh came outside with him, and he and I started talking. Harper and I ended up going with him to Matthew's party and spent the rest of the night there."

"Good. I'm glad everyone else had fun, even though I went a little overboard."

Liv cocks her head. "A little?"

I meet her chiding gaze. "Yeah. A little."

"You told me you saw a deer. Then, you kissed me."

I flick droplets of water at her. "Well, you are *very* attractive. Definitely the best-looking one out of all of us."

Laughing, she splashes me back. "Don't let Astrid hear you say that."

The laughter that bubbles from my chest flows with ease, a welcome departure from the chaos that ensued since I awoke.

AFTER LIV and I head back to the dorms, I text Bianca an apology. The response I receive is curt. *All good. Thursday. Eight o'clock.*

The status quo resumes.

I spend the remainder of the day curled in my bed, catching up on readings for class. Something tells me Steffens owes us a pop quiz in Ancient Myths tomorrow.

Roughly a half hour later, I'm still sitting in my bed, eating lo-mein out of a takeout container as I explain the events of earlier that morning.

True to her nervous antics, Zo paces the floor. "I still can't believe they suspect Nick. It's *Nick,* for Sphinx's sake."

"Say it again," Liv pipes, swallowing a mouthful of rice and broccoli. "Not sure if I heard you correctly the first time."

"Guys," Scarlett says gently.

I take a break from grabbing more noodles to really look at her. Her normally warm hazel eyes are fraught with worry; the space between her eyebrows seems permanently creased.

"We're going to prove he's innocent," Astrid says, catching on to Scarlett's distress. "I've already started going through the files."

"Astrid sent me some too," says Liv.

Scarlett lets out a defeated sigh. "I don't suppose I can be hopeful that you've found anything yet?"

No one says anything.

He's a really good big brother. My brain conjures Scarlett's earlier comment on Nick. I might have an idea.

An insane idea. But an idea.

I jump up, placing the container of noodles on the fireplace mantle. "Instead of proving Nick is innocent, why don't we take it a step further?"

The girls stare at me like I have six heads.

I mean, physically I don't.

"Uh oh," Zo begins, raising a thick eyebrow, "I know that look, Rhi."

"What *look*?"

Liv smiles, pushing a strand of blue hair behind her ear. "The cogs are turning. It's the same look you had when you thought of Operation Charybdis."

Scarlett looks hopeful; Zo, excited. Astrid and Liv, intrigued. Shit. I don't want to get anyone's hopes up, including my own. But here goes.

I lift my chin, squaring my shoulders. "I say *we* catch the killer."

My expectation – and perhaps even my hope– was that at least one of them would tell me I was insane. That this was a bad idea. A very bad idea. But the four of them stare at me like I just told them chocolate mousse cures cancer.

From the other end of my bed, Liv, with her unwavering loyalty says, "I'm in."

"Ditto," Zo calls from the center of the room.

I glance at Astrid and Scarlett, sitting side by side on Scarlett's bed.

Astrid's lips turn in that terrifying smile, waving both black-gloved hands at me. "You know I've wanted to show you what my hands can do."

I rest my gaze on Scarlett, who, surprisingly, is the only one who looks unsure. I thought without a doubt she would be the first to agree, being that Nick is her brother.

"It's going to be really dangerous," she tells me. "I don't think we're dealing with an ordinary monster."

I chew the inside of my cheek. She's absolutely right. We're looking for a full-blown monster. Not a half-breed like the rest of us. Someone who can turn into a thing from our worst nightmares. Someone who actually is the reason children sleep with nightlights and humans whisper prayers and incantations of protection before they go to sleep at night.

But I know the real reason she's hesitant, though I don't voice it out loud.

"I know, Scarlett. But we have to try. If not for Nick, for the next girl. The next victim. It could be one of us."

She winces. The rest of the girl gang looks at her expectantly. It's either we're all in this together, or not at all.

Astrid lays a hand on her shoulder. "There's no pressure, Scar. If you don't want to do this, we won't."

Well, *we* won't. But *I* will.

But Scarlett levels her gaze with mine, face molding into a look of conviction. "No. I'm in."

She says this with a fierceness in her voice that I know isn't entirely genuine. Her mask of conviction doesn't falter, despite the alternative I know she's thinking of. Scarlett isn't scared to do this because it's dangerous. That's not the cause of the fear I sense swimming though her bloodstream.

There's a very small part of Scarlett that fears if we do this and we're successful, the culprit at the end of all of this is...

Nick.

TWENTY-SIX

The next morning, there's a surprise outside my door as I leave for Ancient Myths.

"Morning," Nick greets, handing me a cup of coffee. "Can I walk you to class?"

"Depends." I eye the fancy Styrofoam cup. "What's in this?"

"Eye of newt, blood of a cursed prince, bones of a witch..." He taps a finger to his chin. "Let's see, what am I forgetting? Oh, sugar."

I shove him playfully. "Sounds about right." I take a sip as we begin walking. "It's perfect. Where's this from?"

He raises one eyebrow and the corner of his mouth.

"Oh," I say, dropping my voice to a conspiratorial whisper. "Your secret special place."

Nick laughs. "It's a part of my thank you."

"What are you thanking me for?"

He pushes open the dormitory door, and I clutch my jacket tighter as the late October chill whips against my face.

"For yesterday," he says, wrapping a warm arm around my

shoulder. A different kind of heat spreads throughout my chest and travels to my toes, curling them in my boots.

I snuggle into the crook of his arm, ignoring the gawking stares of people passing by. It occurs to me that even though I'd seen Nick walking around campus with plenty of girls, I'd never once seen him display any kind of public affection.

"I should be thanking you," I tell him. "I never thanked you for helping me Saturday night and taking me to breakfast yesterday morning."

He lets out a mischievous chuckle. "Technically, it was lunch. And do you really think I would pass up the opportunity to have a beautiful, half-naked girl in my bed?"

My cheeks heat but I can't help the laugh that follows. "Stop pretending to be a tough guy. If I recall correctly, all you did to this half-naked girl was give her a tender kiss on her forehead."

Nick pauses on the foot of the steps to the classroom building, people shooting us curious glances as they ascend the stairs around us. He faces me, the arm around my shoulder sliding down to my waist, his opposite hand rising to take my chin between his thumb and forefinger.

The heat I felt earlier magnifies. His amber eyes are dark and serious; his face relaxed but considerate. "Do you remember the day I brought Kieran to your room?"

Like I could forget. I nod.

"Do you remember what I told you?" His voice is near guttural.

"You said..." I can't keep my voice from shaking. "You said..."

Nick brings his face close to mine, so close his breath caresses my cheek. "I said I would never touch you like that," his voice drops lower, huskier. "Unless you asked me to."

If it weren't for his hand on my waist, I'd melt to the floor in a puddle of raging hormones.

"Hey guys!" A friendly voice calls from a few feet away.

Nick is the first to turn his face towards the voice as I struggle to keep standing upright. I expect his features to twist in annoyance at the disturbance, but instead his mouth breaks into a smile.

"Hey Josh. Liv."

At the mention of Liv, I finally look in their direction. The two of them walk hand-in-hand, the portrait of the perfect campus couple, all bright smiles. Josh's cheeks are rosy from the cold, where Liv's dark olive skin begins to redden upon seeing me and Nick.

"Morning!" I greet enthusiastically as they approach, trying to untangle the chords of lust sewn into my voice from Nick's last statement.

"I feel a pop quiz coming from Steffens," Liv says grimly.

"You're probably right."

"Does he still let you drop the lowest grade?" Nick asks.

"Yeah, thank gods," says Liv.

Josh looks at her incredulously. "What do you mean, 'thank gods'? You've aced every single one!"

I glance at Liv questioningly. Just how close have she and Josh gotten since Saturday night?

Nick checks his watch. "Well, if you guys are anticipating a pop quiz, you better get going."

We head up the stairs in unison, Nick opening the door for everyone. I let Liv go in first, then motion quickly for Nick to follow as I tug Josh to stay behind.

"What's up?" He says warily when the door closes behind Nick.

I jut my chin toward the closed door. "You really like her?"

His honey eyes narrow in suspicion. "Yeah, I do."

"Good," I give him an assuring smile, reaching for the door. "But Josh, have you ever heard of being caught between Scylla and Charybdis?"

Josh returns the smile, a little sharp at its edges. "Don't worry, Rhi. I won't hurt her."

We both step inside and turn the corridor. Josh places a hand on my arm. "But honestly? Being caught between Scylla and Charybdis...I don't think I'd mind it." He shoots me a grin and walks ahead, leaving me to process the end of his statement.

Cheeky bastard.

My Thursday night lesson with B arrives quickly, and I didn't realize how much I'd dreaded seeing her until I open the door to the gym and find her practicing.

Though her last text to me wasn't anything out of the ordinary for Drill Sergeant Bianca, I can't help but feel there is some sort of rift between us. I'd even thought of canceling the lesson for tonight, but if she didn't already hate me after Bacchanal, canceling on her today would have undoubtedly sealed the deal.

"Hey," I say as I pass her, dropping my stuff near the wall.

No response.

Oh, I am *so* fucked.

I start to put on my padding when B's cold voice interrupts me. "No padding tonight."

I crease my eyes in confusion but grab my foil and head over to her. "Why not?"

"We're going to focus on footwork tonight, not parry attacks, so you can lose that too." B doesn't once look at me when she says this, her eyes traveling from my feet to the foil, but never my face.

"Okay," I say hesitantly. Something is wrong here. "Look, B, about Saturday-"

"Saturday was fun," she says in a placid tone that rivals Astrid's. "Heard you ended up at Nick's." There's a bite at the end of that sentence.

"So what if I did?" I challenge.

B shrugs nonchalantly. "Good for you." The sneer is audible.

I bite my tongue, refusing to fight over a boy. If B has a problem with where I ended up and who I ended up with on Saturday night, she should just spit it out. I won't give her any more ammunition.

"Shall we?" I hold my palm out as a gesture of invitation.

We move through the footwork, which is essentially us sparring without our foils. B uses this as an opportunity to get closer and land physical blows, something that is highly illegal in the fencing world. A small shove here, slight push to the shoulder there. Even if I didn't know something was bothering her, her aggressive handling of me would be a dead giveaway.

My anger is a slow mounting wave, building far off in the distance and growing larger as it approaches the shore. One more "accidental" shove and it's going to crash.

The wave of anger crashes before I know it. B uses her shoulder to send me stumbling back. My cheeks are a blaze of fury, the wrath in my chest exploding like a pressure cooker.

"Ok, you wanna do this? Then let's go." I charge at her, shoving her hard with both arms. "What's your fucking problem?"

B's scowl is back, but for the most part, she remains eerily calm. "I don't have a problem." She steps closer, the threatening look on her face enhanced by the cold fury in her brown eyes. "And if you touch me again, you'll regret it."

That last line of hers is bait. A clear invitation. She *wants* to fight.

Luckily, so do I. The Scylla head hisses in gleeful anticipation.

I crack the whip, sending her stumbling back several feet. She narrows her eyes. "I should have known you would fight dirty." Her claws unsheathe, twice as long as mine.

A small shiver of fear sits at the back of my neck. I have no idea what kind of monster B is.

She closes her eyes. Cracks a taunting smile. "What are you waiting for, Scylla?"

I don't question her choice to have the world go dark. The whip whirls, going for her feet. She effortlessly dodges it, swiping for my face at the same time. I barely move fast enough to avoid it. I unfurl the whip again, trying for her middle, to knock her down, but she gracefully twirls out of the way.

All with her eyes closed.

And then I realize: she can *see* where the whip is going to strike. Whatever power she has, as long as her eyes are closed, she sees where the whip will land.

I do the only thing I can: I wrap my arms around her middle and knock her to the ground. Her eyes open too late; she lays sprawled beneath me as I raise a clawed hand to strike.

With inhuman swiftness, she grabs my raised wrist and uses the leverage of her free arm and the strength of lower body to knock me sideways. She's on top of me before I can even catch my breath, pinning both arms above my head as she puts the weight of her body on my legs.

I can't move. I have no idea how to physically fight, and obviously, B does. "Go ahead, B," I snarl. "This is your moment.

Punish me for whatever it is that you don't have the courage to say out loud."

A strange look passes across her face. Her grip on my wrists tightens. She leans down, and I expect to see a mouthful of razor-sharp teeth or feel the embedment of her claws in my skin.

Instead, I feel her lips as she presses her mouth to mine. Her lips are soft and warm and hesitant, a kiss almost of relief. I don't know if I'm fully in control of my brain when I kiss her back.

A surprise gasp escapes her mouth, her body going rigid as she straddles me. But then her grip on my wrists loosens, her hands traveling to cup my face and pull herself closer as she kisses me harder.

It's then that I sense it; the feeling of relief melts into happiness, into a sensation of reckless abandonment as she sheds her insecurities and trepidations about me and her and latches on to the idealization that this is real.

But it's not. I'm placating her as I kiss her back, thinking I'm doing her a favor by not pulling away, by not stopping, but all I'm doing is giving her false hope.

I place a hand on her shoulder and gently push back. She pulls her lips from mine, her face hovering inches from my own.

"B," I whisper. "We have to stop."

Her heart thunders beneath my palm, and I don't meet her eyes, afraid I'll see traces of resentment in them.

B says nothing as she lifts herself off me, settling beside me cross-legged. She places her head in her hands.

"B, I'm sorry-"

She cuts me off as she raises her head, eyes bright and glassy. "Don't apologize, Rhi." She lets out a long breath. "I should have said something. I just..." She toys with her shoelace. "I just didn't think hearing about you and Nick would bother me so much. I thought I could let it go, and we could just be friends."

"We can be friends, B. We *are* friends. I invited you to Bacchanal because I consider you a friend, and I'm sorry if just now I let you think I want something more."

"I really was worried about you that night," she says quietly. "Not just because you were so drunk, but because I knew where you would end up. And I know how Nick is with girls."

Of course. She knows what everyone else knows about Nick. What he wants everyone else to think.

"B, if I told you it's more complicated than that, will you believe me?"

An unsure scowl. No, she won't.

I wrap my arm around her shoulders, earning a surprised look. "But thank you for being concerned. I heard you went looking for me, and I'm sorry I didn't listen to you about the Dionysian Frenzy."

She sniffs in disapproval, but then her lips purse into a strained smile. "You freshmen never learn, do you?"

I nudge her playfully in response.

"So, did you and Nick…"

"Nope," I say, a smug smile on my mouth. "He was quite the gentleman."

B stares at me, eyes searching my face. "You know, despite his reputation, any girl I've ever spoken to about him says the same thing. And he's never been anything but nice to me, and I can be a hard person to like."

I feign shock. "You don't say."

I'm rewarded with actual laughter as she tips her head back. "Fine. I deserve that." She stares down at her shoes once more. "I wouldn't have hurt you, Rhi."

I give her shoulder a reassuring squeeze. "I know. I wouldn't have hurt you either."

She brings her face up, glancing at me from beneath her eyelashes. "Bullshit."

I press my lips together, removing my arm from around her shoulder and drop my hands in my lap. "Okay. Maybe I wanted to get a punch or two in. But *you* got touchy with me first."

"That's fair."

"What are you by the way?"

Her dark brown eyes crease warily. "You mean, am I a lesbian?'

I snort. "No, B. I mean what kind of monster are you?" It doesn't matter to me what her sexual orientation is, but I find it amusing that the only time sexual orientation takes a back seat in conversation is when you can trace your heritage back to a mythical monster.

"I'd rather answer the lesbian question."

I hold up my pointer finger. "First of all, I never asked that question." My middle finger joints the pointer. "Second, why don't you want to tell me?"

B shrugs. "Just don't like talking about it."

I scrutinize her while she continues gazing at the floor, but I don't push.

"Very well. Do I dare insist that we continue?"

B smiles, the awkwardness and tension forgotten, evident by how her eyes dance, as though she'd been waiting for me to say that.

I return the smile, my own heart skipping.

I have my friend back.

TWENTY-SEVEN

Following Poisons Lab the next day, I head straight for the library, finding Kassi exactly where she'd been nearly a week ago.

"Here," she says by way of greeting, handing me a familiar thick tome. "Start with this one."

It's *Hell's Princes: A Biography*. "You really seem to like this one." I settle in next to her.

She doesn't look at me as she smiles, eyes scanning the open book on her lap. "I remember how much *you* liked it."

"Okay, what am I looking for?"

Kassi jots down a few notes on the pad to her right. "Each time a new prince is introduced, write a brief summary of him."

"You mean *it*," I correct as I pull a notebook and pen from my bag.

That causes her to glance up, dark blonde brows furrowed. "What are you talking about?"

"You called a prince of hell 'he'. It's a monster, so technically, shouldn't we be calling 'he' 'it'?

Kassi blinks. "We're monsters, Rhi. Would you like being called an 'it'?

I'm thoroughly confused. "No, but we're at least partly human."

"Being partly human doesn't put you up on a pedestal, giving you the right to demean other creatures to abstract ideas." She flips to the next page.

Damn Sphinxes.

Instead of arguing, I begin reading. I skim the introduction, as I did last Sunday when I first came upon the book. The first prince presented is Lucifer, and I nearly skim over his passage as well, when I realize this particular Lucifer is not equated with the Christian version I'd come to know.

According to this book, Lucifer was a *god*. Born of Aurora and Cephalus, he was charged with heralding the dawn. I guess that's where the name *Morningstar* comes from.

The passage doesn't go into his transformation from god to "prince of hell" but does touch on the fact that his post in hell is 'of the East' and he is considered the Lord of Air, a title that has also been attributed to Zeus, Greek god of lightning and thunder, and the King of the Olympian Gods.

I glance up from my reading, my brain mashing together bits and pieces of this puzzle of information.

"Interesting, isn't it?" Kassi's gaze is still consumed by the book in her lap, but she nonetheless acknowledges my contemplative look.

"Yeah," I admit, turning my head to face her. "What's all this for?"

Kassi places her pen in the spine of the book, using it as a bookmark. She stares at me, brown eyes cautionary yet somehow eager. "Rhi, if I tell you something, can you *promise* me you will keep it to yourself?"

What's with everyone getting the urge to trust me with

their secrets? But I consider Kassi, a girl who probably wishes she had a person to share things with. "I promise."

A small part of me is secretly hoping she's about to share Nick's prophecy.

"I know about the death of Amanda Reynolds," she starts, licking her lips. I'm about to ask how, but I bite my tongue. Of course, she knows. She's an Oracle.

"I saw her, as a Shade," Kassi continues.

I raise my eyebrows. Now *that's* intriguing.

"I don't know who killed her or Sasha Nichols, but I think it's something bigger than a monster gone rogue."

I eye the book in my lap. "That's why you're researching different kinds of monsters. You don't think it's one of us."

She shakes her head.

I let out a relieved sigh, thinking of Nick. "Not even a monster who is half god?"

Kassi's gaze flicks down to the book in my lap, then back up to me. "What do you think they are?"

Oh fuck. That's not reassuring at all.

"You're thinking of Nick, aren't you?" she asks.

"Is it that obvious?"

Kassi rolls her eyes. "*Nick* is obvious. It's not him. Both victims can be traced to him. Whoever is doing this is trying to frame him. But it's *why* they're trying to frame him that I haven't figured out yet."

I squint as something Kassi said jogs my memory. "What."

Her eyes crease in confusion. "What...what?"

"Not who...*what.* That's what you said to me on Sunday. One of your creepy prophecies."

"Rhi, *all* of my prophecies are creepy."

I give her a quizzical glance. "You told me: 'he's not what he says he is.' And then you or the *Dark Phoenix* or whatever that thing was clarified and said, 'not who, *what.*'

Kassi furrows her brows. I chew on my thumbnail in anticipation of her response.

"That doesn't necessarily mean it had anything to do with the murderer. Maybe it really was talking about Nick. He's got a reputation, you know."

It's my turn to roll my eyes. "Yes, yes. I know. He's a regular Casanova."

"You must really like him."

I decide to answer honestly. No more sarcasm and jokes as a smokescreen. "I do. I'm trying to help him." After all, my entire plan is, at its core, a plan to help him. I might as well just own up to the fact that I have...do I dare say it?...*feelings* for Nick. Feelings that are tipping far beyond lust.

Kassi cocks her head. "Help him, how?"

I give her a rundown of Astrid and the girls checking the student files to see if anything strange or out of the ordinary that jumps out at them about the heritage of any particular student. But I leave out the part that we are trying to single-handedly catch the killer.

"You know," Kassi says as she opens up her book and slides the pen out, "the best way for you to help him is to stay away from him, but I have a feeling that's just not going to happen, so I give up."

"What are you talking about, Kass?"

"Never mind," she says, eyes still on the book. "If you really want to help him, there might be something in the crypt."

"The what?"

She turns the page. "Rumor has it there's an underground crypt where Talbot keeps a *ton* of hidden shit."

I tap her on the shoulder to draw her attention back to me. "A, why don't I know about this, B, why didn't anyone else mention it, and C, how do I get there?"

A smirk. "I always forget that I know so much more than everyone else."

A smug Sphinx. Great.

"No one else knows about it," she continues. "And as for getting there, the entrance is through the Echidna Fountain."

"Anything else?" I press, attempting to keep a lid on my excitement.

Her eyes go from left to right as she tilts her head pensively. "Oh," her face lights up. "Another rumor is that a monster guards the entrance." Kassi goes back to her reading.

"Kass," I stay sternly. "A monster...like...us?"

"Definitely not like us." She doesn't even spare me a glance — just continues reading.

I try to get back to reading, but my thoughts are scattered from deciding if it's worth it to brave the alleged monster that guards the crypt to deciding who I'll ask to come with me.

Within minutes I have my answer.

"So, there's a secret room beneath the Echidna Fountain, guarded by a monster that may tell us who or what is murdering my former lovers?"

"Crypt. A secret crypt," I correct Nick as we walk back to the dorms after fencing this Saturday morning.

Clad in a gray Alystair sweatshirt and black shorts, he runs a hand through his sweat-soaked hair. "I don't know, Rhi. It seems risky."

My heart falls. I thought with certainty he'd be willing to come with me.

"It's okay," I say as we enter the dorms and try to hide my disappointment. "I can ask the girls."

"I didn't say 'no'. Look-" he breaks off as we approach my

room. "Why don't we go to the Odyssey? We can eat and talk about this more."

"The what?"

He smirks. "The diner," he says, complete with air quotations.

"Oh," I say with realization. "Is that what it's called?" He nods. "I like calling it your secret special place better."

Nick shoves his hands in the pockets of his shorts. "Call it whatever you want. Just say you'll come."

"Of course, I'll come." I pull my hair from its tight ponytail, massaging the crown of my head. "Just let me shower first."

He bites his lip, one of the rare occasions I see a glimmer of uncertainty in his eyes. "You can use my shower, if you want."

"Oh. Um..." How do I answer this? Showering in his bathroom is amazing. It offers privacy, peace, the pipe dream that he'll sneak in and surprise me.

"By yourself, of course," he adds with the corners of his mouth curling, as though he'd been reading my thoughts. "But I mean, if you were thinking of inviting me to join you, I certainly wouldn't turn down the invitation." He smiles with his teeth, letting me know he's only half-joking.

Flustered, I grab the doorknob. "Let me grab my clothes." He starts to follow me inside. "No, no," I say, placing a hand against his chest. "You can wait here. Just like you can wait for your shower invitation." I give him a demure smile worthy of Liv and disappear into my room.

ALMOST AN HOUR LATER, we sit at Nick's secret special place at the exact same table we sat at the first time I came here.

I order eggs, bacon, and toast this time. Nick raises his eyebrow once I've finished telling Minerva my order, but then proceeds to order an omelet with bacon, sausage, and home fries.

"So, the crypt. Let's weigh the pros and cons," he says, sipping his coffee astutely.

I place my palms flat on the table. "Let's."

He taps a finger on the side of the coffee mug. "If we go, there's a chance we die."

Nick says nothing further, and I furrow my brows. "Not to point out the obvious, but that's one con, and zero pros."

He sits back in his chair. "I don't see any pros."

"Well, let me enlighten you." I fold my arms and lean over the table. "If we go, there's a chance we find something help-ful, something that can help solve this murder mystery. If we go, there's a chance that we find something that proves beyond all measure, you are completely innocent. If we go, there's a chance we find something that can *stop* this monster and save its next victim. And since you pointed out earlier that it seems to be targeting your former lovers, I might be on that list."

Nick stiffens at my last statement, fingers tightening around the handle of the coffee mug.

"First of all, I would *never* let that happen." His eyes flash dangerously. "Second, while you make some valid points, what if we go to the crypt and get attacked or *killed* by this monster?"

I hold up a finger. "But what if this monster doesn't exist? Kassi said it was a rumor."

"Rhi, there has to be something guarding it. They wouldn't keep things down there if anyone could get to them."

"Maybe it's a unicorn," I suggest somewhat wistfully.

Nick's lips twist in a frown. "That wouldn't necessarily be a good thing."

My mouth drops open as Minerva sets our food down and

tells us to enjoy. Nick picks up his plate and dumps half of his home fries on mine.

"Hey, you don't have to-"

He holds up a hand, silencing me with his wolf smile. "You know you're going to ask for some eventually, so I thought I'd save you the trouble."

I try to hide my own smile but fail as I shove a forkful of home fries into my mouth. I take a sip of coffee then clear my throat meaningfully. "Listen, I'm going to be transparent with you, which is a rarity for me, so keep that in mind for future reference." Nick raises an eyebrow, pulling one side of his mouth with it. "I'm going down there whether or not you decide to come with me. And if you don't, I completely under-stand, but you should know that I'm doing this with or without you."

His face turns blank, but he stares at me intensely. "I should have expected that. You wouldn't be the girl I-" He releases a huff of air. "You wouldn't be the girl I admire if my decisions stopped you from doing what you want to do."

I try to hide another smile, but I can't. "So, does this mean you're in?"

Nick takes a bite of bacon. "When do you want to go?"

The grease from the bacon coats his lips, and my eyes linger on them, wondering what those lips would feel like against my own. Against my bare skin.

"How about tonight?" I say, nearly breathless.

He crunches another piece of meat between his teeth, flashing me his dazzling grin. "It's a date."

TWENTY-EIGHT

The Echidna foundation is illuminated the same way it had been the night the gang and I threatened Kieran. Painted in moonlight, Echidna looks ethereal. It's almost as if the moon itself is paying homage to the Mother of Monsters, the Queen of the Night.

"Now is probably not a good a time to point out that midnight is not the recommended hour to begin an investigation into a secret crypt that may or may not be housing a terrifying monster," Nick says as we stand staring down at the fountain's pool.

"Really? I think it's a perfect time considering there's no one around, and we might raise a few eyebrows wading around the fountain in broad daylight."

I hear his defeated sigh. "Point taken."

We're both wearing black, Nick's ensemble making him look like some dark god of night, the color making the luminous glow to his eyes even brighter.

His eyes flick to me. "Black is a good color on you. Your eyes look so green."

I feel a smile on my lips. "That's just what I was thinking about you."

"That my eyes look green?"

I push him, rolling my eyes. "No, idiot." When I glance at him, he's looking down, a soft, easy smile on his face. It disappears when he brings his gaze back to the fountain's pool.

"Alright. So, do we just step in and...I don't know...knock?"

I frown. "I have no idea. Maybe we should check around the fountain first."

The two of us search the fountain's edge and around its side, using the flashlight on our phones. I don't know what I'm expecting to see. I doubt there's a set of instructions to enter a secret crypt just casually engraved somewhere on the fountain.

"I think I found something," Nick's voice calls from the other side.

I walk over to join him, squinting at strange symbols etched into the stone. "What is it?"

"Ancient Greek, I think." He squats down, eye level with the writing, running his fingers along the engraving. "Hold your breath."

"Why?"

"No, that's what this says. Hold your breath."

"You can read Ancient Greek?"

Nick stands, giving me a coy smile.

"Yeah, yeah. I know." I wave my hand at him. "Super awesome monster god and what not." I pause, staring once more into the dark water of the fountain's pool. "Nick, you don't think..."

Nick's gaze follows mine, the smile fading. "No way. There isn't enough water in that pool for us to fully submerge ourselves underneath. What is it? Like two feet?" He leans over the fountain's edge.

But I'm already climbing over, one foot submerged in the

cold water, an icy chill shooting up my leg and numbing me all over.

Nick's strong fingers wrap around my arm. "What are you doing?"

"Nick," I begin, bringing my other leg into the pool, my lips chattering, "what do you know about what happened to Kieran?"

His eyes whip behind me to the water. "Not enough, apparently."

"I lured him here, to the fountain. Liv used her abilities to create a whirlpool, and I threatened to throw Kieran into it."

At first, Nick studies me, his face a mix of shock and something like pride. But then his brows furrow. "What does that have to do with you taking a midnight swim in a freezing fountain?"

I want to throttle him for missing the obvious. "Nick, that whirlpool was *deep*. I couldn't see the bottom. If the fountain is truly only two feet deep, Liv's whirlpool wouldn't have scared Kieran the way it did." I sweep my hand across the surface of the pool. "This has to be an illusion. A glamour."

Nick ping-pongs his gaze from the fountain, to me, then back to the fountain. He releases my arm and steps inside with me. "Gods this is freezing." He shudders, then looks at me. "Okay, *Lara Croft*, what do we do next?"

I giggle at the reference, then focus my attention on him. "We do exactly what the instructions said: hold our breath."

"Rhi, do you feel that underneath your feet?" The ripple of water around his shin lets me know he's tapping his foot to the floor. "That's hard stone. Not another twenty feet of depth, but stone."

I grab his hand. Despite the chill of the water, the feel of his fingers in mine sends waves of heat throughout my entire body. "Just trust me, okay?"

Nick licks his lips, nodding.

I go down to my knees, and Nick follows. Still holding hands, we plunge only our faces into the water.

Instinctively, I hold my eyes closed as the freezing water slaps me across the face, but a squeeze of Nick's hand prompts me to open them.

Though I kneel on a hard stone floor, the floor of the fountain disappears into blackness.

Nick yanks his face up, pulling me with him. I use my free hand to wipe the water from my eyes.

"You were right," Nick breathes. "Holy shit."

"How far down do you think it goes?" I look down at the surface of the water grimly.

"I think 'hold your breath' is your answer."

The uncertainty in his voice prickles my skin. "Nick," I start, keeping my eyes on the water, "if you don't want to-"

I feel his fingers on my chin and turn towards him. His eyes are blazing, fierce. Similar to the way they looked after he'd taken off his fencing mask the first time I'd seen him duel with B.

"Rhi, I know you said you would do this with or without me. And I know you're doing it for me. But I want to do this for *you*. Because you're right. If whatever is doing this is targeting me, and the women I've been with are collateral damage, I won't let you be the next girl it takes." He draws a murderous gaze down at the water.

There's a tightness in my chest and a flutter in my stomach that's not quite nerves. Nick's words feel layered with something so much more than affection and protectiveness. I squeeze his hand in support, smiling at him when he finally looks at me.

"Hold your breath."

CHAPTER
TWENTY-NINE

Darkness envelops us as we plunge into the fountain. Though darkness itself has never bothered me, the inky blackness surrounding us is a completely different matter. It's the fear of not knowing which way is up, of never making it out.

Of drowning.

Nick's hand in mine is my only comfort, keeping me on course and stopping me from flailing and kicking in a desperate attempt to get back to the surface.

I'm not sure how far down we've swum. Maybe ten feet. But I know I won't be able to hold my breath much longer. Scylla might have been a sea monster, but I never read anything that said she was able to breathe underwater.

Several more feet down, my lungs start to burn. I panic, squeezing Nick's hand. He squeezes back, tugging me further downward, then gives me another squeeze, a more purposeful grasp.

A little further in the distance, I see light. It's small, but it's enough to let me know that we're approaching something - an opening. I swim harder, Nick's strong strokes propelling me along much faster than I'd be able to swim on my own. The small burst of light grows, and I realize the light is flickering.

We finally break the surface, and I take in as much air as my lungs will allow, coughing and sputtering as Nick guides me to the stairs of a silver ladder. I place my hands on the ladder's railing, struggling to pull myself up. Nick's hands grab my waist, and he hoists me up. I nearly collapse once my body is completely out of the water, holding myself up on all fours, breathing heavily.

"Hey, Rhi," Nick's hands are at my back, his voice raspy and breathless. "Look at me."

I slump into a sitting position, eyes closed as his hands move my wet, matted hair out of my face.

"Rhi, talk to me. Are you okay?"

"Yup," I cough. "Never been better."

His thumbs stroke my lips and cheeks, jolting my eyes open.

Another strange situation where he looks like Scarlett, his eyes fraught with worry. They search my face, and then he removes his hands and places two fingers against my neck, to the side of my windpipe.

"Listen, I know I might look terrible, but I'm not dead, so you don't need to check my pulse."

Nick's grin comes with a sigh of relief. "Your lips are blue. Just making sure your heart is still pumping as it should, and since you're still spewing your endearing witticisms, I think you're perfectly fine."

I slam a fist into my chest and wince. "Strong like bull."

He chuckles and holds out a hand to help me up. Warmth once again ignites my blood. *Actual* warmth. I take a moment to study him. Aside from being soaking wet and still stunning, he looks fit as fiddle. Not like he just swam thirty or forty feet into darkness and held his breath for longer than any creature other than a mermaid should be able to. He doesn't even look *tired.*

"What?" he asks, acknowledging my scrutiny.

"Why are you warm?" I feel like that short question sums up most of my previous thoughts.

"Ah," he says sheepishly, "that's some of the god powers. I can regulate my body temperature."

I gaze skyward and sigh. "Of course, you can." When I glance down, I finally take in our new surroundings.

We stand in a long corridor, lit by torches that hang on the walls. The corridor is made of dark stone, the flickering embers casting eerie shadows that dance down the walls. Despite the flames, the other end of the corridor disappears into blackness.

Nick's hand finds mine once more, and I take another look at him. He smiles encouragingly. "We've made it this far."

"I know." I say, but I can't help but shiver.

"Say the word and we'll go back. We'll find another way."

Even if we could go back, Nick's right. We made it this far. I give him a small tug. "Let's go."

We walk in silence for a few moments until the warmth of his hand prompts me to speak.

"So, what are your other godly powers? Aside from being a heating pad." *And drowning people in their own blood,* I add in my head.

"Well, I can heal myself a lot faster than you, even though you can heal yourself quickly."

"I can?"

He side-eyes me but makes sure to return his gaze quickly in front of him.

"We all can heal ourselves, Rhi. If you broke your arm, it would heal itself within like two days. If I broke my arm, it would heal in two hours."

"Huh. I guess that's why I've never once been sick in eighteen years."

The corridor still hasn't changed, the blackness ahead of us still seemingly endless. But we continue walking, hand in hand.

"It happened on your eighteenth birthday right?" Nick asks. "Your claws and the urges."

"Yeah," I say, my cheeks heating. "At my party. I wanted to eat my friend, Jesse."

I expect Nick to laugh or grin, but his expression remains stoic. "He was just a friend, then?"

I see where this is going. I'm not sure I want to go down this road, but since Nick opened up about his past, I guess it's only fair. "Jesse and I were friends since grade school. We started dating at the end of sophomore year of high school but went back to being friends at the beginning of last year.

"Why did you break up?"

Nosy Nelly. "After we, uh, slept together, he told me he loved me." I slide my gaze to Nick, finding he's clenched his jaw. "I didn't love him. Not like that. So, I broke up with him." I shrug. "I thought it was the right thing to do."

Nick slows his pace. "Why don't you sound sure about that?"

"Because even though I'm not in love with him, I still love him as a friend. And I wanted to keep that friendship. And I'm not sure if that's selfish or not."

"It's not," he says quietly. "It's not selfish to spare someone unrequited love and to continue to love them in a different way."

I contemplate his words, finding a small weight lifting as they settle within me. He's right. I did the right thing by breaking up with Jesse and being honest with him. Both about not loving him the way he loves me and admitting that I only loved him as a friend and wanted his friendship.

But then, I remember, he no longer wants anything to do with me.

"It doesn't matter," I tell him. "When Jesse found out I was coming here, he wrote me off."

"Then he's a dick." Nick words come out fast and sharp.

I catch myself smiling.

"So, he's the only guy you ever…"

My smile turns into a frown. *Geez.* How long is this corridor? I pause before I answer, thinking I might be saved by us coming upon something other than more length of hallway.

Luck is not on my side. "Yeah." I turn my neck to look at Nick. "What about you, Casanova?"

Nick simply side-eyes me, his mouth twisted in a half-grin.

I roll my eyes, and my mouth parts in an attempt to push him for an answer, but he interrupts me.

"Do you smell that?" he asks, eyes widening.

The smell of burning wood enters my nose.

"We must be getting close to something," Nick continues, pushing me behind him. "Stay behind me."

I pull at the back of his shirt, stepping beside him once more. "Really, Sir Lancelot?"

His expression is stern, brows drawn together and lips in a tight line. "Rhi, you've seen what I can do. If there really is some sort of monster up ahead guarding the entrance to the crypt, how will you defend yourself?"

My answer is a crack of the whip around his neck - not enough to threaten, but enough to get my point across.

His lips curl into my favorite smile. "So, the rumors are true, Scylla."

"About time you acknowledge my monstrous heritage." I let the whip unfurl.

Nick nods. "Ok. From this point on, we proceed slowly. With caution. No talking."

I salute him. "Aye aye, captain."

I receive an eye roll in return.

Just as Nick instructed, we proceed warily, our footsteps barely making a sound on the floor. The blackness unfolds into a dim twilight, revealing an ancient wooden door with a brass handle set in a stone arch.

The lack of protection surrounding the door sets off a ton of red flags. Not only is there no so-called monster guarding this door, there isn't even a *lock*.

"This seems too easy," Nick murmurs, sharing my thoughts.

"Maybe the monster is on the inside?" I suggest.

"Maybe." The skepticism in his voice is not reassuring.

Still, we move towards the door, and I don't protest this time when Nick grips the handle and pushes me behind him.

With a soft *click*, the door opens, and Nick pokes his head inside. He's so still that for a few terrifying moments, I think something decapitated him and his body is just standing there, ready to slump the ground.

But my imagination has run away with me again, and Nick pulls his head back and opens the door wide. Though there didn't appear to be a lock on the outside of the door, I now notice there's one on the inside.

We step inside a large room, about the size of the dorm's common room and similarly decorated. The smell of burning wood I'd scented earlier comes from a roaring fire set in a fireplace made of gleaming chestnut, brick and mortar making up the inside. A brown leather couch sits in front of the fire, facing the wall opposite. A square claw-footed table is placed directly in front of the couch, the same chestnut color as the fireplace, and another brown leather sofa sits on the other side of it. The walls of the room itself are lined floor to ceiling with books, with only the very last section of the shelves to the far right cut off at the bottom quarter, revealing three drawers.

This looks nothing like a crypt. This looks like a lounge.

I look at Nick the same time he looks at me, his expression of wonder and confusion mirroring my own.

"What's the plan?" he asks.

"You mean because there's no monster for us to take on, and we've somehow stumbled into a cozy den rather than a creepy crypt?"

"Not in so many words, but yeah."

I consider our new course of action. "I guess we just search the room. See if there is anything we can find. The books, the drawers over there. There has to be *something* here." At least, I'm hoping I didn't nearly drown only to find Professor Talbot's secret getaway for self-care.

"Okay," Nick agrees, but grabs my hand before I venture further into the room. "Rhi, let's do this quickly. Even if there is no monster guarding this room, the fact that there's a fire going suggests that someone or something was here, left, and will probably be back soon." In saying that, Nick turns the lock on the door.

I nod in agreement then head off to the right, my eyes glued to the drawers on the last shelf. I run my fingers along the smooth wood finish, sliding my hand underneath the hanging pull, and softly open the drawer.

I hold my breath, waiting for something to happen. Booby-traps to spring. Alarms to go off. This alleged monster to appear.

Nothing.

Inside the drawer I find an array of manila folders and pull out the first one my fingers touch.

I flip open the file, finding nothing inside. No papers, no

notes jotted down on the file itself. Not even the top tab has anything written on it. I pull out a few more folders, all of them exactly the same as the first.

Closing the drawer, I open the second. It's filled with the same empty file folders as the top drawer. Out of a defeated curiosity, I open the third drawer.

Same thing.

Frustrated, I slam the drawer closed with a loud *bang*. Nick looks up from a book on the other side of the room.

"These books are empty," he tells me.

"So are the files in these drawers." I run a hand down my face, walking towards him. He stands in front of the brown leather couch, looking more intrigued than frustrated, like I am.

"This makes no sense," he says. "And yet..."

"Yet?" I press, standing in front of him.

"Yet there has to be a reason all of this is here."

"Yeah, to waste our time." I let out an aggravated huff.

Nick closes the blank book and tosses it on the end of the couch. He rubs those warm hands down my arms. "Relax, Rhi. We'll find something."

Just as the tension in my chest eases at his words, the door handle rattles. Nick and I both whip our heads towards the door, the lock jiggling.

"Hello? Is someone in there?" A velvet smooth voice asks from outside.

Nick looks back at me, his brows creased in confusion. "That's no monster," he whispers.

I gulp. "No. Could be a professor." Which means if we're caught, we're in deep shit.

The door handle rattles again. "There's no way I locked myself out," the strange voice contemplates.

The hands on my arms travel down to my waist, gripping

tightly. "Rhi, please don't punch me in the face for what I'm about to do, okay?"

Before I can ask Nick what he means, he pulls me into him and crashes his lips down to mine.

I'm too startled to do anything, so I go rigid, my arms at my sides, hands clenched into fists.

But then I understand what he's doing. If we're caught, he's trying to make it look like we ended up down here for some sort of hookup. I play along.

His lips are soft, and I wrap my arms around his neck, pulling him closer. He clenches my waist in surprise, then relaxes and deepens the kiss.

With his tongue.

A small gasp escapes my lips, as his hands move from my waist to the small of my back, pressing me closer still. Nick steps backward, falling into the couch, pulling me on top of him.

The threat of being caught long forgotten, I shift my body to straddle him, earning a soft groan from the back of his throat. I cup Nick's face as his hands, scorchingly hot, send shivers throughout my body while they move under my soaked shirt.

My own fingers aching to explore him, I shift again so I can tug the hem of his shirt up and slide my palms underneath to his hard stomach.

"Ah," he hisses, breaking the kiss. Then, laughs softly. "Your hands are cold."

"Sorry," I say, biting my lower lip, swollen from his mouth. The dark look in his eyes coupled with the roguish smirk on his face and his hands on my skin are going to completely unravel me.

"Come here," he says huskily, adjusting his hips so that my lips once again hover tantalizingly close to his own.

With the movement of his hips, I feel the hard press of him against me, setting my blood to boiling. I grind against him, and Nick exhales sharply against my collarbone.

"*Fuck,*" he growls.

I bring my face forward, eager to feel his lips. He pushes wet hair from my face, his gaze lasered on my mouth.

"*Quiero besarte hasta la muerte,*" he whispers.

Gods, I'd forgotten how fucking sexy that sounds when he says it. Especially now, with my legs straddling his hips and our pelvises grinding against one another.

"Are you finally going to tell me what that means?" I breathe.

Nick runs his tongue over his bottom lip, his hands shifting to grip my ass. "For all intents and purposes, it means 'I'm dying to kiss you,' but word for word?" He slides a warm hand up my back, melding my body into his. Nick's lips brush mine as he speaks. "It means, 'I want to kiss you until death.'"

I want to kiss you until death. I know without a doubt I would let him. I would stay here with his hands and mouth on my skin and our bodies pressed together until I drew my last breath.

Nick moves his mouth in slow, teasing kisses from the base of my ear down my neck. I let my head fall back, giving him access to my throat. His fingers peel the wet shirt from my skin until it's pushed above the swells of my breasts. He palms my left breast and takes my right nipple in his mouth through the fabric.

I release a guttural moan. My nipples harden beneath the heat of his mouth and his hand. My claws emerge and dig into his shoulders.

A primal groan hums in his throat, and he yanks my bra strap down to completely expose my right breast, his tongue and lips now devouring the bare flesh and sucking ferociously.

I cry out, not from pain, but from the sharp ache that shocks my core. His hard cock is so tormentingly close to my center the monster in me wants nothing more than to tear our clothes into shreds and ride him into oblivion.

And that's exactly what I plan to do. But then my eyes catch the door behind us. The one that's now open.

"Nick," I gasp, pushing myself off him. I'm quite impressed with how quickly he manages to stand, given his...er...fragile state.

He turns in the direction I'm still staring, mouth agape. He faces me, shaking his head. "What-"

As soon as the word is out of his mouth, he breaks off, shoving me behind him. I fall into the couch face first, the graceful ballerina that I am, and whirl as fast as I can to see what caught Nick's attention.

His claws unsheathed, I stare past him. Past the coffee table, and onto the opposite couch.

Where there's a giant golden cat, smiling at us like it just found dinner.

CHAPTER

THIRTY

"Please, don't stop what you're doing on my account." The giant cat licks his chops. "You two are the best entertainment I have had in *years*."

The voice of the cat – or is some sort of tiger? – is the same smooth drawl we heard outside the door, the one trying to get in after Nick had locked it. It lounges languidly on the opposite couch, its short fur a beautiful gilded color with light green eyes ringed in gold.

I adjust my bra and shirt so that I'm fully covered and slink around Nick's body to stand beside him. Nick remains perfectly frozen, his hands at his sides. His nostrils flare wide, scenting the air around us.

I wonder if all my wolf comparisons are not so far off after all.

"Rhi," he growls softly at me. A warning.

The cat *laughs*. In so much that a cat can laugh, I suppose. But it's melodic, carefree.

Knowing.

"Relax, my dear boy. I have no wish to harm you or your mate."

What did this thing just say?

It must notice the confusion on my face, because those glistening green eyes flit over to me. "Is that not what the two of you were doing before I came in here? Mating?"

Oh, good grief.

"We weren't mating," I snap, heat blooming high on my cheeks. Mostly because this giant house cat is not completely wrong.

The creature's jaw – large enough to swallow my head whole – twists into what looks like a frown. "Oh. My apologies. It's been some time since I've mated, myself. I guess things change."

"What are you?" Nick asks, clearly the only pragmatic one in the room asking the important questions.

The cat tilts its head in a small bow. "King Lyncus, at your service."

Nick's jaw twitches. He obviously recognizes the name. "But you're a..."

"Lynx?" he finishes for Nick. "I guess you are unaware of my fate."

Nick says nothing, just continues to watch the Cat-King warily, still untrusting of the creature.

King Lyncus yawns, as if the story he's about to share bores him. But the fire in his eyes says otherwise.

"Tripoletmus came to me, possessing the gifts of Demeter. I tried to take them for myself, and Demeter changed me into this."

The explanation is curt, lacking in detail for something that should probably merit more of a description. "Why do I get the feeling you're leaving out something very important?" I ask.

"Yeah," Nick agrees. "Maybe you can elaborate?"

I study him again. He hasn't moved his gaze from King Lyncus since he spotted him, but he's a bit more relaxed.

King Lyncus grins, flashing a mouthful of sharp feline teeth. "I like you, boy. What's your name?"

"Nick."

"No, it's not."

That seizes my attention. He told me Nick wasn't his real name when we first met, but how would this creature know that?

"It might be what you call yourself, but that is not your born name. It is not the name your father gave you," King Lyncus continues, the wicked, feline grin still on his lips.

"How do you know that?" Nick's voice is edged with suspicion.

King Lyncus puts two man-crushing paws on the floor, lowering the rest of his feline body off the couch. He pads towards us, stopping next to the coffee table when Nick emits a low, warning growl at him. The King merely smirks, eyes settling on me. They narrow, but not in a threatening way. More like interest.

He then stares at the books lining the walls. "Do you know what some Native American tribes called lynxes?"

When neither one of us answers, the King returns his gaze, this time finding Nick. "Keepers of Secrets."

Realization floods through me. "That's why the books, the files, they're all empty. It's all for show." I step toward the King-Cat, brushing away Nick's hand attempting to hold me back. "You. You have all the knowledge. All the secrets."

King Lyncus opens his large mouth and lets a pink tongue loll out in another bored yawn.

But also a confirmation.

"Please," I implore, "we need to-"

"You want to know the name of the creature that is taking the lives of your peers," he answers, his tone heavy with disinterest.

"You know?" I gasp.

An incline of his head and another flash of sharp teeth is my answer.

"He won't tell us, Rhi." Nick says, eyes still glued to the King. "Not without a price."

"Clever boy," the King purrs.

"Well, what's your price?" I ask eagerly.

His feline pupils enlarge in anticipation, and he grins wider, pinning his stare on Nick. "I want your true name."

Nick sucks in a sharp breath. "You know I can't tell you that," he says quietly.

My mouth drops open, and I grab Nick's arm; he tears his gaze from the King to me. "Nick, tell him! It's just your name!"

"I *can't* Rhi." I hear the exasperation in his voice, the sorrow. "You have no idea what you're asking."

"Nick," I plead, "this is our only chance."

Nick faces me, closing his eyes in what I know is a cop out, so he doesn't see the look on my face when repeats, with exaggerated despondency, "I can't."

I turn from him, biting my tongue to keep from screaming.

"There is something else…" the King's voice slithers through the air, touching on the fragility that's formed between Nick and me.

"What?" I snarl.

"When I told you I wanted to take Demeter's gifts for myself, you were right, I left something out. I was tired of the gods and goddesses showing favoritism, picking out mere peasants to bestow their gifts upon. I was a *king,* and even that wasn't good enough for the Goddess of the Harvest." The King pads towards us again, stopping inches from where we stand. I can see his eyes clearly now, the green in them checkered with blue, and I realize with the absence of the ring of gold encircling them, these are his human eyes.

"So I attempted to slaughter Triptolemus while he slept under my roof. Just as I was about to plunge the dagger into his chest, I found my human body gone, and this to be my permanent form, courtesy of Demeter."

"Sounds like you got what you deserved," I say coolly.

The King's eyes narrow and he growls. "Careful, girl. It is my help you seek, is it not?"

I press my lips together to keep from having another "no-filter Rhi" moment, but the King is back on all fours, curling up on the coach just beside me.

Nick pulls me into him and away from the Lynx, leaving the King looking amused "And what is *your* name, girl with the sharp tongue?"

Figuring my name is not as important as whatever Nick's real name is, I have no problem telling him. "Rhiannon."

He inclines his head in curiosity. "A monster girl with a witch's name. How peculiar. Yet that makes you perfect for what I'm about to ask."

"Which is?" Nick snarls from behind me, arm still protectively wrapped around my waist.

The King sits back on his hind legs. "I've been trapped down here for centuries, keeping the secrets of your kind. I want my freedom." He licks his chops. "Find Circe. Only she has the means to free me."

"No fucking way," Nick says.

I push Nick's hands away from my waist and move to his side, anger flaring in my chest. "What's the problem now?" The name Circe rings a familiar bell in my brain, though I can't place it.

"Do it," the King entices, "and I'll tell you about the creature you seek."

Nick opens his mouth, but I crack my whip around his neck, silencing him as I say to the King, "Done."

I relax the whip, anger radiating off Nick in waves. I feel his scathing glare and sense of betrayal in his eyes.

"What did you just do?" he whispers harshly.

I ignore him, focusing instead on King Lyncus, eyes darting back and forth between us in amusement.

"What a pair you two make," he comments. "A monster-god, together with...," the King inhales deeply, eyes closing as though savoring a delicious scent.

But then he whips them open, shock widening those golden, green-blue eyes. He pads closer to me, still inhaling. "What *are* you?"

"A Scylla," I answer, assuming that's what's setting his bells off.

"Scylla, yes," he says slowly, cat-eyes flicking across my face and down the rest of my body. "But..."

"But what?" Nick's voice holds a hint of residual anger, but the emotion is trumped by curiosity.

The King ignores Nick, still staring at me. "Rhiannon, how I would love to keep your secrets," he purrs, nuzzling my ear.

"That's enough," Nick says sharply, stepping between King Lyncus and me. And even for all our earlier contempt, I don't stop him, feeling unsettled at the King's speculation of my ancestry.

"Very well, *Nick*," the King drawls pointedly. "I look forward to seeing you both again. Perhaps by that time, I'll have opposable thumbs." I hear the laughter in his voice and get the message: *Find Circe or don't come back at all.*

Looking over Nick's shoulder, I watch as the King slinks

back to his perch on the brown sofa where we first encountered him.

Nick reaches behind for my hand, not bothering to look back at me. His anger at me is palpable, a thick shroud enveloping the space between us.

But I'm not without anger of my own.

As we head toward the door, the King's voice rings out at our backs. "You can take the stairs, you know."

We both turn, me being the one to speak. "Stairs?"

The King nods his head in the direction of the last bookshelf, where I'd been searching the blank files, and in the wall next to it appears a door.

A door which was not there earlier.

In silence, we move toward the door. King Lyncus watches us with laughter in his eyes. We climb the stairs without speaking, the silence deafening, a noxious pressure building between us with every step.

"Will you come back to my room?" Are the first words Nick speaks.

I don't answer at first, wondering if some space between Nick and I would be better so I can make sense of the chaos that just occurred.

"We need to talk," he insists, his tone commanding.

First of all, I *hate* those words. I hated saying them to Jesse before I broke up with him and being on the opposite end of that now isn't any better.

Second, the pure male authority laced within those words is enough to set my teeth on edge and has my mouth open to tell him to go fuck himself.

"Please," he says softly.

"Fine," I reply, putting a loose lid on my temper in case I need it when we get to his room.

There is another door at the top of the stairs that when opened, leads right to Nick's floor.

I scowl at the hallways. Traitors. Even the walk to his room takes all but three seconds, when I know it should have taken longer. Just whose side are they on?

"Do you want to shower first?" Nick asks once we get inside his room.

"No. Let's get this over with."

He clenches his jaw as he tosses his key card onto his bed. "It's like that, huh?"

"What do you want me to say, Nick?" I throw up my hands. "You didn't want to tell King Lyncus your name – fine. I won't even pretend to understand why."

"That's just it, Rhi," he says sternly as he steps towards me. "There are so many things you *don't* understand. So many things you don't know."

I narrow my eyes. "Don't give me that shit. You weren't even going to wait to ask me about finding Circe. You were going to take it upon yourself to decide for *both* of us that it wasn't a good idea."

The left side of his mouth pulls, not into my favorite smile, but into one of taunting arrogance. "Oh, you mean exactly like what you did to me? When you choked me and made the terrible decision to agree to find Circe, who by the way, is the most dangerous witch that has ever existed."

My lip twitches. I didn't know that. But that still doesn't make it okay for him to think he has the authority to make my decisions for me. Even *he* admitted it was the reason he admired me. Because I do what I want.

Nick moves closer, encroaching into my personal space. "Would you like it if I used my powers on *you*, Rhi? If I persuaded you to do whatever I want?" His warm breath caresses my cheek, and I hate the fact that my body heats, my blood rages, and my core tightens at the suggestive tone in his voice. I think of those moments before King Lyncus, when I straddled his lap and felt his hard length, how thoughts of what we were supposed to be doing were nothing more than a fleeting dream, and it was just him and me and his mouth on mine.

Damn him. I don't know if I want to punch him, fuck him or scream at him; I'm feeling way too many things at once.

"Go ahead. Try it," I challenge, adding a seductive edge to my voice that matches his.

At first, he looks uncertain, his amber eyes darkening and his breath quickening against my skin. He takes my right hand, gently turning it over, tracing his thumb over my pulse point.

Which is racing faster than a Triple Crown winner.

But other than my body reacting normally to him, the way it always has, I feel nothing. Nothing other than the strongest urge to pick up where we left off before King Lyncus made his appearance, but something tells me that's not what Nick was going for.

"It's not working, is it?" I ask with an arrogant smirk that puts his to shame.

His face reveals nothing, but something sparks in his eyes. "Well, my actual Persuasion powers didn't work, no."

I grin wider in smug satisfaction.

"But obviously I don't *need* to use them with you," he finishes, my favorite smile gracing his face.

Nick is still close, close enough that with one upwards tilt of my face, I could brush his lips with my own, wiping that infuriating yet endearing wolf grin from his mouth. But our previous conversation needs attention, and I don't mean the one we had with our tongues.

"Tell me about Circe," I distract him, her name doing its job in getting him to straighten, then back away. "Tell me why agreeing to find her was a bad idea."

"There's always been bad blood between our kind and witches." His eyes blaze with anger. "They're deceitful. Liars. Some of them are even responsible for how our ancestors came to be what they were."

Something ominous twists in my belly. Something that reminds me why the name Circe rang a bell.

"Circe is not only powerful, but also cruel. She tricks and toys with creatures for her own twisted amusement." He rakes his fingers through his hair. "She's also insane. I wouldn't want you near her for that reason alone, but she'll have it out for you, especially when she finds out what you are."

The coiled dread in my stomach explodes as I remember what I read the day I discovered what I was. "She'll have it out for me because I'm a Scylla. And Circe is the witch that cursed her."

THIRTY-ONE

Nick and I decide – *together* – to put off going to find Circe until after Thanksgiving. We wouldn't want to ruin our families' holiday by one of us not returning. Or, as Nick stated, "being turned into swine."

Since Thanksgiving is my favorite holiday and being turned into a pig is not high up on my bucket list, I agreed with him.

Still, telling the girls everything that happened was like trying to explain aerodynamics to a bunch of toddlers. They couldn't believe there was an underground room with a King-turned-lynx that kept the secrets of the entire school.

"I *have* to meet this King Lyncus," Zo insists, as I hush for her to keep her voice down in the dining hall.

"If we don't get what he wants from Circe, that's out of the question," I tell her, biting into a slice of pizza. "He basically told us not to come back unless we found her."

"And do you know where she is?" Liv asks between mouthfuls of salad.

I swallow. "Not a damn clue."

Zo stares at me intensely. "So, you guys are going to do it, then? Find Circe?"

"That's the plan, yeah."

She shakes her head. "I don't think you should do it, Rhi. Circe is a monster."

I choke back a laugh. "That's the pot calling the kettle black, no?"

"Rhi," Liv intercedes, tucking a bright blue strand of hair behind her ear, "Circe is the witch that cursed Scylla."

"I know," I say, a bit harsher than I intended.

"Then why are you so eager to walk into a death trap and bring Nick with you?" Zo demands, ice lacing her words. Her black hair is pulled back into a low bun, accentuating the sharp features of her face, full dark purple lips turned into frown.

Scarlett and Astrid finally take their attention off each other and look to me for an answer. All four of them stare, waiting to hear my answer to Zo's question.

I prop my elbow on the table, rubbing my fingers across my forehead. "Because," I begin, letting out a heavy sigh, "because it's our only chance. The files you've been going through reveal nothing. So, who's going to be next, huh? You, Zo?" I nod my chin in her direction, then look at Liv. "Liv? Astrid? Scarlett? Me?" I take turns meeting the gaze of every girl as I say their names.

"And then what?" I continue. "Nick gets framed for murders he didn't commit, and his life is over?" I lick my lips, shaking my head. "No. We can do this. I know we can."

A hand squeezes mine; I look to my left to find Scarlett, a warm, grateful smile on her face.

For a few awkward moments, no one says anything. My stomach drops as I consider that I might be alone in this. That this is a road the girls won't follow me down. And I realize how much I rely on their support, their strength. For all my bravado, for all my "fuck everyone else" mentality, I needed them, and I'd be lying if I said I didn't want them behind me on this.

"Alright then, new plan." Zo's voice breaks the silence. "We get as much information about Circe as we can, so Rhi and Nick don't go in there blind." She glances at Liv. "Find out whatever you can about protection charms." Her gaze goes to Astrid. "Astrid, find out where Circe might be." My mouth tilts upwards as Zo takes charge, giving orders. "The rest of us will look up anything and everything we can find on this witch. Her strengths, her weaknesses." She fixes me with a shrewd smile. "Leave it up to our Rhi to want to take on the baddest witch in the history of witches."

My mouth twists into a smirk. "If I didn't have you guys, I wouldn't have the courage to," I admit, again looking at each one of my girls.

My girls. My friends. My strength.

THE DAY before we leave for Thanksgiving break, I lie in my bed nursing the glorious symptoms of getting my period, which include a pounding headache, a twisting stomach, and aches in nearly every muscle of my body. Basically, the exact same way I'd felt on the night of my eighteenth birthday party, without the throbbing of my fingertips or the urge to eat someone.

I guess that's an improvement.

Scarlett sits on her bed, thumbs sweeping across the keypad on her phone.

"I'm going over to Astrid's for a bit," she tells me, rushing to leave.

"Where's the fire?" I ask.

Her eyes go wide as I startle her. "Oh. Um. Nothing.

Nowhere. Astrid needs help with something. I'll see you in a bit."

I stare after her in confusion as she rushes out the door, realizing too late that she's headed off to Astrid's alone, and wasn't it decreed months ago that not one of us would go anywhere by ourselves?

Though, Astrid's room is on this floor, just around the corner, I reason. Maybe that's Scarlett's reasoning for heading out in such a hurry and –

The soft rap of a knock sounds on the door.

Half groaning, I get out of bed, cursing whoever is making me move more than I need to as I open the door, disrupting my Sailor Moon marathon.

Nick stands in the doorway, a plastic bag dangling from one hand, dressed in gray sweatpants and a black *Nirvana* T-shirt. His godly powers must be what allow him to look perfect in everything he wears, even when he looks like he just rolled out of bed.

Me, on the other hand? Loose black sweatpants and my favorite Sailor Moon T-shirt, and my hair has seen better days. Much better days.

"Hey. Can I come in?" I don't miss the trepidation in his voice.

There's been a small distance between Nick and I since our excursion to the crypt. We never hashed out what happened: his authoritative decision-making followed by my impulsive actions.

And we never discussed what happened *before* King Lyncus: The "fake" make out session that almost turned into what King Lyncus called "mating" and what that means for both of us as far as where we stand relationship wise.

"Maybe," I answer, eyeing the plastic bag in his hand. "Is that for me?"

His mouth splits into my favorite smile, and he waves the bag tauntingly. "Why don't you find out?"

I attempt to snatch the bag from him, but he jerks it back effortlessly. "Need to work on those Jedi reflexes, I'm afraid."

I narrow my eyes. I want to tell him it's not wise to pick a fight with a girl during that time of the month, monster or no. But I'm also not about to tell him I have my period.

"I'm sorry, Nick. I'm indisposed."

"This will make you feel better, trust me."

I cock my head in interest, then sigh and step aside to let him in. He heads right for my desk, his broad shoulders blocking whatever he's removing from the bag and setting atop its surface.

When he moves to the side, the most glorious thing I've seen since I laid eyes on him awaits me.

"Rocky Road ice cream, chocolate syrup, sprinkles and whip cream. Did I forget anything?" Nick stares at me expectantly, a hopeful glimmer in his eyes.

"Spoons?"

He fishes around in his pockets and pulls out two spoons, grinning like an idiot.

I march over to him, mouth near drooling, and pluck a spoon from his outstretched hand. "I'm on to you, Nicholas."

Nick merely smirks, handing me the coffee mug that sits on my desk. I immediately start scooping out ice cream while he heads over to Scarlett's desk and grabs her mug.

"Consider this a peace offering." He grabs the canister of whipped cream and sprays some straight into his mouth. I stare at him bewildered, but he holds the can out to me.

It's pretty much impossible to stay mad at him or hold a grudge or whatever I was doing. I roll my eyes and smile, opening my mouth.

Nick sprays a dollop of whip cream onto my tongue then

goes back to making his ice cream concoction. The amount of chocolate syrup he pours over the whip cream is sinful.

"Would you like some ice cream to go with your syrup?" I joke as I pour sprinkles on my own three scoops of Rocky Road.

"Says the girl who has more chocolate sprinkles in her cup than anything else."

I glance down. The whip cream is nearly invisible underneath all the sprinkles I added.

"Besides," he adds, "one can never have enough chocolate *anything*."

"I won't disagree with you there." I sit down on my bed, drawing my knees in and curling against my pillow. Nick sits at the base of my feet as I shove a spoonful of ice cream into my mouth.

Oh gods, this is *good*.

"How did you know I liked Rocky Road?" I ask, my stomach fluttering with the realization that he took the time to find out my favorite ice cream flavor.

The wolf grin greets me. "Liv."

I pause dipping my spoon in the cup. I assumed he'd asked Scarlett, but then remembered it was Liv I told. Hers is strawberry. Sometimes it's hard to remember the mundane conversations amidst the ones about murder and witches.

"Well, as far as apologies go, this is a wonderful start," I tease.

Nick licks his spoon pointedly. "I'm still waiting for mine, you know."

I make a show of looking around the room as if I don't know what he's talking about. I bring my gaze back down to my ice cream, about to dip my spoon in, when his hand grabs my wrist.

"Rhi," he says, his voice low and serious. His strength is incredible. I can barely move my wrist to get the spoon remotely near my ice cream, and he isn't even using a firm grip. And boy, do I want another spoonful.

"Fine," I groan. "Just release the spoon please."

Nick relents, and I eagerly plunge the utensil into a mound of ice cream, scooping out as much as I can.

"Mime sowwyy." My apology comes out muffled through a mouthful of Rocky Road.

Nick laughs. "I'll take it." He looks down, his expression turning from playful to remorseful. "I'm sorry, too, Rhi. I'm sorry I couldn't give King Lyncus my real name."

Regret punches me in my stomach. I'd forgotten how cruel and nonchalant I'd been after Nick refused to give the King his true name, dismissing the severity of the situation. That clearly, there was so much more to his refusal to give it up. And I should have known better. Should have known that Nick would sacrifice it in a heartbeat if he were able. But I'm still curious as to what keeps him from revealing it.

I place the mug down and crawl to him, sitting back on my knees as I cup his face and turn his chin towards me.

"Hey. You don't have to apologize for that. I know you would have given it up if you could, Nick. I just want to know why."

His eyes search my face, hesitant. For a moment, I think I've broken down the wall he's built. *Let me in,* I plead internally. Nick licks his lips, eyes despondent. I know then he won't tell me. I make sure his amber eyes are locked on mine. "I just want to protect you. I thought if you told the King your name and he told us who this monster is and how to stop it, this would all be over. And you wouldn't have to worry anymore."

He swallows. "And you know that's all I was trying to do right? My main priority is to protect *you.* I've heard so many horror stories about Circe, and the minute her name was mentioned, my blood boiled at the thought of you anywhere near her."

Nick takes the mug between his legs and places it on the floor. I let my hands fall to my lap as he returns those bright, beautiful eyes to my face.

"Rhi," he continues, "I know I was angry with you after you agreed to find Circe, but I wasn't lying when I told you I admire you for your boldness. For your fearlessness, and for the way you don't let anyone – and I mean *anyone*-" he says with emphasis, "tell you what to do." Nick strokes my cheek with his thumb, and I pull my bottom lip into my mouth. "Don't lose that, Rhi. People, especially other men, will try to take that from you. Will try to tear you down." His gaze is ferocious, intense. "Don't let them."

Nick continues to look at me, eyes so piercing it might make someone else cringe. But I consider his words, the power behind them, and I can't look away from him. In a world where women are often told they're too bossy if they're assertive, too aggressive when they speak their mind, just *too* much of every-thing, Nick is telling me to be exactly that. Too Bold. Too Fear-less. Too Unapologetic.

And I think I love him for it.

My answer is a brush of my lips on his. Nothing as desperate or demanding as our last kiss. A simple whisper of gratitude.

I break the kiss, smiling demurely. "Now, when you refer to other men, are you implying that you don't want to be the only man in my life?"

My favorite smile and a hint of wickedness in his eyes. "I thought I already was the only man in your life."

I flick his nose. "For now, Nicky Boy."

He playfully tackles me down to the bed, sliding next to me

so I can curl against his chest. "Then, let's keep it that way. Because you're the only girl in mine."

I don't know if he can see the sublimely happy grin that splits my face, but I don't care. In this moment, all the prior chaos is long forgotten. There are no secret rooms. No monsters with murderous agendas. No plans to thwart evil witches. In this moment, I'm just a girl whose heart soars, because the boy she likes finally admits to liking her back.

CHAPTER

THIRTY-TWO

"What time are your parents coming?" Nick asks me the next day, as he, Scarlett, Astrid and I hang out in mine and Scarlett's room.

"In about an hour, I think."

Nick glances at his watch, then looks up at Scarlett and Astrid. "Think we can wait until Rhi's parents come?"

I stiffen – not at the look of sheer annoyance on Astrid's face – but because I am nowhere near ready for Nick to meet my parents.

"That's okay," I give him a winning smile. "Traffic into Manhattan is probably going to be nuts. You guys should get going."

"Oh Rhi, we don't mind," says Scarlett, oblivious to Astrid's grievances.

Astrid pulls up her phone. "Actually, she's right. Look at this." The Gorgon shows Scarlett her phone then holds it up for Nick and me to see. Whatever app she's using displays a map of nothing except blaring red lines heading in every direction towards New York City.

"Shit," Nick huffs. "We're going to be sitting in traffic for hours."

"You should go," I urge, leaning into him. "I'll see you on Sunday."

He nuzzles my ear, speaking low. "Get any closer, and I won't be going anywhere."

Blood rushes to my face as Astrid moans. "Ugh. The honeymoon phase." She sticks out her tongue in a gag-like manner.

"What are you talking about?" Nick admonishes, nodding in both her and Scarlett's direction. "You guys have been going out for four years and are *still* in the honeymoon phase. Speaking of, try keeping it down this weekend, okay? My bedroom isn't that far from Scarlett's."

I choke on laughter as Scarlett looks supremely mortified. Naturally, Astrid's expression remains stoic, as though Nick didn't just imply that he is able to hear her and Scarlett's bedroom activities.

"You're such an ass," Scarlett retorts.

Nick shrugs before turning to me and plants a quick kiss on my lips.

"Call me when your parents pick you up, okay?"

"K." I follow him starry-eyed as he rises from the bed, grabbing Scarlett and Astrid's bags.

Scarlett comes over to me and gives me a hug, unsurprisingly. "I'll miss you, Rhi!"

"It's only four days," I tell her, but feel warm and tingly by her admission nonetheless as I hug her back. "But I'll miss you too."

She waves a hand dismissively. "Oh, please. You're going to miss Nicky more than me."

"Well, he *did* bring me ice cream," I reply, mouth curling up at the corners.

Scarlett smiles, wide and bright. "Yes. Yes he did." She

follows her brother who is waiting by the door, leaving Astrid, who does not hug me.

Also, unsurprisingly.

"I guess I'll miss you too, Scylla," she says. With a wink and a smile, Astrid leaves, and it's then I notice Nick lingering by the door.

"You sure you don't want me to wait?" A flicker of worry crosses his face as I move toward him.

I lean back against the doorframe. "And risk Astrid's wrath? No way." My fingers grasp the fabric of his shirt, this one with the band name *Sublime* on its front, and pull him toward me. Nick rests one hand on the doorframe and brings the other to my waist, lowering his face to mine. The tame kiss we shared earlier was for Astrid and Scarlett's benefit, and there is no way I am letting him leave for four days without sharing something more.

Nick takes the hint and kisses me hungrily, his tongue sweeping in my mouth at the first brush of his lips. I unhook my fingers from his shirt and slide my hands around his neck, pressing him against me. A guttural sound emits from deep in his throat, and he pulls back slightly.

"Rhi," he whispers against my mouth, "I'm not sure I'm going to be able to stop if we keep going."

I grin, opening my eyes. Amber ones stare back at me, bright and rapacious as his chest rises and falls against my own. I can't help but caress the back of his neck, tangling my fingers in the hair that falls at the nape. He shivers beneath my touch, leaning further into me, and I understand his meaning of losing all self-control as the hand at my waist toys with the hem of my shirt, stroking bare flesh underneath.

I don't know how long we stay like that, staring at each other, weighing the pros and cons of taking a chance. His gaze flits to the side, eyeing my bed, and an electrifying thrill runs through me.

But in the end, Nick kisses me, deep and long and regretful, before pulling back and whispering in my ear, "Not like this." His voice is a lazy caress. "I am going to take my time with you, Rhi." He nibbles on my ear lobe, and I bite my bottom lip hard, failing to contain the low whimper that escapes my mouth.

He releases an arrogant chuckle before straightening, amber eyes smoldering, and brushes a knuckle across my cheek. "To be continued." He gives me one more quick kiss, then grabs the bags and takes off.

I stare after him, dumbfounded. Well, dumbfounded and frustrated, to be precise. How unfair is *that?* I run my fingers through my hair and blow out a breath. Maybe I should take an extremely cold shower.

The sound of footsteps coming down the opposite end of the hallway is the only reason I tear my sight from Nick and find Liv walking toward me.

"Hey, you're still here," she observes.

"And so are you." I fold my arms. "My parents should be here soon. What about you?"

She stops right in front of me, the combination of her bright pink sweater and aquamarine hair conjuring the perfect image in my head of a *My Little Pony* figurine.

"I'm staying here for the holiday."

I raise my eyebrows. "What do you mean? Why aren't you going home? Is Josh staying?"

Liv laughs. "No. And we're not at that stage yet, to be spending holidays with each other." She twirls a strand of hair around her finger. "My parents are in Europe, so they won't be celebrating anyway. And I don't feel like spending six hours on a plane each way just for a four-day break."

My phone chimes with a text message from my mother,

letting me know my parents are in the parking lot. I thumb a quick message back to her then look at Liv.

"You're coming to have Thanksgiving with me," I tell her, in an I-won't-take-no-for-an-answer tone.

Liv goes wild-eyed. "Oh, no. Rhi, I couldn't possibly-"

"Too late," I grab her hand and tug her toward her room down the hall. "I already told my parents you were coming, and they're so excited to meet you."

Behind me, I hear a defeated sigh, and I smile victoriously.

THIRTY-THREE

Thanksgiving has always been my favorite holiday. My mother makes enough food to feed a small army, even though it's usually just myself, my parents, my uncle and occasionally, my absurdly obnoxious cousin. Since I was blessed with his absence last year, I'm anticipating having to deal with his blatant snobbery today; unless, through divine intervention, my uncle has somehow misplaced his only son.

There's nothing wrong with being hopeful.

When a sleek black BMW pulls in front of my house, I shoot a cursory glance out the bay windows and to my dismay, watch my cousin glide impertinently out of the car. He is by no means unattractive, which only makes his egotistical personality worse. Tall, with chestnut brown hair and green eyes, the sharp angles of his face accentuate the perpetual sneer of his mouth and his upturned nose, which, I'm convinced he wasn't born with. It must have gotten that way after all the times he'd turned his nose up at me.

True to his blue blood heritage, he wears his Princeton colors whenever he can, today donning a black V-neck sweater with a white collared shirt underneath and an orange pin that no doubt represents whatever fraternity he pledged to ass kiss.

My cousin, Charlie, is what I like to call a 'done-it-all.' Someone has a story about rock climbing? He's scaled Everest. Someone can speak another language? He can speak six. Charlie has always done it before and done it better. He's spent his life making sure to one-up me and has always made sure to remind me that we are most certainly *not* related since I was adopted.

Charlie strides toward my front door holding a bottle of wine, and though he's only a year older than me, I'm sure he'll somehow convince my parents and his father that he should drink with them. Maybe this month he's a wine connoisseur.

"You have a Scylla look," Liv informs me.

"A what?" I face her, incredulous.

She giggles. "Who just got out of the car, and why is it making you look like you want nothing more than to rip them to pieces?"

Sheesh. I hadn't realized my facial expression had gone into monster-mode. "It's my uncle and my cousin. We don't get along. My cousin, I mean. Not my uncle. He's cool."

The doorbell rings and I begrudgingly open it, planting a huge false smile on my face. "Hey Charlie."

"It's Charles," the prick answers, patting my shoulder and walking inside.

"Oh, *pardonne*," I reply, with the air of someone of inflated importance. Charlie – excuse me – *Charles* ignores me, and I greet my uncle. "Hey, Uncle Pat."

My uncle Patrick has the same green eyes as Charlie, but darker hair and my mother's smile, which he flashes at me.

"Hey kiddo." He sweeps me into a hug. "I am so proud of you! Alystair! Can't wait to hear all about it!"

"Thanks, Uncle Pat." My uncle heads inside and goes

straight to the kitchen to greet my parents, where I assume Charlie is also. But after I close the door, I realize Charlie is walking into the living room, heading straight for Liv.

My first thought is that his pompous ass is going to make some rude comment about her ostentatious hair color. But as I hurry in after him, I catch the side of his face: mouth agape, eyes wide, staring at Liv with pure wonder, like he's never before seen anything so beautiful.

Which, he probably hasn't.

And then Liv smiles.

I look at Charlie and think: *sucker.*

"Hi, I'm... I'm Charlie," he stammers, holding a hand out her.

Oh *now* he's Charlie. What a fucking idiot.

"Nice to meet you, Charlie." I swear Charlie's knees buckle when she says his name, and I have to bite my tongue to keep from exploding into hysterics.

"I'm Liv," she says. "Rhi's friend from Alystair."

"I didn't know Rhiannon had any friends," the ass has the gall to say, still drooling.

"It's Rhi, *Charles.* And I'm surprised you can string together a subject and predicate, considering your jaw is still on the floor." I stand next to him, glaring at him from beneath my lashes.

Charlie blushes, to my sublime entertainment, and scowls.

"I'm going to see if your Mom needs any help," Liv says, leaving Charlie and I alone in the living room, which I'm not sure is wise on her part. Because if I murder him, she might be considered an accomplice.

Charlie stares after Liv as though in a trance, and I roll my eyes. "Never going to happen, Charlie." As I walk past him, he grabs my arm.

"You *have* to hook me up with her." He's still not even

looking at me. He looks past me, craning his neck to see if he can get another glimpse of Liv inside the kitchen.

I wrench my arm from his hand. "That's a hard no. Besides, she has a boyfriend."

That information causes my cousin to finally draw his gaze to me, green eyes narrowed and his mouth turned up in an arrogant "oh please" expression.

"Who? Some loser freshman?"

Anger flares deep in my chest. The Scylla head stirs. "None of your business, Charlie. She's too good for you. And her boyfriend will eat you alive." I storm away from him just as my mother calls dinner, and the Scylla gives a low approving hiss in my ear.

"So," my uncle Pat says, stabbing his fork around his plate, "tell us about your first semester, Rhi. Alystair must give you a considerable workload."

I think of my first Poisons Lab. Of the incident in Trans with Robert and the arrow. Of the secret room underneath the Fountain and my new mission to track down an infamous witch.

"Considerable workload" is a severe understatement.

"You can say that," is all I offer. I shove mashed potatoes into my mouth as my cousin glowers across from me.

"Your parents told me you've taken up fencing, as well." He takes a sip of wine, eyebrows raised in admiration. "I'm very impressed."

Charlie snorts into his water. "*You* fence?"

"Yep." I pop the 'p,' and when no one else is looking, I give him the finger. Liv snickers beside me.

My mother clears her throat peacefully. "She practices

outside of her classes, too. Who did you say is training you again?"

"Bianca Ramos."

"Never heard of her," Charlie says with an air of dismissal, reaching for the bottle of wine.

I'm seconds away from using my telekinesis to shatter the bottle all over him for insulting Bianca, but my uncle puts out his hand. "Charles, even if you illegally drink on campus, that doesn't mean you can drink at family gatherings."

My cousin stiffens, pink lightly coloring his cheeks. "Dad, I told you, Brandon and I are planning to travel to Italy for our semester abroad and do a wine tour. I just want to be familiar with the different grape varietals."

I nearly spit out my iced tea. What did I say? Wine connoisseur.

"Charles," my uncle says, exasperated, "this wine is from Burgundy, not Italy, and if you think I'm paying for you to go to Italy to fuck around for a semester, you're sorely mistaken." He plucks the bottle from my cousin's hand and refills his own glass before placing it down in front near himself.

Charlie's cheeks are so red they're almost purple, the same color as the wine he was denied.

My father's voice breaks the awkward silence. "Rhi, I thought you were training with a boy?"

I almost choke on my drink. "Oh yeah. We uh, switched partners for a little bit. He said I was getting too familiar with how he moves."

Next to me, Liv suppresses a laugh, no doubt a sexual innuendo playing in her head with my last sentence. I lightly kick her underneath the table.

"What was his name?" My mother presses. "Nate?"

"Nick," I say, and my cousin's fork clatters to his plate.

"Nick Cervallos?" He asks in shock.

I stare back at my cousin with equal surprise. "Do you know him?"

Charlie scoffs. "He's only the best fencer in the entire city. Second only to Madeline Fitzgerald, who's probably the best fencer in the country."

It shouldn't come as a surprise to me that Charlie knows or knows of Nick. Before my uncle and aunt divorced a few years ago, Charlie lived in an elegant brownstone on the Upper East Side of Manhattan. He had it all – the fancy prep school and the classy extracurricular activities. Charlie was probably one pair of Ferragamo loafers away from eating yogurt on the steps of the Metropolitan before the start of his first prep school class. And since Nick and Scarlett live in Manhattan, it's possible they may have run in the same circles growing up.

"Nick was at Dalton Prep, a year ahead of me, before he left to go to Alystair for high school," Charlie continues, solidifying my assumption.

"Madeline's the Fencing Club's President," I tell him, hoping to steer the conversation away from Nick.

Charlie pins me with an incredulous stare. "No way Nick Cervallos chose you, out of what - twenty other students – to train."

There's a burning in the back of my throat, the same one I'd gotten when Jesse told me I didn't belong at Alystair. It's amazing how I'm barely phased at the idea of seeking out a vengeful, powerful witch, but my cousin's words tear me down faster than one of Wilde's poisonous flowers.

"Oh, he chose her for more than that," Liv softly quips, batting her pretty eyes at Charlie. "Nick Cervallos is Rhi's boyfriend." She bites into a whole turkey leg, cleanly tearing meat from the bone, and I swear I see a hint of sharpness in her teeth.

The table is now in a frenzy. Charlie looks as though Liv

just told him there's no such thing as Santa. My father is choking at hearing I have a boyfriend, while my mother preens, talking over my coughing father trying to garner as much information from me as she can. Meanwhile, my uncle has more or less finished the bottle from Burgundy by himself.

I turn to Liv amongst the chaos. "I don't know whether to kill you or kiss you".

A ruthless smile. "Oh Rhi, please don't kiss me again. You were terrible at it."

THIRTY-FOUR

After returning from break, the gang, Nick and I spend the next three weeks searching for Circe's location while preparing for our final exams. I'd also had to make my schedule for the spring semester, which Nick was all too happy to help with.

"Is there no other Professor besides Wilde that teaches Poisons?" I groan as I add Intermediary Poisons to my schedule. I shift my laptop on my legs, stretching them out on Nick's bed.

He turns from his desk chair to face me, his expression solemn. "Afraid not. At least, not until your junior year." He rises to sit beside me. "I thought you were doing well in that class?"

"I am. Extremely well, actually, but don't you remember the first day of lab? She nearly killed the entire class just to teach me a lesson." I shake my head and frown. "I can't imagine what she'll have in store for me next semester."

Nick playfully ruffles my hair. "Don't worry. The first semester is the hardest. You'll be fine next semester."

My frown remains, and I start to fiddle with the ends of my hair.

His eyes flick to my hands, then rest on my face. "Rhi, what's really bothering you?"

I shut my laptop and move it to the side, chewing the inside of my cheek. "We still have no idea where to find Circe."

"I know, but there also haven't been any more murders," he states.

"For now," I argue. "I just can't shake the feeling that whatever this thing is doing, it's waiting for something. That this isn't over."

Nick's fingers tip my chin, and I tilt my head up. "Rhi, it's going to be okay. We'll find her, and we'll get the answers we need."

"I hope so," I say with an aggrieved sigh. Nick goes to his desk, pulling open the middle drawer. He reaches in and returns to my side, a small box in his hand.

"What's this?" I ask, trying to peer through his fingers at the box.

A soft smile turns his lips, and he opens his palm. "It's an early Christmas gift. I was going to wait, but..." he shrugs, still smiling.

I tentatively take the box from his fingers; black velvet tied with a blood-red bow. I give the bow a slight tug, letting the ribbon fall onto his silken sheets. Nick watches my every move with such stifling focus, I wonder if he can see the slight tremble to my fingers as I open the box.

On a small black pillow lies a bright gold necklace, its delicate chain pooled into a gilded puddle around a pendant. I gently pick up the pendant, a design of swirls that nearly resemble a heart, but not quite. Three brilliant gems glitter where two of the swirls meet: a pearl, a moonstone, and alexandrite.

"Nick, this is..." I trail off, staring in awe at this beautiful piece of jewelry that includes all three gems that pass as my birthstone.

Nick takes the necklace from my fingers and motions for me to turn around. I oblige, feeling the warmth of his fingers sweep across my neck, pushing my hair over my shoulder. Once he's done, the pendant sits right below the hollow of my throat.

"Do you like it?" His voice is a worried whisper.

"Like it?" I face him, rising on my knees and cup his face in my hands. "I love it. It's perfect." I kiss him, long and hard and deep. His arms wrap around my waist, pulling me tighter before Nick shifts on the bed, guiding my body down to the mattress. Fingers trembling, I reach for the hem of his shirt, helping him pull it over his head. For a moment, the only thing I focus on is the steady rise and fall of his chest, the rapid beating of his heart as I slide my hands up his chest to wrap my arms around his neck. Nick brings his lips back to mine, one hand sliding up my shirt to cup my breast, and I release a low moan in his mouth.

I reach down to grab the hem of my shirt, having just tossed it to the floor when I hear a soft rap on the door.

Nick and I freeze. He jerks back on his knees, but his eyes don't leave my body. They travel slowly, sweeping across my stomach and up to the swells of my breasts through my black bra, a dark hunger lurking in them. The knock appears again, and Nick grabs his shirt and twists in frustration, the corded muscle wrapping his arms flexing with each turn.

When he turns to meet my eyes, I see the question in his. The longing. It would be a lie if I told myself I didn't feel the same way, wasn't wishing and wanting this to happen for a while now.

"Ignore it," I whisper, breaking the last of his resolve.

Nick releases a throaty, relieved sigh, but just as he presses his body down on top of mine, the person knocks again. More insistent.

"Nick, it's Scarlett and Astrid." His sister's voice reverberates through the door.

Without speaking, we throw our shirts on. He gives me one quick kiss with a smoldering look that says, "This is far from over," and we head toward the door.

Scarlett and Astrid blink in surprise to find us standing before them once the door opens. Scarlett had been out with Astrid when I went over Nick's earlier, so she hadn't known I was here.

Her cheeks flush noticing our ruffled state, no doubt figuring out the reason we took so long to come to the door. Astrid, true to form, smirks knowingly.

"What's up?" Nick asks casually, as if he and I had just been playing Jenga before we were interrupted.

"We found her," Scarlett says, eyes darkening.

Nick's fingers tighten on the door, bits of it crumbling beneath his fingers.

"You're sure?" he asks.

Scarlett nods, but Astrid's sapphire eyes flash. "Yeah, we're sure. We've found Circe."

WHEN I THINK of where an infamous witch with insanely jealous tendencies might live, I expect to have to search for her in a lair. Or a dark tower. Or some equally disturbing place that could possibly require grappling hooks and/or a spine of steel to break into.

Turns out, the notorious witch can be found lurking in one of New York City's most famous nightclubs.

I should also probably mention that she owns it.

"Well, isn't that some shit," I murmur, reading over all the information the girls had printed out on Circe.

"Right?" Zo gets up from her bed, reading over my shoulder. "It was no wonder we had so much trouble finding her. She doesn't go by Circe."

No, she doesn't. And very smart on her part, considering Circe probably isn't making the top one hundred most popular names for girls anytime soon.

The witch now calls herself Tamsyn du Pont, from an aristocratic family that owns substantial real estate in all the wealthiest neighborhoods Manhattan has to offer. Her nightclub, *Strega* - far less inconspicuous than her fake name - means "witch" in Italian.

"How did you find all of this out?" I ask none of the girls in particular.

Unsurprisingly, Zo, with that quick-fire brain of hers, answers. "I thought it would be a good idea to search the newspapers for any odd disappearances or occurrences. While nothing was reported on the club itself, a lot of weird shit has been happening just around it."

"What do you mean?"

"People disappearing for months, then turning up right near it, dressed in party clothes, which has been the most common occurrence," Zo answers. "So I decided to delve deeper into *Strega*. Astrid was able to get property records and deeds to the Club, and although the Du Pont family is well known in Manhattan, it was strange that there wasn't any record of Tamsyn Du Pont until a few years ago. The building hosting the club was leased until it was bought by -

"Tamsyn du Pont." I finish.

Zo nods.

"It's possible that this isn't her," Scarlett chimes in. "But it's the only lead we have."

I nod, fully aware that we could be chasing a dead end. But like Scar said, it's all we've got.

I review the notes Zo prepared, describing Circe's various powers, her physical description, and the horrors she's inflicted over her many, many years of petty sorcery.

"Any weaknesses?" I ask, noticing that detail is nowhere to be found.

"Not that any of us could find," Zo says, leaning against Liv's bed. "Just the mention of an herb called moly, with a white flower and black root. According to Homer's *The Odyssey*, Hermes had Odysseus eat it before he went to Circe, and her potions had no effect on him."

"Does the herb actually exist?" Astrid asks, sitting on Liv's desk.

"I doubt it," Scarlett tells her, perched as usual, on her lap.

Liv, sitting on her own bed near Zo interjects "Well, we only really need to worry about finding Nick some protection. Rhi is taken care of."

I shoot her a quizzical glance. "I am?"

She nods to the pendant at my neck. "Your necklace. It's your..." she tilts her head, seemingly searching for the right words. "Captain America shield," she finishes with a smile.

My fingers absently toy with the pendant. "Nick didn't tell me that. Does the symbol mean something?"

Scarlett rises from Astrid's lap and walks over to me, tracing the swirling design. "It's not really the symbol, Rhi. Nick had it specially made for you. And that means something."

The end of her sentence carries such a weight I can't help but continue to wonder exactly what that something means.

"Hey guys, check this out." Zo says beckoning us over to her desk, we crowd around her as she points to a description on her laptop. "It seems that medical historians have been trying to figure out if moly actually exists for centuries." She pulls up a picture of a plant with small white petals attached to a long dark green stem with a white bulbous root at its base.

"This is called a snowdrop," Zo continues, pushing night black hair back over her shoulders. "*This* is the plant believed to be Homer's version of moly."

I lean in, intrigued. "And it's something that's attainable? Like, it grows on this continent, and not somewhere in Antarctica under the waxing moon or something?"

Zo points to a random line halfway down the page. "Northern Hemisphere," she says with a triumphant smirk.

"Uh, we may have a problem," Astrid directs our attention further down the page. "It blooms in springtime, on or around the vernal equinox, which is months from now."

I clench my jaw in frustration, turning away from the girls. Perhaps bringing Nick, bringing *anyone* along with me is a mistake. This was my idea, after all. And if I'm the only one with protection, it makes sense that I should go alone.

Of course, I have to get past Nick first. There's no way he'll let me do this by myself. But I'll worry about that later.

Committing to my new course of action, I face the girls again, preparing to tell them my change of plans, when Liv places a delicate finger near the screen.

"Its species is *galanthus nivalis*," she announces mundanely.

"What does that mean?" Scarlett stares at her curiously.

Liv looks up, a victorious expression on her face.

"It means," she says, flashing her ruthless smile, "that I know exactly where to find it."

THIRTY-FIVE

"The greenhouse?" Nick questions skeptically. "This is the magical plant that will protect me from Circe's witchcraft, and you found it in the greenhouse?" He glimpses the picture on my phone of the snowdrop.

We sit at our usual table in Nick's secret special place, digging into our lunches: cheeseburger and fries for him and a BLT for me.

Obviously, Nick's fries are also mine.

"Yeah," I tell him because there really isn't much else to elaborate on. "Actually, Liv found it." Her time in the Garden Club had proved more useful than anyone could have ever expected.

"Well," he says with a sigh, "I guess that's it then. Off to Circe we go," he adds grimly.

I take a French fry from his plate. "Cheer up. Maybe she won't care what I am. It's been thousands of years. I'm sure she's moved on."

He stares at me bewildered. "Rhi, your ability to see the

glass half-full in every situation might be considered a superpower."

I chew thoughtfully. "I don't think it's *every* situation."

"Yeah it is. You tried to convince me that a unicorn was the alleged monster that guarded the crypt, remember?" He takes a sip of soda through a straw.

"And look at that. There wasn't even a monster at all. Unless you count creepy King Lyncus and his voyeurism."

Nick laughs for a moment before his face turns serious again, and I don't think it's because I'm helping myself to more fries off his plate.

"I'm thinking winter break would be the best time to do this, but once again, a major holiday ruins our plans."

Right. Christmas is in a few days. Once more, we wouldn't want to disappoint our families by dying before then or showing up to dinner as pigs.

"Sounds good to me," I say cheerfully, through a mouthful of food. Nick's grim expression doesn't lift. Trying to lighten the mood, I add, "Since you think I have a superpower, and you and I are going off on these missions, whaddya say you and I have Avenger nicknames?"

Nick raises a dark eyebrow in amusement. "Sure. Which Avenger do you want to be?"

I don't hesitate with my answer. "Iron Man."

He dips a fry in ketchup, chuckling. "Makes perfect sense."

I throw my crumbled straw wrapper at him. "What about you, huh?"

"Isn't it obvious?" He answers with a sly grin.

I frown, wracking my brain through the various Avengers and which one would be the obvious choice.

"Oh gods, really?" I say when I've figured it out.

"Really." He takes a bite of his burger.

"You want to be Thor, because he's a god."

Nick holds up a finger. "No. I'm going to be Thor because he's ridiculously good-looking, and I mean..." he trails off, using both hands to gesture to his own ridiculously good-looking face.

I roll my eyes and laugh. "You're something else, you know that?"

His answer is another large bite into his cheeseburger. Before I continue eating my own sandwich, I find myself toying with the pendant at my neck, remembering how Scarlett told me he had it specially made for me, and that it meant something.

"Nick?" I draw his attention, and he pauses before taking another bite. "Scarlett told me you had this specially designed. What did she mean?"

His bronzed skin leeches of color, and he places the burger down on his plate before wiping his mouth with a napkin.

"Nothing. I just had it commissioned. I didn't walk into a store and buy it, that's all." He doesn't look at me as he says this, finding twirling his straw around his cup very interesting.

Lying is certainly not Nick's forte, but I'm curious as to why he's lying at all. "Then how does it offer me protection from Circe?"

Color further drains from his cheeks, his body stiffening. But then he looks me right in the eye and says with absolute sincerity, "Didn't Liv tell you? She was researching protection charms and came across that one. I thought it would be a nice gift for me to turn into a necklace you can always wear. And it has your birthstones, so the necklace contains something that's a part of you."

His words are strong but clipped, the explanation sounding almost rehearsed. A knot forms in my stomach, twisting with tension. *Something that is a part of you,* echoes in my head, to which I want to say, *You're a part of me.*

An ill-boding sensation snaps at my skin.

I open my mouth to press the issue, but Nick beats me to it.

"Rhi," he says, amber eyes boring into mine, "remember that night at the Fountain, when you asked me to trust you?"

"Yes."

"If I ask you not to push this, to just trust me, can you do that?" Nick's eyes are all but pleading for me to say yes. I don't say anything at first, the memory of his earlier words rolls around my head.

The imploring look in his eyes travels to his face as his lips part and his breathing quickens, and I say, "Okay, fine."

But I can't help but think, *Oh Nick, what did you do?*

I LEAVE the issue alone for the rest of our meal together and go back to my own room after. Nick has another one of his society meetings tonight, so we plan for him to come get me after.

I spend the remainder of my time reading over the information the girls found on Circe. Physically, the witch is described as having "hair like flames," which I can interpret as having red hair, or, considering my current reality, actual flames. But then I remember that she's changed her name, she may very well have changed her appearance.

Seeking her out in this nightclub is going to be difficult. Due to her dangerous reputation, it would be stupid for me to ask around for her. And in an age where you can find a picture of pretty much anything and anyone, no pictures of the witch herself exist.

Circe might be insane, but she's also clever, and that always makes for a perilous combination.

Still, I have this naïve idea that she won't care about me. I mean really, who am I to her? Sure, she cursed Scylla thousands of years ago, but that was because she wanted the affections of the same man that loved Scylla. I highly doubt Circe will be vying for Nick's attention.

"Nick's coming here, right?" Scarlett's voice pulls me from my contemplation.

"Yeah, he should be here in-" I grab my phone, realizing it's about fifteen minutes past when Nick should have arrived. "Actually, he's late."

Scarlett shrugs. "Maybe the meeting ran later than expected."

"Maybe," I say, though unease creeps into my belly.

"I was going to go to Astrid's, but I can wait with you if you want."

"Nah, that's okay." I smile at her reassuringly. "I'm sure he just got tied up. I'll call you if he doesn't show up soon."

Scarlett says goodbye and leaves. Our group became lackadaisical with our chaperone duties due to the murders quieting. Going to each other's rooms alone doesn't seem too dangerous when we are all on the same floor, just a few doors down from one another.

My phone rings, and I pick up without glancing at the Caller ID, assuming it's Nick.

"Rhi, it's Zo," she says, voice panicked.

My grip on the phone tightens in response to her tone. "Is everything okay?"

"I don't know. I just got to Andrew's, and he said that Nick never showed up to the meeting. Has he been with you?"

My stomach takes a sharp plunge. "No. Zo, let me call you back." I hang up before she responds, finding Nick's number in my recent calls.

The call goes straight to voicemail.

"Fuck," I murmur, scrambling for my door.

I don't know why my mind automatically assumes the

worst. But ever since Professor Talbot told me I can sense things, I've been inclined to listen to my instincts.

And my instincts tell me something is very, very wrong.

I take the stairs to Nick's floor two at a time, but as I clear the third landing, I slam forcefully into someone.

"What's the hurry, Rhi?" a slimy voice slithers over my skin.

I step back, staring into the poison-green eyes of Kieran.

"Get out of my way," I hiss, attempting to shove past him.

He blocks my path, a wicked sneer on his lips.

I'm truly amazed at the audacity of this asshole. Evidently, almost dying doesn't deter someone from making the same stupid mistakes.

I spread my arms in an invitation. "You really want to do this again?"

"You know," he whispers, stepping closer, sour breath hot on my neck. "I've spent the last few months wondering how to pay you back for what you did." His eyes flick to my wrist. "You were all smart enough to get the tattoo that keeps me out of your dreams. But I kept thinking, what would hurt them the most?"

The sensation of a rapidly depleting hourglass hangs over my head, and Nick's face burns the front of my brain. "Kieran, I don't have time for your hypothetical revenge plots." I try to move past him again, but he whips an arm out to hold me in place.

I don't yell. I don't even squirm. I simply lower my gaze to the bony fingers clasping my arm, then lift my eyes to the prick holding me captive.

"Are you fucking kidding me?"

Kieran pays no attention, laughing, even as I strike with the invisible whip, pinning him against the opposite wall.

"You see," he keeps with his tirade, a maniacal gleam to his eyes. "I kept asking myself, what could I do to hurt her? But I was wrong. It's not about hurting *you*, Rhi."

I go rigid at the implication of his words.

"What did you do, Kieran?" I whisper, voice shaking.

Another maniacal cackle. "The best way to hurt you, *really* hurt you, I decided, was to hurt *him*."

The whip barely loosens from around Kieran before I take off up the stairs, Kieran's sinister laugh following me with each step up.

"You're too late," his cackling echoes behind me. "They wanted him gone, and I was happy to help."

That last sentence nearly has me stop to question him, but the nerves churning in my gut tell me I don't have time. I burst into the hallway, the few people lingering outside of their rooms showering me with looks of astonishment.

"Nick!" I yell as I run towards his room. I press against the handle, the door unmoving as I throw my fists and my body against it.

"Nick!" I yell again frantically, pounding my fists against the door, but it's no use. I glance at the two boys who had the courage to move closer.

"Get me somebody that can open this door!" I scream at them.

They don't move.

"NOW!" The inhuman snarl that erupts from my lips sends them running in the opposite direction.

Despite my earlier fruitless efforts, I continue fumbling with the handle, interchanging throwing my entire body at the door with pounding on it until my knuckles start bleeding.

I've just about given up, resigning to wait for the two boys to come back with a way in, when I hear a low sounding hiss in my ear.

Not just one hiss but *two*.

One strike of the whip isn't strong enough to break down this door, but the combination of two...

I back away, the hissing in my ear loud and urgent, like rattlesnakes about to strike. My heart pounds furiously in my chest as I wonder if this is at all even possible.

My vision narrows to the gray slate door, the obstacle in my path. I envision Nick behind it, dying or possibly dead, and my knees buckle under the weight of fear.

The Scylla heads hiss in disapproval, so I steel my spine, knowing that I won't be able to handle both heads without innate strength, and Wilde's words replay in my brain: *There's no room in your life for fear.*

I pull together whatever courage I can muster, thinking first of Nick, of his smile, of whatever sacrifice he made for me in obtaining this necklace. And then I think of Liv and the rest of my girls. My friends. My strength.

And I strike.

THIRTY-SIX

The force of two Scylla heads is *significantly* stronger than one. So much so that at their release, I stumble forward and fall face first to the floor.

A crunching sound echoes throughout the hallway, and I lift my head to find two large dents in the center of the door, in the uncanny shape of monstrous, inhuman heads.

I push against the handle, the door still immovable.

I back away and tell them: *again.*

They move in perfect unison, the unchecked strength of them a marvel to behold. I don't fall this time, having steadied myself enough to withstand their brute power.

Both whips hit the door in the exact same spot, rattling it enough that it cracks open under their pressure.

I race inside and get no further than the threshold, the sight of Nick lying on his bed with terrifying stillness stopping me in my tracks.

My breath comes in rapid spurts, my eyes zoning in on the ashen, pallid color of his skin, the thin, white trace of foam at his mouth. The bile in my stomach lurches as one thought flashes through my mind over and over again: *He's dead. He's dead.*

Though my heart is crumbling, shattering into a million pieces, my brain and body work independently of it, to the point I'm not even sure I'm in control when I inch closer to him.

His motionless chest gives me another jolt of terror. And yet I continue to move, placing two fingers alongside his windpipe, just as he'd done to me.

For a few horrifying moments, I feel nothing. But then...a flicker. The smallest pulse of his heartbeat beneath my fingers.

I loose a shuddering breath as I examine him, looking for any telltale sign that will clue me in on what Kieran did to him.

Aside from the foam at his mouth, which could be from a number of things, his face is unmarred. In fact, Nick appears to not have engaged in any sort of physical struggle. He looks like he was dressing for the meeting. Black pants, white collared shirt, gold cufflinks glinting-

And that's when I see it. Right underneath his gold cufflinks, the veins that map his wrists are black.

Poison.

Without wasting another minute, my teeth emerge, venom filling my mouth seconds later, and I sink my teeth into Nick's neck.

I THROW up for two hours.

The poison laced within Nick's blood burned my tongue, like I'd swallowed hot liquid at its boiling point. An acrid taste lingered after, reigniting my nausea again and again.

The moments after I sunk my teeth into Nick's neck were a

flurry of people, noises and questions. Questions that I couldn't answer.

Professors Talbot, Cicero and Wilde barged in, pulling me off Nick and checking his pulse just as I'd done, firing question after question at me like loose cannons.

The first time I threw up was on Cicero's shoes. I then ran to Nick's bathroom, continuing to hurl my guts up, the voices of the three professors carrying over so that I picked up fragments of their conversation.

"…shirt of flame…"

"…poisoned clothes…"

"…note…"

"…infirmary…"

Then there was a skirmish of movement and other voices I didn't recognize. Soon I was back to throwing my guts up, the sound of my retching drowning out everything else.

At some point before the two-hour mark, two people came to sit by my side. Too sick to even lift my head, I kept my eyes closed, clutching the toilet with a death grip.

It's not until I finally rest my sweat-soaked forehead on the cold bathroom floor that I hear a soft voice whisper: "Rhi, can you open your eyes?"

No. It hurts. Everything hurts. My throat is dry and scratchy. My head swims and pounds. The mere thought of lifting my eyelids is agony.

Something cold and wet presses against my forehead, soothing the burn, wiping perspiration from my skin.

"Rhi," a harsher voice says, demanding. "Open your eyes."

The command in that tone has me force one eye open, then the other. Astrid's sapphire eyes stare back at me, bright and burning. I should have known it was her voice that pulled me from my sickened stupor. Yet despite her exigent tone, it's her that holds a cold washcloth against my forehead, with all the concern and delicacy of a mother.

Aquamarine hair and a serene, beautiful face enter my vision as Liv softly places her hand against my face, moving the sweat-matted hair away.

"Hey," she says, eyes creased with worry, "you're okay. Wilde told us you'd be sick for a while. Your body was just purging the toxin that was in Nick's blood."

Nick. The sound of his name breaks open a dam of memories. His face drained of color and life. The foam at his mouth. The black veins at his wrists.

"Is he..." I croak, voice raspy and brittle.

"He's in the infirmary, sleeping," Astrid says. "But he's alive, thanks to you."

My eyelids flutter closed in weary relief. A weird, light scent of citrus floods my nostrils.

"You need to drink this," says Liv.

I open my eyes to find an opened bottle of Gatorade sitting under my nose. I groan, pushing the beverage away.

Astrid grabs my wrist. "Rhi, you have nothing in your system. You need hydration. Or you're going to end up in the infirmary with Nick, and possibly worse off."

I stare beseechingly at Astrid, who gently lifts me from the floor to lean my body against the sink. It's an arduous struggle just to keep my head upright. Liv places the lip of the Gatorade bottle to my mouth, tipping my chin back to take some of the liquid. It soothes my throat, and I take down a few more gulps.

"Easy," Liv scolds. "A little at a time. You don't want to make yourself sick again."

When I've taken enough sips that my throat feels a little less raw, I speak. "It was Kieran."

Astrid and Liv share similar looks of shock mixed with rage.

Astrid's face twists into an expression of such stone-cold murder I swear it's Medusa herself looking back at me.

"Let's get you in the shower. Once you're clean and comfortable, we'll take you back to your room, get you something to eat, and you can tell us what happened," she says with utter calmness, despite the storm brewing in her eyes.

The girls help me undress, but I manage a shower on my own. After throwing on the comfy sweats Liv brought me, we pass through Nick's room on our way out.

For all Professor Talbot's mockery of present-day crime shows, the room looks like something straight out of *Law and Order* or *CSI*. Yellow tape bars anyone from coming close to his bed, and there's an outline of his body marked with some sort of clay across his sheets. Black tape is placed in the shape of an 'X' on a spot on the floor near his bed, as well as another one on his dresser.

Too exhausted to verbally ask, I shoot Astrid a questioning glance.

"Liv and I will explain later," she says with finality, and we leave.

A tray with a silver cover sits atop my desk once we reach my room. Liv peels back my covers as Astrid plucks the note from the tray.

"Make sure she eats all of this. From Wilde," she crumbles the note and tosses it in the trashcan next to my desk, then removes the cover.

Steam curls from a bowl of what deliciously smells like chicken noodle soup. I settle into my bed, Liv fussing over tucking the covers around me, and Astrid brings the tray over.

"You eat," she commands. "And we can talk." The two girls sit on either side of me. I pick up the spoon and start shoveling soup into my mouth.

"So, you're telling us that Kieran is responsible for poisoning Nick?"

I nod, watching Liv and Astrid exchange a look of skepticism.

"Is it so far-fetched to believe the kid that attacked Zo and me, and whom we threatened to kill, is responsible for poisoning Nick?"

Liv shakes her head. "It's not that we don't believe he's capable, Rhi, but the type of poison he used and how he did it..." her lips twist into a frown. "He doesn't have the means to."

"Maybe we should get Wilde," Astrid suggests upon seeing the confusion on my face.

Liv agrees even though I remain silent, and Astrid leaves to fetch the Poisons professor.

"Where's Scarlett and Zo?" I ask.

"With Nick," Liv says. "Zo stayed with Scar. She's inconsolable right now."

Fear creeps up my spine. "Astrid said Nick was sleeping. For how long?"

Hesitation spreads across Liv's face.

"Liv, please?"

She sighs, averting her gaze. "The poison worked fast. Wilde said Nick was probably unconscious within seconds. But as far as killing him..." she trails off, tentatively lifting her gaze to mine, just as I shudder at her words.

"The poison wasn't perfect. Once it entered his bloodstream, it slowed down, taking its time." Liv reaches forward, squeezing my free hand. "It was your venom that saved his life, Rhi. It stopped the poison from spreading and stopped whatever permanent side effects it might have caused if it was left untreated."

I drop the spoon into the bowl, closing my eyes as tears fall in steady streams down my face. I hear Liv shift on the bed and feel the tray being lifted from my lap. Liv's fingers wipe the tears from my cheeks, then she pulls me into a hug.

"Let it out, Rhi."

I burst into tears on Liv's shoulder, her arms tightening around me with every shuddering sob released.

It feels like my body waited for this moment to tremendously exhale, realizing it needed to perform at optimal levels to gather the strength I needed to use the two Syclla heads to break down the door, to keep my wits about me even when I thought Nick was dead. To not break apart at that fact and use my brain to push forward to get him. To save him.

And I'm just so, so tired.

Liv's embrace never loses its protective strength, and she doesn't let go until my sobs quiet into silence.

"Thank you," I tell her once we break apart.

Her hands still rest on my arms, eyes bold and breathtaking. "I've got you, Rhi. Always."

A knock at the door keeps me from dissolving into a puddle of tears again. Liv leaves me with a smile and lets Wilde in, Astrid trailing behind her.

The Poison professor's eyes go straight to the empty bowl of soup. "You ate it all. Good." She stands at the side of my bed, and though she looks impeccable as always, there's a weariness to her granite gaze.

"I suppose you have questions," she says as she pulls my desk chair beside the bed and sits.

"I do."

"Are you well enough to talk?"

I push myself to sit further up. "What happened to him?"

"The poison in Nick's bloodstream was very advanced, administered in a way I don't think anyone has used since the nineteenth century." She blinks, tilting her head. "Did you know that one way to poison your enemies is to do so through their clothing?"

"No."

She nods, pressing her lips together. "As I said, it hasn't been done in almost two centuries. But that's what happened to Nick. His cufflinks had been dipped in something called 'Shirt of Flames,' a very old, complicated poison. Next to impossible to replicate without a skilled toxicologist."

My expression is as stony as Astrid's. "Are you trying to tell me that Kieran couldn't have done it?"

"I don't see how, Rhi. He wasn't the best student in my class. He wasn't even *decent* at Poisons."

"But he told me he did!" I exclaim, clenching the sheets in my fists.

Wilde looks at me pityingly, but her eyes are troubled. "The only other explanation is that he had help."

I dart my gaze to Liv and Astrid, their faces telling me they are thinking exactly what I am.

The monster that killed those girls to frame Nick. Whoever it is in its human form is who helped Kieran. *They wanted him gone, and I was all too happy to help,* he'd said. Which means Nick has a target on his back, too.

Another puzzling issue crosses my mind. "How did Kieran get Nick's cuff links in the first place?"

Wilde's face softens. "There was a box with a note on Nick's dresser. I think he thought they were a gift." She takes a breath. "From you."

I feel sick all over again. I hadn't given him his Christmas gift yet. He probably thought that was it.

In a rare gesture of compassion, Wilde places a slim hand on my shoulder. "This is in no way your fault, Rhi. You saved Nick's life. He would have died if you hadn't gotten to him and used your venom."

I bite my tongue so hard I taste copper. Being reminded that Nick would have died if I'd arrived a modicum of a second later envelopes my body with tremors of terror.

Wilde removes her hand from my shoulder. "I have a few questions of my own, if you're up to it."

I nod. She interrogates me first about what Kieran told me, then the line of questions follows my ability to break down Nick's door, to which I reveal I now have control of two Scylla heads.

As I expected, Wilde widens her dark gray eyes in disbelief. Astrid and Liv stir beside me, no doubt just as shocked as the Professor.

"Incredible," Wilde murmurs. "Cero didn't think you'd be able to manage one."

"His faith in me is always appreciated," I mutter wearily. "Where's Kieran now?"

"The dungeons."

Pity. I was hoping she'd tell me something more exciting, like burning in the fiery pits of hell.

"What are you going to do with him?" I ask.

"Question him, of course. Then expel him."

I laugh mirthlessly. "He's just going to get a slap on the wrist?"

"What do you suggest, Rhi?"

"Is being drawn and quartered no longer an acceptable form of punishment?"

The corner of Wilde's mouth lifts. "Not for a longtime now, I'm afraid." She sighs heavily, patting my hand as she stands. "Have a little faith in us, Rhi. Kieran won't walk out of here unscathed and without providing us with answers."

My eyes follow Wilde as she leaves, the wheels in my head turning.

Astrid cocks her head in intrigue. "What are you thinking, Rhi?"

I throw the sheets off my lap. "I want to see Nick."

"And then?" Liv asks.

I face the girls, my expression as cold as Nick's skin when I'd placed my fingers against his neck. "And then I'm going to pay Kieran a visit."

CHAPTER

THIRTY-SEVEN

It's two in the morning.

I should sleep. My eyelids are heavy with exhaustion, and weariness rattles my bones as I dress. My muscles are stiff and sore, and even though I've drank some water since the Gatorade and the soup, the sharp stabbing in my head hasn't gone away.

But I know sleep will come fitfully if I don't see Nick. And the Scylla in me is just begging to get a glimpse of Kieran, to see him imprisoned in a cell quivering like easy prey.

Astrid, Liv, and I head across campus to the infirmary in the Southgate building. I shiver despite my heavy coat as December licks the air with an icy tongue, my breath forming clouds of smoke in front of my face.

The Southgate building has an air of melancholy surrounding it, an oppressive tension that comes with housing the school's infirmary. Even though the halls are marble and stone and gleam just as bright in the moonlight as Northgate's halls, the air here is cloying, the sweet smell of sterile sickness wafting through the halls.

I push open the door to the infirmary, Astrid and Liv flanking me like soldiers. White beds with curtains line each wall, some drawn closed to hide the patients within, others pulled open to empty beds.

Of about fifty beds, I count only five with the curtains drawn. Astrid and Liv lead me further into the room, stopping about halfway through.

I pause before entering, afraid to see the toll my venom took on Nick's body in fighting the poison. Liv puts a comforting hand on my shoulder. Reaching with shaky fingers, I draw back the curtain and step inside.

Nick lies as still as I saw him when I first entered his room. With an overwhelming surge of relief, I take in the steady rise and fall of his chest, the golden-caramel color of his skin.

My knees nearly give out at the weight that lifts from my shoulders. This time, Astrid is the one to steady me, and my eyes drift across the bed to where Scarlett sits, hazel eyes rimmed in red and swollen, cheeks blotchy and tear-stained. Zo sits beside her, perking up when she sees my face.

"Rhi, you're okay," Zo lets out a breathy sigh.

"I'm okay," I echo. "How are you doing, Scar?"

Scarlett's lips quiver as she closes her eyes and a single tear falls down her cheek. She gets up slowly, Zo flashing a worried glance behind her as Scarlett makes her way around the bed.

Scarlett stops right in front me, chest rising and falling, then throws all her body weight into wrapping me in a hug.

"Thank you, Rhi," she sobs into my chest. "Thank you for saving him."

Once again, I hear: *he's a really good big brother,* in my head, and start immediately crying with her.

Liv is the first to join the embrace. I can tell by the smell of fresh blossoms that interrupts the smell of sterile bleach from the infirmary. Next is Zo, as I slit my eyes open and catch a glimpse of midnight hair, bracelets jangling with her move-ments. Finally, Astrid follows, her arms long enough to wrap around all of us.

I don't know how long the five of us stand there, huddled together in our little shell where it feels like nothing can hurt us or anyone we love. How agonizing it is to have to pull away, to return to the state of sick siblings and lovers and secrets abound. We form a tight knit circle around Nick's bed.

Scarlett looks at me, trading the tears in her eyes for a firm resolve.

"We're coming with you to find Circe," she says in a steely tone that leaves no room for argument.

I flit my gaze to Nick. "So, he won't wake up for a while?" The thought threatens to shatter my bones where I stand.

"Three days," Scarlett tells me. "But he will be too weak to move or do much of anything for at least two weeks. The poison was vicious."

I grit my teeth, my brain conjuring Kieran's face and poison-green eyes, the person responsible for nearly killing Nick.

I make sure to look at each one of the girls. "Then we'll go together. When do we leave?"

"How about right after Christmas?" Zo suggests. "Liv and I have decided to stay here for break. Astrid and Scarlett were already staying to be with Nick."

"That Saturday, then," I clarify, deciding here and now that I will also stay behind. I'd just seen my parents at Thanksgiving.

Zo nods. Astrid moves to put her arm around Scarlett, who has gone back to looking at Nick, a small tug at the corner of her mouth.

"You know he won't like this, right? All of us going instead of him?" She lifts her gaze to Astrid, then to the rest of us.

"No, he won't," I tell her, watching Nick's eyelids flutter. "But that's because he's a really good big brother."

Scarlett blinks at my words, *her* words.

I lift the curtain. "I'll be back tomorrow, but if anything, and I mean *anything* changes before then, call me."

I duck underneath, hearing the girls whisper, and a voice call, "Where are you going?" It's Zo's. I don't answer, just quicken my pace as I leave the infirmary as I head towards the Westbourne building.

Light footsteps echo behind me, but so does a familiar scent.

"Why are you following me, Liv?"

In a few quick strides, she's at my side. "Do you really think I'd let you go alone?"

"No," I say with a small smile and keep my pace.

She grabs my arm just as we reach the stairs to Westbourne and turns me towards her. It's then I get a glimpse of the monster beneath the beauty, the one that swallowed ships whole. Her eyes flash, sparks of blue moonlight in their own right, and her teeth are sharp. "I've got you, Rhi. Always."

I reach for her hand. Give it a squeeze. "And I've got you, Liv. Don't ever forget that."

She smiles.

We enter the Westbourne building, the atmosphere just as dark and ominous as Southgate. The stairs wind down...down, down, down, in what seems like an unending spiral before we hit the bottom, and Liv squeals at the creature guarding the door.

"What are *you* doing here?" I ask King Lyncus.

A feline grin. "Rhiannon with the sharp tongue, it's so nice to see you again. I don't suppose you've seen Circe?"

I give him an "are you kidding me look" coupled with a low growl.

He sighs mournfully. "I didn't think so." The cat-king's gold and green eyes flit over to Liv, and he cocks his head. "Aren't you lovely to behold, beautiful sea monster."

She actually blushes.

I let out a frustrated sigh through my nostrils, nodding to the steel bolted door behind him. "We need to get in there."

"I'm afraid that's not possible." A bored yawn, revealing his large man-eating jaw and bone crushing teeth. "I have strict orders that no one goes beyond that door."

I step into the King's personal space, shrugging off Liv's warning hand. Even perched on his hind legs, the King sits nearly a head taller, smiling down his muzzle at me. His human-yet-not eyes snap with intrigue at my boldness.

"Even me, the monster girl with a witch's name, who's found Circe?" I taunt.

King Lyncus remains unmoved. I take another step, all but spitting in the King's face.

"You don't believe me. I understand. After all, Circe isn't a fool. Tamsyn du Pont was incredibly hard to track down."

The King stirs, eyes widening at the mention of Circe's alias. The knowing smile vanishes but then is replaced by one of victory. He licks his chops, pink tongue larger than my hand.

"I knew it would be you, Rhiannon with the sharp tongue." He closes his eyes and inhales, the same way he did at our first encounter, like he's savoring something succulent. King Lyncus's eyes flutter open, shifting between Liv and I.

"Where is your mate? I smell him on you. His blood is in your veins, yet he is not here."

I bristle at the word "mate." Not only because Nick and I haven't yet *mated* as the King refers to it, but it just implies something so formal, so...

Intimate.

"He's occupied." I say curtly.

Another knowing smile and a tilt of his head. "An answer worthy of a lynx, Rhiannon. Now, what is your business with the prisoner?"

"Just thought we'd drop in and say hello."

The feline grin widens, teeth sharp and threatening. "The anger raging through your blood tells me you won't aid in his escape, but you cannot kill him, either."

I shoot Liv a disappointed glance. "Aw shit Liv, he guessed it."

Liv grins in response, showing her own pointy teeth.

King Lyncus rises on all fours, a mammoth of a creature. Liv lets out a small, startled gasp.

"Five minutes," the King says. "It is my gift to you, the monster-girl who found Circe."

"It wasn't me. I had a lot of help."

The King smiles. "You have a pack."

"Yeah, she does," Liv answers, stepping to my side.

The King once again tosses his gaze between Liv and I, his knowing smile unwavering.

From the way he keeps looking at Liv, I can't shake the sense of foreboding.

"Five minutes," he repeats, and the steel door unbolts itself and creaks open.

Liv and I step into a dim room, a chill sweeping through the air that I know, instinctively, never dissipates. It sets my teeth clattering, and I clench my fists, warming my cold fingers.

Crude, barred cells sit every few feet from the other, lining the room on both sides, the one's visible to me empty. Torches burn every four or five cells, allowing darkness to permeate. I get the message. There's no light here. No hope.

But there's only one cell I'm interested in, the one with incoherent murmuring. As we approach the cell, Kieran's head snaps up from between his legs, and though his face and arms are filthy, his body shaking with tremors from the cold, his eyes are like green fire.

"Is he dead then?" Are the first words out of his mouth.

Liv's claws unfurl faster than I can blink. I rest my hand on her arm.

"I'd say I'm sorry to rain on your parade, but that would be a lie," I answer.

Kieran laughs. Cold. Cruel. Calculating. "But you're *so* good at lying, aren't you, Rhi?"

I stiffen, not just at the truth in his words but the fact that he knows it. I want to explore that, question him further. But that's not why I came here.

"Who helped you, Kieran?"

The incubus tilts his head back against the wall, eyes closing, an evil sneer turning his lips.

"It doesn't matter," he says. "I failed, and I'll be punished for it."

Ice flows through my veins at the resignation in his voice, at the sheer calmness of it.

I try a different approach. "Kieran," I say, moving so close to the bars their frigidness slaps my skin. "Tell us who helped you, and we'll ask them to be lenient."

He bursts into maniacal laughter, falling over on the floor to a fetal position, shaking uncontrollably. I glance at Liv, whose dark olive skin is near porcelain, taking in the frightening sight of Kieran appearing to lose his mind. Her expression mimics my own. I don't know what to make of this. Have they tortured him within an inch of his sanity? Is that the cause of his behavior?

Faster than a crack of a whip, Kieran is up, hands gripping the bars, and though his face is twisted with lunacy, smile abhorrent enough to scare the devil, his eyes hold no trace of mania. They burn with an unwavering flame. I know then that this monster boy is not crazy.

"You think I'm frightened of Professor Talbot? Cicero? Wilde? Pawns. They're all pawns. Pawns in a much larger game, Rhi. A game of kings and queens, gods and monsters," he continues babbling, chuckling every now and then.

I'm tempted to step back. Liv already has. But I can't show fear. Wilde was right. I don't have room for it.

"You're speaking my language, Kieran. You wanna talk chess? Let's talk chess. Who's moving the pieces?"

Kieran flashes a terrifying grin, pushing his face against the bars. "Gods and monsters, gods and monsters. But you're asking the wrong question, Rhi."

I chew the inside of my cheek in frustration. His previous answer wasn't illuminating, but before I open my mouth, Kieran is prattling again.

"Both sides want the king. The king, Rhi. That's how you win the game. Be the first to get to the king."

"Who is it?" Liv's voice whispers behind me. "Who are they trying to get to?"

The hands at the bars tighten, Kieran's knuckles whitening with the grip. The terrifying smile falls from his face. His eyes dance wildly, darting every which way before they settle upon me.

"Who's the person both sides are trying to get to, Kieran?" I ask again. "Who's the king?"

His mouth curls up disturbingly slow, and he licks his lips with satisfaction of just having had a delicious meal. "You, Rhiannon."

THIRTY-EIGHT

Me? *Me?*

I take it back. This boy is definitely unhinged.

Liv is undeterred by Kieran's proclamation. "What do they want with her?" She's glued to my side, standing shoulder to shoulder with me.

"That's the riddle, isn't it?" He moves his face sideways, still flush against the bars so his pale skin protrudes through the openings. "Perplexing." His green eyes narrow, right at me. "Can you guess, Rhi? Can you calculate that many moves ahead?"

"Bullshit," I spit at him. "You're just blabbering. You're stuck in here for what you did, and you're going to be punished." I slam my hand against the bars. Kieran doesn't flinch. "And it'll be a cold day in hell, Kieran, before I let them keep me from breaking you apart, limb by limb, for what you did to Nick."

Again, nothing but splintering laughter. His eyes dart sideways, contemplative. "Hell *is* cold, Rhi. The kind of cold that burns. The kind of cold that slowly gnaws its way beneath your flesh and buries itself inside your bones, destroying you from the inside out."

Liv grips my hand at his chilling words.

"Like love, Rhi," Kieran continues, his fingers tightening against the bars again, the veins at his temples bulging as he pushes his face even harder against the steel. "Love destroys from the inside out. Nick knows this. You can't love him. It will destroy you both."

I take in a sharp breath, the words a bullet to my chest. I hadn't thought about if I loved Nick or not. I know I care about him, probably more than I ever cared about any boy.

Yet his words hit their mark, the fact that I can't love Nick. It makes me morose and irate and hopeless all at once. Does he mean that I'm incapable of it? Of loving him? Or Nick, being what he is, is incapable of loving me?

Kieran gives me that slow disturbing smile once more. "Checkmate."

I lunge for him, but Liv's clawed hand twists the back of my jacket. "Don't," she whispers.

I seethe, ready to erupt, but will myself to calm down. It must be some act of divine intervention that I hear King Lyncus' smooth drawl.

"Time's up."

Liv loosens her grasp, turning. But I remain glaring at Kieran, too many thoughts ricocheting across my brain and everything he's told me. His smile is plastered, a joker's grin, but in the end, I turn my back on him.

"Watch your back, Rhi," he says, low and haunting, voice dancing with cruel amusement. "Keep your moves to yourself. The people you think are on your side will be the ones to betray you."

I go still as a statue, turning Kieran's words over in my head. Warning or taunt? Truth or lies?

"Rhiannon," the King urges, beckoning me with a single, sharp claw. Liv is already a few paces ahead.

I raise my head and square my shoulders, shooting one last withering glare at Kieran. "I hope whoever you're working for rips you apart, body and soul." That wipes the sardonic grin off his face.

The steel door slams behind me, bolting shut of its own accord.

King Lyncus searches my face. "The answers you received were not what you expected."

"It doesn't matter," I lie through my teeth. "He's lost it. Nothing Kieran said makes any sense."

The cat-king looks pensive. "Someone *will* betray you. The monster-boy wasn't lying about that."

Of all the outrageous things I'd heard from Kieran, I'm surprised King Lyncus chose that to touch on.

"I don't suppose you can tell me who that is?"

A slow, predator's smile. "You can certainly request that information instead of knowing the creature that hunts your peers. It might be more useful, in the end."

I narrow my eyes, contemplating his words. What if the betrayer and the murderous monster are one and the same? Which seems the likely scenario.

And also the one that's the most heartbreaking.

"No," I say. "When I return," I lean into him, "and I will, it will be with whatever you need from Circe to be freed. And then I will finally have the answers I want and can put an end to all this bullshit."

The predatory smile turns razor sharp, not just by the flash of his teeth. "Scylla truly is reborn with you, not only in her likeness, but in her ferocity." The King sits back on his hind legs, bringing his muzzle inches from my face. "I cannot wait to see what you will do, Rhiannon with the sharp tongue. You, who will bring kings to their knees."

Two days after my visit with Kieran, I'm awakened from my uncomfortable sleeping position of lying face first at the edge of Nick's hospital bed, by a squeeze of Nick's hand.

I lift my head, rolling my neck and shoulders, and wipe a trail of crusted saliva from my mouth.

"I told you, you drool," a lazy voice comments, one that I feel I've gone centuries without hearing.

My eyes burst open, taking him in. Nick has pushed himself up on his pillows, his skin perfectly rich and golden.

But aside from his voice, it's his eyes I've missed. Bold and beautiful and burning, those stunning amber orbs look upon me with laughter and tenderness.

I ignore his comment and throw myself at him, catching his lips with my own. I let my fingers trace his strong jawline, the taut muscles of his neck. His arms are strong around me, clutching me with desperation.

"I've missed you," I murmur against his lips.

He grins, pulling back. "I heard I have you to thank for being alive." He kisses me again. "Remind me to add that to what I owe you."

I ignore the heat in those words, shifting so that I sit beside him. "This isn't the first time you woke up?" There's a stab of pain at the thought that I wasn't here for it.

"I woke up this morning for maybe five minutes. Scarlett was here and gave me the world's fastest run down. And then I fell asleep again."

"How do you feel now?"

"Like a million bucks," he says, though I can see the weakness in his movements. Nick's usual effortless agility is gone.

I study him, eyes searching for any physical sign of injury that might have been left behind. The blood at his wrists no longer flows black, but I take one more cursory scan of his body.

And then I see it.

A light purple bruise on the side of his neck, right where I'd bitten him.

His fingers touch where my gaze lingers, tracing the bite mark. Nick raises an eyebrow. "Your handiwork?"

"I'm sorry. I didn't realize how hard I bit you."

Nick reaches for my hand, tugging me down so our faces are inches apart. "You saved my life. Don't ever apologize." His lips graze the side of my neck, traveling to my ear before he takes a small bite of his own. "Besides, it's another thing I can repay you for."

I don't have time to react or to comment, because a surly voice says: "Gods-damn, awake for five minutes, and *this* is the first thing on your mind?"

I whip my head around to find Cicero and Wilde standing at the edge of the curtain, Cicero's face washed with aggravated amusement. Wilde wears her thin, sharp smile.

Cicero shakes his head. "Fucking teenagers."

"I'm twenty," Nick says, unruffled by the fact two Professors caught our sexual banter.

"A twenty-year-old boy might as well be a thirteen-year-old boy where sex is concerned," Cicero argues. "So, I rest my case."

Wilde releases a muffled laugh, stepping towards us. "I'm glad to see you're feeling better." Her granite eyes flick to me. "Both of you."

"How long do I have to stay here?" Nick asks.

"At least another three days in the infirmary, then you can go home, or to your dorm room, where you will remain on bed rest until the doctors clear you," Cicero tells him, large arms crossed.

I feel Nick clench the sheets and face him just as he erupts. "If you think I'm lying in bed for-"

Cicero steps forward, his body so large and brusque his presence fills up the small space. "You don't have a choice, Nicholas. Your body is recovering from almost *dying*. So, you *will* abide by the precautions set forth by the doctors here."

"And that includes not engaging in any sort of sexual activity for that time period," Wilde adds, staring at me.

My cheeks heat to near burning, but Nick just groans.

"I understand your pain, Nicholas. But keep it in your pants until then. And you," he turns that hard stare on me, "keep your hands to yourself."

Despite the burning in my cheeks, I wriggle my fingers tauntingly. "Heard."

Cicero rolls his eyes as Wilde steps forward. "Nick, we've called your mother and told her what happened," Wilde says. "She was traveling abroad, but should be here soon, and we have made arrangements for her to stay if she wishes, so that she may spend the holiday with you and your sister."

Another groan from Nick. "Oh gods. She's going to be a wreck."

"Can you blame her?" Wilde asks in bewilderment. "Her child almost died."

"Did you tell her everything?" he asks.

Cicero twists his lips. "Mostly. We thought you might want to fill her in on some of the other details." He looks at me.

Nick chuckles. "I suppose it's only right that I should be the one to let my mother know I have a girlfriend." My stomach lurches, the feeling heightening with a combination of trepidation and happiness.

"And that she bit me." He adds with a wink.

I let out an embarrassed groan. "You're going to tease me about this for the rest of my life, aren't you?"

There's a hint of mischief in his eyes, and Nick presses his lips together, no doubt to refrain from making another inappropriate comment.

But Cicero is no fool. "Sara, this is our cue to leave, before these two lovebirds make me throw up."

The Trans Professor nods his head in departure, but Wilde smiles at the both of us, wide and welcoming, before she leaves with him.

I shift my attention back to Nick. "Do you want me to bring you anything? I grabbed some of your clothes for you. They're on the chair." I nod my chin to the small stainless-steel chair perched on the opposite side of his bed.

He pulls my hand. "I have everything I need right now."

We kiss again, slow and gentle. But my thoughts are preoccupied, thinking first of his mother's visit, and then of the news I have yet to share with him, news will most likely spark his anger.

I pull back. "Nick, there's something I need to tell you."

His eyes search my face. "You're going to see Circe."

"How did you know?"

Nick's gaze flicks to my fingers pulling at my hair. "Wild guess."

He's eerily calm, which is throwing me off. I expected a protest of epic proportions.

"Say something," I beg, discomfited by his silence.

Nick passes his thumb over the rest of the fingers on his left hand, cracking a knuckle.

"I won't lie to you, Rhi. I'm not comfortable with the idea. But even though I know that wouldn't stop you from going, I also know you can handle anything."

I grin with my sharp teeth, earning a laugh.

"And I'm sure the girls will be going with you, and I know not one of you would ever let something happen to the others. Though, the thought of you and Scarlett near that witch..."

I study him again, taking in his words. It's not the first time he's celebrated my strengths. Admired them. For all his protective instincts, his predatory snarls and gazes when it comes to me, Nick has no problem with my independent nature.

"*I'd* still like to be the one going with you," he confesses.

"Why the change of tune?" My curiosity, as always, gets the better of me.

Nick wraps an arm around my waist, fingers digging into the curve. "You saved my life. How could I ever doubt your capabilities?"

The smile that comes is involuntary, as is usually the case when it comes to Nick. His own capability to make me smile in almost any type of situation is not lost on me.

I lean in closer, the hand at my waist toying with the elastic band of my leggings, his thumb slipping underneath...

And then Nick's eyes widen at something behind me. His hand swiftly disappears from my waist, falling into his lap. He sits up straighter, body going rigid.

I don't have enough time to question him before he clears his throat and says: "Hi, mom."

THIRTY-NINE

The woman I glimpse when I turn my head can only be described as one word:

Breathtaking.

I recall the picture I'd seen in Scarlett's room of the three of them, remembering that although she shares her son's golden-brown skin, her and her daughter share the most similarities.

Large hazel eyes, more green than brown, dance back and forth between me and Nick, and in her wry smile I find the source of both Nick and Scarlett's lupine grin I've come to love. But where Nick's hair is the color of raven's feathers, hers is dark brown washed with red, and her frame is small but curvaceous, like Scarlett's.

She also looks no older than twenty-five, which is freaking me out.

"Is this the girl to whom I owe my thanks?" she says, a hint of a Hispanic accent gracing her voice.

I hear Nick swallow as I rise from the bed to greet her.

"Mom, this is Rhi." A pause as she takes me in, eyes creasing at the name. "My girlfriend."

Nick's mother raises both eyebrows, a new assessing expression on her face.

"Nice to meet you," I say, holding out my hand as blood crashes into my cheeks.

But the wolf grin turns her lips, and before I know it, she wraps her arms around me.

"Thank you for saving my son's life." She pulls back, hands on my arms and squeezes. "You'd have to be a mother to understand the depth of gratitude I have for you." Her eyes are warm. Genuine. They glance behind me to Nick. "Maybe one day you will."

An abashed groan from behind. "Mom. Really?"

She catches my eye, grinning at her son's embarrassment. "I'm Victoria." She releases her hands from my arms, moving to sit beside her son.

Victoria immediately fusses over him. Fixing his pillows. Placing a hand against his forehead. Asking all sorts of questions that range from what he's eaten, to more personal ones that make me want to fall into the small crack in the corner of the wall and never emerge.

"I'm going to let you two catch up," I say, backing away. Nick tosses me an imploring look, to which I can't help but bite my lip and smirk. "It was really nice meeting you, Victoria."

"You too Rhi," she says smiling. "I would love to see you again, under different circumstances of course."

I cock my head, shooting Nick an amused glance. "I think we should make that happen."

By Christmas Day, Nick has finally returned to his dorm room, and he and I have a rare moment alone as his mom and Scarlett leave to pick up food.

Nick and I sit side by side on the edge of his bed, and I hand him a decorative holiday bag, red and green tissue paper peeking from the top.

"Merry Christmas, Nicky Boy."

For all his chiseled features, he looks like an excited toddler. Nick reaches eagerly into the bag, tossing bits of red and green paper about, and pulls out a graphic T-shirt with *Marvel's Thor* on the front.

Nick laughs holding the shirt out in front. "I love it."

I stare at the floor, self-consciously toying with the pendant at the hollow of my throat. "Well, it's no secretly designed necklace with a mysterious backstory, but I thought it suited you perfectly."

His hands clasp over my own, and his finger turns my chin to face him. "Rhi, I love it. Really. And as for that," Nick's eyes slide to the pendant, "sometimes, I'm afraid it will never be enough."

"I'm sure you've noticed by now that I will happily take gifts and adoration in the form of food, preferably Rocky Road ice cream," I say to assuage his apparent distress at not giving me a more expensive gift.

A soft chuckle. "I'm very well aware of that, but that's not what I meant."

I bring our joined hands down, the prior coolness of the pendant now warm against my skin. "Then what do you mean, Nick?"

My voice carries a sliver of pressure, an urge for him to finally tell me the truth behind this necklace.

Nick places a soft kiss on my lips. "Just promise me you will never take it off." Another kiss to the hollow of my throat, right above where the pendant falls. "Promise." His lips move and hover right above the pulse point on my neck.

My eyelids flutter as his lips gently press against the tender area. "I promise." I hear his relieved sigh, feel another brush of air on my shoulder. The tension that I'd buried from our first conversation about the necklace at the diner resurfaces, the pendant now feeling like dead weight.

Kieran's words about love rattle ghostly chains in my mind. There's nothing that is keeping me from loving Nick. In fact, it's just the opposite. The more time we spend together, the more my feelings for him surge past mere butterflies and lust. It feels like my heart is expanding, threatening to spill over with happiness. Yet, when Nick speaks of this necklace in a way that makes me think there was a tremendous sacrifice on his part, my heart caves in at the thought of losing him again. I'd almost lost him once and that's enough for me to decide *nothing* would be more painful than living without him.

SATURDAY COMES AT LAST, and around nine o'clock in the evening, the girls and I discuss our strategy in mine and Scarlett's room while we dress for *Strega*.

"Scar, I hope your Persuasion powers are as good as Nick's." Zo frowns at a card in her hand. "My fake ID is terrible."

"I don't even have one," I chime in, trepidation fluttering about my stomach. All this time I've been worried about meeting Circe, when I never thought twice about how we would get *in* the club in the first place.

"Don't worry about it," Astrid snaps in defense of Scarlett. "She knows what she's doing."

Scarlett smirks as she pulls on tight leather pants over her extremely low-cut body black bodysuit, her voluptuous assets threatening to spill out.

Zo makes a face at Astrid when the Gorgon's back is turned, motioning for Liv to zip up the black cropped shirt she's paired with black pants.

In fact, I realize every single one of the girls is dressed in black. Liv has on a short, long-sleeved black dress that might as well be second skin. Astrid is wearing distressed black jeans and a simple long-sleeved shirt, the only evidence she bothered to dress up lying at her feet with her four-inch heeled boots.

Me? I didn't get the "all black" memo. When I was home, I pulled a long-sleeved blood-red dress from my closet that might be considered modest, if it didn't cling to every curve of my body and stop at my mid-thigh. Liv's crimson stilettos accentuate the dress's look.

"I love that Rhi looks like she's doused in blood," Zo says with an evil grin. "Very fitting, Scylla."

I can't help but grin back, flashing my sharp teeth. If I'm doused in blood, my girls are cloaked in midnight shadows, when the moon is brightest and the darkest shades of black come alive.

I press against my chin, cracking my jaw. "Let's go. We've got a witch to hunt."

STREGA NIGHT CLUB sits on West 20th Street in Chelsea. We arrive around ten-thirty, and the line is wrapped around the block.

The Uber drops us off directly in front of the nightclub, infectious, rhythmic music pouring onto the street from behind the club's large arch double doors. Nick told me the club itself used to be a church, and is reflected in the gothic architecture mixed with new construction.

Leave it up to a centuries old witch to desecrate a church and turn it into one of New York City's most exclusive nightclubs.

We stride up to the front doors, the girls looking cool and

confident as I struggle to keep my fingers from tugging at the ends of my hair, which hangs long and straight down my back.

The patrons in line are all in good spirits, laughing excitedly and dancing to the leaking beats from the club. I wonder if this is part of Circe's magic, making her patrons think they are having the time of their lives waiting in line for hours in the freezing temperatures of almost January in New York.

Their laughter dies as we approach and head straight for the two bouncers guarding the doors. We wear no jackets - Scarlett insisted we were walking in without a fight.

The bouncers are bulky brute men, taller than Astrid in her four-inch heels and as wide as bulls, giving Cicero a run for his money. In unison, their eyes narrow at our group.

"Scarlett Cervallos, plus four guests," she says in a bored tone certainly influenced by Astrid.

The bouncer on the left smirks while his companion checks the clipboard clasped in his gloves.

"There's no one on here by that name, little girl," he says tauntingly, his gaze sliding to Scarlett's chest.

Scarlett doesn't lose any swag. She steps forward, boldly staring at the keepers of the club. "Check again," she demands in a soft, bedroom voice. "I'm sure there's been some sort of mistake."

The girls around me shiver, I suspect not from the chill in the air. Both men frown, and the one with the clipboard flips through it again.

"I still don't see anything," he murmurs, then looks up. "You're right. It must be a mistake. Come in."

Shock ripples through me as the bouncers open the arched doors. Astrid has a knowing look on her face that says, "that's my girl."

We are greeted by a pretty girl with wheat-colored hair that sweeps into an even layer down to her waist and a headset fastened to her ear. She leads us through a winding hallway, the beat of the music reverberating in my ears, the words and rhythm becoming clearer as we approach the main room.

The hallway opens to a large balcony overlooking an expansive dance floor. Girls dressed in nothing more than scraps of clothing dance on large speakers placed throughout the room, the entire club drenched in a silky twilight with interspersed flashes of silver that make it seem like the patrons are dancing among stars.

Astrid and Scar lead us, following our hostess down a spiral staircase to the main floor, passing the club's dancing patrons. I notice they move effortlessly to the music, seemingly losing themselves in the rhythm and touching each other with familiarity.

"What the fuck is this?" Zo murmurs under her breath.

"They're definitely on something," Liv responds, eyeing the dancers. Not one glances up, too lost in their own ecstasy.

We stand before an elevated platform, four stairs leading up to an area situated with black plush couches and circular tables with buckets of ice and liquor.

Something about the platform sends an uncanny ripple of familiarity through me before I realize I'm looking at what used to be the altar of the church.

"Creepy," I mutter under my breath, as our hostess leads us to one of the empty couches.

She gestures to the circular cushion and the bottles within the bucket. We have our choice of alcohol, complete with canisters holding a variety of other beverages for mixing.

"Enjoy," she says before disappearing down the stairs and into the throng of sweaty bodies.

"Damn, Scar," Zo whistles. "I knew your Persuasion powers were good, but I didn't think they were *that* good."

I see her point. Not only did we get into the club without

any opposition, somehow, we made it to the VIP section. I take inventory of our neighbors. Mostly men dressed in black suits, grabbing scantily clad girls off the dance floor, enticing them with a night of exclusivity and free drinking.

In fact, we seem to be the only group of *all* girls, though I notice far across the platform, one of the private areas seats a woman with five men. She sits in the middle of them, daintily holding a flute of champagne between fingers with dark nails as long as my claws, and just as sharp. She smiles wickedly, tossing black hair over her shoulder as she leans into one of the men, licking her lips at whatever he whispers into her ear.

I like her style.

I turn my attention back to my friends, all standing awkwardly around the table.

"What now?" Liv asks.

"Don't drink anything," Zo warns. "Even with the moly in our system, who knows if this alcohol is really alcohol."

"We have to do *something*," Astrid argues. "We stick out like sore thumbs, standing here staring at one another."

Scarlett grabs Astrid's hand. "Come dance with me." She tugs a surprised looking Astrid to the dance floor.

Liv side eyes me as I survey the club. "What are you thinking, Rhi?"

"I'm thinking Circe knows we're here."

Zo pauses her fiddling with a bottle of champagne. "How?"

I continue my scrutiny of the dance floor, making sure I can see Astrid and Scarlett clearly, before I bring my gaze to Zo and Liv.

"It's all too easy. I don't doubt Scar's ability either. I think she got us in with no problem. But VIP? Not only is it random, but it puts us in an area where we can be easily watched." I shake my head. "Circe definitely knows we're here. The question is: what's she waiting for?"

Zo sucks in a sharp breath while Liv chews her bottom lip.

I pluck the bottle of champagne from Zo and grab a flute, flopping myself down on the couch.

"What are you doing?" Liv asks.

I pour the champagne into the flute. "Blending in." I pour two extra glasses for Liv and Zo. "We don't need to drink it. Just hold on to it for appearances."

Zo nods, understanding my game plan. "You're going to let Circe come to us."

"We don't have a choice." I once again skim the dance floor, the balcony above, and our neighbors in the VIP section. "She could be anyone."

Zo and Liv take their own inventory of the people surrounding us, their attention zeroing in on Astrid and Scarlett on the dance floor.

"Go dance," I urge them, noting their restlessness.

"What about you?" Liv asks.

"I'm not really in the dancing mood." I glance down at the bubbles breaking apart in my champagne flute.

A hand rests on my shoulder. "Nick is fine, Rhi." Zo gives me a little squeeze. "Stop beating yourself up over the fact you didn't get to him sooner."

I offer her a tight smile. "Thanks, Zo. But seriously, go dance. I'll be right here. Keep an eye out for anything or anyone unusual."

Zo nods and heads down the steps, but Liv lingers.

"I know what you're doing," she says in an accusatory tone.

"I don't know what you're talking about."

Her cheeks turn crimson with anger, the demure smile and countenance gone, replaced by a feral look of the terrifying sea monster that lies underneath.

"Don't lie to me, Rhi. Everyone else might not see it, but I do."

I raise my eyebrows, playing dumb.

Liv leans down, her face in mine. "You have some sort of hero complex where you think *you* need to be the one in danger, saving everyone else from it." She straightens, shaking her head. "When will you learn to let us help you? Let *me* help you? You don't have to do everything alone, Rhi."

I say nothing, though her words strike a tightly wound chord in my chest that snaps ferociously. Evidently frustrated at my lack of response, Liv exhales an aggravated sigh, then joins the rest of the girls on the dance floor.

Liv is entirely correct. I have no explanation for *why* I feel the need to do things alone, but is it so wrong to not want to put my friends in danger? Especially when they wouldn't be here in the first place if I hadn't agreed to find Circe without thinking it through beforehand.

Since Nick's near brush with death, I've been mulling over my actions. And it seems that everything that has happened to everyone I care about, is a result of a chain of events that began with something *I* did. Kieran had it out for Nick because of the plan I concocted to punish him for Zo.

Even Wilde's first poisons lesson and Cicero's Trans lesson with the arrow put innocent people in danger, all for my benefit.

I'm riding this guilt wave, and I'll be damned if I let it crash and drown any more people I care about.

Satisfied the girls are dancing and ignoring me, I get up and disappear into a dark corridor with the label "Restrooms" blaring in neon pink script above the entrance.

I push the door open to the restroom, narrowly avoiding two women giggling as they brush past me.

I pause in front of the second sink in, noting the sound of someone else in one the stalls, and stare at myself in the mirror. I can't help but think back to the girl in June, the one who thought she was nothing special, certainly not a half-monster. The one who anxiously awaited starting college, wondering how she would fit in, what kind of people she would meet, never guessing she'd fall in with a group of girls she considers sisters.

Am I so different from that girl? Stronger, sure. More rash, maybe. But different?

The door of one of the stalls bangs open, startling me from my rumination. The lone woman from VIP approaches, standing a sink away from me. If Nick is the most beautiful boy I'd ever seen, she's his equal in female form. Her hair is a silk veil of midnight, falling to her waist in soft waves. Large, expressive green eyes watch me in the mirror, and she smiles, pearly white teeth set against flawless dark skin. The woman finishes washing her hands and turns, eyes traveling up and down my body.

"Nice dress. Love the color."

I try not to laugh. For some reason, the women's bathroom in bars and clubs brings out the best in all of us.

"Thanks. I saw you in VIP. I like your style."

The woman laughs, sending odd shivers down my spine. "Why have one when you can have many?"

Her full outfit comes into view as she faces me. Her upper body is wrapped in black strips, two of them crossing over chest in an 'x', exposing much of her midriff and the curve of her waist. They disappear into her low-cut jeans, ripped in so many places I wonder why she bothered to wear them at all. She stands a head over me, despite my four-inch heels and five-foot five frame, the black strappy stilettos at her feet aiding in her height.

Between one blink and the next, she's applying a blood-red hue to her voluptuous lips, not bothering to look in the mirror as she does so. I continue to watch her apply the color with expert precision, not once going outside the perfect shape of her own lips for it to bleed on her skin.

I'm not surprised when she holds out the lipstick to me.

"As I said before, I like your style. And your taste in lipstick colors." I make a pointed glance at my own blood-red dress.

The woman smiles, her hand still outstretched. "Care to try it?"

I smile back and accept the lipstick, hovering it right over my lips. The woman watches with a keen interest, still smiling.

Until I reach into the neckline of my dress and pull out Nick's pendant. Her green eyes flash, her jaw tightening as she takes in the protection charm.

"On second thought," I say, tossing the lipstick back to her. She catches it with one hand. "Who knows where your lips have been. Historical accounts give you quite the promiscuous reputation."

Another smile graces her lips. Slow. Cunning.

Evil.

The Syclla heads hiss angrily as I take a step toward her. "Hello, Circe."

CHAPTER

FORTY

Circe's answering grin is cutting, laced with thousands of years of wickedness and vengeance.

She circles me like a buzzard waiting for death. I feel her penetrating gaze at my back, my shoulders tensing in anticipating the sharp point of a knife.

The Scylla heads haven't stopped hissing, thrashing about in my mind like ocean waves amidst a hurricane. It seems that even centuries later, they recognize an old enemy.

Circe completes her circle of me, recognition marring her flawless face. I don't like the look she's giving me, like she's seen me before, when I know with utmost certainty, I've never seen anyone that looks like her.

"Are you my past come back to haunt me?" she asks with a tilt of her head, her waves undulating.

I frown. "I have no idea what you're talking about."

Circe steps forward, squinting, like she can't quite make out what she sees before her. "It's you, isn't it?"

This is hardly the epic showdown I imagined between myself and the notorious Circe.

"Who do you think I am?"

The witch picks up a strand of my hair, twirling it around her finger. "But you look *exactly* like her. What's your name?"

I swat her hand away. "Rhiannon."

Circe gives a start. "Scylla is reborn and named after a witch?" She shakes her head. "My how the gods love to toy with me."

The bathroom door crashes open, several girls stumbling towards us in a riot of laughter.

Circe glances over my shoulder. "Come, Rhiannon. We have much to discuss."

She walks past me, but I grab her arm.

"What was in the lipstick?"

A curt giggle. "Oh. That. Just Chanel Rouge Allure in Pirate."

I tighten my grip. "Bullshit."

Her gaze slides to my hand on her arm, then to my face. A coil of fear slithers down my spine. I lower my hand to my side, earning a coy smile from the witch. "You're not as stupid as your ancestor it seems."

She continues walking, leaving me to seethe at her comment. I keep the Scylla heads in check, itching to let them loose and strangle her. A brash reaction to her mockery of my ancestor, or a more innate response, I wonder?

Circe glances once over her shoulder to make sure I'm following, and I grit my teeth as I put one foot in front of the other. We leave the restroom and walk down the hallway to VIP in silence, but when Circe sees my girls all standing around our section, she speaks.

"It's no wonder you were named for a witch, Rhiannon." She gestures towards my friends. "You have a coven."

"They're called friends, Circe." As I say it, I come to the realization that this isn't the first time my friends have been labeled. King Lyncus called them my pack. They, themselves refer to us as a gang. Though the words are all different, - coven, pack, gang - they imply the same thing: unity. "I'm guessing you don't know much about that," I taunt.

"Why do you draw that assumption?" Circe breezes past my friends, barely sparing them a second glance. But they catch my eye, and I motion with a jerk of my head to follow.

"I'm going to take a wild guess and say that your penchant for cursing women who draw the eye of men you like doesn't lend well to forming female bonds."

Circe abruptly stops, shoulders tensing, but she doesn't face me. Instead, she addresses the group of men in her section that stare at her adoringly. I can almost see their puppy-dog tails wagging.

"I've grown tired of you all," she says with a breathy sigh. "Get out."

They stare at each other, some fiddling nervously with the buttons on their perfectly pressed collared shirts. It's almost impossible to tell them all apart. One of them, clearly the boldest of the bunch, stands.

"Surely, you at least want some of us to stay." His dark eyes move past Circe to me, then fall behind me. "You couldn't have brought them all here for yourself."

His statement puzzles me at first before I realize the girls have gathered alongside me.

Circe laughs softly, a lover's purr against my ears, and gods-damn, with that laugh, I know exactly why men and women crumble at her feet.

She traces a long dark fingernail along the man's jaw, and he shivers as it travels down his neck, trailing dangerously along the pulsing vein. In a moment of horror, I think she's going to slice his neck open.

Instead she grabs his chin. "I don't share my things. And I happen to find the pleasure of women much more satisfying."

"Can't argue with her there," Astrid says from beside me, her mouth twisted in a smirk.

Circe all but tosses the suits out of her way, plopping down on her now vacant couch as the men file out begrudgingly. Her startling green eyes take in each one of my friends.

"Ladies," she spreads her arms and palms wide. "Make yourselves comfortable."

"And who the hell are you?" Zo asks.

A slight tilt of her head and an arrogant curl of her lips. "I'm the person you all came to see."

Astrid stiffens next to me, her arm instinctively going in front of Scarlett. Liv side-eyes me, jaw twitching. I can't see Zo's expression, but I'm sure it's no different.

"Please," she sweeps a hand across the table in front of her, laden with drinks and treats alike. "Help yourselves."

Zo snorts. "Yeah, like we'd ever eat anything *you* offered."

Circe's eyes narrow, and fear pierces my abdomen. I still have something I need from her, and I won't leave here without it. I can't risk anyone pissing her off.

"You must know you have a reputation, Circe," I explain matter-of-factly.

"Reputation is what others think of you. Something I give zero fucks about." She takes a dainty sip of champagne.

I exchange a glance with Liv. Is Circe implying her notorious reputation that has followed her for centuries is bullshit?

Or, is she just setting a trap?

I take the bait and sit down beside her as she refills her glass.

"You aren't here to discuss the merits of my past, so why don't you get to the point, Scylla."

"It's Rhi."

Circe looks up at that. "Ah. Yes. *Rhiannon*. Still so fascinating, I must say." Another sip of champagne. "I will speak with you alone." She waves her fingers toward the girls in dismissal.

"We're not leaving you." The stern proclamation comes from Liv, to my surprise and everyone else's, judging by the shocked expressions on their faces.

Circe gives a dramatic sigh. "Your witch is wearing one of strongest protection sigils I have ever seen. Even if I *wanted* to harm her, it would be impossible. And you all have enough of the moly in your system that nothing you touch or consume will harm you." She nods her head. "My word."

They still don't move, and my lips tug at a smile. But we have a job to do.

"Guys, I'll be fine." I level my gaze. "Please."

Astrid is the first to move, tugging off her black gloves. Almost as one, Scarlett, Liv, and Zo step back, just as they did the night of the bonfire.

"Anything happens to her and this place will be in the papers tomorrow. And not in a good way."

Circe leans back into the couch, gaze fixed on Astrid's bare fingers. She raises a toast. "Ah. Medusa. Nice to see you again." Takes a sip. "I gave my word. I won't repeat myself."

"Go," I urge.

Astrid tugs her gloves back on and turns as she reaches for Scarlett. Zo follows, but Liv lingers, a ferocious stare skewering Circe.

"Though I don't like repeating myself, Charybdis, I'll do so for your sake. No harm will come to your cousin."

Circe's words fall on deaf ears. I get up and go over to Liv.

"I don't trust her," she says.

"I know. I'm not sure I do, either. But I have to tell her about Lyncus. We need his help."

Liv licks her lips, uncertainty washing over her face, but

she finally relents. "I've got you, Rhi. Always."

"I know."

When I turn, I find Circe curiously watching our exchange.

"So," I say as I return to my seat beside her, "how do you know what kind of monsters we all are, or have you simply cursed so many women you know your own handiwork?"

Circe places her champagne flute down and rubs her temples. "Gods, I am definitely being tortured. You are just as obnoxiously mouthy as she was."

"When you said you wanted to talk, I didn't think you meant to talk shit about my ancestor. Cursing her into a monster form wasn't enough?"

The witch snaps her head up, glaring at me with eyes like sharp emeralds.

"What do you think you know about what happened between Scylla and myself?"

I tug at my hair, discomfited by her intense gaze. "A mortal fisherman came to you looking for a love potion so he could win the affections of Scylla." I suck my lower lip between my teeth as Circe's gaze burns. "But you fell in love with him instead, so you cursed her."

She releases a humorless chuckle. "Leave it to men to muddle the details." She takes a strand of my hair between her fingers, admiring it as she continues to speak. "What if I told you that isn't the truth? That Scylla and I were as close as sisters, and the man that came between us gave me no choice?"

Too nervous at this point to pull away, I swallow thickly, allowing her to continue toying with my hair. "I don't know if I would believe you."

"Of course, you wouldn't. I've heard the stories they tell about me." She lets my hair fall from her fingers, shifting so that I glimpse her side profile and reaches for her champagne.

I'd be lying if I said I wasn't intrigued, or that something in

Circe's voice, in her eyes, tells me she isn't lying. "These stories have been told for millenia. You cursing Scylla. Turning men into pigs. You have a reputation for being insane. Sadistic. If you're saying none of that is true, then why let it perpetuate?"

Circe watches the bubbles dance from the fresh glass she poured. "Rhi, you have been on this earth for what? Seventeen, eighteen years? I have been on it for *centuries*. Women do not obtain the level of respect men do. Not then. Not now. I learned long ago that it was fear – fear that kept my enemies at bay, fear that made both my enemies and my peers respect me."

"Fear does not equate to respect, Circe," I say before I can stop myself.

Circe gently takes my chin between her thumb and forefinger. "No, young witch, it doesn't." She leans in. "But it is better to be feared, then to be hunted."

She releases my chin, her hand falling to her lap and her eyes following. "What is it you seek from me?"

I hesitate, her words pricking like sandpaper over my skin. Hadn't Wilde said something similar? That we are not only hunters, but *hunted*? Could the witch be telling the truth, that all these stories of infamy and jealousy are nothing more than a smokescreen to keep her enemies afraid and away from her doorstep?

It's too large a pill to swallow, but that doesn't change the fact that I still need her help.

"King Lyncus sent me."

Her head whips up, the champagne glass in her hand shattering underneath a tightened grip. I suck in a sharp breath as blood drips from her clenched fists, and my peripheral vision sees the gang take note, all of them ready to come to my defense.

"Listen to me carefully," Circe says, an unearthly growl in her voice. Blood still trickles from her now open palm, cascading down her wrist. "I swore no harm would come to you or your coven, but if you lie to me-"

"What I'm telling you is true: I'm here on behalf of King Lyncus. He's offering me information. Secrets. In exchange for freeing him."

Her bloody hand reaches out and clasps my neck. "Freeing him from *where?*"

In the space of a breath, the girls are across the platform, moving faster than I ever imagined.

The Scylla heads thrash and hiss, and I contemplate releasing them. But then I see the look of heartache and worry in Circe's eyes, and it dawns on me.

"You two are lovers," I say, with the little breath I have.

Her fingers squeeze. I let one of the whips wrap around the wrist that's holding my neck. Circe's grip loosens, but she doesn't let go.

"Where is he?"

"Don't tell her, Rhi." Astrid's gloves are off once more. "I thought we had an understanding?" She waves her fingers as Circe shoots Astrid a menacing glare.

The hand at my throat falls, but Circe turns to me, enraged.

"You *will* tell me where he is."

"He's alive and turned into a lynx. He said to find you. That you would know how to free him. That's all I'll tell you."

Her eyes narrow. "Why should I believe you? I haven't heard from Lyncus in centuries. I was told he was dead."

Some soft part of me feels for Circe. Again, I question whether her earlier speech was a lie, something to gain my trust. And yet, here we are, with the ball in my court as I tell her someone she loved and thought was lost to her is alive.

"Circe," I begin softly, "what would I have to gain from lying to you?"

"Revenge," she snaps so fast it all but shoots from her mouth like gunfire.

I take a deep breath. "I'm not *her*."

I note the shift in Circe's features as her jaw relaxes and her lips part. She releases a shuddering breath. "If what you say is true, then I know what I must give you."

She waves her hand and a vial containing a black liquid appears between her fingers.

"Tell Lyncus to drink this," she says as she hands it to me. "But it must be administered on the vernal equinox. Not before. And certainly no later."

"Vernal equinox? But that's in March!" Zo exclaims behind me.

My heart falls. That's two months from now. Who knows how many more girls will die before then?

"You don't have anything that will work sooner?" I ask.

"That's the best I can do." Circe taps the vial with a dark fingernail, her wrist and hand now free of blood. "It contains my blood, so Lyncus will know exactly where to find me when he is freed."

I clench the vial between my fists. "Thank you."

"Assuming you aren't lying to me, I should be thanking you." The witch brushes her lips against my ear. "And if you *are* lying to me, you will regret it."

I try not to let the threat get under my skin. "Not as much as you will regret what Astrid will do if any harm comes to me."

Circe smirks, glancing behind me to the girls. "Don't take your coven for granted, Rhi. One day you might find yourself alone."

This last statement irks me more than Circe's earlier threat. It reminds me of Liv's accusation that I need to do everything alone. And it reminds me of Kieran's taunt, that someone close to me will betray me.

I stand, choosing not to respond. "Come on. Let's go," I tell the girls, turning to leave.

"Oh, Rhi?"

Reluctantly, I face Circe, the witch now standing, her eyes fixed on my necklace. She motions me closer.

I close the distance between us, and she touches the pendant. "Do not take this person for granted, either," she advises, nail tracing the design. "Whoever made this for you sacrificed a great deal."

My blood rushes from my head at the severity of her words. My fingers find the pendant. "Like his life?"

Circe cocks her head pensively. "Not necessarily. Sometimes, life isn't truly our greatest sacrifice. One can give up something equally important, so much so that living without it would be the greatest burden."

I shudder, unable to imagine what it was that Nick sacrificed, yet slightly relieved that it might mean he didn't bargain away his soul.

"What's his name?" asks Circe.

Tension is a fist clenched inside my chest as I remember how hesitant Nick was to give Lyncus his name. Well, his *real* name. Surely, giving Circe Nick's name wouldn't mean anything...

"Nick," I say with a breathy exhale as though his name off my tongue unfurled that tight fist. "Nicholas Cervallos."

At the mention of Nick's name, there's a tumultuous wrath behind Circe's eyes that makes her earlier rage seem inconsequential. She lets a monstrous hiss that rivals the Scyllas'. Circe grabs my arm, bringing her face close to mine. "Stay away from him. Yours and his is a story that does not end well."

Circe releases me with a small shove, sending me stumbling backwards. Two hands steady me, the smell of blossoms letting me know it's Liv.

Always at my back.

"What was that about?" she asks as Circe disappears down a hidden flight of stairs.

"Just repeating that I better not be lying about Lyncus," I lie. "Come on. Let's get out of here."

Shoulder to shoulder with Liv, we join the rest of the girls and leave Strega, Circe's warning about Nick piercing my brain with roaring alarms.

And piercing my heart with blades.

FORTY-ONE

It's nearly three in the morning when we return to campus, none of us speaking as we head inside Northgate.

My silence is wholly due to Circe's parting words, and how they align with what Kieran told me regarding Nick.

Then, there is the mysterious prophecy to consider, that I *think* I'm somehow a part of, as well as the fact that Kieran told me I have two warring sides after me. Though, he might have been a little too far gone when he told me that.

I have a feeling all this ties together, but how?

The more serious issue that looms over all of us is the fact that we need to wait nearly another two whole months before we have answers. In that time span, half the female population of Alystair could be slaughtered.

As we turn the corridor on our floor, Zo pauses. "Why do you think the murders have stopped?"

We all come to an abrupt halt, circling together.

"There were only two," I offer. "Sasha and Amanda. Two of Nick's former flings."

"But Nick dated other girls. All of them are still alive," Scarlett says, her eyes pinning me. "As are you."

Silence settles over us like a dense fog as we ponder the strange connection between the murders.

Zo purses her lips. "We know someone is out to frame Nick, but what if that's not the whole story?"

I blink. "What do you mean?"

"Maybe framing Nick is just a bonus prize," Zo continues with a shrug. "Maybe the murders serve a different purpose, and framing Nick just sweetens the deal."

"What purpose would the murders serve?" Liv counters.

"Revenge." The word leaves my mouth as fast as it did Circe's.

"Revenge?" Liv echoes. "You think the murderer is one of Nick's jilted lovers?"

I shrug. "Why not?"

"They all know about each other," says Scarlett. "And they're the ones that usually end it."

"That doesn't mean that one of them isn't jealous," Zo protests. "Who was he dating before Rhi?"

"Amanda and Lila, before Amanda was murdered," says Astrid.

Zo turns pensive. "Lila's someone we could-"

"Her file was clear," Liv interrupts. "Lila is a chimera. Nothing more."

Right. Because the "person" we're looking for also needs to be half-god.

"There's also Samantha," I muse. "Nick was with her the night of the bonfire. She's still among the living."

"For now," Zo mutters.

I rub my temples, frustrated that it's taking us so long to figure this out.

"Look," Zo holds out her palms, "it's been a long night. I'm sorry I brought this up. It's just...don't you get the feeling we're missing something *so* obvious?"

Yes. Yes, I'd been thinking that for months now.

I release a frustrated sigh. How could I be so good at chess, at calculating so far ahead, and miss what's happening right in front of me?

Unless, *that's* the problem. I've spent so much time strategizing, trying to plan my moves, that I've been blind to the present.

...And the past.

"What if we look at *when* these murders occurred? See if there's a connection in the time frame to something else happening?" I suggest.

Zo perks up, nodding. "Excellent."

Everyone looks thoughtful. Intrigued. As if we might be close to realizing something.

Everyone except Liv.

"Maybe we should all get some sleep first," she says, her dark olive skin drained of color.

It's so odd for her to look like that, when she's usually the first one on board with whatever I plan. So odd for her to look like...

She's hiding something.

The ones you think are on your side, they are the ones that will betray you.

No, I think vigorously. *Not her.*

The rest of the gang seems to agree with Liv, and we decide to reconvene tomorrow. I try to catch Liv's eyes, usually always so eager to grasp mine, to share a smile, a knowing look. But they remain downward, her subtle shifting making me think she's mulling something over.

Please, I implore again, *not her.* I don't know if I could handle betrayal coming from Liv. But then I think, *isn't that the point?* Betrayal doesn't imply trickery by someone you expect it from. No, the very essence of the word is laced with deceit from someone you care about. Someone you love. Someone you trust.

After all, there's no worse feeling in the world than believing someone has your back before they stab you in it.

FATIGUE CREEPS into my bones with every step I take towards Nick's room to show him what I procured from Circe.

When Nick opens the door, he's shirtless – of course – and drenched with sweat. After a cursory glance at his bare stomach and chest glistening with perspiration, I raise my gaze to find his eyes dragging over every curve of my dress.

I clear my throat.

"Yeah." He blinks. "I mean, come in."

"Why are you so sweaty at three-thirty in the morning?" I sit on his bed and groan with relief as I kick off my shoes.

"I couldn't sleep," he says, standing in front of me. "I kept thinking about you and Scarlett and the girls." He cracks his knuckles, averting his gaze. "I was really freaked out, so I decided to exercise."

I note the ashen color has returned to his skin, remembering Cicero's words that he was supposed to be on bedrest and not partake in any kind of strenuous activity.

"Oh. So, by exercise, you mean you decided to try a Navy SEALs inspired workout?" I screw my face into a look of bewilderment. "You're ten shades lighter, which means whatever you were doing was too strenuous, and-"

"I was scared, okay?" Nick's voice is full of fear, his eyes finally meeting mine. "I *hated* not being there with you. So, it was either I work out my anxiety that way, or I drink, and I chose the route that would less likely end up with me making some really stupid decisions."

"Okay," I say softly. "Though, the last time I drank, one might argue I made some pretty good decisions." I grin up at him. He sits beside me, the smell of sweat mingled with spicy cedarwood and sweet vanilla pushing my weariness aside to awaken a long growing hunger.

"I'd argue that was less of a decision and more of a desperate attempt to find a bed," he grins back.

"How convenient for you then, that I ended up in yours."

Nick leans into me, voice dropping an entire octave. "Would you like to conveniently end up in it again?"

I place my hands on his firm chest, his skin pebbling beneath my touch. Reluctantly, I push him away.

"No strenuous activities, remember? In fact, sex was the *only* strenuous activity specifically mentioned by Cicero and Wilde."

Nick's eyes widen and his mouth falls with false shock. "Get your mind out of the gutter, Owens. I was merely offering you my bed to sleep."

I narrow my eyes and push my tongue against my cheek. "I have nothing to sleep in." Nick's gaze roves down my dress torturously slow, his lips curling with what I know he's about to say next. "And before you make another ridiculous comment regarding me sleeping naked, I have something to show you."

Reaching into my purse, I pull out the vial given to me by Circe, the *real* reason I came to see Nick.

That wipes the fantasizing look off his face. "You did it."

"Of course, I did," I reply, slightly hurt at the surprise in his voice.

He shakes his head. "I'm sorry. I didn't mean it like that. It's just...I really thought Circe would have put up some sort of fight."

"The only fight she put up was when she asked who gave me this necklace, and I told her you did."

Nick balks, face leaching further of color. "What did she tell you?"

I search his face, weighing the pros and cons of telling him the truth.

"Please don't lie to me," he asks, a level of vulnerability in his usual confident tone that makes my heart splinter.

"She told me to stay away from you," I confess. "That our story doesn't end well."

"Like she should talk," he snaps, turning away from me.

I place a hand on his shoulder. "Nick, she isn't the only one that said something to me." His amber eyes darken. "Kieran told me that you can't love me. That it would destroy us." His bottom lip trembles. "What does that mean?"

Nick cups my face, thumb trailing over my lips. "Nothing, Rhi. It means nothing. I found you, and I'm never letting you go, okay? That's all that matters."

He says this with such conviction, such strength and passion, I don't want to argue. Yet...

"But-"

"Please, Rhi," he begs, pressing his forehead against mine, eyelids shuddering. "Please let this go."

The competitor in me wants to keep pushing. Wants to *win*. But I knock her down, remembering that there are more important things at stake than my love life.

Speaking of which, Nick never said he loves me. So, all this worrying might be moot if we go our separate ways at the end.

That thought sends ripples of agony through my veins.

"Two months," I tell him, moving my face from his, his expression contorted with confusion. "We can't give that potion to Lyncus until the vernal equinox."

Nick rubs his palm down his face in exasperation. "Of course, it couldn't be *that* easy."

"It never is."

Nick studies me for a moment before he presses his lips to mine. "I'm going to take a shower." He rises, his back to me as he approaches his dresser, and I swipe away a myriad of inappropriate thoughts.

A white ball of cotton flies at my face, along with a pair of boxers.

"For you to sleep in," he says with a small smile, and heads towards his bathroom.

Eager to get comfortable, I undress almost as soon as I hear the shower running, and gods, these smell like him more than his bed does. I nestle into his pillows, drawing the sheets over me. My eyes droop immediately, until I feel a body alongside me and an arm wrap around my waist. Nick nuzzles the back of my neck, a pleasant sigh escaping my lips. Here, in his arms, it's easy to pretend we're nothing except two ordinary people, wrapped in the comfort of one another. Pacified by that thought, I drift to sleep, the sound of Nick's breathing calming all my fears.

I WAKE ONLY a few hours later to the sound of vehement hissing in my ear.

The Scylla heads are whipping, undulating furiously, urging me to get up and get going. A heavy sense of dread sits on my chest like a boulder, though once I glance at Nick, the tightness in my chest eases.

It's not him that's in danger. Not this time.

My thoughts immediately conjure the girls, and the hissing grows louder, angrier.

It's not them, either.

I pull myself from Nick's arms as softly as I can manage, trying my best not to wake him. He doesn't stir, though I pause a moment to admire the dark lashes that settle upon his cheeks like soft kisses.

A violent hiss.

Alright, alright. I'm going.

I dip into the hallway, pulling the door closed quietly. Judging from the rosy splashes of color painting the limestone walls, the sun must just now be creeping over the horizon.

Is it too much to go back to my room and throw some normal clothes on?

The hissing grows wild. I take that as a 'no.'

I head down the stairs, grateful no one else is up at this ungodly hour on a Sunday to see me donning a boy's black boxer shorts and a white shirt.

I approach the first floor, the furious hissing resuming the further I move away from the doors.

"Are you kidding?" I say aloud. "It's freezing out there! Do you see what I'm wearing?"

My answer is more hissing.

I grit my teeth and step outside, the biting chill of winter slapping my bare limbs and my face.

And then it's gone.

The temperature outside might as well be mid-summer, that's how warm I suddenly am, despite the fact I know it's currently about twenty degrees.

Snapping jaws have joined the hissing, pushing me to move faster. I walk straight, catching a glimpse of Westbourne, and I turn abruptly.

That's where I need to go.

I race towards the building, venom pooling in my mouth. The Scyllas are writhing, excited. They want a fight. Anticipate it.

A coil of fear unwinds itself inside me.

Are they leading me to the monster?

But then I remember the Westbourne building hosts its own version of monsters. The criminals in the dungeon, though only one criminal lurks there now.

Has Kieran somehow escaped?

I throw open the door to Westbourne and practically fly down its winding steps to the dungeons. Lyncus is not there to greet me at the bottom, and though the Scyllas are thumping their sinuous bodies with eagerness and malice, the sixth sense I've acquired tells me something is wrong.

The lock on the steel door hangs off its bolts, swaying with an ominous *creak*. The Scyllas have quieted, as if they too, understand that we're no longer about to fight. Whatever was here came and left. And I have a feeling I'm about to discover what it came here for.

I enter the dungeon, footsteps light on the gritty concrete floor. A sharp tang hits my nostrils, stopping me in my tracks. Every single torch is extinguished, save for one. The one that burns beside Kieran's cell.

The dread that I awoke with spreads from my chest to my stomach, my limbs heavy with fear. I put one foot in front of the other, the closer I get to the bars the more I realize something shiny drips down them, its color becoming illuminated with the flicker of firelight.

Blood.

I peer through the bars, anxiety trickling in with every breath I draw. Kieran doesn't seem to be anywhere in the cell. Kieran -

My eyes finally adjust to the dimness, allowing me to see fully inside.

A piercing scream tears from my throat.

FORTY-TWO

I was wrong. Kieran isn't anywhere in the cell.

He's *everywhere* in the cell.

Bits of Kieran's innards and bones and flesh decorate the dungeon cell like a slaughterhouse. And the blood. There's so much blood.

I turn from the gruesome sight and drop to my knees, vomiting. I squeeze my eyes shut, willing the horrifying image to disappear. But try as I might, it remains, as though burned into the backs of my eyelids.

"By the gods..."

I shakily turn my neck to find Talbot, Cicero and Wilde, staring into Kieran's cell with expressions of distraught horror. Wilde's porcelain skin is gray and Cicero looks like he might join me in being sick. Only Talbot appears to have kept his composure.

"What are you doing here?" he asks, charcoal eyes suspiciously fixed on me.

"The Scyllas..." I breathe. "Led me here."

Cicero snorts. "Right. The kid who poisoned your boyfriend

is now brutally murdered, with you standing right outside his cell, and you had nothing to do with it?"

"Wait a minute," Wilde interrupts. "Where is Lyncus? He's supposed to be guarding the door."

Three skeptical pairs of eyes turn on me. I rise unsteadily, the image of Kieran's grotesque dungeon cell coupled with the accusatory stares of the professors an unbearable weight.

"I have no idea where Lyncus is." I hold up my hands. "And how the fuck do you think I'd be able to accomplish *that*?" I throw a hand in the direction of Kieran's cell, desperately avoiding eye contact with the scene.

Professor Talbot's attention darts between me and the cell. "Your two Scylla heads are perfectly capable of inflicting that."

"Talbot," Wilde says hesitantly, throwing him a surprised look, "there's *nothing* of Kieran left. I highly doubt-"

"Sara," Talbot cuts her off, "find out where Lyncus is, and why he wasn't where he's *supposed* to be. Rhi, come with Cicero and me to my office. We will continue our questioning there."

Wilde opens her mouth but shuts it at the scathing look she receives. Trepidation flutters along my skin. I have nothing to hide, no reason to worry, but Cicero isn't my biggest fan, and I can't help but feel like I'm walking into a trap.

I follow Cicero and Talbot up the stairs and out the door of Westbourne, again grateful it's still early enough that no one is out and about to witness me being herded by two Professors in my "walk-of-shame" outfit.

Like he's read my mind, as we approach Talbot's office, Cicero says, "Whose clothes are you wearing?"

"Mine," a chilling voice answers from behind me.

I don't need to turn to know whose voice that is, but I do, nonetheless. Dressed in one of his many band shirts and jeans, Nick's vicious glare at Cicero and Talbot is enough to send slivers of fear down my spine.

Cicero rolls his eyes. "Of course, they are. Aren't you supposed to be on bedrest?" He shoots me an accusatory glare, as though Nick being out of bed is my doing.

I mean, I guess it is.

Talbot sighs wearily, as though Nick doesn't look ready to tear both professors apart with his bare hands. "Come in, Nicholas."

As two professors file into Professor Talbot's office, Nick catches my eye. "Are you okay?" he mouths silently.

I shake my head, biting my lip. After seeing what I saw, I'm anything but.

Nick's attention snaps to my face, scrutinizing, before trailing down my bare limbs, and I realize he's searching for signs of injury.

Talbot gestures for us both to sit, though Nick puts a hand out to block me before I do.

"No restraints, Mr. Cervallos. Just conversation." He holds out a cordial hand to both chairs.

We sit, and Nick places a hand on my jittering knee to calm it. Every time I blink, I see that awful massacre in that cell.

"So," Talbot begins, "here we are again."

"She was with me all night," Nick says quickly.

"That might be true," Talbot says with a contemplative tilt of his head, "but the fact remains that we found her at the scene of the crime."

"And what was the crime, exactly?" Nick asks.

Talbot sits back in his chair. "Kieran has been killed."

The hand on my knee tightens.

Cicero scoffs. "Killed? Don't coddle them. He was *slaughtered*. There's nothing of him left in that cell."

Cicero's words bring vivid images to my mind, so much so that between one blink and the next, I'm staring at that bloodied cell once more.

I throw a hand to my mouth as bile rises, and I lurch forward, Nick up and behind me.

"Professor Cicero," Nick says, his hand now rubbing my back. "You don't believe Rhi is responsible? I mean, look at her. Just the mention of it is making her sick!"

I bring my hand from my mouth, looking Talbot right in his eyes, letting him see I have nothing to hide.

But the cheerful man I'd met my first day at Alystair is gone, replaced by the determined, hard-faced president of the university.

"Why were you there, Rhi?" His voice is without emotion.

"I told you," I say, narrowing my eyes. And then I launch into the full story – of how I woke up to hissing and thrashing, of how the Scyllas steered me directly to Kieran's cell in anticipation of a fight.

Talbot exchanges a curious look with Cicero.

"I think they knew the monster, the *real* monster was there, attacking Kieran," I finish.

"And why would the monster want to attack Kieran?" he asks.

I bite my lip, knowing I can't lie. But then I'd have to admit that I went to see Kieran which, I'm going to guess, will probably get both me and Lyncus in a shit load of trouble.

"You were going to question him, weren't you?" Nick interrupts, saving my ass.

Talbot glances warily back and forth between Nick and I, then blows out a puff of air. "Yes. We were awaiting the arrival of the Verity Ring. It would force him to tell the truth under any circumstances. Oddly, my abilities have been...lacking when I tried to discern the truth from Kieran 's lies. So, I requested the Verity Ring be delivered here, and I confirmed its arrival early this morning. Wilde, Cicero and I were on our way to Kieran's cell to retrieve him for questioning."

An insidious feeling creeps into my bones. Talbot's lie-detecting abilities didn't work on Kieran, which means whoever is helping him must be *extremely* powerful. "This monster knew it was going to get found out if Kieran was questioned. Who knew about the Verity Ring?" I ask.

"Just Cicero, Wilde, and myself."

I feel Nick straighten behind me, his hand gripping the back of the chair. "Perhaps you should look closer to home, Professor Talbot."

Though I expect Talbot to snap back, it's Cicero that approaches Nick. I turn just in time to see the burly man get right in Nick's face, sparing no breathing room.

"Don't you *dare* accuse one of us," he hisses. "You have no idea what we've been going through to find this monster."

Before Nick can respond, Wilde breezes through the office, the only tell-tale sign of her rattled composure a stricken expression twisting her perfect features. A small wisp of paper is wedged between her delicate fingers.

"Lyncus wasn't at his post because he was called back to the crypt." Her voice holds traces of disbelief, like she can't quite believe what she's saying, as she hands Professor Talbot the slip of paper.

"Who requested his presence back at the crypt?" Cicero asks.

It's subtle, but Professor Talbot's hands grip the paper a little tighter as his eyes move down the page and narrow in on the signature scrawled at the bottom.

"You, Cicero," he says, showing a now red-faced Cicero the note.

This...." Cicero's hands shake, the veins at his temples protruding. "I didn't write this!" He thrusts the paper at Wilde and Talbot. "I *swear* I didn't write this!"

Nick joins my side, jaw nearly hitting the floor. He grabs

my hand, and I sense his muscles tensing, ready to pull me behind him if this gets ugly.

Wilde darts her gaze to Talbot. "Is he telling the truth?"

The Professor stays silent for a moment, smoke-grey eyes studying Cicero. "Yes."

Cicero lets out a huge breath, leaving Nick and I exchanging confused glances.

"Rhiannon was telling the truth as well," Talbot continues. "Which means that this puzzle just continues to become more difficult to solve." He shakes his head. "Ms. Owens and Mr. Cervallos, please return to your rooms. I will call on you if I have any more questions."

I glance at Cicero beneath my lashes as Nick's hand gently squeezes to lead me out of the room. Cicero's cheeks remain reddened, his face twisted into a look of bewilderment. His eyes dance wildly from Talbot to Wilde to the paper in Talbot's hands, as though asking – no, *pleading* – for someone to believe him.

Nick's soft tug makes me realize I've halted, continuing to stare at Cicero. I've never liked the man, and it's no secret he doesn't seem to care much for me either. But right in this moment, a twinge of pity strikes my chest.

We step into the hall, the door closing behind us of its own accord.

"This is insane," Nick mutters as we head towards the doors.

"It's not Cicero."

"No? Then who wrote the note?"

"I have no idea. But this is getting so much more complicated."

Nick stops before the exit. "Let me run back to my room and grab you a jacket."

"No need," I tell him and push the doors open. Once again,

my body is the perfect temperature, though my breath curls in wisps of smoke in front of my face.

It takes a moment for me to realize Nick isn't beside me. He remains on the building steps, staring at me with his eyes narrowed.

"What?"

"You aren't cold?"

"No, though I don't think I'm impervious to frostbite." I glance down at my toes turning blue from the freezing ground.

Nick climbs down the few remaining steps, his face still twisted in a look of confusion. "When did this happen?"

I shrug, walking. "Right when I came outside this morning." The puzzled look on his face doesn't disappear. "Maybe it has something to do with the Scyllas. They wanted me to get here *fast*. I even asked if I could grab more practical clothing."

He stops again, touching my arm. "You talked to them?"

"Yeah. Well, I talked. They hissed."

Nick blinks several times, then resumes walking toward Northgate.

"What's wrong?" I ask, catching up to him.

"Nothing." The response comes quickly. Too quickly. He's a terrible liar. Nick pulls open the door to Northgate. I say nothing as we climb the stairs until I realize we stop on the second floor where my room is, and not the fourth.

"Can I come back to your room?" I hate the fear in my voice, the unease. I'm not sure if our previous conversation left Nick upset or weirded out by me, but right now, I can't fathom going back to my room without him. As it is, every time I close my eyes, the gruesome image of Kieran's cell is there, waiting. All I can think of is Nick's body pressed against my back, his breath tickling the nape of my neck – just as we fell asleep only a few hours ago.

Though I'm reluctant to admit it out loud, I need him to keep the nightmares at bay.

"Of course," he says without hesitation. "I just thought you might want to get comfortable in your own clothes first." Nick reaches for me, combing his fingers through the ends of my hair. "I'm not letting you out of my sight."

I let out a sigh of relief, melting into his arms. "I'm perfectly comfortable in these."

Nick pulls back, thumb sweeping across my lips. Those amber eyes pierce into mine, endearing.

"You're frightened," he acknowledges.

I shudder. "Nick, what I saw…"

He silences me with a press of his lips against mine. "I won't let anything happen to you."

I don't tell him it's not me I'm worried about, despite Kieran's warning of two warring sides after me. Whoever this is could've gotten to me plenty of times, and yet here I am. Instead, it seems the people around me are becoming collateral damage in this dangerous game I'm caught in the middle of. I have to re-focus, re-strategize, if I'm going to save the people I care about. In the game of chess, the King is arguably the most limited piece, moving only one space at a time in any direction. It feels like I've been doing the same thing. Moving along slowly, in different directions, taking too long to put the pieces of the puzzle together. One space at a time. But those are the rules of the game.

Which means if Kieran is correct, and I'm the King, I have to break the game.

CHAPTER

FORTY-THREE

Two months pass swiftly.

Just like the convoluted mystery that Nick, the girls and I are trying to solve, March weather is its own enigma.

One day the sun shines brilliantly, teasing us with hope of an early spring. The following day we're hit with a blizzard that wraps the entire campus in mounds of pristine snowfall.

The vernal equinox falls the day after the rogue snowstorm, on the Friday of an important party called Anthesteria, thrown by Eleusis, the secret society Nick belongs to. The society aptly named the party in honor of the ancient Athenian festival to celebrate the welcoming of warmer weather, to which of course, I scoff.

"It's thirty-five degrees," I tell Nick, as we sit in the library studying. "Warmer weather my ass."

He glances up from scribbling down notes, smiling. "The party is really to celebrate the vernal equinox, which is not about warmer weather, but new beginnings, transitions." He tosses the pen down in between his notebook. "It's why Circe's potion can only be administered then."

"You mean tonight," I say, something that was puzzling me now becoming clear. "Because the potion is not just going to free him from his bonds at Alystair, but the bonds tying him to his lynx form."

Nick nods. "Technically, tomorrow is the vernal equinox, so we can sneak down to the crypt at midnight tonight to give it to him."

"I just hope we don't have to use the fountain again," I mutter, closing my philosophy textbook. Part of my new schedule this semester included trading Economics for Philosophy, which I can't say makes me unhappy.

"I doubt it. That door is still there."

I furrow my brow. "The door we came through a few months ago?"

"Yeah," Nick says, lowering his voice even though he'd already been whispering. "I have a feeling Lyncus has spelled it so only you and I can see it."

"How intriguing."

"I'll say." He closes the notebook, glancing at his watch. "I don't know about you, but I'm done for the day. Want to get something to eat before the party?"

I nod, always eager to go to The Odyssey.

We leave the library, trudging through the snow-laden landscape of campus. I wear my heavy winter jacket, but only for appearances sake. Since the morning of Kieran's death, my body temperature involuntarily adjusts to inclement weather.

Nick and I had various discussions on this. At first, he tried to convince me I was part god. I took my concerns to Professor Talbot who shook his head and pulled my file. "One hundred percent Scylla," he'd said. And since before me, the last known record of Scylla was herself, he assured both of us it was quite possible regulating body temperature was one of her abilities.

That settled that.

Then, there was the matter of the murderer, who had not struck since the death of Kieran. Again, I find this puzzling. Why the hiatus? Where is the pattern? So far, Kieran's death is the only one that makes sense, seeing as he was about to divulge the identity of the monster.

Not to say that the break from death hasn't been welcoming. The girls and I spend more nights studying, laughing and enjoying each other's company rather than talking of murder and betrayal. Yet, every now and then, I think of Kieran's words, and when I catch myself laughing at something funny Zo said or smiling at Liv's adorable recount of her dates with Josh, the word *betrayal* slashes across my brain like a swipe of claws.

And Nick and I only continue to grow closer, which hasn't let me rule out the fact that *he* could be the one that betrays me, and I don't know what would be worse: to be betrayed by one of the girls that are like my sisters, or to be betrayed by the boy who holds my heart and soul.

Because I'm falling in love with him.

"Rhi?"

"Hmm?" I hadn't realized Nick was talking. I blink as a waiter clears the plates of our finished meals.

"You okay?"

"Yeah. Sorry. What were you saying?"

His eyes crease warily, reading my face for any signs of distress. I school my features to neutral. A perfect poker face.

"I said I'll be by around nine tonight to get you for the party."

"Oh. Sounds good."

Nick tilts his head, narrowing his eyes once more, and throws cash on the table.

Promptly at nine that evening, a soft knock sounds upon the door. Scar went out with Astrid, so I give myself one more look in the mirror before I open the door.

The sight of him in a suit will never cease to make my jaw drop. Crisp white shirt flawless against his golden-brown skin, the way his slacks hug his muscled thighs. Black hair swept away from his face, revealing startling amber eyes encased by long dark lashes.

Just as I'm thinking it about him, his full lips part and say, "Beautiful."

At hearing the word, I self-consciously slide my palms down my black dress. I opted for the midnight hue, remembering Nick's comment that black brings out the green in my eyes. The dress is made of fine silk, the curves of my body revealed through the delicate material. A slit travels up the right side, stopping at my mid-thigh. But it's not the front of the dress that caught my eye when I first saw it.

Nick makes a strangled noise in his throat as I step in the hall to join him, the backless dress exposing bare skin. I shiver as he brushes away curled tendrils of hair, one finger drifting lazily down my spine.

"Wait," he says, stopping me. "I have something for you." Nick reaches into his pocket and pulls out a white box with a blue ribbon. I smile as I take it from him, the ribbon coming undone with one small tug. Inside the box are two silver combs lined with gleaming pearls.

I hold up one of the combs to examine it, the smile on my lips growing wider. Nick grabs the other one, sliding into my hair. I hand Nick the other comb and feel it glide softly on the opposite side. I grab the lapels of his black jacket to draw him down for a kiss, before I pause.

"Do these have any special story behind them? Did you get them from a mermaid in exchange for giving her your legs for six months?"

Nick laughs. "No, Rhi. I got these from Amazon. I can show you the receipt if you like. I'm an Amazon Prime member," he finishes proudly.

"Shut up." I kiss him, smiling against his lips. "Thank you.

"Oh, there's one more thing." He fishes around in his right pant pocket and pulls out a dark, delicate material that glints off the firelight sconces in the hallway. Its glistening sheen makes me think it's satin.

Nick lowers his mouth to my ear. "Turn around."

I eye him warily, though an illicit warmth spreads throughout my lower belly, and I do as he asks. Nick's hands come around to my front, and he drapes the material over my eyes, securing it behind my head.

"Be honest, can you see anything?"

I shake my head, a protest on my lips. But then Nick's fingers indolently stroke the base of my spine, before dipping lower, his hand grazing the top of my ass. I let out a breathy exhale.

"Do you trust me?" His lips are once again at the base of my ear, his warm breath trailing down the side of my neck.

Licking my lips, I nod, and I feel his hand flatten against my lower back to guide me forward.

"Why am I blindfolded?" I ask.

Nick chuckles darkly. "We're a secret society, Rhi. We like to keep our meeting room...a secret. I'll take it off once we arrive, but it will go back on when we leave." Both of his hands grip me by my waist to steady me.

I follow his lead, the loss of my vision making my other

senses much more acute. Particularly, the sense of touch. All I can focus on are the feel of his fingers seeping through the sheer fabric of the dress. The thumb of his right hand strokes the bare flesh of my lower back, and although it's the smallest sensation, it manages to send jolts of electricity straight between my thighs.

"It's not so bad being blindfolded, is it?" Nick's voice is still deliciously low.

"No," I admit.

I brace myself for descending the stairs but find that Nick's steerage never veers from a slight turn here and there. In fact, it doesn't even feel as though we've left the building at all. It's not until a familiar chill settles upon my skin, and I inhale the stale scent of blood, that I know exactly where we are.

"We're in the dungeon," I state. My hands suddenly become clammy. Visions of Kieran's gruesome cell bombard my brain, and my breathing quickens along with my heartbeat.

I feel Nick move in front of me. Knuckles gently sweep across my left cheek. "Breathe, Rhi." He whispers. "If you want to go back, just say the word."

He'd said something similar, only a few months ago, when we'd discovered the tunnel underneath the Echidna fountain that led us to Lyncus. *Just say the word, and we'll go back.*

He gave me a choice then, and he's giving me a choice now.

I shake my head. "I'm okay."

His fingers lightly grip my chin. "You promise?"

"I promise."

One of Nick's hands leaves my waist, and the slow creak of bars reverberates in my ears. I'm guided forward, the soft press of stone now crunching around me. The stench of old blood is replaced by burning wood and smoke, the chill entirely suppressed as fire licks the air and fills the space with heat.

Voices permeate the silence and raucous laughter grows louder and closer as we continue to walk.

"There he is!" A cheery voice booms.

Nick's hands tighten around my waist, halting my steps. There's a slight tug at the back of the blindfold, and it falls from my eyes.

The room before me can only be described as a broken throne room. The room itself isn't large, comfortably fitting the thirty or so bodies that currently float about its parameters, chatting idly and sipping from golden chalices. Dark red paper curls away from the wall in various spots like the peel of an orange, and three sparkling chandeliers drip from its high ceiling. The far right wall boasts a long, rectangular table filled with an assortment of meats and various cheeses and steaming vegetables. I notice the opposite wall is lined with curtained alcoves, the drapes a purple so dark they appear black.

In the center of the room boasts a throne, its black cushioned seat frayed and worn. The garish, golden baroque frame is cracked along the top, and one of the arms is missing a section underneath. The voice that greeted us belongs to the body currently perched upon the throne, dark wavy hair falling to his shoulders, and his eyes, darker still, drink Nick and I in salaciously. He sits with one leg drawn up, his forearm resting upon his knee and the sleeves of his black shirt rolled up to his forearms.

"Cervallos," he grins, those dark, enticing eyes lasered on me, "you brought her."

Nick pockets the blindfold, seeming gloriously bored with who I assume is our host. But the hand that hasn't left my waist tightens possessively as he draws me into him. A dark smile tilts my mouth at his claiming.

"I did," he replies, a warning enveloping his tone. "But not for you."

The boy grins impossibly wide, and I expect to see a show of teeth. Instead, he swings his folded leg down and stands from the throne. As he approaches, I notice a faint shimmer around his lower lip, before I realize he has two piercings in the form of rings.

"Rude," he says to Nick. "It's my birthday."

I laugh at that and am stunned when both boys bestow me with serious looks.

"Oh," I say sheepishly. "Is it really your birthday?"

He grins again, and I don't like it. It's too sharp. Too knowing. "Yes." He steps into me. "What are you going to give me?"

"Jordan," Nick warns again. He says the name only once, laced with a threatening promise.

Our eyes lock, and I suddenly want to give Jordan anything and everything he wants. My body heats, flooding with arousal, and...

And it's gone.

I blink. Nick seethes beside me, but Jordan looks both perplexed and frustrated, his dark brows drawn together and a frown on his face.

"What are you?" I ask, with no small amount of morbid fascination.

"A snake," Nick spits.

Jordan laughs at that, meeting Nick's stony glare. "Again, rude." He then seems to think better of it. "But you're not wrong."

A snake? What a letdown.

"Jormungandr." Jordan states, noticing my obvious disappointment.

"I'm sorry, *what*?"

Jordan sighs heavily, like he's used to this reaction and

tired of explaining it. "Nick, would you do the honors? It's my birthday."

"You've said that," I point out. This kid is...odd to say the least. And what does Nick have to do with anything?

"It's the monster he's descended from," Nick explains, his golden eyes dark and brooding and completely focused on Jordan. "Jormungandr is a Norse monster, the Midgard Serpent. Jordy thinks he's special because it's prophesied that he will bring about the final battle between gods and monsters."

Jordy huffs. "I *am* special. Even my mom says so."

I laugh again. I can't help it. "Special, maybe. Ridiculous? Definitely."

Jordy glances from Nick to me, that cutting smile back on his face. "I like her, Nick. "How about you, Rhi?" A forked tongue darts out from between his lips, curling well past his chin, and I gasp. "What do you like?"

He stares at me with those smoldering, dark eyes again, and although I initially fell beneath his spell, nothing happens this time. Jordy squints in confusion, and that forked tongue once again makes an appearance.

"Enough, Jordy. I said she's not for you." Nick gestures vaguely. "There are plenty of women here to indulge your fantasies. Women who are actually susceptible to your powers," he finishes, a taunting smirk on his lips.

Jordy strikes a hand to his chest. "You wound me, Nicholas!" Quick as an adder, Jordy whips his hand out, grabbing Nick's shirt and drawing him close. "But you *do* owe me a gift," he says darkly, eyes flitting toward me.

Nick's hand comes over Jordy's, and I can see the way his grip tightens. "She isn't part of any gift, Jordy. Don't make me say it again." With that warning, he flings Jordy's hand away, causing the snake to tumble back a few steps.

It's then I notice that people have stopped and are staring, some whispering behind their hands and into the ears of their partners. My eyes narrow at Jordy, finding those two rings in his lips.

Anger flares in his eyes, the color changing from depthless black to blood red and then back again. Then, that chilling smile slowly takes form. "Snake bites," he says.

Confusion addles my brain. "I beg your pardon?"

He runs a forked tongue lazily over his bottom lip, still grinning too widely. "The piercings. That's what they're called." His dark eyes glint mischievously. "You seem enthralled by them."

My cheeks heat momentarily before I catch Jordy leaning into Nick, whispering in his ear. Jordy's tongue flicks the inner part of Nick's ear, and Nick barely flinches. I'm both impressed and surprisingly aroused.

Both boys straighten, and Jordy turns to me with a wink. "Enjoy the party, Rhi." He saunters away, throwing his arm around a girl with caramel colored hair and a dress that can be best described as strategically placed scraps of black fabric. Or not so strategically placed, considering she's half-naked.

"What was all that about?" I ask Nick, who continues to stare in Jordy's direction. He releases an aggrieved sigh.

"Jordy's a senior, and the president of the society. Every year, the acting president throws an elaborate party for their birthday, and we're required to bring gifts." Nick wrinkles his nose as he glances after Jordy one more time, who has returned to the dilapidated throne with the girl now straddling his lap. One hand grips a golden chalice while the other has disappeared beneath her dress.

"I'm guessing an Amazon gift card won't suffice?" I try to draw laughter out of Nick, but his expression remains solemn. I won't lie and say I'm not intrigued by the society's practice of gifting, and I want more information. "So you offer them women? Or men?" I add when Nick squints his eyes at me.

"It's more complicated than that." He gestures toward the table laden with food, and we make our way toward it. "It's not always about sex."

"Oh no?" I shoot a sideways glance at Jordy and the girl, who now appear to be fucking, judging by their moans and the fact that Jordy's pants are around his ankles.

Nick laughs and shakes his head. "She's not the gift." He lifts a carafe of dark red liquid and pours two cups, holding one out to me. "Wine?"

I take it and wrinkle my nose, expecting a pungent scent of berries and chocolate, yet something familiar makes its way into my nostrils: french toast, chocolate chip cookies, and cedarwood and vanilla.

"Is this Dionysian Frenzy?"

Nick gives me a wicked smile. "It's laced with it."

I bring the chalice to my lips but pause, remembering what happened the last time I drank too much. Although, considering it led me to spending the night in bed with the man standing before me, it wasn't *that* bad.

Nick must read my thoughts. "Don't worry. It's not as potent because it's mixed with the wine, and you won't get away with drinking that much while I'm around." His mouth widens beneath the lip of the chalice as he gulps the liquid down.

"Oh?" I raise a brow. "And just how do you plan on stopping me? You're not *my* brother Nick, and I don't need a babysitter." I take a large swig of the wine, delighted at the way the muscle in his jaw twitches and his eyes blaze with a challenge. I lick my lips pointedly before giving him my back.

His arm snakes around my waist before I barely take two steps. I feel his firm chest against my back and every hard inch of him pressed into my backside. I know that Dionysian Frenzy works quickly, but the way every nerve in my body fires chaotically and pressure builds so strong in my core that I need to clench my thighs together - that's all *him*.

Nick's tongue traces the shell of my ear. "You're right. I'm not your brother. The things I want to do to you are far from brotherly - far from even *gentlemanly*." He traces a finger down my spine, and I shiver.

"Tell me," I plead shakily.

"You sound so pretty when you beg," he continues to whisper in my ear. "But I'd rather show you."

There's a rush of cold air at my back, and when I whirl around, Nick is gone.

My eyes dart about the room, searching for blue-black hair and piercing gilded eyes, but it's as though he vanished into thin air.

"Annoying when that happens, isn't it?"

I turn toward the voice, full of mockery, now knowing who it belongs to. The corners of my mouth pull in a derisive smirk as I take in Jordy's disheveled appearance. He never bothered to fully tuck his shirt back in his pants, nor did he care to button it properly. The black shirt drapes across his pale chest and abdomen askew, buttons mismatched.

I bounce my gaze between the throne and him. "That was quick."

His eyes flash. I glimpse red. "Her pleasure isn't my concern."

"Said every man ever." I roll my eyes.

His answering grin can cut glass. "Let me rephrase: *her* pleasure isn't my concern." Jordy leans closer, that forked tongue close to grazing my lips. "But *yours* is."

I jerk back. The wine turns sour on my tongue. Panic creeps in like a slow slithering vine, threatening to tie me down as the implication of Jordy's words wrap around me. "But Nick said I wasn't for you."

"Relax, Rhi. Nicholas made it abundantly clear that I'm not to touch you, and I gave him my word. But -" the forked tongue flicks out again. "I have no doubt you wouldn't mind *him* touching you, hmm?"

The panic recedes, confusion taking its place. "I don't understand."

Jordy inclines his head, gesturing for me to follow. We head back toward the food table as he speaks. "You and I are very similar, Rhi. We're both rare monsters, the only ones of our kind. With that, comes rare abilities. You have telekinesis. Aside from hypnosis, I have the rare ability to siphon emotions."

I whip my head towards him, shock rippling through me. My reaction must please him. His lips curve indecently. He pours wine from the carafe into two gold chalices, offering me one as Nick did earlier. I reach for it but don't bring the chalice to my lips.

"I don't need to physically experience pleasure in order to feel it," Jordy explains. "If you give me permission, I can share yours."

I stare at him cautiously, waiting for the other shoe to drop. "So let me get this straight: you want Nick to fuck me, so you can get off?"

"That's my price," he says placidly, as though we are bargaining baseball cards rather than sexual favors.

"And if I refuse?"

Jody's eyes darken. I expect a hint of red, but only depthless black engulfs his irises. "Nick will owe me."

His statement is insidious, and I expect he won't elaborate on just what, exactly, Nick will owe him. My fingers find the pendant at my throat, remembering Nick has already sacrificed something for me. I won't let him do it again.

"Before I agree to this, I have questions."

Jordy raises a dark brow, inviting me to continue.

"Nick will be the one pleasuring me, and no one else?"

A single nod.

"And it will actually *be* Nick, himself? Not you or anyone shapeshifting or wearing his face or a glamour?"

Jordy smiles wickedly. "Clever. But no. Nick and only Nick will be between your thighs." His eyes peruse my body before he brings the cup to his lips and takes a drink. "And wherever else."

Heat floods my face as well as the exact spot Jordy mentioned. "Will you be watching?"

His sinful smile widens, and Jordy leans in. "Do you want me to?"

"No," I answer quickly.

Jordy chuckles. "Relax, Rhi. There's no kink shaming here. Some of us enjoy it when others watch."

I take a moment to scan the room, hoping to see Nick. Hoping that if I catch sight of him, my unease will dissipate and I can accept Jordy's offer, no holds barred. Instead, I toy with the pendant again, a thought worming its way into my brain.

"There's just one problem," I start, and Jordy raises two eyebrows this time. "Most powers don't work on me. You saw it first hand with your hypnosis."

"Ah." He finishes taking a gulp of wine. "Good point, except this ability isn't directly affecting you. In fact, quite the opposite: it's taking something away."

I mull this fact over for a bit. "So you're going to be stealing my pleasure? I won't feel anything?" Seems like a giant waste of time, really.

"Oh, you'll feel it, Rhi. I'm not stealing your pleasure, just... sharing it." He finishes with another too-wide grin and his forked tongue poking between his lips. "Do we have a deal?" Jordy holds out his chalice to me.

I look around the room one more time, still unable to locate Nick. I lick my dry lips, taking a deep inhale.

"Deal." I clink my glass with his and swallow the contents in one gulp.

Jordy follows suit, those dark eyes of his glistening with satisfaction and excitement. "Enjoy the party, Rhi. I'm sure Nick will find you soon." He winks and saunters off into the crowd.

NEARLY AN HOUR GOES by as I drift among the party-goers, making small talk. Some I recognize from fencing and just walking the school's testy hallways. All are older classmen and women, juniors and seniors. I appear to be the only freshman.

The second cup of laced wine hit about a half an hour ago, and I find myself relaxing, no longer looking over my shoulder for Nick. Dance music starts to play, some popular, bubbly tune. The Dionysian Frenzy continues to pump through my system, and I unabashedly dance with another girl. She pulls her tawny hair from the back of her neck and fans herself.

There's a shift in the tone of music as a new song comes on. It's slow but deliberate in its melody, its tune sinuous. Its sharp and obscene lyrics pierce my ears, the words settling themselves within my bones, awakening something primal within me.

Strong hands wrap around my waist. My nose fills with Nick's scent, a mixture of sugar and spice. Warmth spreads like honey from my chest, radiating down to my toes.

I bring one arm up and curve it behind me, grabbing on to

the back of Nick's neck. The two of us move together with the rhythm of the music. I grind into him hard, eliciting a low moan from deep in his throat. His hands stroke my body through the fabric of my dress, and I shiver with delight at the feel of his lips behind my right ear.

"Do you trust me?" Nick's voice is low and rough.

"Yes," I whisper. I'm not surprised when darkness clouds my vision as the satin blindfold is placed around my eyes once again. Nick's hands find my hips, guiding me away from the throng of bodies. I'm acutely aware of the sweat that has pooled beneath my breasts as the air cools the farther I move from the dancing bodies. Again, I marvel at the sensation of touch, of how that particular sense immediately heightens once my vision is obscured. I know the phenomenon occurs in regular humans, but the fact that it happens so quickly for me makes me wonder if it's the fact that I'm a monster with rare abilities.

Or perhaps it's just Nick. His touch. His proximity. His mere *presence*.

One of Nick's hands leaves my waist, and a small gust of air breezes past me. Nick takes my hand, pulling me forward, and my shoulder brushes thick but soft fabric.

The alcove. It must have been a curtain that I felt. He's taken me to one of the alcoves hidden behind the purple drapes. Soft moans and grunts drown out the music, my sense of hearing already heightened thanks to my innate monster, coupled with my loss of vision. Though I had no doubt sex was indeed what these private alcoves were for, my heart quickens at the thought of being surrounded by it, of what Nick will do to me within these walls.

"Wait," Nick says, and I stand idly as I hear him draw the curtains closed. He then stands in front of me, his finger tracing my lips. I exhale shakily, the anticipation coupled with not being able to see driving me insane.

"You agreed to this?" He asks, and I nod. "I want to hear you say it, Rhi."

I bite my bottom lip, fighting a smirk. Always about consent. "Yes, Nick." I reach to take off the blindfold.

His fingers wrap around mine. Tighten. "It stays on." He places my hands down by my sides, and his lips hover above mine. "I'm going to ask you again: do you trust me?"

"Yes," I say breathless.

"Good, because I wasn't lying about the things I want to do to you, Rhi." His mouth moves closer so that with every word he speaks, it brushes against my lips. "I think about you constantly. About the way you'll sound when I'm buried inside of you." He steps into me, forcing me back. "About how those claws of yours will feel tearing my back apart as I make you scream." He forces me back again, and I swear I'm not breathing. "About how you will taste..." Nick pauses as the backs of my knees hit what I assume is a bed or couch. "...when my tongue is between your thighs."

He captures my mouth in a brutal kiss just as I release an embarrassing moan. I try to wrap my arms around his neck but he forces them by my sides again. He tears his mouth from mine and shoves me down. I land haphazardly on my ass, but the fall is cushioned by something soft, and my fingers grip into sheets. A bed, then.

My fingers shake as I reach for him. I want to rip this fucking blindfold off. I want to touch him, to tear my claws down his back like he just said and mark him as mine.

He takes my hand, and for a moment, I think he's going to give in to my desperation and let me touch him. Instead, he pushes my finger past his lips and bites down with razor sharp teeth.

I cry out, attempting to yank my finger from his grasp, but Nick holds firm. Blood drips from the pad of my finger. Then, Nick's tongue is there, slowly licking the blood away. I imagine how he looks, bits of his dark hair falling into his eyes. Him towering over me, his eyes gilded and salacious as his tongue moves over my pointer finger, sucking gently as he licks the blood clean.

I could come from that vision alone.

"Keep your hands to yourself," he growls, taking one more luxurious lick. "For now." Nick releases my hand, and I draw it into my chest. His fingers come beneath my chin, tilting my head up, and his mouth is on mine once more. "I told you once, I wouldn't touch you unless you asked me." Nick flicks his tongue out against my lips. "Ask me, Rhi. Ask me to touch you."

He says it like a plea, desperation heavy in his words. Yet if I say no, or nothing at all, Nick will stop. He'd welcome whatever punishment or debt Jordy would bestow upon him. The plea isn't to save him from that fate. It's something primal. Something born of lust. Something I'm just as desperate for. So I utter the three words that will save us both.

"Touch me, Nick."

Nick makes a strangled noise in the back of his throat. "Lie back."

I lower myself down on my back, my breathing erratic. My heart thumps with such ferocity I expect my ribcage to burst any second. Yet through all of this, my core aches painfully. Even more so as the hem of my dress rises from my ankles and makes its way past my knees, Nick's hands moving deliciously slow over the tops of my thighs.

"Nick," I choke out, propping myself up on my elbows. He merely chuckles, pushing the silken fabric far enough that it pools around my abdomen. Then he pauses, releasing a throaty exhale. I'm reminded of the night I ended up in his room after my first experience with Dionysian Frenzy. My nightgown bunched in my hands, exposing my racy underwear and my naked thighs. I recall the primal look on Nick's face. I imagine that's exactly how he looks now.

The feel of his fingers edging my underwear causes my claws to finally tear free, and my claws tear through the sheets. He pushes my underwear aside and slides a finger down my center, which is already slick with arousal. I buck my hips at the feel of him, but Nick places one hand on my stomach and holds me down effortlessly.

"Fuck," he grinds out. "You're so fucking wet." I whimper at the loss of his fingers, only to hear him sucking them clean. "You taste like a fucking dream. Just like I knew you would."

I press my lips together to stifle another embarrassing groan and feel his fingers hook into the sides of my underwear.

"Lift that beautiful ass for me."

My body can't obey fast enough. Nick pulls my underwear down in one swift tug, clearing it free of my shoes. The sound of his knees hitting the floor stokes the burning ache between my legs, the image of him kneeling before me like an acolyte flooding me with even more desire.

Nick's hands are on my thighs, his grip firm yet gentle as he nudges them farther apart. I tremble, the feel of his mouth inching closer to my center nearly driving me over the edge already. His lips trail over the skin of my thigh, tongue flicking out and licking intermittently. He stops just before he reaches my center, biting the tender flesh of my inner thigh. I cry out again, the sharp pain causing the ache between my legs to become downright unbearable.

"I hope you don't mind sharp teeth, Rhi..." Nick's voice trails, his warm breath tickling my most sensitive area. I brace myself, anticipation nearly causing me to unravel as I await the feel of his mouth and his tongue. "...Because I'm going to fucking devour you."

His tongue slides right into me, and if it weren't for the strength of his hand holding me in place, I would have launched right off the bed. I try to clench my thighs together, but Nick uses both hands to force them open, his fingers pressing into them so hard I know I'll have bruises in the morning.

I feel him pull away, and the absence of his tongue is excruciating.

"If you want my tongue, you better keep these pretty thighs apart," he warns. "Because I have plans for my fingers too."

Proving his point, he plunges two fingers inside me and returns his tongue to the bundle of nerves at my center. His tongue swirls and sucks with just the right amount of pressure, his fingers pumping in and out in tandem with the rhythm of his mouth. And his *teeth*. He wasn't lying about his teeth. They graze my sensitive flesh, my body wracked with jolts of electricity from the intensity.

My core tightens as pressure wraps around my spine, my orgasm building. He told me not to touch him, but I could fucking care less about his rules right now. I tangle my fingers in his thick hair, pressing his face even harder into me. Yet Nick doesn't flinch. Doesn't pause consuming me with his mouth and tongue, *devouring* me like he promised. Instead, a laugh reverberates against my clit.

"So fucking needy," he murmurs, his tongue still working. I grind against his face, hardly able to conceal my moans any longer. "Come for me, Rhi." Those four words cause me to unravel entirely. I arch my back and cry out, Nick's hand still holding my hips in place. His tongue continues to lick and suck well after my orgasm subsides, and I lie writhing beneath his palm. He finally pulls away and gently guides me upright.

My fingers shaking, I push the blindfold off my eyes, the sight of him leaving me breathless. He stands before me, his lips glistening with my arousal. Nick's eyes never leave mine as he swipes a thumb across his lower lip and dips the finger into his mouth, savoring it.

Savoring *me*.

I lunge for him like a savage beast. I throw myself at his body, frantically clawing his clothes. I take his mouth in mine, tasting myself on his lips. Nick pulls back, eyes dark and gilded. The question is there. The longing. All I have to do is answer it. But the arch of my body into his isn't enough, the grip of my fingers into the back of his neck, nor the fact that his mouth and tongue just devoured the place where I now want his cock. None of that is enough. Nick wants a verbal response.

He wants *permission*.

I open my mouth, ready to give in. Ready to give us both something we've wanted for way too long.

A strange chiming interrupts my speaking. I reach into his pants pocket to retrieve his phone. An alarm sounds, drawing both of our gazes down to the numbers on the screen.

Midnight.

"Lyncus," Nick exhales.

I nod, regret flooding me as I understand that the moment between Nick and I is broken. This comes first. Finally, after months of waiting, it's time. Finally, we will discover the monster that hides within these walls and put a stop to it, once and for all.

CHAPTER

FORTY-FOUR

I slide my underwear back on, the heat of Nick's gaze searing me. He watches intently, as though in a daze, those bright amber eyes trailing up my thighs, lasering in on the exact spot his face was only moments ago.

Nick shakes his head, as if he's clearing his thoughts. "I swear, once we find out who and what this monster is, I'm taking you back to my room to finish what we started."

"Is that a threat or a promise?" I grin slyly.

He dangles the blindfold in front of me. "Both."

Nick secures the blindfold around my eyes and once again guides me from the alcove. The sounds of the party fade as we make our way through the dungeon and away from Westbourne. We've been walking only five minutes before he gently squeezes my waist, halting me from going any further. Nick pulls the blindfold from eyes, and there it is: the door we'd come through months before in the same spot I'd seen it, a few doors down from Nick's own room.

We descend the stairs hand in hand, my stomach a tangle of chaos. This is it. The question that has been haunting our lives since the day before classes began will finally be answered.

The door at the bottom of the staircase is already open, as though Lyncus knew we were coming.

The Cat-King rests in another lazy position, this time on the couch Nick and I were...what did Lyncus call it?

Mating.

As we approach, he grins with a mouthful of fangs, an eagerness to his eyes. "Don't the two of you look smashing."

Nick reaches into his pocket and holds the vial before Lyncus. The emotion in his green and gold eyes shifts from eagerness to hunger. "Here it is, as promised."

"I'll need you to open that vial." He waves a large paw. "These can be very cumbersome when dealing with that sort of thing."

"First, tell us about the monster," I demand.

"No can do, Rhiannon with the sharp-tongue. I want the potion first. Then, and *only* then, shall I tell you what you wish to know."

Nick snatches the vial from Lyncus's line of vision. "You must *really* enjoy being a lynx."

The Cat-King offers one of his wide, lazy smiles, sharp teeth gleaming like the deadly point of a blade.

"I've been in this form for centuries. What's a few more?" The King climbs off the couch, circling Nick and I the same way Circe did me. Slow. Predatory.

"*You* on the other hand, have much more to lose. The incubus won't be the last to die." Lyncus concludes his circle of us, gaze resting on me. "Don't you want to know who is going to betray you Rhiannon?"

I still, squeezing Nick's hand.

"What's he talking about, Rhi?" Nick turns his head to me.

I keep my eyes fixed on Lyncus, coils of dread unwinding in my chest.

"You're worried it's him, aren't you?" Another flash of his teeth in a mocking smile. "Or perhaps it's one of the girls you love so dearly, whose lives you hold above your own." Lyncus brings his large maw close to my face. "I can tell you this: the monster will lead you to the betrayer. Not right away, but in time, much will be revealed."

"Give him the vial, Nick." I feel Nick's penetrating gaze, so I meet it. "Circe will be looking for me if Lyncus remains missing. We can't afford another enemy, especially not someone with her power."

Understanding dawns on his face, and his eyes fall to the pendant at my neck. Nick pops the cork off the top of the vial.

Grinning, Lyncus sits on his hind legs, tips his massive cat head back and opens his large mouth.

Nick looks at me one more time for assurance, and I nod. He steps forward and pours the black liquid down Lycnus's throat.

Lyncus's mouth closes, his body shuddering from what seems to be the effects of tasting something foul. But the shudders continue to wrack his body, turning into horrifying convulsions. The King screams in agony as his bones twist and break, his form starting to become more human than animal. I grip Nick's arm in terror.

It ends nearly as quickly as it began, with a stunning human man standing before us. Bare chested, his waist is draped in a combination of red and brown leather and cotton, muscled legs wrapped to his knees in brown cords that give way to sandals. His defined arms are encased at the bicep with shimmering gold cuffs, as are his wrists. A brilliant gold ring adorns the ring finger of his left hand.

"Is that...." I trail, allowing myself to fully take in the King in his human form.

Lyncus pants wildly, staring wide-eyed at his palms as he brings them in front of his face. He turns them over, wiggling his fingers, and then runs one hand through a corn-silk mane that falls to his shoulders.

"A wedding ring?" he answers me, smiling. "Yes, it is."

I attempt to pry, wondering if his wife is Circe, before he interrupts me. "We haven't much time." Lyncus glances around nervously as Nick and I exchange our own glances of unease.

"The monster you seek is one of the ancient ones, thought to have been imprisoned, but was set free."

"Set free why? And by whom?" Nick questions.

"He was released to retrieve something of great value, hidden where they cannot tread." The King's gaze, now blue and green absent of the gold ring, pins me.

"Pay attention, Rhiannon. You are a key piece in this monster's blood path. *You* are the endgame."

I shake my head. "Then why am I still alive?"

He grins, and even without his mouthful of sharp teeth, it's still deadly. "It is not your death it seeks."

A tremble rattles the floor; Lyncus snaps his head up, eyes darting frantically before they once again settle on me. "We're running out of time. You've been researching Rhiannon. Revisit your work. Watch those closest to you. The answers are right before your eyes."

King Lyncus's body shimmers at the edges. The floor violently shakes. Nick grabs to steady me, while we both fight to keep from falling.

"What the hell is that?" He exclaims.

"That," Lyncus says, "is another monster. Leave. *Now.*"

"What other monster?" I ask, mouth agape. And then, realization strikes. "The one that guards the crypt?"

Lyncus's body is nearly translucent, and I realize whatever magic was in that potion is causing him to disappear.

"No. The monster that guards *me*," he finishes, before vanishing completely.

Nick and I only have seconds to look at each other in horror. An inhuman growl echoes beneath us, and before we have a chance to react, the ground erupts, bits of dirt and floor spraying in every direction.

I'm thrown backwards and away from Nick, landing roughly on my side. I roll over swiftly, just in time to see the body of a giant, white worm emerge through the wide hole in the ground.

Dirt falls into its wide-open mouth, a pair of crude fangs protruding from its upper and lower lips. Its body is sectioned in ring-like segments of bulging white flesh. The worm lets out a ravenous cry before it lands with a thud that once again shakes the entire room.

And the smell...Gods, that smell. It's putrid, foul. Death incarnate.

The Scylla heads are hissing wildly, writhing and thrashing. I leap to my feet, just as the worm turns its head in my direction. It appears to sniff, though I can't make out any semblance of a nose. But its mouth drops, pools of saliva dripping from the corners.

It's hungry, and evidently, I smell fabulous.

My own venom gathers as my teeth descend and my claws unsheathe. Far away and almost incoherently, Nick screams my name. The only audible sounds are my own rapid heartbeat and the thrashing and hissing of the Scylla heads.

The worm lets out an angry screech, charging for me on its

belly. It's fast, but my whips are faster, and they lash out at the body of the worm just as it opens its mouth to devour me.

They don't just strike the worm. They *eat* it. It cries out in pain and rears back as two bite marks the size of an automobile mar its flesh, black blood pouring from the wounds and spilling to the floor.

"Rhi!" I finally hear Nick yell, his voice coming from somewhere else in the room. The Scyllas rear back, preparing for another strike, when something crashes into my right leg. Searing pain engulfs my thigh. I scream in agony, falling on my back, my head swimming with blackness as it slams against the floor.

The pain in my leg is burning, and I gingerly touch my outer thigh to discover a deep gash. I feel serrated skin and muscle underneath, and nearly pass out from that thought.

A large *splat* lands on my forehead, and I force my eyes open. The worm hovers above me, inhaling my scent, lips curling back to further expose its fangs. My scream catches in my throat.

Then it stills as a squelching noise floods my ears. The worm's mouth agape, it jerks forward, like it's choking, and then its head falls, completely severed from its body with a sickening *thump* to the side. The body slumps at my feet.

My eyes are immediately drawn to Nick. He stands with his claws unsheathed, sweeping to the floor in jagged, pointed tips. His shirt is splattered with red and black blood, as is his face, and his eyes, normally so gilded, are wholly black, absent of pupils. He breathes heavily, chest rising and falling, as those black orbs remain fixed on the worm. Nick draws back his lips in a terrifying snarl, his teeth no longer flat and square but sharp and jagged, and like my dream, I see *rows* of them.

And that's when I realize he must have transformed into this. The monster. The one he's always so afraid of letting out.

Nick doesn't look for me. His stare lingers on the worm, sizing up his victory. His expression is completely feral, and I don't know if I should speak to coax him into returning to me or if I should let him return on his own.

A surge of pain sparks against my thigh and I gasp, gritting my teeth. Nick snaps his attention to me, eyes creasing into dark slits. The Scylla heads are up and squirming again, hissing at him. My teeth throb and an influx of venom invades my mouth. My body recognizes him as a threat. A predator.

And every inch of him screams it. The way he tilts his head, ever so serpentine, a snake considering its prey. Power encompasses him like a magnetic field, darkness and shadows swirling about him as though they are his to command at will. He is death, terror, a creature born of nightmares.

He is the most beautiful thing I've ever seen.

I will my heart to slow, my breath to still. I cannot come across as prey to him. If anything, I have to be his match. His equal.

I force myself to stand, leaning heavily on my left leg. Air rushes up against my right thigh, the slit of my dress having been made even deeper by a further rip. I feel the blood pouring out, trickling down my leg. Nick's still black eyes follow the blood and his nostrils flare, mouth twitching.

"Come on," I say, beckoning him with a claw. "I'll go easy on you."

Nick's face doesn't change, nor do his eyes. Any hope I had that he would recognize my voice is lost. He prowls toward me, the Scylla heads loud and urgent in my ear. As he gets closer, he cocks his head, listening. He smiles.

He is the most terrifying thing I've ever seen.

There's no space between us now, the Scylla heads snapping their jaws at his proximity. Nick continues to slowly tilt his head from left to right, his smile the curve of a serpent's tail.

And then it dawns on me: *he can hear them.*

Those black eyes whip to my face. Stare into my eyes. He reaches with deadly claws into my hair and pulls out one of the pearled combs.

The smile falters.

His eyes are back on me, and finally, *finally* I see the tiniest spark of recognition. Nick's gaze trails down the bridge of my nose, outlines my lips.

The black in his eyes recedes.

Now almost fully amber, they find the pendant at my neck and go wide.

His claws disappear. His fangs vanish. Staring back at me are the bright eyes I know and love.

Nick falls to his knees.

CHAPTER

FORTY-FIVE

I sink to the floor and reach for Nick's hands. They sit limply in his lap, his head bowed in either shame or exhaustion – maybe both – black tendrils of hair dipping toward his brow.

He breathes shakily, and I cup his cheek with one hand, lifting his face. Nick's lips are parted, eyes wide and glassy. His bottom lip trembles as he continues to search my face.

Nick swallows. "Did I...Did I hurt you?"

"No," I whisper. "You saved me."

"It," he says weakly. "It saved you."

"No," I argue. "*You* did." I bring my other hand to fully cup his face. "And you came back to me."

Nick exhales deeply, eyes fluttering closed. "I was pinned down by a piece of the floor. I saw the Indus worm go after you, and I didn't think. I just reacted. I needed to get free." His eyes open. "I thought I could just draw some strength from the monster, enough to move the debris off me. But I couldn't control it." He lets out a shuddering breath, dropping his head once more.

"Keep your head up," I scold and tilt his chin towards me. "You don't have to apologize for what you did. For saving my life. The point is that you *won*, Nick. You beat it. You came back to me."

"I came back to you," he repeats, voice tinged with relief. His eyes search my face, looking for reassurance and finding it.

I glance around the wrecked room. "Let's get out of here. I'm sure the Professors will have been alerted to the disturbance by now." Nick lets me help him to his feet, and I do my best to hide the pain shooting down my leg.

"Lyncus played us, you know," he says as we carefully skirt around the gaping hole in the room.

I let out a deep sigh. "I know. I should have expected he wouldn't have just *told* us who the monster is." I pause for a moment, mulling over the King's parting words. "He said the monster was one of the ancient ones. Does that mean anything to you?" I glance at him.

"I would have thought it meant something to *you*," Nick side-eyes me as we ascend the stairs. The pain in my leg is agonizing as the serrated skin pulls further apart with my movements.

I scowl. "I've been doing research with Kassi, but I don't remember anything about any-" I throw up air quotes – "'ancient ones'. I'll grab my notebook from my room tomorrow and see if there's something in there that can help us."

Nick pushes open the door to his room, and my bravado of ignoring the pain comes to a crashing halt. I drop to my knees, biting my tongue to keep from crying out.

He's beside me in a flash. "Where are you hurt?"

I stretch my legs in front of me, pulling the dress open to reveal the wound.

Nick lets out a low hiss. "Why didn't you tell me you were injured?"

"I didn't think it was that bad," I lie, my breath shaky.

Nick carefully hoists me up in his arms and places me on his bed, blood traveling in rivulets down my leg and landing in dark droplets on his floor. I grimace as I sit, the wound opening as my leg bends.

Nick curses, gathering his black sheets and pushing them against my thigh. "Keep that pressed against your leg. I'll be right back."

I do as he says, closing my eyes, gritting my teeth through the sharp sting – though it's fading.

Nick returns with a towel, kneeling in front me. "Let me," he says, and I drop the sheets, revealing the wound. He starts patting the area around it, wiping the blood away. I bite my lip as I anticipate the burning that will come once he applies pressure, but nothing happens. Aside from slight tenderness, the stinging is absent.

He continues to pat the wound slowly, eyes creasing then enlarging as he takes in the gash. "It's healing," he says, voice laced with marvel.

"Let me see." Nick removes the towel, and sure enough, the angry gash has now receded to a thin red line.

I breathe a sigh of relief, but Nick stands abruptly, chucking the bloodied towel to the corner of the room.

"What's wrong?" I ask, as he places his back to me. I stand up slowly; though the gash itself healed, putting pressure on my right leg is still a little painful. "Don't we all heal quickly? Being terrifying monsters and all." I try to put a touch of humor in my voice as I approach him.

When Nick faces me, he has a probing look, like he's been illuminated to something he was unable to see before. "Not that quickly." His voice is low, contemplative.

"Oh, not this again," I tell him as I head toward the bathroom to wash the blood from my hands. I have a feeling he's going to revisit the "you're part god" argument.

His fingers wrap around my wrist, spinning me to face him. "Who are your parents, Rhi?"

I step back, my wrist still encased by his fingers. "They're humans."

Nick steps into me, breath quickening. "I mean your *real* parents."

"I don't know," I whisper, halted from moving further back by the wall. Nick presses up against me, every hard inch of him melding into my body.

My own breath hitches as he releases my wrist and his hand brushes the tear in my dress, thumb stroking the light scratch that was once a gaping wound.

Every nerve in my body fires at once, his eyes darkening to burnt gold. The thumb of his other hand strokes my cheek, tracing the curve of my lips before his entire hand settles behind my neck.

"There's something Lyncus said that bothers me." The hand on my thigh moves inward, tracing lazy, indolent circles as it moves higher...higher...then pauses.

I can barely think. "What?"

Nick brings his face to mine, lips brushing my own as he speaks. "Do you really think I would betray you?"

He has me in a vulnerable position, one where I would say anything just to feel his fingers travel inward. But I try my best to shake it away and take this moment to look at him. *Really* look at him.

His beautiful face, all sharp angles and chiseled features. The face that not so long ago was twisted into an expression of undiluted terror. The eyes that were night-black and depthless. The dark power that emanated from him, threatening to consume me where I stood.

And yet he fought it. And came back to me.

Do you trust me?

"No," I whisper. "Not you. It would never be you."

Nick's shoulders relax, releasing tension. I lean up to brush my lips softly against his – a silent invitation.

He teases me with his wolf grin, fingers resuming their soft exploring. "My tongue in between your thighs earlier wasn't enough for you?"

"No," I pant.

He tsks. "Greedy." His mouth trails my jaw until it reaches my ear. "You know you need only ask."

I glide my palms up his shirt, fingers resting lightly on his chest before I grip the fabric and jerk him forward. "I'm not asking you, *Nicholas*. I'm telling you. Fuck me," I whisper against his lips.

His hand disappears completely underneath the dress, and I bite my lip as his lithe fingers skim the edge of my underwear, before hooking inside them. Nick groans in approval when he slides one finger easily inside me and wastes no time adding another.

I let out a low moan as I lower one hand to grip his waist and bring the other to his face. Blood still paints my fingers, leaving bloody trail marks where I touch him. I start to pull my hand away, but Nick presses harder into me, letting out a sensual growl as he thrusts his hand at a maddening pace.

"Don't." His voice is a low rumble of thunder. "I want to see exactly where you touch me."

Nick cuts off another moan from the back of my throat when he crushes his lips against mine. My grip on his waist tightens, the hand at his face slipping around his neck to pull him closer. His tongue sweeps into my mouth as I open for him and taste him hungrily. Those fingers of his are deft, clever, a spiraling ache making its way to my core.

My claws unfurl, tearing through the side of his shirt. Nick chuckles as he moves his lips from my mouth and traces them along my jawline...to my neck...and then the soft spot between my neck and shoulder as he slips the thin strap of my dress down to my elbow. His hand comes to squeeze my breast as he drags his sinful lips lower to the tender flesh, taking my nipple in his mouth. I cry out as I feel the sharp point of teeth, but the pain only serves to bring me closer to the edge as Nick pumps the hand in between my legs in tandem with my ragged breaths.

He pulls back enough for me to see blood dripping from his lips. *My* blood. Rather than feeling disgusted, the sight of my blood coating his mouth fuels my own unwholesome appetite. I lean forward and lick those sensuous lips, the taste like a sweet ambrosia, driving me further toward oblivion. Nick's fingers curve and hit a spot inside me that has my vision nearly blackening. He captures my mouth and again draws blood as he sinks his teeth into my lower lip.

"I want you to come again for me," he demands against my lips, his tongue lapping up the blood dripping from my mouth. I dig my claws into the skin at his waist, flesh tearing beneath my fingers. My body obeys Nick's command as my back arches and my hips grind against his hand.

"*Fuck.*" I breathe into his shoulder as my body comes down from the wave of pleasure, and I let my teeth sharpen just enough to return his love bite.

Nick lets out a dark chuckle, and the hand that was between my legs tightens on my thigh. He directs my attention by taking my chin between his thumb and forefinger.

"Menace," he says, his golden eyes dark and ravenous.

It's that look that sets my body fire again, and I know I need more. I need his hands, his mouth, gods, even his fucking *teeth* everywhere, fangs and all.

I sheathe my claws and place both hands under his shirt, fingers exploring the hard lines of muscle, the dip that falls perfectly beneath his pants.

Gods, why are there *so* many buttons? "You have more of these, right?" My breath is ragged and rough.

He's still wearing his wolfish grin, which used to infuriate me, and now only makes me want to bite into those sensuous lips. "Go for it," he says, understanding exactly what I plan to do.

I take a clawed fingernail and tear down the front of his shirt, buttons falling off left and right until there are none in my way, and I push it from his shoulders into a puddle of ivory on the floor.

My hands rest against his chest, his heart thundering beneath my palm, matching my own fiercely pounding heart beat for beat.

But not from fear. Only from desire. From want. From... something else. Something that's making my chest tight and my throat burn and something I know I've never felt for anyone else.

My bloodied fingers hook into the skin at his chest, and the other strap of my dress falls. Nick's hands peel the gown off slowly, torturously, as he leaves a trail of kisses from my collarbone, to the top of my breasts, down to my navel, his tongue flicking, leaving me trembling with every graze.

When the dress is nothing but a heap of silk at my feet, I look down, Nick's grin still fiendish as he slides those wicked hands up the sides of my legs and hooks his fingers into my underwear.

"You have more of these, right?"

I bite my bottom lip as I smirk. "Go for it." He lets his claws loose, wild and long and beautiful as they tear through the thin fabric, and my underwear are now nothing except shreds of lace.

I stand before him completely naked yet have never felt more beautiful. More comfortable. More *empowered*. Nick rises, those beautiful amber eyes taking in every inch of me, as though he is memorizing every curve, every dip, every scar that adorns my skin. His lips part, hands shaking as they reach for me, caressing the arc of my waist. Nick takes his time, pressing his lips back to mine, tongue sweeping inside my mouth in slow, agonizing strokes that have me wondering what it could do elsewhere on my body.

My hands find the waistband of his pants, fumbling with the belt buckle before I all but yank it loose and tear the button along with it. I hear the slump of the fabric falling to his ankles, the shuffle of his feet as they kick the pants loose. Yet never once does his mouth leave mine, lips and tongue caressing with expert precision, as if this is a language he is more than fluent in.

His hands are as skilled as his mouth, stroking my body with just the right amount of pressure, and I slide my entire hand below the elastic band of his boxers, savoring the long, hard length of him in my palm as he says my name. Low. Raw. Guttural.

The only article of clothing left between our bare bodies disappears, and I'm hoisted against the wall in one swift movement, Nick pressed against me and the blazing fire roaring inside me all gloriously unbearable.

Then his bed is beneath me, and I'm beneath him, wondering why his head is turned and I no longer feel the heat and demand of his lips or both of his hands exploring my skin with such urgency they might leave handprints.

And then I realize where his one hand has gone, and what his eyes seek. The drawer of his nightstand is open, and I hear the tear of foil once his fingers find what they're looking for.

A delicious thrill runs through me as Nick shifts his body, eyes darting downward just once between us before his gaze settles back upon mine.

I continue to trace my hands down the hard muscles of his back, feeling the crevice of his spine before the base of it dips.

Both of his hands are now on either side of my head, Nick bracing himself on his forearms. His eyes, saturated with hunger but also hesitation, search my face.

I take his face in my hands, drawing him back down to me, making sure that with each stroke of my tongue against his lips, his ear, his neck, I erase any worry, any uncertainty.

And then there's no room left for uncertainty for either of us as Nick pushes inside me with one hard thrust.

A small gasp escapes my lips as my body adjusts to him, my arms hooked underneath his own and my hands – free of claws – grip his upper back. Nick moves slowly at first, his gaze upon me reverent, and for all the times I'd closed my eyes before, I can't take my eyes off his face.

"Gods," he breathes, his voice gravelly. "You're fucking perfect, Rhi."

The slow pace he sets I know is for my benefit, but I don't want him gentle. Tame. I want him *unleashed*.

I want him monstrous.

I let my claws pierce the skin around his shoulders, a small amount of blood pooling underneath my fingertips, and I lock my ankles around the small of his back. Nick drops his head to mine, growling. "I'm barely holding on to my control."

"I know," I say against his lips, taking a bite of them for good measure. Nick's golden eyes flare with heated longing. "I don't want you in control. I want you unhinged, Nicholas. *Ruin me.*"

Those last two words are all it takes for him to abandon his restraint, slamming into me with such force it drives both of us up the bed. We move together, the feel of his lips against my own, against my skin, adding to the overwhelming sensation that I'm aflame and would gladly burn for him. Nick pays attention to my every gasp, every shudder, every moan, shifting and reacting so that waves of ecstasy build so deep, I find my claws unfurling, and I tear through the sheets as though not to harm his skin.

Nick's hands join mine, bringing them back beside my head, gripping so fiercely it's as though he's doing everything to keep us conjoined. And just as the blaze threatens to engulf me, he crushes his mouth on mine, a subtle hint of darkness, of the monster, reflected in his otherwise bright eyes.

My spine ripples with pleasure, and I grind against him as the orgasm overtakes me, Nick's mouth swallowing my cries of ecstasy. He pounds into me with one final, powerful thrust, chasing his own wave of pleasure before he removes his mouth from mine and collapses against my chest. Nick shudders as I run my fingers through his hair, my body still humming from the feel of his skin against mine, of him still being inside me.

Nick finally looks up at me, eyes bright and still ravenous. He reaches to wipe sweat-matted hair from my forehead. "That was..."

"I know," I say, breathless.

"I still can't get enough of you."

"Yeah?" I smirk, raising a brow. "Think you can go again?" I know he can. I feel him hardening inside me already.

Nick flashes me his signature grin, a devilish glint to his eyes. He pulls out of me slowly, turning toward his nightstand to retrieve another condom. I prop myself up on my elbows, my eyes widening when he turns to me and is already fully erect. My mouth waters with the idea of him inside me again, of his mouth and hands on me.

"Get up," Nick commands, voice laced with a delicious darkness that has my blood roiling and wetness pooling between my thighs.

I stand up just as he demanded, gazing up at Nick from beneath my eyelashes. He meets my stare, the beast in his eyes unmistakable, and I know that I'm going to get the version of Nick I'd wanted from the beginning. The one that's going to ruin me.

The monster.

Nick takes my hand and guides me toward the wall across from the bed. The wall where all of this started.

"Turn around."

I shoot him a defiant glare, despite knowing it will only rile the beast. I'm counting on that. "Make me."

Nick's nostrils flare, eyes darkening hungrily. I don't have a chance to protest - not that I want to - when his firm hands grip my waist and spin me to face the wall. I throw my arms out to brace myself from falling forward. Nick has already positioned himself behind me, and I realize that I'm right where he wanted me all along: bent forward and primed for his taking.

His hard length is pressed against my entrance, and Nick leans forward so I can feel his breath at the base of my ear.

"Good girl," he praises, sending an illicit thrill down my spine. As though he can see me tremble, he traces that shiver with the tip of a claw. A sharp sting follows the path he makes, and the feel of his tongue replaces the pain as he licks the blood from the base of my spine to in between my shoulder blades. I grind my ass back into him, silently begging for him to take me.

"What was it that you said earlier, Rhi?" His arm hooks

around my waist, and his fingers work the tight bundle of nerves at my center.

"Fuck," I hiss. Why the fuck is he asking questions? Earlier? Earlier when? "I don't know."

His hand disappears from between my legs only to wrap around my hair and tug. My neck arches, and Nick's lips are at my ear again. "Think, Rhi."

I can't think. Not when he's doing exactly what I wanted. Handling me exactly like what I am - a formidable monster and not some breakable damsel.

Oh.

"I said I wanted you unhinged."

Nick growls in approval, and he pushes himself inside me. "Do you still want me to ruin you?"

I whimper at the sinful promise in his voice, wriggling my hips to get him to move, but Nick doesn't budge.

"Yes."

Nick pulls out completely, the loss of him more punishing than his tight grip on my hair. "Then beg for it."

"Fuck you," I snarl. Nick presses his cock against me again, just enough so he's barely inside me. Oh gods, this is fucking *torture.*

Nick makes another sharp tug at my hair like it's a reign and a splinter of pain lances through my scalp. "You already did, but this time, I'm fucking *you.*" He slides in a little deeper. "Now, *beg.*"

I give up, the ache between my legs unbearable. "Please."

I can almost see the smug, conquering grin on his face as he says, "Please, what?"

I use the wall as leverage to push back and impale myself on him. "Please, Nick. *Ruin me.*"

I barely get the last word out before he slams into me. He pounds into me with such ferocity I can hardly use my hands as leverage anymore. But Nick holds me in place, his sharp clawed-hands digging into the skin at my waist and the other wound tightly in my hair.

"You're fucking perfect, Rhi. Taking my cock like it was made for you." Filthy phrases continue to spill from that unholy mouth, and my core tightens as another wave a pleasure crests and threatens to crash with each punishing thrust. My arms give out, and I rest against the wall on my forearms. Nick removes his grip on my hair and grabs my chin, turning my face towards his. He places a brutal, savage kiss against my mouth rich with the taste of blood and dark promises.

"Don't give up on me yet," he says with his lips brushing against mine. With each thrust more and more ruthless. "I want those pretty lips screaming my name as you come around my cock."

My body shudders and stars explode behind my eyes as a powerful orgasm ripples through me, and I come undone just as Nick demanded.

Screaming his name.

FORTY-SIX

I wake the following morning to a soft whisper in my ear: "You owe me new sheets."

I peek at the surface of the bed with one eye, then open both fully.

Nick's sheets are nothing more than scraps of black ribbons lying in erratic strips across my skin. The warmth I'd felt all night long was from his body alone.

""You might want to add a new desk lamp to that tally," I observe, noticing his desk is also in disarray. The poor lamp hangs limp and broken. Thank gods we had the sense to move his laptop before we took our activities from the wall, to the desk, to the floor, and back to the bed again.

He smiles against my neck. "I needed a new one, anyway." His teeth graze against tender flesh, tongue flicking out intermittently. My skin pebbles beneath his mouth.

I put a hand to his chest. "Whoa, sir. We have important business to attend to today."

Nick groans, flopping down on his back. Sunlight peaks through his curtains, illuminating the sculpted muscle of his chest, his defined abdomen. Strips of darkness cover him from the waist down, though my brain conjures up a perfect recollection of what he looks like beneath those scraps, the feeling of tracing my fingers down those lines, the sounds he makes lost in sensation...

I grab a long strip of silk and straddle him, the surprised look on his face spreading my lips into a smile. "I guess we could give ourselves one more hour," and tie his hands above his head. I lean down and whisper in his ear, "And this time, I'm going to make *you* beg."

ROUGHLY AN HOUR LATER, I shower and leave Nick's room, having had the sense to leave clothes there before the dance. I'm about to slide my key card into my own room when I remember the last time I entered unannounced.

This time I knock, silence the only response. I open my door to an empty bedroom, and retrieve my notebook from my bottom desk drawer, leafing through the pages. I reread the sections on the Princes of Hell, lingering upon the notes I took of Lucifer, Belial, Leviathan and Satan. But nothing about the fallen princes correlates to what Lyncus had said: That the monster is one of the ancient ones, and that pieces to the puzzle are right under my nose.

With a sigh of defeat, I grab my bag, throwing the notebook inside as I head to the library. Just as I close the door, familiar soft footsteps approach.

"Hey, Liv," I say as I turn to greet her.

"Hey."

Ever since the night at Strega, there's been an awkwardness between us. That's not to say that we don't still joke and laugh, or that I don't still feel close to her. It's something else. Something that looms like a swinging pendulum above my head waiting to drop.

But I chalk that up to the fact that I've been told someone will betray me, and if it's Liv, that will hurt worse than all the others.

Liv shifts uncomfortably, her blue hair vibrant against her simple white sweater. She chews her bottom lip, aquamarine eyes filled with trepidation.

"What's up?" I ask.

"I need to talk to you about something."

I war internally. Liv appears extremely bothered, yet I don't want to put off checking my notes. If Lyncus said they will lead me to the true identity of the monster, then whatever Liv needs to talk to me about can wait.

"There's something I need to do first that's really important. It has to do with the monster," I tell her, and the tightness in her expression softens. "I think I'm really close to figuring this out."

Liv widens her eyes, relief flooding her features. "Oh. Of course." She nods. "This can wait then. Just call me when you're back, okay?"

"Of course," I reply. "I shouldn't be long."

I turn from Liv, nearly down the hall when I hear her catch up to me.

"Do you need any help?"

"Nah. Like I said, this won't take long."

She startles me by drawing me in for a hug. "I've got you, Rhi."

I pull back only a little, catching her gaze. Any doubt I had about Liv betraying me disintegrates as I witness the genuine sincerity in her eyes. "I've got you too, Liv." I give her hand a squeeze. "I promise I won't be long. I'll call you in like an hour, okay?"

Her lips part into a smile that lights up her entire face and my whole heart.

It being a Sunday, I expect to see Kassi when I reach our usual reading spot nestled behind the stacks, but I'm greeted by an empty space. Piles of our books remain, so I take my usual seat among three book stacks that tower over my head when I sit down and pull out my notebook with the *Hells Princes* tome I grabbed from one of the book mounds.

I have this nagging feeling that I'm missing something, something right in front of my face as I stare at the words on the page. But these are words I've seen before. They are –

There.

Right in the introduction. How could I have missed it? The words nearly explode from the middle of the page – the page that I'd skimmed because I thought it of no consequence. I assumed the more interesting and useful facts would be in the meat of the book itself, describing each of the four princes in earnest.

But here they are screaming at me like a banshee:

Four princes known as the ancient ones. Monsters, they are. Born of earth, air, fire, and water, they ruled in a time before the Titans, before the gods of Olympus, and the gods of old. No, these are the gods of dust and bones, nightmares and shadows, ruling long before the chosen walked the earth. But their number is now three, for one among them could not be contained by the power of the others. The one born of water to the west, his wrath like that of a storm-ravaged sea. Imprisoned him, they did, for he would have brought about the destruction of all four.

I whip my head up and reach for my notebook. Lyncus had said the monster we seek was imprisoned but had been set free. Which means this monster is not merely half-god, half monster. It's a fucking *Prince of Hell.*

Lyncus was right. It was in front of my face the whole time. I flip the notebook open, scanning through the notes I'd taken on each Prince: Lucifer "of the east" and "Lord of Air." Nope. Not him.

Satan is the "Lord of Fire" and is "of the South." Not him either.

Next is Belial: "Lord of Earth" and "of the north."

So, that leaves...

I flip to the page of *Princes of Hell* that features Leviathan. Lord of Water, of the west. *The one born of water to the west.* The monster's corresponding graphic is ghastly and disturbing, making the pictures of Scylla and Charybdis I'd seen look like nothing more than garden snakes. In this drawing, Leviathan rises from a tumultuous sea, more dragon than serpent, its mouth open and ready to devour souls. Three large eyes, two a sickly yellow, the middle one bright blue, stare back at me through the drawing, knowing. I study the curve of its tremendous body, segments appearing on the surface of the water, the deadly tail in the forefront of the picture capped with spikes large enough to impale Scylla herself.

But the body, I notice, is not one of scales. No, the body is depicted as if it was made of *human* bodies, entwined together, their mouths twisted in never-ending screams of torment.

I shudder, slamming the book closed. *This* is the monster we're after. A creature so deadly, so untamed, his own brothers were forced to imprison him.

But that still begs the question of *who* it is. I reach for my notebook, scanning my notes on Leviathan. Represents envy. Sower of chaos. An unstoppable force from mankind itself.

This isn't helping. I close my eyes and rub my temples, wracking my brain. The girls initially targeted were Nick's former lovers. But that's where the tie to him ends. After Amanda Reynolds was killed, the next murder was Kieran. No one else has been killed by the creature since, though I would assume I'm next on the list, despite Lyncus' reassurance that I'm part of a larger plan.

I keep coming back to this idea of envy. Of a jilted lover. Leviathan embodies the very sentiment of envy. Would it be so wrong to assume it could be Samantha? Astrid and Liv had yet to check her file. Maybe it's her. That would certainly have been under my nose the entire time.

I gather my things, eager to get back and share my discovery with the girls and Nick. I'm almost at Northgate when my two Scylla heads hiss uncontrollably.

I know this warning. The monster is near. *Leviathan* is near. I pass Northgate, heading in the direction of the archway between Northgate and Westbourne, the area where the bonfire was held. The hissing turns to screeching wails, something I've never heard from them. My heart stops, fear catching it in a tight fist. Theirs is a cry of sorrow.

Nick, I immediately think, racing down the steep hill. I curse as my feet sink into the snow, slowing my pace. My pulse races, heartbeat now pounding ferociously in my ears as a familiar scent makes its way into my nostrils.

Blood.

I see it then, staining the pristine white snow like grotesque scarlet puddles. Small droplets are sprinkled between the puddles, leading me to believe the victim was attacked, tried to move, fell, then moved again. My eyes follow the trail of blood behind a large oak tree, its base wide enough to hide whoever lies behind it.

I swallow thickly, sucking in large gulps of air as I approach the oak tree. Snow crunches beneath my boots in the most penetrating manner to my ears, as though warning me I won't like what I see.

I place one hand on the bark of the tree, drawing one final breath. Trembling, I peer behind the base of the tree.

My brain takes time to come to terms with the body I see lying against the bark, propped up like a porcelain doll. Throat slit. Blood staining her shirt so it's no longer the color I remember. Her hands and fingers are saturated with it, hands I squeezed only an hour ago. Fingers I painted Thanksgiving night in my bedroom a pretty blue, darker than the color of her now blood-stained hair.

Her beautiful aquamarine eyes are open and lifeless, mouth frozen in shock.

I don't scream. I sink to my knees, warm tears falling to my cheeks. Wet snow seeps into my jeans, but my blood has already chilled. My heart stopped beating. There's no breath for me to draw, not while she doesn't.

I hold Liv's lifeless body in my arms, silent tears streaming down my face. *My fault.* This is all *my fault.* Why didn't I just push off going to the library? If I had, Liv would probably still be alive. I made her second to the research, yet I didn't do the same for Nick last night. I could have insisted he and I get my notebook *then.* Head to the library *then.* But I let my desire for him win. And the result is more catastrophic than I could have ever imagined.

I do my best to try and think of Liv *before* - her skin a dark olive. Her eyes are bright and endearing. Her beautiful yet ruthless smile.

But the only image that I see when I close my eyes is this one. Her skin ashen and pale. Her eyes empty and cold. Where I used to see blue I now only see red, her body so coated with blood it's like she bathed in it.

This is the image that will haunt me, and it's nothing less than what I deserve.

And as though she were kneeling here beside me, not lying lifeless in my arms, I hear the words: *I've got you, Rhi.*

Finally, I scream.

FORTY-SEVEN

I lie in my bed, covers drawn up over my swollen, blood-shot eyes.

I haven't moved from this spot in three days. Nick has been in and out, just as distraught as I am. I wish I could say I've drawn comfort from his presence, from his arms wrapped securely around me. But nothing alleviates the sharp pain in my chest. Nothing fills the void that formed in my heart knowing Liv is truly gone from my life.

A sophomore found me sobbing, holding a lifeless Liv in my arms. It took Wilde, Cicero and Talbot to pull me away from her. Professor Talbot tried assuring me it wasn't the monster that attacked Liv, as the nature of Liv's death didn't coincide with the rest of the murders. I suppose the small silver lining of the situation is that she wasn't in pieces like the others. But I know better. My Scyllas know better. They sensed it. And I was too late to stop it.

A body climbs into my bed, tugging the covers down. Scarlett snuggles against me, sniffling as she joins me under the sheets. For the last three days, her and I took turns crying in one another's arms. Sometimes, I gather whatever strength I have and crawl over to her bed. Sometimes, I find her in mine. Other times, I find all four –

I mean *three*...girls in our room. A tear falls onto my pillow. There's only four of us now. Four of the girl gang.

Scarlett wraps her arms around me, as though my last thought radiated such sorrow, such heartbreak, she could sense it.

Astrid and Zo show up to our room. And though Liv is gone, though the picture of her death has not once left my memory, I glance at the door, waiting for her to show up. Bright blue hair and eyes. Ruthless smile. I wait for it.

The silence from everyone else tells me they all do too.

Zo clears her throat. "I am the king of shovels," she says shakily. "I have a double. I'm thin as a knife and I have a wife. What am I?"

I know what she's doing – trying to draw us away from our heartache, distracting us with a riddle. It's working, as I find my brain picking apart the words and phrases.

But then a voice inside my head whispers, *Liv would know the answer,* and I fall into the dark void once more.

"The King of Spades," Scarlett says meekly. "You told us that one before." She blinks, eyes red-rimmed and swollen. "Liv knew it."

I bite my lip to keep more tears from falling, to keep myself from falling further into that darkness.

"They said it wasn't the monster," Astrid says from her perch at Scarlett's desk. "But it was, wasn't it?" Though her eyes are tear-filled and red just like the rest of us, her stony glare is resolute, directed right at me.

I nod. "The Scyllas knew. They took me to her. I was too late," I finish with a shuddering breath.

"Why the change in murder tactics?" Scarlett questions from beside me.

"Because it probably sensed Rhi," Zo offers. "It had to do the job and do it quickly."

The result was a quick slice to the throat. This very conversation was something I couldn't bear to think about. But I owe it to Liv to finish this.

"Why her?" Scarlett says, and I can hear fighting back a sob.

We all look at each other because the answer is beyond our reach. Liv doesn't fit into the pattern of killings. She wasn't one of Nick's former lovers. Wasn't a threat to the monster...

But she was there with *me,* the night we questioned Kieran. The night Kieran spilled numerous secrets. And Liv, with her demure smile that always held the monster lurking underneath, might have started to figure out just exactly *who* the monster was.

"It's my fault," I blurt out, fingers gripping the sheets upon my sinking realization.

"Oh, by the gods, Rhi," Zo starts to approach me. "Of course, this isn't-"

"I'm the one the monster is after." I don't raise my eyes at first. I feel Scarlett shift away in shock, hear the surprised, hurt gasps of the others.

When I glance up, it's Astrid that hovers near me. "What do you mean?"

I stand up, taking a deep breath and perch near the wall, so that every single one of them is in my line of vision. So that when I finally tell them everything, every look of betrayal and hurt will be right before my eyes. I've decided that will be my punishment.

"When Liv and I went to see Kieran, that's what he told me. He said two sides were after me, comparing it to a chess game, and that I was the King. I didn't think anything of it at first. It seemed like he was insane. But then he was murdered right before he was to be questioned. And Lyncus told me something similar. That the monster didn't want me dead but wanted me nonetheless."

I take in each of their faces. Only Astrid's eyes are narrowed. Zo and Scarlett are wide-eyed, mouths parted. I expect the first backlash to come from Astrid, but it's Zo that lashes out. She finishes the few steps she took earlier, closing the space between us.

"Why are you just *now* telling us this?"

I lick my lips, breath coming out in short spurts. "I didn't..." I swallow, mouth dry and tacky. "I didn't think, Zo. I thought Kieran was nuts. And I didn't want to worry anyone-"

"You didn't *think*?" she spits. "You didn't think that by Liv being there, a target was painted on her back? That when you were told *you* were the cause of *all* of this," she waves her arms frantically, "with Liv right by your side, that she wouldn't end up as collateral damage?"

I try swallowing again - to no avail - as I shake my head.

Zo scoffs. "You did know, Rhi. As smart as you are. You knew perfectly well. You kept us in the dark like you always do because you need to be the hero. And *you* need to be the one figuring things out. Saving the day. Liv knew it. And because of that, because of *you*, she's dead."

Zo might as well have sucker punched me in the stomach, that's exactly what her words feel like. And the truth in her words is heavier than a boulder on my chest.

Because she's right.

I let out a choked sob as Zo storms out of the room. My eyes find Astrid, and Scarlett, both of them looking exactly how I pictured. Betrayed. Hurt. I thought I was prepared for the punishment I imagined by seeing their expressions. But the heaviness in my chest, in my heart, is dead weight, crushing me with each breath I draw.

Astrid is the first to step toward me, hands clenched at her sides. But then she blinks back tears, one sneaking down her cheek, and she leaves.

It's just me and Scarlett, who remains seated on the bed, silent tears streaking down her cheeks.

"Scarlett," I finally manage to get out, my voice choked up in sadness, "Scarlett, I'm so sorry."

She just looks at me, hazel eyes so morose and defeated, and a face that is so like her brother right now, it's going to kill me.

Oh gods, what will Nick think of me when he finds out?

Scarlett rises and walks past me, then turns and sighs. "I don't blame you, Rhi. But I think we all need some time right now."

Tears tumble out of my eyelids as I nod and watch the last of my friends disappear. I bury my face in my hands and sink down the floor, continuing to sob uncontrollably until I hear a knock at the door.

I don't answer; I'm not in the mood for company right now.

"Rhi, it's me. Please open the door."

Oh, that voice. My heart sheds a bit of the weight at hearing that voice. *Does he know?* I wonder. Did Zo or one of the girls run to him and tell him what I kept from everyone? If he doesn't, he'll find out soon, and I'm sure he'll turn from me, too. Just another one of my betrayals. Another one of my lies by omission. Only this time it got someone he loved killed. How could he love me after knowing that? How does he love me at all, knowing how much I lie? Would it make a difference if I told him I loved him? No. I've waited too long to let him know.

And telling him now would only drive the knife deeper when he tells me he could never love me back.

"Go away, Nick," I say softly.

Another knock. Harder this time. "Rhi, please."

"Go away!" I shout, then bite my clenched fist to keep him from hearing me cry.

"Rhi-" his voice cuts off, followed by muffled protests. There's a loud thump, then silence.

Dread quickly replaces the sorrow and the guilt, and I leap to my feet, running to open the door. I scream his name, only to find empty space. No sign of Nick. No sign of struggle.

I peer from left to right. Something is wrong. It's just past noon, but the hallway is dark. Sunlight should be streaming through the windows, lighting up the corridor. Yet the hallway looks as though darkness has descended upon it, as though night is in full bloom.

I step into the hallway, the Scyllas letting out low, warning hisses, reminding me to keep my guard up.

Yeah. Something is *very, very* wrong.

My claws unsheathe, teeth sharpening and venom pooling. I continue down the hallway, noting there are no sounds – no TVs blaring from dorm rooms, no music, no conversations. Whatever this is reeks of some sort of magic.

I push open the door to the stairs, descending slowly until I reach the first floor. The Scyllas continue hissing, guiding me outside Northgate. The campus is just as dark as the dorms, as though night descended upon day without warning. And just like the dorms, not a soul roams the lawn or walkways.

Just as they'd done previously, the hissing grows louder with each wrong direction, and I find myself heading towards Southgate, where the Auditorium is.

Just as I'm about to enter the building, a figure bursts from the library doors, charging toward me.

"Rhi!" Kassi yells.

"Kass, what's going on?"

She slows as she approaches, glancing around wide-eyed. "It's some sort of glamour. A *very* strong one. Whoever is doing this is very powerful."

So, not only is Leviathan incredibly lethal, but magically adept. Great.

"It's Leviathan," I tell her, while we stand on the steps to Southgate.

Color drains from her face. "The monster is Leviathan? You're sure?"

"Yes. And I'm wasting time. I think something happened to Nick." I head up the steps, Kassi following. She grips my arm as I grab the door handle.

"Rhi, I saw Liv."

I crane my neck slowly. "As a Shade?"

Kassi bites her bottom lip, nodding. "She didn't say anything – they never do, but after she appeared, I had the strongest urge to find you." Kassi steps into me, grabbing my hand. "I think whatever is about to happen, I need to be there with you."

After what happened with my friends, it feels good to have someone by my side. Someone that doesn't look at me like they're waiting for the next lie to escape my lips, or for the next betrayal.

I squeeze her hand. "Okay, Kass. But be careful. I can't lose any more people I care about."

She smiles halfheartedly, something that doesn't sit well with me, but I nonetheless open the door to Eastbourne and step inside.

"Why are we the only ones affected?" I ask her as we walk.

"I think it's more that we are *unaffected*. The glamour seems to be on everyone else. They can't see what's happening.

I'm going to guess and say you aren't affected because of your immunity to certain powers and poisons. As for me?" She shrugs. "I have the ability to see things no one else can."

We stop in front of the doors to the auditorium, my stomach bubbling with dread. The Scyllas are emitting warning hisses, not because I'm in the wrong place, but because they know a battle lies beyond those doors.

Kassi and I enter the auditorium, engulfed in such an inky darkness it's impossible to see two feet in front of me. But as my eyes adjust, I notice a figure lying on the floor, blood marring his face and shirt.

Nick, I think, but as I move closer, I realize it's not Nick.

It's Josh.

I rush toward him, dropping to my knees. Josh remains unconscious, hair sticky and wet with blood. His lip is split, his shirt splattered with scarlet, but I can't make out where it's coming from.

"Josh," I shake him gently, relieved to hear his soft breathing. "Josh, please wake up."

Kassi's hand falls on my shoulder. "Rhi, something isn't right."

"What do you mean?" I face her as she turns toward the door. The hand at my shoulder trembles.

"I'm not sure. It's a feeling..." When she looks at me, her features transform into pure terror. "Rhi-" she gasps, her eyes taking in something past me.

I glance down, a gasp escaping my own lips.

Josh is gone.

"What the-"

A blur flashes before my eyes, snapping my attention. I see nothing, only a whirl of color traveling towards me.

Kassi leaps in front of me, her body at an odd angle.

The sound of sliced flesh fills the room.

Blood pours from Kassi's throat.

She lands in my arms, blood now coating her neck and chest, painting my own hands as I cradle her head.

Tears spill down my face. Kassi grips my shirt, and though I expect her eyes to glass over, for her to deliver one last terrifying prophecy, they remain clear and dark brown, filled with a mixture of terror and sadness.

Kassi pulls me towards her and slides a folded piece of paper in my hands. Her lips brush my ear as she whispers her final words to me. Words that shake me to my core.

With her last words, Kassi reveals Nick's prophecy before her body falls back, lifeless.

FORTY-EIGHT

"Kass," I shake her gently. "Kass." I plead, though I know it's no use. The light in the Oracle's eyes is gone.

With bloodied hands, I shut her eyes and lay her down on the floor, hugging my body. My bottom lip trembles as tears continue to fall.

"Oh, come *on*. Is she really that big of a loss?"

As though he materialized from thin air, Josh hovers above Kassi's body, peering over her with a grotesque sneer on his face.

Startled, I leap to my feet.

"She was *so* morose, so morbid." He walks around her towards me. "How could you stand being around her?" Josh glances behind him.

Shock settles over me like a cold chill. "*You?* It's been *you* this whole time?"

"Afraid so." He chuckles. "Honestly, I thought you would have figured it out *much* sooner."

Without thinking, I lunge, Liv's beautiful face at the forefront of my mind. I grab Josh by his shirt before I swing my fist back and connect it with his jaw.

The Cyclops goes down like a dummy, legs folding beneath him. But he laughs, a cruel, cold thing, blood trickling from his lip.

"Such rage," he says, meeting my gaze. I notice his eyes have gone from their honeyed tone to a gleaming, sickly yellow. "Rage and impulsiveness. I can see why they think you would make a great weapon."

"Who?" I snarl, stalking toward him.

He stands, tongue flicking out the corner of his mouth to lick away the blood that drips. Josh closes his eyes and sighs with pleasure. "I'd forgotten what the blood of the human body tastes like. Us *true* monsters just don't taste the same, wouldn't you agree?"

"I'm not like *you.*" I take a step back, though his words strike a chord deep within me.

"Aren't you, though?" He steps toward me. For every step I retreat, Josh advances. "You should know better than anyone that the word 'monster' encompasses so much more than teeth-" he flashes yellow, sharp fangs, and his mouth widens to accompany them. Like Nick, he has rows of them, and the disjointing of his jaw to the rest his face is uncanny to behold. "...And claws." His hand unfurls, revealing wide curved talons – dragon's talons. "The girl who lies. Who keeps her friends in the dark, telling herself it's for their protection. But that's not true, is it? You love the command of power. Of authority. You love being the one with all the chess pieces in your palms, moving them as you like."

My back is against the wall, my breath coming in rapid gasps of fear. And not just because of Josh's –Leviathan's – proximity or what he might do, but because once again, there's a sliver of truth to his words. But I remain silent, letting him talk, hoping he doesn't realize how close I am to wrapping my hands around a foil that must have been abandoned from one of the fencing lessons.

"We're not so different, you and me. I had dreams of power. And I was punished for it."

Leviathan turns his head, and I seize that moment to grip the foil and swipe it across his cheek, sending him stumbling back.

The monster laughs again, though this time, the laughter is tinged with a dark growl.

His brows shoot skyward. "Are you challenging me to a duel?"

I keep the foil aimed at his chest, amazed my hands are steady. "You killed Kassi. You killed Sasha and Amanda." I sob. "You killed Liv. For that, I will tear you apart with my bare hands."

Leviathan shivers, yellow eyes glowing. "Oh. Such vicious ferocity. Yes. A true monster indeed."

I swipe again, hitting the other cheek, a matching line of red forming.

The monster's lips curl, fangs protruding. "Very well. A duel then. But let's make it more interesting."

The weight of the foil in my hand changes, becoming heavier as the thin instrument widens by several inches. I adjust my grip on the hilt as the base itself enlarges. The small tip at the end of the foil elongates into a sharp point.

In my hands, I hold an actual sword.

"Our own little fencing competition," Leviathan grins at me, grasping a sword in his right hand, sharp teeth mocking and deadly.

Nerves wrack my entire body as I turn the sword over in my hand, getting a feel for the weight distribution. I'd come a long way in fencing thanks to B, but the idea of a *real* weapon in my hands, something that will easily drive through flesh, is unsettling.

Leviathan settles into position.

"En garde."

I toss formal duel etiquette aside with my silence, raising my eyebrows, inviting him to make the first move.

He accepts, raising the sword and bringing it down swiftly, a loud clanging ringing out in the air as I raise my own weapon to block it.

Leviathan smiles.

I shove him off, knowing I can't be too hasty. One of the very first things B taught me was to bide my time and not tire myself out, leading my opponent to exhaustion first.

The monster takes the bait, charging and lunging at me in quick movements as my feet whirl, dodging him blow by blow and meeting his attacks strike for strike.

We circle one another, the frustration on his face evident in the upturned sneer of his mouth and his heavy breathing.

"Human body isn't so great with stamina, is it?" I taunt.

"Coward," he bites back. "You play defense well, but do you avoid attacking me because you know you can't truly land a blow?"

I give him a smile worthy of a true monster – sharp teeth dripping with venom and all.

"Nah. I just figured I'd go easy on you. I wasn't even using my good hand." I shift the sword from my right hand to my left, his mouth thinning into a tight line with my movement. "Don't you remember that day in fencing class? Scylla was ambidextrous. And so am I."

I finally strike, catching Leviathan off guard as he stumbles to meet my sword. Just like the day in fencing class, my series of attacks are swifter and more natural with the sword now in my left hand.

It truly is a dance, sword play, as our weapons cling and clang, filling the air with a delicate melody. Leviathan continues to tire, clearly not used to exerting himself in a human body, even if it is part monster.

I finally swipe his sword away, the point of my blade resting against the hollow of this throat. Again, I'm merely met with a sardonic smirk.

"Well done. Unfortunately, a human blade won't kill me." Leviathan grabs the tip and squeezes, drawing blood from his own hand as he bends the steel blade like a wet noodle.

I freeze, a smile curving his mouth. "Besides, if you kill me, how would you ever know what came of your precious Nicholas?"

"Where is he?" I growl, jerking the bent blade away and tossing it aside.

Leviathan licks his bloody palm. "I was going to keep him hidden, but I suppose a little motivation might be good for you." His yellow eyes flick behind me, to the far back corner of the room. Before I turn, I hear the rattle of chains, the struggle of gasping breath.

Bound in chains by his wrists and neck, Nick is on his knees, face bruised and bloodied. His amber eyes are fierce when they spot me; the veins in arms protrude as he tries to break free of his hold. His mouth falls open emitting no sound, cheeks reddening. I take a step toward him when Leviathan's voice calls to my back.

"I wouldn't do that if I were you. If you so much as take one more step in his direction, the brace around his neck will continue to tighten, choking him within an inch of his life."

I feel the Scyllas writhing beneath my skin. My neck turns. Slow. Reptilian. "What do you want from me?"

"I want nothing from you, Rhiannon. It's not I, who seeks you. I am merely the vessel sent to retrieve you."

I face him fully. "By who?"

His grin is a thing of nightmares – rows of crude fangs and a forked tongue darting out to clean the remaining blood from his lips. "You'll see." His head cocks to the side. "Your Scyllas are uncharacteristically quiet."

I hold in a sigh of relief. I'd purposely kept them silent, assuming he'd be able to hear them the same way Nick was able to in his monster form. I'll keep him talking, letting the Scyllas fill with ravenous hunger and rage until I release them when Leviathan is least expecting it.

"I guess they don't find you threatening."

He laughs. "Oh, Rhiannon. Such an incredible liar you are. You lie to everyone around you. You lie to yourself. Does it ever end?"

"Why now?" I ask, changing the subject. "Why wait until this moment? You could have taken me at any point. You didn't need to kill anyone."

Leviathan moves ahead contemplatively, as if weighing my words. "You are partially correct. I didn't need to kill the first two girls. But Liv needed to be disposed of. And of course, Kieran.

"You see," he circles me, "the boy whose soul I devoured, the boy you know as Josh, he was filled with such betrayal and rage when I ate him. The girl he loved, Sasha, left him for your Nicholas." He jerks his head behind him. "I used his anger as fuel and killed her first."

I'm usually the jilted lover, Josh's words to me at our first fencing class. Gods, it really was right in front of my eyes the whole time.

"And Amanda?" I question, eyes sliding towards his movements around me.

Leviathan's gleaming eyes focus on Nick. "I knew Nicholas

would give me trouble in my quest for you. I wanted him gone."

"So you killed Sasha and Amanda to inconvenience him. To frame him. And used Kieran to attempt to kill him -"

"Ah. Ah. Ah." Leviathan waves a taloned finger at me. "That wasn't *my* doing." His lips curve wickedly at the confusion on my face, eyes ping-ponging between me and Nick. "It appears Nicholas has been keeping *many* secrets from you." Leviathan takes a step forward, head cocked unnaturally to the side. "Don't you know who he truly is?"

My attention snaps to Nick, my brain reliving all our past conversations, and all the vague answers to my questions he'd given me. Why he couldn't tell Lyncus his true name. What he'd sacrificed to make the powerful pendant that sits at the hollow of my throat. The reason why Circe warned us to stay apart, that I now know has everything to do with prophecy Kassi revealed with her dying breath.

His amber eyes are imploring - not to save him, but to forgive him. Nick's secrets have nothing to do with the monster before me, or the deaths at its hands. I direct my gaze back to Leviathan.

"Stop trying to distract me. Wanting Nick gone doesn't explain the deaths of Liv and Kassi. And it doesn't explain why you didn't try to take me sooner."

"They wanted you to have fully blossomed into your powers. So, I waited. And waited. But Liv started to suspect me." His body is near flush against mine, eyes a bright, glowing yellow. "I was there the day she tried to tell you. The day I killed her. The day you brushed her off."

It feels as though a large stone sinks to the bottom of my stomach as I consider his words. Liv had wanted to talk, and I remember the relieved look on her face when I told her I thought I knew who the monster was. My knees buckle under the weight of this new truth.

I swallow against a dry throat, my eyes darting to the body lying prostrate on the floor, a pool of blood surrounding her. "And Kassi?"

Leviathan shrugs lazily, a cruel smile still splitting his face. "Don't blame me for that. She was trying to defend you. Her body caught the wrong end of my tail. It would have knocked you out, but it cut her throat open."

I let out a strangled sob, Leviathan continuing to grin mockingly. "Just another tragic death because of *you.*"

My anger burns like a molten lava.

I lose it, attacking with both Scyllas. Leviathan's blood-curdling scream tears through the air as I turn my back, racing towards Nick. His eyes are wide with terror, and I nearly reach him, falling to my knees just as he disappears before my eyes.

"No!" I scream, slamming my fists against the floor. A maniacal cackle prickles my skin, and I once again face the monster. The demon. The Prince of Hell.

My Scyllas did a number on him. He's entirely coated with blood, torn flesh dangling from his arms, legs, and neck. But Leviathan only laughs, those lurid eyes too bright.

"You didn't think I would make it that easy, did you?"

Between one blink and the next, his face is right against mine. "Look at you, Rhiannon. All this power, for what? You're alone, in the end. No Nicholas. No friends. No one to help you. Don't fight me. If you come willingly, it will be so much easier."

I meet his stare, tears brimming at the edge of my eyelids. I will them to stay put as his words strike my heart, blow after blow. Nick is once again suffering because of me. And I took my friends, my strength, for granted, just as Circe warned me not to.

You may find yourself alone, in the end. She spoke those

words like she knew they would come to pass, and here I am standing before the monster that murdered for sport, and killed the closest friend I'd ever had – my sister. Here I am standing before him helpless.

And all alone.

I drop my head, ready to concede. It's the one thing I can do for them. I can go, and my friends, Nick, the rest of the school – they'll be safe.

"She's not alone."

I whip my head toward the stony voice I know so well, the usual hardness replaced with something like...love.

Near the doors, standing shoulder to shoulder, a barricade of strength and power, are my girls. My brain stutters as I count four, not the three I had left.

Astrid, Scarlett, Zo, and Bianca.

FORTY-NINE

"You're not alone, Rhi," Zo says, her gaze somehow both soft and hard at once. "Not now. Not ever."

Leviathan tsks. "You girls should have minded your own business. What a pity I'll have to kill the rest of you."

The sight of the four of them standing there gives me a formidable new strength. *This* is what true friendship, true sisterhood is. Despite your differences, your disagreements, in the end, you are always there for one another.

"Over my dead body," I growl.

The Prince of Hell's eyes move like a lizard's over to me as he remains facing my friends.

"Unfortunately, you are wanted alive. But they said nothing about unconscious – or unscathed."

Zo is the first to attack.

She comes in swinging – long sharp claws out and teeth bared, managing to tear through the flesh on Leviathan's arm before she's tossed like a limp doll across the room.

I release the Scyllas just as the rest of my girls charge him. The first head to reach Leviathan wraps around his neck, and though they have always been invisible, Leviathan seems to know exactly where each one will strike as he slices his own claws through the whip, the Scyllas screeching in agony.

But it gives Scarlett enough time to come behind him and sink her teeth into his neck. Bianca and I charge simultaneously, the Scyllas rearing and striking wherever they can.

Despite four girls attacking him on all fronts, Leviathan seems to be concerned only with keeping Astrid away from him, who I notice is now glove-free.

Astrid with the deadly hands. Even now she circles him, looking for a way to grab a hold of the Prince without touching any of us.

With a mighty roar, Leviathan tosses each one of us clear across the auditorium. I land on my side, pain splintering through my hip bone. Rolling over with a groan, I shakily get to my feet and search for the creature.

Leviathan's eyes are wide and murderous, blood dripping from every limb. He stands, palms facing outward, his hands growing larger – much too large for a human body. As I stare wide-eyed, I realize that his entire body is growing, changing. Shedding its human skin into what looks like scales. It's as though Leviathan unzips himself from Josh's body, as if the human body he stole was nothing more than a suit.

An unholy beast emerges from the carcass that was Josh, taking up nearly the entire auditorium. It's body writhes and coils, mounds upon mounds of scaly flesh separating me from my friends. His snout resembles that of a dragon, long and pointed at the tip and as large as an automobile, saliva dripping from its corners.

My gaze continues to travel up and past the long snout, the sharp teeth, and finds that between its two large yellow eyes, lies an electric blue one.

The terror that floods my veins arrests me to the spot. How

can we defeat *this?* This is no monster. This is a demon from the darkest depths of Hell. A creature even its own brothers feared for its ruthlessness and destruction.

"Look at me, Rhiannon." Its voice booms and shakes the foundations of the building itself, though it seems he's merely whispering in my ear. "You cannot defeat me. And now, I am going to make you watch as I tear each one of your friends from limb to limb, eat their entrails, and paint the walls of this school with their blood." It snaps its jaw as though calling me to pay attention. "And then, I am going to destroy the rest of this school and eat everyone in it." The snout of the beast widens into something resembling a smile.

I don't move an inch. I don't utter a sound. Not when Bianca is lithely hopping unnoticed toward the demon, those familiar long claws out and ready to tear through its skin. My heart skips as I realize she's heading for one of the coils of its body that sits just below its heart.

She swiftly lands on her destination, arm raised and ready to tear out Leviathan's heart.

I hold my breath.

A whoosh of air causes me to gasp. A blur moves through the auditorium. I don't have time to tell Bianca to watch out before she screams and crumples, her legs completely severed from her body.

B's piercing cry urges my feet to finally move. I'm racing toward her, hearing Leviathan's maniacal cackle, both in my ear and echoing throughout the room.

Leviathan's coiled body serves as a labyrinth. I leap and duck through the coils as they rise and unfurl, closing off the space behind me just as I make it through. Inside one of the coils I find Astrid. She lies on the floor, blood pouring from a wound on her head.

No, no, no. Please, no. With trembling fingers, I find the pulse point on her neck and feel a subtle pounding beneath my fingertips. I breathe a sigh of relief.

Bianca wails again.

I take off on the next opening of coils, finally reaching B. She drags herself along the floor, her legs cut cleanly below the knee.

"Rhi," she gasps for breath. Sweat plasters her hair to her forehead.

"B, it's okay," I soothe. "It's okay." I dare trail my gaze down her body to the stumps at her knees to assess the damage and discover something *very* strange.

"B, are...are your legs *growing back?*"

"I'm a Hydra," she says, breath coming in short gasps.

A Hydra. The monster whose heads grew back in multiples each time one was severed.

"B, Astrid is unconscious. Scarlett and Zo..."

"Scarlett is knocked out too," she continues breathlessly. "I think...I think I'm going to pass out now."

B closes her eyes as I cradle her head in my hands, smoothing her hair away from her face. Astrid, Scarlett and Bianca are now unconscious. But what of Zo? I say another prayer that the worst-case scenario is that she also lies unconscious somewhere.

Leviathan's low growl snaps my attention to the beast, fear encasing my heart. But it's not me he's focused on.

Through one of the lifting coils I see Zo rooted in place with fright. She gazes up at Leviathan, lips trembling.

"Zo!" I scream.

She doesn't take her eyes off Leviathan. He continues to growl, dragon lips peeling away from his mouth so his fangs gleam.

"Zo, scream! You have to scream!"

"I can't!" She yells back, darting her eyes frantically to me. "You-"

"*Just do it!*" As I yell that command, Leviathan opens his mouth wide, ready to devour my friend.

Zo opens her mouth in return.

I cover B's ears in case she isn't fully unconscious. A shrill like I've never heard enters the atmosphere, not so much a scream, but more the sound of millions of nails scratching a chalkboard at once. Or forks and knives scraping across china. It's grating. Irritating. Makes me clench my teeth and wish it would just fucking stop. But I don't feel any pain.

Leviathan, however, rears back and thrashes, letting out a wail of agony so piercing I feel it in my bones. He shakes his head rapidly, as if to wrench free of the noise. I use this moment of distraction to unleash the Scyllas. Both fire at once, tearing through his flesh as the wailing turns deeper.

A whoosh of air brushes against my skin, and Zo is lifted from the ground and thrown against the far wall. I feel it once more, this time a force so heavy against my chest that lifts me as well and pins me to the side wall. I clench my eyes shut, wincing at the pain and the need for air. When I finally open them, I see what imprisons me: the tip of Leviathan's barbed tail. Spikes protrude from either side of it, spikes that were clearly the cause of B's severed legs. These same spikes form a cage around me, and if I move an inch, I'll impale myself on one.

Think, Rhi. The barbed spikes have me imprisoned. Every single one of my friends lie unconscious between the body of this monster. My Scyllas barely put a dent in this massive crea-ture. This has to be the moment I admit defeat. This has to be checkmate.

Or is it?

My teeth are out and venom spills from my mouth, dribbling out of the corners of my lips and down my chin. I watch the rise and fall of Leviathan's coils, waiting for one to get close enough for me to take a bite. I don't know if this will work, but I have to try. My venom is only life-saving when counteracting another poison. But on its own...

It's deadly. Wilde's words replay in my head.

A piece of Leviathan's tail slithers upwards and caresses the side of my face. I turn my head and bite.

Hard.

Leviathan wails as his spiked tail releases me from my cage, and I narrowly miss getting swiped across my body. I duck, rolling haphazardly underneath. I push myself to stand, watching the scaled coils undulate and writhe as Leviathan convulses, rearing his large head in agony.

I spit, black blood splattering across the floor, the taste of something putrid and foul lingering on my tongue. At first, I fear it doesn't work. Leviathan continues thrashing, but the beast only looks murderous. Then, the creature shakes, coils unfurling, as his body shrinks into that of a human body. Josh's body; but only Josh's body from the waist up: his torso gives way to a long, scaled tale that travels the length of the side wall.

He coughs and shudders, black blood pouring from his mouth, the veins in his now human arms as black as the blood he chokes on. Leviathan carefully pushes himself up on his arms, skewering me with a glare.

"Come on, then," he taunts. "Finish this."

I walk toward him, the Sycllas hissing, eager to tear the rest of him apart.

He flashes a terrifying smile, black blood staining his teeth. "Don't you want to know who's coming for you, Rhi? Don't you want to know *who let me out?*"

My steps falter. I stop and consider his words.

A moment too long.

Because a third Scylla head emerges, this one allowing me to see *behind*, like eyes in the back of my head. The end of Leviathan's spiked tail whirls toward me at impossible speed. I won't react in time. It's going to strike, and there's nothing I can do about it.

Until I see Astrid, blood leaking down the side of her face, creeping alongside the wall as she comes upon Leviathan. Her hands are bare and splayed, and the beast follows my wide-eyed gaze to look behind him, but it's too late.

Astrid grasps Leviathan around the neck, his mouth frozen in a scream.

In the flicker of a heartbeat, Leviathan has turned to stone.

strid with the deadly hands. I stare at her in wonder, a stone statue of the end of Leviathan's tail a centimeter from my back.

Breathing heavily, she says, "I told you that one day I would show you what my hands can do."

I offer her a smile. A ghost of one answers me. Astrid scans the room, eyes finding Scarlett, and she rushes over to her. I take that time to assess the room. Bianca and Zo still lie unconscious in the same spots they'd been in. Bianca has a new full set of legs. I crouch beside Zo to check her breathing.

"Rhi!" Astrid's surprised gasp causes me to look up.

The statute of Leviathan has disappeared.

I glance nervously around the room, until another voice draws my attention.

"His brothers have taken him back to Hell."

I whirl, finding Nick on his knees, free from chains, though crude marks brand his wrists and neck. I run toward him, falling to the ground as I bury my face in his neck and just breathe in the scent of him.

"Are you okay?" he asks.

I pull back, my face wet with tears. "Kassi is dead." Nick's face leeches of color. "Scarlett and the girls..."

Nick looks past me at the mention of his sister, eyes darting around the room. He brings me up as he rises, and we race toward his Scarlett.

"She's fine, Nick," Astrid says, black leather gloves back on, as Nick crouches down with a panicked expression. "All of them are fine. They just need to wake up."

"How's your head?" I ask her.

Astrid scratches dried blood from her temple. "Still attached to my body, so that's good news."

I manage a tight smile, but my eyes find Kassi's body lying in a vibrant pool of blood. I immediately remember the last words she whispered in my ear. My gaze flits to Nick, his focus lasered on Scarlett.

"What the fuck happened here?" a voice demands.

Cicero, Wilde and Talbot all stand at the auditorium doors, faces washed with horror and disbelief.

I sigh, not ready to iterate the horrific events that just occurred but figure I should probably get it done sooner rather than later.

"We need medics here," Astrid says before I start. "Now."

"Absolutely," Talbot answers.

No one says anything as the three teachers inspect my friends, eyes scanning the rubble strewn about the floor. Wilde lets out a cry when she sees Kassi.

The medics arrive in almost ten minutes, bags and stretchers in tow. Scarlett, Zo, and Bianca are lifted onto the beds, with Nick, Astrid and I being offered to lie on our own, which we decline. I take one last look at Kassi's body being zipped up in a dark body bag before I blink back tears and follow my unconscious friends to the infirmary.

. . .

AFTER BEING POKED and prodded by several doctors, who eventually turn away satisfied that all I have are a few cuts and bruises, I'm visited in the infirmary by Professor Talbot. I peer around his body.

"Where are your trusty sidekicks?"

He smirks, sitting beside me. "How are you feeling?"

"Fine."

"Good. Does this mean you're up for explaining what happened?" He stares at me expectantly, and with a reluctant sigh, I launch into the full story.

I explain about finding Lyncus, even setting him free. I explain how Kassi and I researched every week, and continue with my visit to Kieran and what he told me. I end with Nick and my second visit to Lyncus, the Indus worm, and my confrontation with Josh/Leviathan.

"Kieran said there were two sides after me," I say. "Leviathan was one of those two sides. But what would the other be?"

Talbot takes in a deep breath. "I don't know, Rhi. Perhaps the other side isn't bad. Maybe that's the side that wants to see you safe."

I don't buy it. "Why am I so special?"

He smiles. "With great power..."

"I know, I know." I wave my hand. "With great power comes great responsibility or something like that."

Professor Talbot's smile turns. "No, Rhi. With great power comes a fuck-ton of enemies."

My thoughts turn to Circe. *It is better to be feared than to be hunted.*

He pats the side of the bed. "Thank you for explaining everything. I have much to do. For starters, new protection wards need to be placed around this entire school."

"How was Leviathan able to breach them in the first

place?" I ask.

"Our school will welcome anyone with a trace of monster heritage. Obviously, Leviathan fits that bill, but I never made the protection wards strong enough to deter a Prince of Hell. His brothers would have no cause to harm us, and the Lord of the West had been imprisoned since nearly the dawn of time."

I chew my lip thoughtfully. "Then, what do the wards protect us against?"

Professor Talbot's gray eyes turn stormy. "Gods and the demi-gods. Only they have reason to wish for our destruction."

"Even after all of these years?"

"Yes, Rhi," he answers wearily. "Some biases carry themselves through blood and time, ingrained with each new generation. Hatred is taught, and the gods and demi-gods teach nothing but animosity for our kind."

Gods and demi-gods...something Zo said at the beginning of the semester surfaces. "Professor Talbot, who are the Sons of Hercules?"

For the first time, Talbot's face pales. "Where did you hear that name?"

"Someone mentioned it months ago."

His eyes turn dark and smoky, a characteristic I've come to know means he's not happy. "The Sons were an extremist group of demi-gods that dedicated their lives to purging monsters in all forms, even those like us, who are partly human."

"Were?"

Talbot folds his hands on his lap. "They were eradicated almost forty years ago."

I chew my bottom lip. "So, you don't think they are responsible for Leviathan?"

He shoots me a look of disbelief. "I can't see how a group of bigoted monster hunters would release a deadly monster to do their bidding. Seems rather hypocritical. Besides, as I said, they no longer exist."

"You're certain?"

Talbot eyes me curiously. "I am, but if I weren't, what makes you believe they would come after you?"

They're coming for you. I hear those chilling words as if Kassi were standing next to me, and I believe her. I'd be a fool not to. After all, the first prediction I'd ever heard her make came true: *one of you is going to die.* If only I listened then. Maybe Liv would still be alive. I won't make the same mistake twice. Not that I now know Nick's prophecy as well.

It may not be the Sons that are coming for me, but someone is. Or *something* is. And next time, I need to be ready.

Whispers carry over from behind the curtain. Talbot inclines his head with a smirk. "I've taken up too much of your time. You have impatient visitors."

As Professor Talbot leaves, my friends take his place, surrounding my bed.

"B!" I squeal. "You have new legs!"

She laughs, stretching a limb out in front of her. "They'll take a little getting used to."

"We have permission to go back to our rooms," Scarlett tells me. "I thought we could all meet at ours and talk."

I nod. "Where is Nick?"

"They released him already," she says. "He wanted to give you a chance to rest and knew we wanted to see you first."

I get myself cleared to leave, and the girls and I gather in mine and Scarlett's room. Without prompting, I tell them everything. I gave Talbot an abridged version, but I leave out no details with them, learning from my mistakes.

"Gods, Rhi," Astrid says when I finish. "That's a lot."

I sigh, lowering my head. "I know. And I'm so sorry I kept

you guys in the dark about so much. I thought I was protecting you all. I thought I was doing the right thing."

A hand falls to my shoulder. "You shouldn't have had to bear all of that alone, Rhi." I look up and see Zo. "That's what friends are for."

"I know that now." I make sure to look every one of them in the eye. "And I promise, I'll never lie to you guys again."

"So, was Josh the betrayer?" Bianca asks.

I think about Josh before I knew he was Leviathan. I liked him, but I never felt close enough to him that his revelation of being the monster felt like a betrayal. Besides, from what Leviathan explained, from the moment I met him, Josh had never really been *Josh*. The real Josh had been devoured, his life stolen before I knew him.

"No," I say, fully aware that this means another heartache is imminent. A silence settles upon the room.

"None of us will betray you, Rhi." Bianca says, standing shoulder to shoulder with Zo. Astrid has her hand wrapped in Scarlett's, her usual stony glare replaced with genuine loyalty. Bianca and Zo stare at me with the same unwavering devotion.

"We've got you, Rhi. Always," Scarlett says.

Hearing Liv's words, the ill-boding sensation that followed me ever since I was told someone close to me would betray me alleviates. With complete certainty, I answer, "I know."

AFTER THE GIRLS LEAVE, there's one more thing I need to handle, one that I've been dreading.

I stand before Nick's door, fist raise to knock. How is it that I fought a centuries old demon yet can't muster up the courage to face him?

Because this will kill you, a voice inside my head whispers.

I drag my fist against the door.

Nick answers, facial features light with relief. He pulls me against him, shuts the door and crashes his lips against mine.

I don't pull away at first. *Let me have just a few more moments of this. Of him.* But when he draws back, beautiful eyes filled with happiness, I know it was a mistake to steal even those moments.

I swat his hand away as he attempts to brush hair back from my face. Nick steps back. "What's wrong?"

I clench my fists, drawing my body further from him. "Nick," I meet his confused eyes, "I don't want any more secrets. I want to know everything." I'll give him this one chance to answer all the questions he'd previously dodged.

Nick straightens. Licks his lips. His breathing is ragged. His eyes search my face, considering. Finally, his shoulders sag in defeat. "I can't, Rhi."

This time, I step into him and raise my chin, challenging. "What did Leviathan mean when he asked if I knew who you *truly* were?"

I'm met with silence, though Nick's eyes are screaming, pleading. Still, I press the issue, leaving no space between us. My own eyes search Nick's face, questioning. "Who are you, Nicholas Cervallos?"

Nick licks his lips and pushes my hair behind my ear. I feel his other hand at my waist, his fingertips curving in, trying to pull me even closer. He leans in, lips grazing my ear, "I'm yours."

My teeth pierce my bottom lip in an attempt to keep the tears at bay. I need to get this over with. The longer I stay here, in his arms, the more my resolve weakens. The more his words and his touch chip away at what little willpower I have left to do what I came here to do.

"That's not good enough," I say against his cheek. "I can't do this anymore."

Nick jerks back as though I've slapped him, eyes narrowing. "What are you talking about?"

"You and me," I say, commanding my voice to remain steady. "Us. The secrets we keep...they're...dangerous." I start rambling.

His shoulders sag with released tension, the corners of his mouth lifting. "We're monsters, Rhi. It's not our secrets that make us dangerous." He chuckles and steps into me, fingers trailing down my cheek, tracing my lips.

Godsdamn it, Rhi. Stop this. Nick leans down, his eyes locking on mine. "And I don't care. I'd face all the dangers of Hell to find you before I'd choose peace in Heaven without you."

My lips tremble. I let my claws pierce my palms inside my fists to steady myself.

"I love you," he whispers against my lips.

I close my eyes, fighting the tears that threaten to fall. *Say it back!* My heart screams. *Say it back!*

But I can't.

I shove him away, feeding him the words to a song he once sang to me. "'Love's a state of mind,' remember?"

Color drains from his cheeks. In judging his expression, I might as well have just punched through his ribcage and ripped out his heart. I pray he doesn't hear my own shattering.

Those amber eyes search my face for what feels like hours, before they settle and harden. "You know," he whispers.

I step back, feeling smothered. "I don't know what you're talking about."

He advances, growling, "*Stop lying.* You *know.* Kassi told you."

At the mention of her name, I see her throat cut before my eyes. Her body lying in a pool of blood. I use that as fuel.

"Kassi told me *nothing*," I snarl. "She died right in front of me, collateral damage for just being my friend. Stop trying to make excuses. I don't want to be with you anymore." I spit the words in his face like daggers.

I'm breathing heavily, my heart thundering in my chest. I need to leave before the tears come. Before I fall apart. I turn, but Nick clasps my wrist.

"Just tell me one thing, Rhi."

I hesitantly face him. His breath is warm on my skin, his familiar and comforting scent threatening to unravel me. My wrist is still in his grasp.

"What?" I whisper.

Nick brings his face to mine, eyes piercing right through me. "Tell me you don't love me."

Time stands still. I feel the rise and fall of my chest, counting each inhale and exhale, hardening myself, before I tell the biggest lie I have ever told.

With my free hand, I fiddle with the ends of my hair. My voice is calm and steady as I say the next words: "I don't love you."

Nick blinks. Inhales through his nose. Nods once and releases my wrist. I leave his room fully composed, but as I open the door to the stairwell, I sink down to the floor and sob.

Stop lying. You know.

He was right, but I couldn't tell him that. I needed him to believe me. Needed him to think that I didn't love him.

I pull a folded piece of paper from the pocket of my jeans, my fingers shaking as I open it fully. One of my tears falls upon the page, smearing the ink. But it doesn't matter. I know exactly what they say. As I laid in that hospital bed, I read these words over and over and over.

A monster with secrets bound to keep,

· · ·

HIS GOD-TOUCHED blood runs ocean deep,

CURSED to love without love in return,

UNTIL SHE FINDS HIM, for love he'll yearn.

THE MONSTER by whom Gods shall fall,

CURSED BY THE WITCH, Scylla she's called.

BOUND by a love unrelenting and unbidden,

EVEN DEATH CANNOT unmake what stars have written.

BUT DEATH, envious of a love he will never attain,

CRAFTS A CURSE of his own to relieve his disdain.

THE SCYLLA WILL LOVE the Monster beyond her dying breath,

UNAWARE IT IS her hands that cause his death.

. . .

When Kassi told me Nick's prophecy, she revealed that he would fall in love with a Scylla. And she would love him, too, irrevocably.

And I do love him. It's because I love him, that I had to lie. Had to break his heart, as well as my own, because that wasn't the end of Nick's prophecy. Despite how much I love him, how I would put my life before his every time, in the end, Nick is going to die.

And I'm the one that kills him.

EPILOGUE

NICK

Bass-heavy music drums angrily through my head as I step through *Strega's* doors. I wince, following a tawny-haired girl through a corridor to an open balcony overlooking the dance floor. The scene is the same from the last time I'd been here; barely clothed dancers ripple across the floor like lapping waves, swaying with the music. I wonder if some of these people were here the last time I came.

I wonder if they ever left.

My hostess leads me down a spiral staircase, and we wind our way through the gyrating bodies, some so drenched in perspiration I imagine they've been dancing for hours. Days, even. Just one of Circe's many methods of torture.

The VIP section has been remolded from an old church altar, and still resembles it somewhat. I climb the few steps to the platform and sit next to a familiar face. Flashing lights illuminate his golden hair, casting an almost angelic glow about him. Though there's nothing benevolent about this man.

"Nicholas," his smooth voice drawls, "I wondered when I might see you again."

"I thought about not coming at all."

Lyncus flashes a feline grin despite his now human form. "That would be poor manners. What would your father say?"

I raise an eyebrow skeptically. "He probably would encourage it."

Still smiling, Lyncus reaches forward to grab a lamb chop from the table. He places the meat entirely in his mouth like one would a lollipop and pulls out a clean bone. "How is your Rhiannon?"

I tense immediately at hearing her name, even more so at the possessive pronoun before it. After all, she isn't *mine*. Not anymore.

Lyncus picks up on my body language, raising his own gold-dusted eyebrows. "You two are no longer...what do the youth call it? An item?"

"No." I grip the edge of the seat cushion. "Why don't we just get on with our exchange?" The King strikes his chest as if maimed, collapsing into the couch. "But what a tragedy! A twisted gift of the Magi story if I've ever heard one!"

I say nothing, my chest tightening. The sacrifice I made to ensure Rhi's protection cost me a great deal, and in the end, she tore my heart out with her claws.

And I'd do it all over again.

Another figure sits beside Lyncus, and I stifle a groan. I'd hoped to be in and out of here

before she had a chance to interrogate me. The Circe I know has waves of long dark hair and smooth brown skin with piercing green eyes. An appearance meant to draw you in like nature's most fearsome predators: the more beautiful they are, the more dangerous.

I can't help but think of how Rhi fits that bill.

"What are you carrying on about now, Lyncus?" Circe purrs, running dark nails through his hair.

Lyncus simply smiles at me, eyes twinkling.

"What are you doing here?" Circe asks me.

"I have business with him," I gesture to the King.

"What kind of business?" She presses.

"Business that's none of your concern, Aunt Circe."

Her eyes narrow in warning. She picks up a lamb chop and like Lyncus, places the whole piece of meat in her mouth and comes away with a clean bone. "This business wouldn't have anything to do with the Scylla, would it?"

When I don't answer, she huffs angrily, the music in the club abruptly shifting from some sort of electronic dance tune to angry rock. "What is it, exactly, that you don't understand? *She is going to be the death of you.* Is it really that hard to comprehend?" Circe shakes her head.

"I love her." I've never offered a simpler explanation for anything. And yet, those three words hold a myriad of complications.

Circe stands and faces me. Without warning, she slaps me across the back of my head. "Ow!" I rub the back of my scalp. "What the fuck?"

"I'm trying to knock some sense into you." She grabs my chin between long fingers. "Now, you listen to me, and you listen closely. This isn't a game. The best thing for the both of you is to stay apart. Do you think Rhiannon will be able to live with herself if she kills you? Do you want that for her? Does she even know what happens when you die?"

I swallow against a dry throat. I hadn't thought of that. Not about dying, exactly. I'm not afraid of it. But about what it would do to her. How it might break her. "No, she doesn't," I answer.

Circe straightens, nodding her head, reading the expression on my face. "Good. Well, at least that's one thing we don't have to worry about."

Her back turned, she misses the subtle clench of my jaw. But Lyncus makes a strange noise in his throat. Circe turns her neck, shooting him a scathing look. "What are you not telling me?"

Lyncus crosses one leg over the other and folds his hands on his lap, deferring to me with an expectant look.

I sigh. "Lyncus helped me make the protection sigil that I gave to Rhi as a pendant in exchange..."

Circe is fully facing me again, eyes wide as saucers and wholly dark. "In exchange for what, Nicholas?"

I brace myself as I say the next words: "My true name."

The club pitches into complete darkness, music fading to silence. I don't even hear the alarms of the club patrons, just my own unsteady breathing.

When the lights finally come back on, the club is cast in an eerie red glow, ominous and foreboding. All the scantily-clad dancers and club patrons have disappeared. Circe still stands before me, outrage washing her features. This, *this,* is the witch from legend. The feared sorceress bested by no one.

Every muscle in my body stiffens as she steps toward me, my body preparing itself for a blast of power that might knock me into the next century. The monster inside me stirs, awakening with the thought of facing a fierce competitor.

But Circe cups my face gently. "Oh, my boy. My stupid, stupid boy. What a fool you are." She turns to Lyncus. "And *you.* You knew the consequences. And you let him do it anyway?"

Lyncus looks neither abashed nor reproachful. He meets Circe's murderous stare. "I am the Keeper of Secrets, my love. It is my curse. And that secret," he flits blue-green eyes at me, "is worth more than you know."

"It's done, Aunt Circe," I say with as much conviction as I can muster.

She lets out a regretful sigh. "She won't be the last girl you love, Nicholas."

"She's the only girl I've loved." As I say it, I know with every fiber of my being that it's true.

"You only love her because of the prophecy-"

"The prophecy has nothing to do with it. I would have found her and loved her regardless. And I will still love her." I say the next sentence with fervor. "Even if it kills me." Circe regards me with sorrow. "It will."

"Then so be it." I lean into Lyncus, who looks as eager as a starved man about to devour a meal. I cup my hand around my mouth and his ear, aware of Circe watching our every move. And I whisper my true name.

Lyncus and Circe remain silent as I rise from the couch and exit the VIP area. I move across the dance floor, the absence of dancers allowing me a straight departure to the winding staircase.

Once the cool air of the city hits my face, I take a deep breath. It's done. My name is revealed. Rhi will be forever protected as long as she continues to wear that necklace, and I believe she will.

I know she knows about the prophecy. I know that was the reason for her coldness, for her breaking my heart. She is the best liar I've ever met, but the night that she came to my room and told me she didn't love me, she made one mistake: the tugging on the ends of her hair. A dead giveaway. People always have their ticks, their mannerisms, that reveal their deceit. Most people aren't as good at hiding them as Rhi. But either she let that slip, or she wasn't aware of just how much I pay attention to her, how much I *know* her, to realize that when she lies, or when she's unsure, she fiddles with her hair.

I'm not without my own secrets, my own lies, of course. Circe is my aunt, a fact that I kept from Rhi and even my own sister. Though, I wasn't lying when I told Rhi how dangerous Circe was, and am still surprised my aunt let her walk from her club unscathed.

I'm surprised *I* walk out of there unscathed.

Well...physically at least.

Circe's haunting words about whether Rhi knows what happens when I die rattle their ghostly chains. She loved me as the monster, but will she love me if she knows I will become more than that?

Who are you, Nicholas Cervallos? Her question sears my brain.

Rhi had been right about one thing. Leviathan murdering those girls was an act of revenge. Not against me. Not because Josh, the *real* Josh, was a scorned lover. Leviathan's vendetta is against my father, because of what he did. Because of what I will become when I die.

"I won't let that happen," I say, the words disappearing into the frigid wind. Hands in my pockets, I stop as the whistling wind stills, and my heart stutters with disbelief that I've been heard.

After a few moments of silence, the wind picks up again, bringing with it a biting chill and the cold, evil laughter of my father.

My father's bargain with my mother was that she would raise me as long as I never told anyone my true name, the name my father gave me. But if she or I broke that promise, once I die, I would join him to take his place.

As the ruler of Hell.

ACKNOWLEDGMENTS

I wrote *Monstrous* in six months, when the world was falling apart. My husband, myself, and my one child at the time were quarantined in our little condo, unable to see our family and friends. And that's when the girl gang came along. Rhi came first, but the girl gang formed so organically as I wrote, they became my family when I missed my own terribly. So, I suppose it's only fair to begin by thanking Rhi, Liv, Scarlett, Astrid, and Zo. Their friendship and love for one another gave me the strength to continue to write this book even when I wanted to give up.

Brekke, this book would not be what it is without you. You have single-handedly helped me perfect my craft. I can't thank you enough for pouring your heart into this book with me. I have to admit, when you suggested rewriting the entire begin-ning, I nearly fell off my chair, but I'm so glad I listened, and I'm so lucky to have you in my corner.

Kristen, who knew our mutual love for *Kingdom of the Wicked* would blossom into a beautiful, horny friendship? Thank you for agreeing to beta read *Monstrous,* and for allowing me to harass you on an almost daily basis. I promise to send you every copy of *Monstrous* that is ever printed, and I won't even tell you it's coming.

WTS, where would I be without all of you? I'm so fortunate to have such an amazing writing group. Alaina, thank you for guiding me through this process, and letting me ask you a million questions about self-publishing. Morgan, you have been a lifesaver on more than one occasion! Thank you for your incredible formatting job. Taylor, thank you (or should I be thanking your hubby) for the Spanish translation (and suggestion).

Nikki - You have made these last few months so much fun amidst the chaos before release. I never dreamed I'd find another author friend with so much in common (literally - everything from our favorite Linkin Park song, to being born 5 days apart, to having the same name). Thank you for your enthusiasm for *Monstrous*, and for sharing your incredible talent with me to make the amazing stickers and Alystair logo. I can't wait to see what else you come up with, and where your stories take you. I hope I can return the favor one day.

My (now) four children: Ralphie, Jules, Izzy, and Nick (no, you were not named for *that* Nick), watching you grow is a constant joy in my life. Jules and Izzy – you were growing in my belly while I wrote this book. It's as much yours as it is mine.

To my parents, as always, thank you. I couldn't do any of this without your unwavering support and your belief in my writing. Mom - you are the reason I write strong women. I learned how to be one from you.

My (now second) favorite twins, Alex and Greg: I enjoy writing sibling dynamics because of you two. I'm so glad Mom didn't listen when I asked her to bring you both back only three days after she brought you home. You've really grown on me after 34 years. Now, what are the odds you'll actually read your older sister's book?

To everyone who has picked up *Monstrous,* reviewed it, shared it on their socials, or just helped spread the word: THANK YOU. Thank you for welcoming my weird little monsters into your hearts. Rhi, Nick, and the girl gang are yours now.

And last, but certainly not least, to my husband, Ralph. You're the reason I write tales with epic romances. You are every fictional male character I've ever read come to life. How lucky am I that I get to live a fairytale? I love you, and "I'd face all the dangers of Hell to find you before I'd choose peace in Heaven without you."

ABOUT THE AUTHOR

Nicole Rubino is a lover of fantasy – the darker the better - though she loves a steamy contemporary romance for good measure. Monstrous is her debut new adult novel and is the first of a three-book series. Morticia Addams is her role model, and you will often find Nicole belting out the tunes to any Stevie Nicks or Fleetwood Mac song (alas, not well). The mother of four young dragons (children), Nicole manages the beautiful chaos of her home by channeling it into her poor characters instead. Nicole lives in New York with her 100% Aries of a husband and the aforementioned dragons.

FOLLOW ME

Instagram & Tik Tok: nic_reads_and_writes